Nice Words

Cynthia Hoskin's *Fall's Bright Flame* is one of those rare works that causes a reader, immediately drawn in by the book's irresistible story, to find her or himself simultaneously, almost effortlessly, reflecting on the meaning of family and friends, the passage of time, and the many things that, although largely beyond our control, create a plot of their own wherein we can find ourselves and perhaps begin to understand who we are. Hoskin provides us with both an escape, and a homecoming. *Sonja Rethy, Editorial Director, Hebrew Union College Press*

+++++

Cynthia Hoskin is a master storyteller. Her plot moves quickly with interesting twists and turns. But mostly it is her dialogue, sparkling with wit and wry humor, that captures the reader. One is caught up with the brash openness of her protagonist. In her descriptions of even the most apparently superficial conversation her narrative voice points out the smallest details revealing nuance, critique of social convention and depth of character. In this she follows in the giant footsteps of Virginia Wolf. *Jacob D. Lindy, psychoanalyst and author of "Invisible Walls" (Routledge Press); "Vietnam: a Casebook" (Guilford Press); "Trauma, Culture, and Metaphor: Pathways of Transformation and Integration" (Routledge Press)*

+++++

Cynthia Hoskin takes the reader on a compelling page-turner of a ride with one-of-a-kind characters not easily forgotten. Through realistic dialogue and an original plot culminating in a surprising turn of events, the energy of *Fall's Bright Flame* remains afterward as a flavor for one to savor. *Mary Anne Sanders, Author of "Miss Ollie: Tennessee Madam" and "Nearing Death Awareness: A Guide to the Symbolic Language, Visions and Dreams of the Dying"*

+++++

Cynthia Hoskin is a masterful storyteller. Through dialogue and description she weaves a tale of drama and intrigue, making her novel impossible to put down. *Connie Sullivan, internationally known fine arts photographer and author of "Petroglyphs of the Heart".*

Fall's Bright Flame

ISBN 13: 978-0-9863339-9-6

This is a work of fiction. All incidents and dialogue and all characters with the exception of some recognizable figures, are products of the author's imagination and are not to be construed as real. Where real life characters appear, the situations, incidents and dialogues concerning those persons are fictional and not intended to depict actual events or to change the fictional nature of the work.

The Cornish Chronicle, Publisher
Cold Spring, Kentucky

Cover and photography by Cynthia Osborne Hoskin

All requests and questions can be addressed to choskin@osbornehoskin.com;
Web site: osbornehoskin.com

ACKNOWLEDGMENTS

Fall's Bright Flame benefited enormously from the in-progress suggestions and encouragement of the following people:

Credit goes to Daniel Brown, *AEQAI* Editor, for originally suggesting I write about this era and group of men and women that mainstream literature largely passed by, one in which I took part.

Major thanks to my friend and Hebrew Union College Editorial Director, Sonja Rethy, for her incisive and constructive response to reading the book not once, but twice, as well as for her recommendations and enthusiasm for the project along the way.

For invaluable help with particulars, thanks to Elizabeth Armstrong Downing for her take on today's best London shops and restaurants; Dr. O. Redmond McNeil and Dr. Jacob Lindy for keeping medical information accurate; and Diane Bellamy of Tregrill Farm Cottages in Cornwall for helping me with locating local hospitals as well as for her beautiful description of Cornwall in the spring, embedded as a note from Lady Bromley in the chapter *Life Moves On.*

My appreciation goes also to Dottie Rockel, Alice Weston and Connie Sullivan for their astute comments and sensitivity to nuance. Thanks, too to Leslie McNeil, Ethan and Barbara Stanley, and Vince and Mary Aug for their helpful comments on various parts of the book along the way.

Special thanks goes to Mary Anne Sanders who patiently critiqued the novel as it unfolded and offered penetrating criticism as well as encouragement.

This list would not be complete without mentioning the delightful Monday Morning Writers Group of Cincinnati and especially those who took the time to provide me with written suggestions as I read chapters aloud.

And lasting gratitude to my husband, Richard John Collins Hoskin, for being an ongoing and intelligent sounding board, dauntless BBC-trained proofreader and wholehearted supporter. I have my creative sons, Daniel, David and William Hewett to thank for their encouragement and indispensible help with cover design.

Not least is the contribution by our Scottie, Abigail, who played the major role in concluding the story with her usual verve.

Preface

Cynthia Hoskin has written a very sophisticated novel, her first, titled *Fall's Bright Flame*. Realizing that almost no fiction has been written by or about women of her generation, who matured in the fifties, her work continues in one of American literature's most fertile territories: the American suburb, with forays in and out of various Eastern seaboard cities: Boston, New York, Baltimore in particular. These are cities where the old tradition of Social Registers still held sway and had a lot of clout, and Hoskin's narrator and most of her characters come from that world. Hoskin is particularly astute in her understanding of the mores and language of said world, as she not only understands it, but also suggests its strengths and weaknesses throughout her novel.

While reading *Fall's Bright Flame*, a very fast-paced novel zipping back and forth between the cities mentioned, I saw echoes of John O'Hara, John Cheever, and John Updike, those superb chroniclers of upper middle/upper class suburban American life; the roots of their writing, too, harkens back to both Henry James and Edith Wharton, and I see more Wharton in Hoskin's writing than I see James, and that's a compliment, as Hoskin's female characters manifest the strong willed characters of the women from that background. Friendship between women is a strong point in Hoskin's novel; her women characters speak in a kind of assumed code, and their closeness is lovely to observe. In Hoskin's world, people have dinner parties all the time – it's what friends do – and homosexual men, for example, are easily integrated into their world, questions left unasked; civility reigns.

Hoskin's narrator, whom we meet just after her mother's death, is an independent-minded woman, presented in the novel as a fiction writer of increasing renown, with a most ambivalent relationship with her sister, who works in the film industry: one of the strong points in the novel is this sisterly relationship, maddening yet still close; they know one another almost too well, but defer to one's another's strong and weak points. And neither is overly emotional about their mother's demise. They come to suburban Boston to clean up her affairs, sell her house, move on (wills are of more interest here than the mother's character, but I found that kind of detail very true to life). The narrator, too, will meet a male neighbor of her mother's, mysterious and vexing, and we know that these two will eventually come together, whether temporarily or permanently is difficult to know throughout the novel, which thus keeps the plot moving along quickly. Hoskin also introduces a subplot, so the readers don't know who this man is, where he comes from and the like; I found this subplot diverting and amusing, as it also involves wills and money and unknown (but protected) identities.

And as the plot develops, we are privy to some serious growth and internal dialogues of the narrator, which are strong and well delineated. The narrator's closeness to her first husband and to her children is very credibly done, too. Hoskin knows her restaurants and her hotels and what her characters eat, drink, and discuss. Fascinatingly, the moral code by which the narrator lives neither cracks nor breaks, and that's quite a feat on Hoskin's part. People in this novel find themselves equally at ease in London as they do on the East Coast of America, and Hoskin knows her territory well.

"Fall's Bright Flame" is extremely well written, and it speaks to a world mostly gone, now, and lets us ruminate about what we may have lost as well as where we were headed. It's a terrific read, and it has some real depth to its characters. I couldn't put it down; it's a serious novel about manners, of course, and it works on many levels, which Hoskin intends. *Daniel Brown, Editor AEQAI.com, Art Curator and Literary Critic*

FALL'S BRIGHT FLAME

Part One, 1995

Chapter One

Death

Karl and I were having one of our rare arguments when the news came that my mother, Elizabeth McKenna, was dying.

"You'd better leave as soon as possible. I don't know how much longer she can hold on," said the voice of a stranger, Dr. Creighton.

I was stunned. I didn't know Mother was ill. Of course I started asking questions.

"She had cancer," came the cool reply. "She did not want you or Suzanne to know or worry."

"But, but, I don't understand," I spluttered. "I mean if you knew, then . . ."

"Mrs. von Sturnheim, I am her doctor."

I didn't know what else to say except that I'd leave within the hour.

"Good," was his answer. "I'll meet you at her house." We hung up.

I relayed the news to Karl who was standing with his back to me, looking out the kitchen window of our Baltimore townhouse at our garden, now curled into brown fall sleep.

"Well, then, I expect you'd better do as you are told and get up to Hopwood as soon as possible," he said without turning around. "That's horrible news."

"Karl . . ." I started. He finally turned and looked at me.

"Forget it, Elise," he continued in his crisp Austrian accent. "We don't argue. This is silly anyway. I do my job, you do yours. We are happy that way, no? I will try to get home before Thanksgiving, I promise."

"Karl, yes, no, oh damn. I'm in a muddle. All I asked before we argued was that you be around for Helene's party; fifty is an important birthday, and they're our oldest, dearest friends."

"Well, I can't. That's final. My work is in Denver, and this is the critical period of staging and rehearsing for the opera. You're making a molehill out of a mountain."

Karl had been in America for years, but he still couldn't untangle American idioms. "That's a talent I've tried to master," I said.

Realizing what he had said, he chuckled in return then held out his arms. We hugged.

"I'm truly sorry about your mother," he added.

"I know." I broke away. What lay ahead would be easier to deal with alone anyway. During our thirty years of marriage, Karl's involvement with my family was minimal. An only child, his parents lived in Austria where he visited them rarely. He had come to America in 1948 for graduate school and stayed. Family attachments, except for our own children, were of little interest to him. I'd never understood his rigid hierarchy of priorities, but I did see how they left him to pursue what he chose, when he chose to. There was no pushing Karl, whatever the issue.

I looked at the clock. "I'd better pack; it's already ten." I immediately called my sister Suzanne, and we compared the few details Dr. Creighton had shared with us. She said she'd catch the red eye night plane from Los Angeles and gave me the time. "I'll call you at Mother's tonight if I can't get on that plane; otherwise expect me in the morning. You can meet me?" I assured her I would.

By eleven I was on the road north to Massachusetts and drove straight through with only one stop, although there were delays from rush hour traffic. I arrived around seven-thirty in the coastal Massachusetts town where I had grown up and where Mother and Dad retired after living for years in Boston to be nearer his work.

Lights were on in Mother's house, and Dr. Creighton was waiting. After briefly saying hello, he gave me the news that Mother hadn't waited but had died hours before I arrived. I sighed. She always had her own rhythm, a beat ahead of the rest of us.

So, Elizabeth McKenna was dead, and the funeral in the familiar little churchyard would be in a couple of days. Suzanne would no doubt, in her brisk way, reorganize any plans I made.

"I know you're disappointed. I'm sorry," Dr. Creighton said.

The house was empty and silent with the familiar aroma of beeswax furniture polish pervading. Excusing myself for a moment to use the bathroom, I hurriedly combed my hair and walked back to where Dr. Creighton stood near the front door. Mother's presence was palpable.

Faded roses drooped from a crystal vase on the round mahogany dining table in the low-ceilinged room. The window at the far end was a now darkened eye, and I went to it, squinting to catch a glimpse of the ocean beyond. All I could see were shards of moonlight dancing on restless water. Dr. Creighton came and stood behind me but did not speak.

"How did it happen?" I finally asked.

"She knew she had cancer, as I told you, didn't want medication, wouldn't let me tell you or your sister for fear of your insisting on treatment. She painted on with a rigid schedule and determination; her art was all to her."

"Don't you think you might have told us anyway?"

"No, I don't. I am — was — her doctor and respected her wishes." He paused and drew a breath, so close behind me it sounded like a hiss. "Did you know about my friendship with your mother, Elise?" he asked. "Apart from my professional involvement in her life?"

"She mentioned your family from time to time as neighbors. That was all. Something about your wife too, her kindness to Mother, I think — Peg is it?"

"My wife is Anne."

"Oh, Anne," I said. "Well, no we didn't know much about you." I was still staring out the window and trying to still the chaos in my brain.

"So you understand, she was my patient and really my dearest friend," he said. "She talked a lot about you and your older sister, how different you are. I was also able to discuss my own life as with no one else."

"Strange," I muttered, still not turning around to look at him. I couldn't think of anything to say and wished he would leave. Whatever he and mother had enjoyed was meaningless to me, even offensive.

Finally I turned and faced him. "Was she resigned or was she angry?"

"She was a realist as you know." The dispassionate way he spoke was grating. I turned to look at him. He was tall — a fact that had escaped me at first — and had a straight narrow nose, blue eyes, slightly olive skin and wide lips. I gauged him to be in his late forties, a few years my junior. His black hair, flecked with surprisingly little gray, grazed his shirt collar.

"Okay," I said. "You and Mother were, I don't know what, friends. Still don't you think her children had a right to know? Wasn't there ever a time when you thought of us, our feelings, how we'd like to be with her? I mean if you were so close, you could have talked to her, persuaded her to tell us." I knew I was being rude, but his detachment rankled.

He stepped back, away from me, and folded his arms across his chest. "No," he said. "There are loyalties and ethics involved here." He wasn't exactly patronizing, just annoyingly cool, and it had been a long day. I suspect there was more than a creeping discomfort in the realization that he had known Mother in ways I never had. This was *my* mother, and I felt I had a right to question the decision of a stranger with regular access to her.

"Oh, I see," I said. "Well, where is she now, this best friend of yours? I mean we'll have to plan a funeral, and we'll need a body, of course." This was unpardonably snide; I was setting up a nasty situation. The thought of Mother dying without family near whittled away my self-control.

He merely looked disappointed. Moving back to the round dining table, he propped himself against it, his arms still folded over his chest. "Okay, Elise, here's what I know: she wanted to be taken to the Addison Funeral Home here in Hopwood. That is being done as we speak. She also wanted to be cremated, as I expect you know. That can be done tomorrow." He paused. "Unless of course you have other plans, in which case I told the people at Addison to wait for a call from you and Suzanne before proceeding."

I sighed. "I'll call Addison's tomorrow after Suzanne and I have time to talk."

"Fine," he said, straightening his back and heading for the door. "I'll leave now. I've left a list of phone numbers for you in the kitchen by the phone: the funeral home; caterers you might want for after the funeral; her lawyer Davis Hopkins; the private number and name for the gallery owner in Maine where her paintings are; things like that. Please call my wife, Anne, or me if you need anything. I'll be in touch." Handing me a card with his home and mobile phone numbers penciled on the back, he reached for the doorknob.

Still chafing, I threw up my hands. "Leave? Perhaps you'd better."

He paused and stared at me for a long moment, his eyes narrowed, his lips pinched. I looked down and took a ragged breath.

"Oh, damn, I'm clearly out of my depth here." I reached out to touch his arm. "I'm sorry." His stiff formality made me feel clumsy, so I drew my hand back.

He looked down at me, his expression softening into a crooked, amused look.

"It's fine. You're upset. Good night."

And he was gone, invisible in the misted black air, the crunch of his well-polished shoes on the gravel lane betraying his rapid departure. I felt rejected and angry, and glad to be alone. Looking at his card, I read: Alex Creighton, M.D. *Alex. Alex Creighton. Okay, Alex Creighton, we'll deal with this later.*

Chapter Two

Suzanne Arrives

Morning found me reliving the botched encounter the night before. The doctor had tried to be kind and helpful, hadn't he? Why my hostility? I did blame myself for a breach of good manners. Then, it struck me that this habit of self-condemnation in the face of conflict was wearing thin. Why didn't I have the same right to assert my feelings as others? Why always back off to avoid conflict? Why, in fact, did I accept Karl's rigidity simply because he seasoned it with little kindnesses and was a good father? The confrontation with Alex had pushed me beyond polite reserve, and this was new — new and oddly liberating. I decided that this time I would not take the blame or apologize. He could have been more forthcoming and sympathetic.

Abandoning further reflection, I padded into the kitchen and found only a stale English muffin and a bag of coffee in the refrigerator. With the coffee maker bubbling to life, I attempted to make sense of the days ahead, jotting tasks on a pad of paper I found on the counter. After two sips of coffee, I glanced at the time, dropped the pencil, took another gulp of coffee and rushed to dress. Closing up the house, I headed to Logan Airport in Boston to meet Suzanne.

Once through the Sumner Tunnel, I quickly parked the car and rushed into the airport. The arrivals board showed that Suzanne's flight had landed.

"Lixie, Lixie!" I heard her shout my childhood name before I glimpsed her blonde head emerging from the crowd of bag-toting travelers. A film director for Universal Studios, my older sister was a blur of energy and elegant clothes as she breezed through long workdays, parties, and busy weekends.

"Do you believe," laughed Suzanne, "that man back there, the one with the red tie, tried to pick me up?" She was visibly pleased. "Tell me all," she added, grasping my arm. "Dr. Creighton wasn't particularly illuminating on the phone, rather abrupt in fact."

I held her off long enough to retrieve her recognizable Louis Vuitton suitcase from the circling belt and led the way to the car. Once on the road, I described my own conversation with Dr. Creighton.

"Ethics?" Suzanne shouted. "Good Lord, the man ought to be hung out to dry. That's absurd. We should have been with her."

"I agree, but our conversation was over before I knew it, and I'm afraid I was downright rude. I felt guilty, but don't now."

"Ridiculous. I don't blame you. I'll call Davis Hopkins — this has to be unethical. As a lawyer, he'll know what to do. So what if Mother decided to spare us. What about how we felt? The doctor obviously had influence over her, could have convinced her." She paused and then added, "He sounds like a pompous ass." I shot her a quick glance and noticed the familiar nose wrinkle proclaiming her aversion to anything from vulgar taste to boring people.

"Suzanne, we shouldn't jump to conclusions. Leave Davis out of it. Dr. Creighton was Mother's friend and doctor, and I've already been beastly to him. No need to add your venom to the mix." She sniffed.

Traffic was dreadful. There had been an accident, and it took a long time to get out of the Boston area. Finally nearing Atlantic Avenue along Hopwood's coast, Suzanne took a deep breath. "The salty air smells wonderful, doesn't it?" she sighed. "I'm so, so sorry I didn't see Mother before she died. I did try to come east three weeks ago, but she was preparing for that show in Miami and said she couldn't take the time. It was like that, wasn't it?"

"Yes." I then expanded on what little more I knew of Mother's relationship with Dr. Creighton.

"So, in a way she did have a sort of patched-together family here. Is he married?" she asked.

"He mentioned a wife, Peg or Anne I think. Yes, it's Anne." We were quiet for a while. Then I asked, "How are Philip and the boys?"

"Philip's off dove shooting in Mexico. Group of boring executives." She turned and smiled at me, and continued. "All's well with Jamie and Paul. Baby Will has returned from another trip to find himself. I told him if he stayed in one place long enough, *himself* might pop up without all the work. He rewards me with a dreamy tofu smile and nonsense about lacking maturity to finish med school yet. He may be right. And Karl and your litter?"

"Karl's going out tomorrow to do the set for *Flying Dutchman* in Colorado. He's thrilled of course. He'll be away at least until Thanksgiving."

"Well, that's standard in your life; I mean Karl away and you not exactly whining."

"Harsh, but yes, I have plenty to do with my writing, and being alone is easy for me." I continued. "Enid and Evan are still in England, not likely to marry and dead set against having children as always. She's handling two important legal cases at the Bradley and Clark office there, and he's had two sales of his mammoth sculptures this month. You already know about the one that went to the museum in Wisconsin. And Penny I told you about months ago — pregnant again and hobbling around with a sprained ankle."

"What's young Matthew up to? Haven't heard much since we went to his graduation."

"He's accepted a job with a newspaper in Cincinnati," I said. "Funny thinking of him living in the Midwest, but the opportunity was too good to resist."

I guided the car down the lane toward the ocean. On the left, a lofty glass and wood house rose from the dunes. "I think that's Dr. Creighton's house," I told Suzanne.

"Looks awfully *Architectural Digest* for Hopwood," Suzanne observed. "Reeks of show and tell. Quite out of place. Now, in California, you could understand . . ."

"We should have a look at the rest of the town," I interrupted, anticipating chapter and verse of a familiar diatribe. "How long since you've been here?"

"At least five years. Not since our trip together to Paris."

Suzanne teetered along the gravel path to the house in red high heels, carrying her suitcase, and we went into the brown-shingled cottage together. Faded blue Boussac-covered furniture, once the height of fashion, rested in pools of light and shadow, and the surfaces of Elizabeth McKenna's beloved antiques gleamed. A mist of sadness overtook us both, and I didn't know whether it was our youth peeking from behind the curtain of years or mourning for Mother that made my eyes smart.

Suzanne roused herself and let her bag fall with a thump on the floor.

"Time for a drink," she said, heading for the cabinet where Mother kept the Beefeater, Chivas, and Remy Martin that she considered fundamental staples on a par with flour and sugar. Retrieving the scotch, Suzanne headed for the kitchen, a modern oasis carved out of the center of the house. I heard the rattle of ice cubes.

"Good idea," I said, "however there's nothing here for lunch. Pour me a scotch too, and then later we'll see if Annie's Diner still exists. I'm longing for fried clams."

A few minutes later we settled on the sofa at the end of the room, the reflection from Mother's favorite Meissen lamp in the window competing with the grey glow from the ocean as waves calmly rolled towards shore and landed with a soft throb.

"So," said Suzanne, "talk to me. What ideas do you have?"

I retrieved my list from the kitchen and gave her a quick rundown of what I'd been thinking. She pulled a notebook and gold pen from her purse and started writing, with an occasional, "umhum." When I was through, she looked up.

"That it?" She took a long drink and replaced the glass forcefully on the table.

"Yes," I answered waiting for the inevitable overhaul.

"Well," she started, taking another sip of scotch. "First of all, I think the hors d'oeuvres after the funeral should have more hot things. It's October after all. Also, did you list the right minister? I know she didn't go to church, but there was one around here she liked."

"Suzanne," I interrupted, "Why don't you take over? I've had no time. And the 'right' minister? Mother said he left town three years ago — a scandal concerning four women in the choir. I knew this would happen. First you ask me what I think, and now you . . ."

She plowed on. "Calm down, Lixie, please. I am trying to make this occasion worthy of Mother. So, we need to be sure that the cemetery has her placed on Dad's right, not the left. They both talked about that at one time or another. Don't know why it mattered, do you?"

"Maybe because that's how their beds were?"

"Something only they knew, whatever. Anyway, let's be sure to mention it."

"Right," I answered. "So, why don't you take over from here? Drink up, and let's go to lunch." I found my purse and headed for the front door.

Suzanne followed me and leaned against the doorframe, hands on hips. "Maybe we should let the helpful doctor do it all, huh?" She looked so funny, standing there grinning at me that I found myself smiling back.

"A perfectly splendid idea!" I said, pulling my coat off a hook on the wall. "You're a bitch, you know that?" I turned and opened the door, brushing rapidly past her.

We drove into town and found Annie's Diner, a favorite haunt during our teenage years when we spent hours playing the pinball machines and chewing on Annie's tender fried clams or hamburgers. I parked the car, and we went in.

Memories fled when we saw the restaurant. Gone were the red plastic and chrome counters and stools, replaced by a décor of white and green wooden booths. Gone too were the pinball machines and huge chrome jukebox, the cigarette machines and posters of tan Marlboro cowboys. Instead, pale seaside scenes in white frames marched along the walls.

We ordered large platters of fried clams, tartar sauce and coleslaw but were able to eat only a small amount. Idly dipping the clams into the sauce and slowly munching, we lapsed into silence, flipping the pages of the local paper. After lunch, we decided to have a walk along the pier to the harbor where a few lobster boats were tied up, their pots drying on the sand. Gulls swooped overhead, blurred in the afternoon glare, screaming to the sky. The briny smell of kelp heaped on the shore brought back, not so much specific memories as an overall feeling of place.

"Wow, this never leaves you does it?" asked Suzanne.

"No. Do you remember Pat, the lobsterman, and his dog — how he used to throw food out into the water and make the dog fetch it? Wasn't he a Harvard graduate? Why do I remember that?" I asked.

"He was, or at least said he was. I have no idea how he went from that to lobstering." She turned and headed back to the car, and once we were seated, she said, "Let's go to the funeral home now and get it over with, then we can ride around town."

We hadn't called first so had to wait for the funeral director to return from lunch. The place was hushed, candle-like sconces lighting mushroom colored walls. There was a little chapel off the main hall. We wandered in there.

"I wonder where they've put Mother," said Suzanne.

"Hard to tell. They won't have done anything yet, as we have to give them permission for a cremation."

We heard the director come in and speak to his assistant in low tones. Presently he came into the chapel.

"You are Mrs. McKenna's daughters?" he asked shaking first my and then Suzanne's hand.

We went through the platitudes and followed him to his office where we discussed what we knew of Mother's wishes: a graveside ceremony, cremation, and a simple urn. When the details were covered and papers signed, he asked us if we wished to see Mother's body before cremation. Suzanne and I looked at each other, startled. Would it be heartless to say 'no'? Suzanne spoke first.

"Is the casket open?"

"Yes."

"Well, then, let's do it," she said, rising and walking briskly out to the hall, swinging back to scoop up her purse.

I swallowed hard and followed her and the director towards the back of the building. In a small room with a scattered gilt chairs sat a simple coffin with Mother laid out in it looking surprisingly well, if a little more tidy that usual. She had on a brown dress — one of her favorites — and her hair had been carefully styled. We stood gazing down at her. The humming of a remote motor emphasized the overall breathless quiet. Suzanne reached out and took my hand. I heard her sniffle and felt tears springing to my own eyes. I leaned over and placed a kiss on Mother's cheek and jumped back, not prepared for the terrible cold, waxen feel of dead skin. Suzanne did not kiss her, simply stood staring, and presently we bestirred ourselves and went back out into the hall where the director waited with hands folded behind him.

We said our farewells and once out on the street, jumped into the car as if pursued.

"Let's take that drive," I offered.

"Yes," said Suzanne and pressed back into the seat, looking out the window.

We drove for a while in silence. Dr. Creighton's words had suggested a part of Mother's life unknown to us, and I remembered times when I intruded upon her restraint with a personal question, only to find evasion: "I merely want to know that you are well and happy," she would say. "That's all that matters. Please, darling, don't worry about me. Don't misunderstand me, but having uninterrupted time to paint is a luxury." Dr. Creighton had been part of that. We had not.

Finally Suzanne said, "Wow, this is a changed town. Many of the same New England houses, but a huge influx of suburban mishmash." She stretched her arms upwards and sighed. "Lixie, actually I'm tired. Let's get groceries and go back and have a nap, okay?"

"Sounds good to me," I said, making a U-turn and heading back into town. As we entered Central Market, I added, "We've got work ahead of us; kids coming in. We need to stock up. Then before naps, we should call the caterer and the minister."

"You already know who?"

"I told you. Dr. Creighton gave me names. We can start there," I said.

"Oh, Dr. Creighton. What's his whole name?" She giggled. "I'll bet it's pretentious, along the lines of William Woodruff Archibald Creighton."

"Well, at least his list was helpful. Please let's try to be pleasant if we see him again, as we surely will at the funeral."

"I'll try," said Suzanne as she veered off into an aisle of canned goods. "Got to have olives," she muttered.

"It's Alex," I called after her. "Alex Creighton."

Chapter Three

Coffee in a Slicker

At seven the next morning the ship's bell by the front door clanged. I glanced at Suzanne in the next bed. A fluff of blonde hair poked out from under the down comforter, but she didn't stir. I put my feet on the cold floor. *Who could that be at this hour?*

Halfway across the living room I realized I was wearing only my nightgown, so expropriating Mother's yellow slicker from the pegs near the door, I slid the bolt back. Dr. Creighton stood there in a grey pinstriped suit, black hair damp with comb marks. His tie had pink and yellow flowers on a blue background, a bright note.

"Hope I didn't wake you," he said. "I wanted to tell you a few things. Sorry for the early hour, but we're up for mass. Anne's insistence, since the boys are home for your mother's funeral."

"Oh," I said, stepping aside. "Do come in. Cold, isn't it?"

"Yes. It's been a mild October so far, so this is not surprising." He walked into the house and glanced around.

"Your sister arrived?"

"She's asleep."

He stood there awkwardly.

"I'm sorry," I said. "Would you like a cup of coffee? Excuse my costume. As you said, it's a bit early."

He hesitated and then smiled. "Yes," he said, "I'd like that." Stooping slightly to accommodate the low doorframe, he followed me into the kitchen and pulled a stool from under the counter, apparently a routine gesture. Perching his body on it, he watched as I filled the coffee pot and plugged it in. Conscious of my comical costume — bare feet, slicker over a nightgown and hair an untidy mass of curls — I pulled the slicker tighter around me. Under the circumstances, waking Suzanne by going back to dress was not an option.

I looked at him. "I feel a little self-conscious, sorry." I pushed the hair out of my eyes. He was silent. I looked at my bare feet and added, "I was rude on Friday."

He stared at me a moment. "You were — beyond rude — actually hostile is more how I'd describe it. I couldn't figure out why."

"Could we leave it that you were a shock? I mean you've got to admit that your popping up spouting arrogant gibberish about friendship, ethics and confidentiality could be taken as offensive. For pity's sake, this was my mother."

He nodded. "Okay. I see. I did hope it wasn't a visceral reaction to me, I mean me personally. Sometimes happens, doesn't it?"

"It does," I said and turned to check the progress of the coffee, for that's exactly what I felt.

"Okay, I didn't handle it well," he cast into the silence. "You walked into an unusual situation. I'm sorry. I was absorbed in my own feeling of loss and not particularly considerate of yours." He looked away and started fiddling with the notepad with the list I had started.

The coffee was ready, and I busied myself with cups and saucers. "Do you want a piece of toast?" Again I spoke over my shoulder, so I wouldn't have to look at him again.

"No thanks. Black is fine. I've had breakfast," he added.

I handed him his coffee and picked up my own. We were silent. I watched him blow steam off the hot surface before taking a sip. He looked up, caught my eye and shrugged, a sort of puff escaping his lips.

"If my stopping by like this is a nuisance, tell me. I brought you the names of a few people you might not know who will be at the funeral, mainly people connected to your mother's art world. He reached into his jacket pocket and handed me a list. "You're very like her, you know." He stared at me for a moment then roused himself. "I have to get going to church for what passes for a soul-enriching sermon. What are your plans?"

"The children will be trickling in, mostly coming by car. I'll meet my daughter Penny's plane at six. She's flying in from Hartford, and aside from being pregnant, she has a sprained ankle so couldn't drive."

"Well, why don't I meet her and bring her home?"

"It's Sunday. Surely you're not going to Boston?"

"I am actually. I have an afternoon meeting with the doctors in our practice. My office is not far from Logan. What time is her plane?"

I picked a notebook out of my purse to check "Five-ten. Will that work? I don't want you to go to any trouble."

"That's fine; I'd enjoy meeting her." He took his still full cup to the sink and seemed ready to speak, but stopped. "What does she look like?"

"Blonde, pregnant and limping."

"Hard to miss in other words." He walked to the door. "Thanks. Am I forgiven?"

"Please, let's leave it alone, okay?" I answered. "And thanks for offering to bring Penny back."

I heard the front door slam as I padded down the hall to the now sunny guest room. "Time to wake up," I said to the lump in the far bed.

"Oh, hell," Suzanne groaned as she pushed back the covers. "What time is it?"

"Nearly eight. There's a lot to do."

"Oh, is there any coffee?"

"Yes, I've already made it," I answered as I pulled off the slicker.

"What the devil are you wearing that for? Is it raining in here?" asked Suzanne as she rose out of bed and stretched her plump, comfortable body in an arc.

"We had an early caller. Dr. Creighton. I made him coffee." I stripped and started poking in the suitcase.

"You're joking!"

"Unfortunately not. He brought a list of people Mother knew that we might not. It was awkward, but he did apologize for his earlier frostiness."

"And you forgave him?"

"Not really. It didn't get to that. I still don't want him hanging around being helpful. Being Mother's friend doesn't exactly make him ours, does it?"

"No." Suzanne watched me for a moment. "You'll never be fat, will you? It's unfair. You have the body of a thirty-year old."

"And what grief you've given me over the years about my body." I laughed, ignoring her question. "'She's always measuring her waist,'" I said, imitating her early taunts that had hurt me in front of strangers.

"I didn't say that. Ever."

"Yes, you did. One time when I had a crush on that friend of yours from New York and was so painfully shy that I couldn't speak. I came through the living room in my bathing suit, and he said I had a nice figure, and you said that. I was mortified."

Suzanne thought for a moment. "That really bothered you?"

"You bet it did. Now get dressed."

Chapter Four

The Funeral

Thirty-one hours later we buried Mother in an informal graveside ceremony. Seating myself, I spotted Alex Creighton and nudged Suzanne, pointing him out. She nodded and wrinkled her nose.

The fall day was unusually warm with rain imminent in the thin light. Grey metal chairs around the coffin were filled, and many people stood behind and around them. I could just hear the sea rolling in at the end of the point.

As Mother was never a regular at this or any other church, the minister knew her only casually. He spoke of Dad, their long and loving marriage and Mother's painting. He spoke in a slow, monotonous drone.

A few remaining orange and yellow leaves landed on neighboring gravestones in the soft breeze, and an answering whisper rose from the living as they moved on the metal chairs. The setting was fitting, as Mother's religion was of the earth and the sky and a universal higher being. This was the anti-doctrinal clarity that infused her paintings, a detachment like the long look in a sailor's eyes gazing toward the horizon.

There were people there neither Suzanne nor I knew, dressed in denim or tweeds with others in smart formal clothes. Milling children and a few elderly jolting along in walkers were scattered around. Mother and Dad had moved back to Hopwood fifteen years before, where they wanted to be after Dad retired from his banking career. He died of a heart attack a year after they'd bought the cottage, situated not far from where our old house had been. Mother, always obsessed with her art, had eventually launched herself like a small ketch heading out to sea, and from that time receded into her own longed-for world. Her paintings were in museums and private collections, and people now said such things as, "Of course you know McKenna's work. I once met her in Edgartown at a friend's house. Forthright and amusing, but private too."

I found myself weeping. Beside me, Penny reached over and squeezed my hand. I wasn't so much mourning the mother I knew as the mother I was discovering, the one who had eluded me. But I understood. In a way, my commitment to writing was as deep as Mother's to her art. I looked at my pregnant daughter and thought about the future human life growing in her lovable body. Clearly Mother thought she had done well by her family and thus moved on to a life of her own with diminished emotional obligation.

Her slow disengagement had really started when I was twenty and left college to work for a magazine in New York. Suzanne was already in California, married. Mother would have been forty-five at the time, and she went to Switzerland for a year to study with the American landscape artist, Charles Meager Coffin, who had a school in Zurich.

At the time I thought Dad remarkably patient and supportive but later realized he was happily immersed in his job and had a comfortable life, with a roomy apartment overlooking Boston Common, a daily maid, friends, and his pleasure in fishing, his literary club, and his weekly cribbage game with old cronies from Harvard, among them the author, Arthur Schlemmer, who now lived in Hopwood.

The minister was slogging into concluding remarks, platitudes about loss and the comfort of knowing Elizabeth McKenna was 'in a better place.' *She was already in a pretty good place*, I thought irritably. *When would he cease these interminable bromides?*

Finally, as the last prayer drifted into silence, one large golden leaf detached itself from the maple tree above and fluttered onto the coffin. We all stood, and as I headed back towards my car I noticed Alex Creighton standing off to the right of the chairs. He was crying. I couldn't very well backtrack to avoid him so I stopped, intending to say a few polite words. He looked up and put his hand on my shoulder.

"It's hard to think of her, I don't know, gone," he said. I pulled away and looked up.

"Yes, it is," was the best I could do. As I turned to leave, a group came across the grass towards us.

Alex drew the woman to him. "Anne," he said, "this is Elise von Sturnheim, Elizabeth's daughter." We shook hands.

Anne, tall with short red hair and sharp features, was wearing a silk paisley dress with a cashmere sweater thrown around her shoulders. Flickering on her hand was a large diamond. The contrast between her stylishness and my own black dress, wool coat and head of scarcely restrained curls was obvious, at least to me.

And," Alex added, turning sideways, "these, Elise, are my sons, Edward, Drew, and David." Later, I remembered that he said 'my' sons, not 'our' sons. I looked at three handsome young men.

"Hello, all of you," I said, shaking hands in succession.

"I'm so sorry about your mother's death," Anne said, her voice cultured and gentle.

"Thank you," I said nervously. "Look, I hope you'll all come back to the house. There'll be a lot of uneaten food if you don't." And smiling thinly, I walked away. If the truth were known, Anne Creighton made me feel old and not a little dowdy.

"Nice of you to console the doctor," said Suzanne, as we finally made our way through the crowd and got into my Honda. We left our various children to climb into my son Matthew's old Datsun.

I glanced at my sister staring straight ahead with a vile little grin on her face.

"And what kind of remark is that?"

"Simply an observation," she said.

"Well, what would you expect me to do? He was right in my path, and then his family came up."

"Oh, Lixie, lighten up. He's sort of cute if you can ignore how obnoxious he's been."

"Oh, for God's sake, Suzanne!" We came up behind a long line of cars leaving the cemetery and had to stop. I turned to her. "Astute observation! I've watched our mother's funeral, and now I'm pondering whether Alex Creighton is cute or not. Really, you are intolerable."

"Ooooooh," giggled Suzanne. We crawled up the hill to the gates, and she added, "Well, what did you think?"

"Good, but not really Mother, if you know what I mean."

"I suppose if the minister didn't get it, he can't be blamed. A few clichés were all he could do, poor man."

Traffic had come to a halt again. "Pull out to the right here," suggested Suzanne, "and take the dirt road that comes out by the Black's farm."

I made the turn, and we bumped along up the hill and out the back road, leaving the rest of the cars idling. At the end of the lane we found Alex Creighton and his family. Their green Range Rover was stopped, and Alex was getting out. He glanced back and shouted, "Only be a minute. The gate is closed." We waited while he unlatched the gate and waved us forward. Anne took in our presence with a smile. The boys waved.

"Lovely couple, don't you think?" asked Suzanne.

"Give your mouth a rest," I growled.

After we had pulled through the gate, I drove off.

"Do you remember," asked Suzanne settling back again, "when you and I got lost here riding the Black's horses? We got back to Mother's after dark and thought everyone would be frantic. Instead they were drinking and playing bridge. Even our husbands barely looked up when we came in. I've never felt so utterly inconsequential in my life."

"Yes, but do you also recall why we got lost?" I asked.

She glanced at me. "No. No, I really don't."

"Well, my darling sister, it was because you were trying to scare me. You took a trail I'd never seen and several more turns, and when we had ridden for about ten minutes, you galloped off ahead of me."

"Oh, yes, I could have left you there too, but I didn't." She smiled. "Wasn't that the same visit when the laundry blew off the line and landed on the beach? A dog took off with Karl's undershorts, and he was furious. Pretty funny."

"He does have a commitment to modesty," I said.

"Understatement," pronounced Suzanne as we turned into the lane to find a few cars already parked on the lawn.

Chapter Five

Gathering

We rushed into the house where people stood around talking, drinks in hand and food already laid out by the caterers. One of the servers came over to us. "And will you be Mrs. McKenna's girls?" she asked in a strong Irish brogue.

"Yes," we answered in unison.

"And which one will be Mrs. von Sturnheim?"

"I am," I said.

"Ah, yes, you take after your dear departed mother. I'm to deliver a message from your husband. He said give her my love and tell her to call when she can, and that was it."

"Well, thanks. Everything going all right here?"

"Oh, yes, mum, we've got it under control. It's a sorrowful occasion, it is. But we're making the best of it, good food and good drink. The living must go on and enjoy the Lord's bounty."

Suzanne put her hand on my arm. "Elise, give me a second before we get involved here. What I'm thinking is . . ."

Adelaide Black, Mother's lifelong friend, interrupted us. "Oh my, it's good to see you both. We're going to miss Elizabeth. There aren't many of us left."

We both gave her a hug. "You look wonderful," I said.

"Oh, do save the flattery." she said. "When the good ones die, you're left with the old bores. Doesn't matter what you look like."

Her kind old eyes twinkled as she took a sip of her martini and glanced from one of us to the other. "Remember the time you two got lost on our horses? We were worried sick."

Suzanne and I exchanged raised eyebrows. I slipped sideways saying, "Excuse me, I've got to see where the watercress sandwiches are," leaving Suzanne to talk with Mrs. Black.

The room was filling up now, quiet conversation giving way to the higher pitch of voices loosened with the nudge of alcohol. There were a few bursts of laughter, and the younger people smoked and drank beer on the terrace, caught like a frame from a silent film in the large window. I could see my daughter, Penny, sitting on the wall, resting her sprained ankle. Enid couldn't get away from her job in London, but I was glad Matthew had made it in time for the service.

I yearned to go outdoors myself, past the chattering young, to smell the soft salty air and feel the sand grind up between my toes. *Later*, I thought. *And later too I will think about calling Karl and trying to describe all of this to him.* The trouble was that Karl's impassive reactions to what I told him made me over explain. Then he would patiently summarize what he thought I was trying to say. I found Ellen, one of the servers, and ordered a scotch on the rocks.

Out of the corner of my eye, I saw Alex and Anne talking with Mrs. Black. Anne held white wine in one hand and a little sandwich in the other.

The closeness of people and the din were suffocating, and I longed for time to reflect and absorb. The full impact of Mother's death gripped me — the loss of precious and unconditional love and the realization that I had taken it for granted.

Alex was at my elbow when I refocused on the room. "We have to go. Edward and Drew are leaving in the morning, and Anne has made reservations at Keenan's. Thank you for this. It was a goodbye your mother would have liked. I'll miss her sorely."

I looked up at him. "We all will," I said. Anne moved in beside him, looping her arm through his.

"Elise, it has been a pleasure meeting Elizabeth's daughter, and thank you for the nice get-together."

"You're very welcome, both of you," I said. "Perhaps we'll meet before I leave." I smiled. Anne turned and saw Mother's lawyer, Davis Hopkins stride across the room towards the front door.

"Oh, Davis," she called, "tell Patsy that we want her to sub in Wednesday's bridge game."

"I'll do it." He disappeared out the door, slamming it so hard, several people looked up.

Penny begged for bed when everyone had left. "Mother, I've had enough food. My ankle hurts, and I love you. I'm heading for Nan's bed." She kissed me, and with a hug for her brother Matthew, her cousins, and her Aunt Suzanne, she departed to the big Victorian bed in her grandmother's bedroom. Mother had always been Nan to the children.

Later, when the remaining young had departed for various neighborhood beds and even the slit of light under Penny's door had vanished, Suzanne said, "What I was going to suggest earlier was that you stay here for a while. It's not that I don't want to help with the packing up, but I can't. Shooting starts Monday, and you have free time right now. Did you bring your computer?"

"Well, yes, as a matter of fact. But I assumed we would get through this together."

"Maybe we can start tomorrow, but then I've absolutely got to leave. Darling, I do want to help. Please don't misunderstand. If you'd prefer to wait, I can come back in January, after Christmas and all. Is that what you'd like?"

I thought a moment. "Right now, Suzanne, what I want is to have a walk on the beach. I'll tell you when I come back, OK?"

"Good enough," said Suzanne. "You have your walk. I'm going to get into bed and read for a while. See you later."

Chapter Six

A Walk on the Beach

I retrieved a heavy sweater from the bedroom and let myself out the door to the terrace. The diffused light lit my short walk through the sea grass to the beach. The breakers were louder now and once over the dunes, the night became blue-black. I was isolated from the sanctuary of warmth and family. *I should have brought a flashlight*, I thought. A fine mist skimmed my face, and I plunged toward the edge of the water. I could see lights flicker far out at sea in the dense atmosphere, and a car horn trumpeted in the distance. A dog barked. Racing clouds intermittently revealed a hazy moon. No stars. The pulse of the sea and its thud as waves landed on the beach mercifully eased my tangled thoughts. I tried to pray, but the words collapsed inward.

I felt rather than heard footfalls on the hard sand — an unexpected intrusion into my black world. I wanted to run, not from fear, but from a reluctance to share the moment with anything alive, man or beast. The beam from a flashlight wobbled its way toward me. When it was within twenty feet, I called out. "Who is that?"

"Elise?"

"Yes, over here." The beam fell full on my face and then swept aside.

Alex was standing in front of me, the wind blowing his hair. He snapped the flashlight off and took my arm, steering me along the beach. "Let's walk," he said.

Too surprised to answer, I was propelled into the wind at a rapid rate. "I couldn't go to bed yet," he said.

"I didn't try," I answered.

"Right."

I pulled up and disentangled myself from his grip. "Look, Alex, I know you're upset. So am I, and I'd really prefer to be alone right now. The day, the people . . ."

"Yes, of course," he answered. "I get it, Elise."

With that he swung around and headed back towards his house. I paused for a moment trying to grasp the situation. I didn't think I'd been overtly rude, simply honest. I plunged ahead along the packed sand and took deep breaths of the damp air, letting my thoughts float away from Mother, Suzanne, Karl — the insistent way my choices and reactions had a habit of referring to them before moving into action. And now Alex was beginning to insert himself into this next chapter. *Would he continue to show up, to remain impervious to my resistance? Why? What did he want?*

I could barely make out the edge of the water and realized I should start back if I wasn't to lose myself in the blackness and walk straight past Mother's house. Then the clouds cleared and the still watery moon shone down, making of the damp sand a pewter path ahead of me. When I was halfway to Mother's house, Alex called out. He was sitting on a dune to my left. This was the limit. *The nerve of the man!*

I walked over to him. "What the hell do you think you're doing?"

He grinned. "Being a pest I suspect. Am I right?"

It was comical; Alex crouched there in the dune grass, swinging the flashlight back and forth along the ground with his face lifted towards mine, his teeth glinting through his smile.

"I'd say you got it right, a miracle of clear thinking." Hands on my hips, I glared down at him.

"Could I come in for a drink?"

"No, Alex, you could not. Now trot home and go to bed like a good boy."

He stood up. "I do think you're being unreasonable, Elise, offensive in fact."

"I am nasty — no one you want to know. I don't know why you keep trying."

He stood up and grasped my shoulder, hard. "Okay, game's off. Let me be clear. I had hoped we could be friends, maybe not as your mother and I were, but at least friends. You're so like her Elise; it's uncanny. She was everything to me."

"Okay, Alex, but right now I've got a lot on my mind. Suzanne and Penny are asleep in the house, and I don't want to wake them. Tomorrow Suzanne and the kids leave except for Penny, and the next day I'm taking her back to Hartford. I'll be back later. Perhaps we can attempt this again, and I'll try to be nicer."

He leaned over and gave me a quick kiss on the cheek and before I could react, he was loping along the beach. I turned and climbed the dunes in front of Mother's house and went in. I flipped off the few lights in the living room and found Suzanne fast asleep in the guestroom. I'd tell her in the morning that I would come back and do the packing and lists.

Chapter Seven

Family

The next morning I telephoned Karl. His voice was furry with sleep. "Hello, darling," he said. "How is it going? Was the funeral the way you wanted it?"

"Yes, it was — simple, a lot of Mother's friends."

"I'm glad. Things are great here. Carlos arrived last night, and we were up until two working on the sets. They're going to be splendid. We've already got a tentative offer to rent them to two other productions next year, which should offset the expense. Do you miss me?"

"Of course," I said hurriedly. "The children were sorry you weren't here, but they understood. Karl, what will we do about Thanksgiving this year? Will you be able to come home, or shall I come out there?"

"I'll come home. Aren't Penny, Christopher, and Fiona coming?"

"I don't know for sure. They did say they might, and I know Christopher's parents are going to Germany for a month."

"And Enid? Matthew?"

"Probably not Enid; she and Evan are too busy; and I doubt Matthew. It's a long trip for him, and he's barely gotten into his new job."

"Well, it will be a good one anyway," he said, "with the five of us. Remember how much Fiona ate last year?"

"Oh yes. And Karl, I wanted to let you know that I'm planning to drive Penny back to Hartford tomorrow and probably go home for a few days. I'll need to come back here, though, to clear out Mother's things. Suzanne and I have to decide what to do with the house too."

"Will she be there to help you?"

"No, she's shooting right through December. She can't be here, but I don't mind, really."

"Seems unfair as usual, Elise." Karl had never trusted Suzanne's motives in anything. She was too ornate a creature for a set designer whose career revolved around illusion. Karl liked the tangible and provable in his daily life.

"We've talked about it. It's fine. I have time, and it's a good place to be alone and write."

Really, we were a well-oiled machine, the two of us, locked in timeworn patterns, managing to stay content. And that was the word: *content.* We loped along parallel paths, periodically uniting over family issues and celebrations, dinners with friends and occasional musical or theatrical performances. We nattered on a while and then said our usual "Goodbye and take care."

The coffee pot did yeoman's duty that morning, and Suzanne had exhausted the supply of pastries from the local bakery. Children, in a flurry of departure stopped by, stayed to question, discuss, hug, say good-bye. Friends came too. Suzanne and I moved through the house in a daze, our plans to do any work derailed. Penny would stay over one more day, so we could drive south together. She was looking forward to being alone with me on the way back to Hartford. Four-year old Fiona was a handful, and it was a respite for her to be a lazy, pregnant adult for a while.

"Mother," called Penny from the kitchen. "Where do I find more coffee?"

I went through to find her rifling through cabinets. "In the refrigerator," I said. Leaning against the counter, I added, "Penny, I thought we'd try to get an early start in the morning and stop in Boston to see Kristina for lunch."

"Fun," said Penny, retrieving a can of Maxwell House from the refrigerator. "How long since you've seen each other?"

Kristina Arnold was my best friend at Beaver Country Day and later my roommate at college. With an American father and Danish mother, Kristina was an international child of divorce. During school and college I spent several summers with her in Biarritz, where her mother's second marriage had landed her in a large restored farmhouse, built around a courtyard and not far from the sea. Good memories there, funny times.

"I guess it's been eight years," I told Penny. "I don't know why, but our lives swing away from each other for extended periods. It never matters. It's always the same when we get together again."

By late morning, Suzanne, Penny and I were alone, the waving, hugs and kisses over. I leaned against the kitchen counter. "Whew," was all I could muster.

"Your friend the doctor called earlier", said Suzanne. "You were out saying goodbye to the kids, so I took it. He said he'd take me to the airport."

"What?" I asked. "Why is he home today? His office is in Boston."

Suzanne shrugged. "He mentioned a dentist appointment. He's heading in at around two-thirty, so I grabbed his offer. Bit early for my plane, but I don't want you to have to drive in then turn around and go back tomorrow. Penny said you're going to have lunch with Kristina."

"Well, Suzanne, that's very thoughtful of you. I mean it. You will be nice to him, won't you?"

Suzanne giggled. "I've stashed a kitchen knife in my purse in case in comes to violence."

Penny glanced down at Suzanne's oversized bag on the floor and said, "It's certainly big enough to hold a knife and rations for a week."

"Very funny," said Suzanne. "Well, since I've already packed, let's take a quick look around and figure out what needs to be done."

The three of us went through mother's room, checking the closet, bureau drawers and furniture. Everything was tidy, and the shelf in Mother's closet held a pile of scarves, sorted by color with red on the bottom, three hatboxes and a row of purses. Then we looked in the hall closet. The shelf there held a run of photograph albums by date, and we got sidetracked looking through a few of them. I set an early one when Suzanne and I had been babies on the dining table, as I had not seen it before and wanted to go through it. After a while, Suzanne looked at her watch and said,

"Let's get the hell out of here and go to Annie's for lunch before I have to leave," which is what we did.

Chapter Eight

Penny and Kristina

Suzanne called the next morning before Penny and I left for Boston, to say she'd made it home all right.

"How did the drive with Alex go?" I asked.

"You'd have been proud of me. We chewed on politics and current affairs — not his or mine," she giggled. "He's pretty liberal, and I was very well behaved."

"I'm reassured to know that's possible," I said.

Penny and I reached Kristina's Beacon Hill brownstone around noon. It took us several minutes to find a cramped parking space and several more to back and fill into it.

Locking the Honda doors, we mounted the steps of Kristina's house. I lifted the brass knocker and let it fall. We heard the beat of high heels on a wood floor, and Kristina flung the door open. "Darlings, come in, do. I'm on the phone but won't be a minute. Go in there," she said waving to her left. "Pour a drink," and she disappeared down the hall.

We entered a large drawing room fitted with French antiques, pink, green, and blue chintzes and Impressionist paintings. Light flooded in through a bay window, and a Pekingese sleeping on the sofa opened its eyes, cocked its head, and let out a sharp yap. It jumped down and bounded over to us, sniffing and wagging. Another one stood across the room, eyeing us suspiciously and finally walked primly away. Penny reached down and patted the first one, and it followed her as she circled the room, admiring the paintings.

"Wow, Mother, these are real! This is a Degas. And that's a Mary Cassatt. Aren't they wonderful?"

"Exquisite," I agreed. "Kristina and Carter lived in Paris when he was ambassador. And of course her mother had houses in France, Greece, and England. I imagine these paintings were mostly hers."

Kristina came into the room from the dining room beyond. "Isn't this too marvelous. I'm rich, finally rich. Dear Mommy's fortune. All from a distillery." She laughed, fitted a cigarette into a black holder and sat down, immediately bounding up again. "Come, let me show you everything. I see you've met Pandora and nasty Bozo. Bozo hates everyone but me and has nipped Carter on more than one occasion." As if bidden, Bozo reappeared and circled around Kristina's feet.

We toured the house, every room in perfect taste. Only Kristina's bedroom seemed familiar, the bed littered with books, notepaper, needlepoint, underwear, and a full ashtray. I knew that Kristina stayed up until the wee hours of the morning, slept late into the day, and armed with strong coffee, pursued her phone calls and daily organization from her bed. She always had her own bedroom, and it appeared that her second marriage to Carter was perfect in every way, each of them independent and mutually complex in their interests. "It's wonderful, Kristina," I ventured. "Not you, but wonderful."

"Not me? Well, maybe, but I decided that if I let a decorator do it, I'd spare myself the agony of indecision. Actually," she said with a conspiratorial smile, "I spend most of my time playing games on the computer. Do you have a computer? It's the most marvelous thing. Carter and I each have our own, and we compete from separate rooms."

"Are you writing?"

"Oh, yes. Recently had a travel article in *Town and Country*. It's amazing. You simply take wonderful trips, stay at five-star hotels, eat glorious food and then write about it. Such fun, you can't imagine. Nobody has good taste any more, so I provide it."

The kitchen was an amalgamation of modern, pale, and costly. We stood aside while Kristina banged and chopped, and then we finally sat down in the dining room to fresh mushroom soup and watercress salad accompanied by crusty French bread.

"So, tell all," said Kristina between substantial mouthfuls. "Are we mournful after the funeral, or is it a relief? I wasn't sad when Mother died; she had turned into the worst sort of bitch. Really always was. Spent half my life trying to imitate her ruthless self-centeredness and then gave up. From a distance it looked sophisticated, clever. Close up it was horrid."

"Not my experience of my mother," I answered. "Losing her was numbing, pointed up the missing pieces in our relationship. There was a great deal I never knew about her."

"Well, really, how much does Penny here know about you? Surely not the juicy little tidbits I do. And I'm sure I missed a lot. The real question is what do we really want to learn about our parents? How we've annoyed them at times? That Mummy didn't love Daddy every minute of every day for umpteen thousand years? Or vice versa? No, of course not." She paused to nibble at a sprig of watercress held in her fingers. "Aren't I right, Penny?" she added.

"I guess so," answered my circumspect daughter.

"And why should we?" pursued Kristina. "We bring out different parts of each other and in turn show what we wish about ourselves. Who am I to you? Dear eccentric old Kristina is different from Carter's view of silly game-obsessed, sometimes insecure, sometimes brave Kristina, or your mother's view of conspiratorial, lazy, funny Kristina. You see what I mean?" Without waiting for an answer, she ploughed on. "Well enough of that serious talk. Tell me, Penny, what are you and that attractive husband up to?" She reached over and patted Penny's stomach. "Aside from the obvious," she added with a wide grin.

Lunch continued with cheerful gossip, the news that Carter had been asked to be on a presidential committee to make economic sense of European trade under new agreements, and a sense of well-being and connection with my life returned. Alex Creighton faded into a vague and mildly uncomfortable part of a crazy few days.

After lunch we left, and I edged the car out of the parking space and headed for Hartford. Penny went over various members of our family, showed resentment at Suzanne once again leaving me with the responsibility for practical details, and spoke unenthusiastically about a new class on parenting she and Christopher had taken at the insistence of her obstetrician.

"What actually worries me," she said switching subjects, "is that children are exposed to more hype than we were. I mean they have television, and now the Internet looks like it will take over. But even if we limit their exposure, their peers have it all, and they hear it. It's the violence and the silliness. Christopher hates it. Of course we know what a purist he is. Architecture will never satisfy him. He hates his clients. He can't convince them that architecture is using space in both practical and imaginative ways. They want their pillars and Jacuzzis. Everywhere you see instant Taras. God's little house seeds, I call them, because where one sprouts, it germinates and casts seeds everywhere." She paused. "Of course Christopher should be a poet or a priest. Mum, I do love him, but I wonder if he was meant to live in the real world."

"Love him," I said. "You'll not change him. Change is for you. If it's raising babies you want, do it. If it's social contribution you want, do it. Christopher is Christopher. People don't merge, and when they try, they end up hating the result. The best you can do is encourage him to be his best self, and do try to be kind. It's often hard. We're good at seeing room for improvement in others; terrible at honestly assessing ourselves."

I didn't expect Penny to answer, and she didn't. As I sped along the highway, she turned her face to the flying countryside, her mind grinding away.

Once I'd hugged Fiona, and carried various bits of luggage into the house, I left. Back on the highway for the home stretch to Baltimore, I wondered why I was doing this when Karl was gone. Mother's house needed attention. My computer and enough clothes were in the car. I made a U-turn on the median strip, searching for state troopers, and headed north again. I realized I had simply used the break in activity as a signal to move on.

It was evening before I turned once again into the narrow lane. Alex and Anne's house, on a rise above Mother's, was a blast of light, and I heard the faint sound of people talking and music through my slightly open car window. I decided to stop to look and turned off the car's headlights. A man and woman came out onto the deck and lit cigarettes. I heard the woman say, "Oh, George, you know you'll never train that dog. You want a servant, not a dog."

Then I saw Alex. He emerged onto the deck from another door and walked to the railing, looking in my direction, although I was sure he couldn't see me in the darkness. A woman walked out to him and put her arm around his shoulders and gave him a kiss on the cheek. He turned to her and started talking. I saw him throw his arms upward and bring them down on her shoulders, shaking her in a gentle way. She turned and went back into the house. He followed minutes later. The woman was not Anne. I put my car into neutral gear and glided into the double parking space in front of Mother's house.

This time the house was dark and cold. I found switches, turned up the heat and brushed aside the recent ghosts. Once surrounded by peace and light, I laid on the sofa simply glad to be there, glad not to be heading for Baltimore. I pulled an old afghan off the end of the sofa, wrapped it around me and fell asleep.

Chapter Nine

A New Day

The sun was high in the window over my head when I woke, and the afghan had fallen to the floor. I uncoiled my stiff legs and went to check the thermostat, and giving it a push upwards heard the furnace cough to life. I went down the hall to the bathroom. Sun washed over the floor and tub. Gulls bawled overhead. A beautiful morning, well advanced, probably around ten. I turned on the taps and steam rose as the tub filled. Snatches of the last few days came back to me: confusion of course, everything happening in a rush, but also a vague sense of release, a gentle longing for an undefined future, a ray of light out of my grasp but looming. It was a wholesome feeling; one that had been absent in recent years and was so at odds with the present that I didn't pause to analyze it.

Pushing the door closed, I looked at the full length of my naked body in the mirror. Age had not exactly passed me by, but the overall impression wasn't alarming, gravity's impact being as yet minimal, anatomy blurred but not wilted.

Sinking into warm water, my toes tingled while radiators crackled with rising heat. I lay back and submerged my head, running my fingers through my hair, letting it float out around me. Baths had always been a special pleasure to me. Mother's shampoo was still on the side of the tub beside an empty bottle of bath oil. I squeezed out a dollop of thick blue liquid and rubbed it into my head, working it into lather, then slipped backward, rinsed and washed the rest of me, dipping my head under the tap for a final rinse of my hair. As I emerged I heard the phone ringing, reinforcing my conviction that bath taps and phone lines have their own form of symbiosis.

I leapt out, grabbed a towel and ran into the kitchen. "Hello."

"Mum! I was desperate. What are you doing there?" It was Penny.

"Oh, darling," I answered, "I'm sorry. I would have called you in a few minutes. I got it into my head to turn around after I dropped you off. I have clearing out to do and thought, why not now?"

"Well, you might have let me know."

"You're right, but I didn't think any of you would be looking for me late at night."

Penny relaxed her stern tone. When do the roles shift between parents and children? This, of course, was what my mother refused to acknowledge.

She would not be pinned down to accountability except on her own terms. After a moment of irritation with Penny, I realized a lifetime of checking up on each other's welfare couldn't very well be regarded as intrusion. It was what the child had been taught by me, her predictable and concerned mother.

"Enid called at six," Penny went on. "She tried to reach you at home, but obviously . . ."

"Oh, dear," I said, "how is she?"

"Fine. She wanted to know how the funeral went and any news we might have. I told her it was what Nan would have asked, simple. It seems so quick now, like a mirage," she added. "Anyway, Enid got a promotion and is moving to Paris."

I noticed a puddle of water growing around my feet as my legs dripped. "Paris? How exciting! Or is it? Is that what she wants?"

"You know Enid. The only direction on her career compass is due north. She'll be managing partner of Bradley and Clark before we can blink." She paused. "She sounded lonely though, said she wished she could have been with us. Mum, I wonder if she'll ever regret not having children once she's got this ambition thing out of her blood."

"Who knows? Life is not a sequential journey. We do have choices, and speaking for myself, I didn't make enough of them. Life happened to me; not me to it. Enid's different." Penny didn't answer, so I went on. "She's happy with Evan. Is he going with her?"

"Of course. He's at home anywhere. She did say he has a one-man show in Dublin in January. It's not easy for him. People hardly make impulse buys of sculpture the size he creates."

I chuckled, thinking of the huge stone figures Evan Forester created, mostly mothers and children. I had always found his subject matter ironic in view of his and Enid's complete lack of enthusiasm for parenthood or marriage. "Well, darling, I'm dripping bath water over the kitchen floor, so I best go dry off. I love you. And give my love to Christopher and Fiona."

"I will. Take care. I'll call this evening or tomorrow."

Immediately I realized that I had caused thoughtless worry to my family, so I quickly called Karl. I got his answering service and left a message as to my whereabouts.

Chapter Ten

Central Market

After giving my hair a good rubbing, I threw the towel around my shoulders, made coffee and opened the refrigerator. In addition to condiments and leftovers we'd forgotten to throw out were a box of baking soda, three bottles of Perrier, and a bottle of wine with a green ribbon tied around it beside a wheel of Brie. A scrap of paper was tucked inside the ribbon. *Strange, I don't remember the wine and cheese being here before we left,* I muttered.

Who on earth would have known I came back here except perhaps Alex? And if he had, how had he gotten in the house without my knowing it? I reached for the paper.

> *Elise, forgive my intrusion; thought you'd gone and used my old key. Saw your car and then you asleep on the sofa. Apologies, but glad you decided to come back. My key is on the counter, so I won't be tempted to break in again. Best, Alex.*

The key was there. I picked it up and rolled it over in my hand. *Alex Creighton seems to come with the house*, I thought wryly. It was faintly humorous, but I didn't want him hanging around or popping up at odd hours if I was going to be there for any length of time, which it appeared I was.

Instead of clearing the house, I took the day off, found an Agatha Christie mystery of Mother's and curled on the sofa by the window with the afghan wrapped around me. At noon, I retrieved a solitary can of chicken soup from the cupboard and heated it for lunch, then napped and read the rest of the afternoon. By late afternoon, I felt refreshed and headed out to Central Market for food.

Mrs. Black was at the butcher's counter when I came in. "Well, Elise, what a surprise! I thought you'd left."

"I did. I got as far as dropping Penny in Hartford and then turned around and came back. The house needs attention, and I realized that doing it now makes sense."

She smiled at me. "Impulsive, but probably sensible. Is Karl away?"

"Yes, in Denver doing the *Flying Dutchman*. Gone until Thanksgiving. So . . ."

"As good a place to settle in as any," she said. "Well, why don't you come and have dinner with Dick and me tomorrow night? Six thirty-ish?"

"I'd like that," I said.

She picked up a small package from the counter and wiggled her fingers. "Until then," and she left.

"What'll it be?" asked the butcher.

"Hello, Clarence," I said, "I'm Elizabeth McKenna's daughter, Elise."

"Well, for pity's sake," he stood back, hands on hips, and smiled. "I guess it's been years since I last saw you. I was sorry to see her go — a lovely lady. We'll miss her."

"We will." I agreed. "I'd like a couple of loin lamb chops and a quarter pound of dried beef, sliced paper thin," I said.

While he was preparing the meat, I skimmed the shelves, picking up anchovies, tuna fish, olive oil, bread and eggs, bits of food I thought would get me through the next few days.

Finishing at the produce counter with a head of lettuce and other vegetables, I heard Clarence say, "Evening, Dr. Creighton."

Good Lord, is there no escaping the man? He immediately broke off and gave me a smile that started slowly and widened to what appeared to be genuine delight before he turned back to Clarence. It was a trivial gesture but clearly more intimate than our history supported.

As I was checking out at the front of the store, he came up beside me. "May I stop by this evening when I take my walk? I should explain. I walk a lot at night. Can't sleep. Got used to late night talks with your mother."

I didn't welcome the prospect but thought it would be churlish to refuse when added to my incivility of the last few days.

"If it's not too late, I'm really tired," I lied.

I paid for the food and carried it to my car. Taking the long route back gave me a chance to look at the town of my childhood. After meandering around the familiar old parts of town, I went off towards the water. The architecture here was on a grand scale, a mix of rambling two-story houses with truncated protrusions like stillborn wings. The abundance of construction materials crammed on the front elevations — stone, brick, half-timber, wood, and concrete aggregate — were at aesthetic odds with the plainer and more economical brick or aluminum sides and backs.

At the center of one web of streets stood the old house that had belonged to family friends, the Milnes. It had once commanded acres of lawn and a view of the harbor, a Georgian brick residence with a flight of steps up to its oak door. A sign now pronounced it the *Harbor View Clubhouse.* I had played on the third floor of this house as a child, my friend Tom and I racing Irish Mails (four-wheeled vehicles propelled by pumping the steering column up and down) over the vast attic floor. There was a slot machine in one corner that gave us a wicked sense of pleasure as we inserted dimes purloined from our mothers' pocketbooks. We waited in vain for a windfall of coins from the old machine. Spending several hurricanes inside its solid walls, Tom and I would sit at the top of the winding stairs when we were supposed to be sleeping, listening to the hilarity of our parents as they chattered and drank champagne while the wind howled, rattled windows and tore the harbor boats from their moorings.

I proceeded to the Yacht Club. Time had not altered this neighborhood, and ghosts of my long scattered friends hovered in doorways. First was the house where we buried rusty nails among the white hydrangeas, turning them a gratifying garish blue over time.

The club itself was also as it had been, a straggling heap of weathered boards culminating in an array of docks. Six Rookies, single-mast, seven-foot Marconi-rigged dinghies in which we had learned to sail, were still tied up. Surprising, as we always took them out of the water after Labor Day.

I parked in the empty lot, walked down to the docks and looked out over a few remaining sailboats. The marshes beyond had been filled in, and a line of low warehouses rose along the skyline before the channel opened to the vast Atlantic Ocean that had been our playground.

Back at Mother's, I unloaded my groceries. The house now felt familiar, although I had not been there that often. Our original place, a short walk from the main beach, had been turned into apartments and several smaller lots with one-story houses.

I put the meat in the refrigerator. The last of the day flickered on the horizon as I walked out the back door and smelled the breeze, heavy and briny. Picking my way along the path, I cleared the dunes with their stiff grass and now leafless beach plum bushes, from which Mother used to make jelly every summer.

Chapter Eleven

A Walk in the Past

Low tide had left an expanse of smooth wet sand scalloped with brown lines of kelp. A yellow Labrador ran along the beach towards me, and a ship moved slowly across the water, far out. A foghorn wailed its doleful song. I saw these moments as a bridge between the old and the new, a demarcation in my life with the edges of the unknown unfurling towards me, and the shadows of the old dissolving behind me.

"May I stop by this evening?" rang in my ears along with my frosty reply.

Foamy waves rolled in along the water's edge as I thought about Karl. We met while I was working for a culinary magazine in New York, having quit Sarah Lawrence College after two years. I was twenty and found it exciting to be going out with a well-known set designer fifteen years older than I.

"Ah," he had said at a cocktail party, "I find you American girls charming, so natural and yes, outspoken."

He didn't take me to the places I used to frequent with boys my age: The Little Club, The Stork Club, and The Maisonette. Karl's taste ran to quieter places with superb food. After one such dinner, as we walked along Fifth Avenue, Karl stopped in the middle of the sidewalk and bent over, appearing to pick something up.

"Oh look," he said, standing in front of me holding out his hand. "What a pretty little box!"

He handed it to me, and glancing at him in surprise, I opened it. It was from Tiffany, and in it was a ring with a sapphire set in a braided gold band.

I loved his Austrian accent, was swept away with the glamour of getting married before most of my friends, and my family was delighted. Karl was everything they thought would give me a solid secure life; being wife to a successful man was the ideal of my generation.

The yellow lab reached me and wheeled around, bounding from side to side and then rubbing up against me.

"Hello, big man," I said, stooping to pat him. He looked up, his tail wagging, and then fell into step behind me.

It was clear after a few years Karl did not want or need intimacy. He liked my presence in his life, but his own remained cloistered. He discussed his work in the most fleeting way. He worked hard and enjoyed the company of other people in opera.

When Enid and Penny were born, he surprised even himself with his enthusiasm for fatherhood. He took the girls, and later Matthew, into his life in a way he had not me. He had infinite patience with their awkward practice sessions on various instruments and conducted little family musicales in which each of the children performed for friends at dinner parties. They went with him, each in turn, to opera rehearsals. They knew everyone with whom he worked.

My need for companionship carried me into more activity than if Karl and I were more connected: volunteer work, lunches with friends and finally, when the children were older, into intensive writing. It took five years to publish a short story; my first novel still lay in a heap on my desk, a rambling tale that now looked undisciplined and depressingly naïve.

I was happy raising the children. Enid was smart and beautiful, but boys found her strength and willfulness daunting. She was twenty when she finally fell in love with Evan Forester, a sculptor from Seattle.

Penny was the opposite — carefree, lagging at school, popular with boys and girls alike, not in the least intimidated by conventional standards of talent as she tried both music and acting.

Matthew never knew a moment when he didn't want to write. His proficiency won him summer jobs until he graduated from Dartmouth and moved to Cincinnati as a business reporter.

My third novel had amazingly made it to the *New York Times* bestseller list. Now my fourth novel, *Gone Crazy*, was out, and I had already started a new one.

The day was flickering low, and I turned and hurried up the beach. The yellow lab followed me, and I gave him a stern refusal as he tried to follow me into the house. With dark, Alex Creighton would appear yet again.

Chapter Twelve

Alex Out of the Storm

By the time I arrived back at the house, it was dark. I took out the lamb chops and chopped garlic, spreading it over their surface. Pouring myself a scotch and water, I lit the fire. The wind was rising and the dry crackling of the few remaining leaves on the oak and maple trees at the front of the house mingled with the snapping of the fire. The phone rang. It was Karl.

"Hi, darling. I see you had a change of plans."

"Yes," I answered. "I'm glad you got my message. It's glorious here, and I can kill the proverbial two birds: writing and packing up. I'll stay a few days and call Ruth to come in and clean our house while I'm away. Of course I'll go back for Helene's surprise party — Anthony would never forgive me if I missed that — and then come back. So we'll both be home near the same time for Thanksgiving."

"That works for now. I'd enjoy having you here, but the days are full, and you'd be bored. We've been working straight into the evenings, and I wouldn't feel I could do that if you were here. I'd want to be with you."

"That's fine. I think I'm getting like Mother, enjoying the solitude. This house doesn't make one feel lonely, simply alone. I've got ideas about the new book that I need to work out."

"Good!" Karl always used that word as punctuation. "So, my dear, we are happy with our work. You can't believe how the whole production has changed in a few days. We've thrown out the idea of using rigging to hint at the ship, and we're building the whole front deck. It will take up the entire stage. Carlos is brilliant, fascinating to see him work."

"Sounds fun, Karl. I've no particular news, except that I ran into Mrs. Black at the market this afternoon, and she invited me there for dinner tomorrow night. I also drove around town — a lot of new construction and most of it out of proportion, tacky."

"Does the village look the same?" he asked.

"Amazingly so. Wright's Drugstore is still there, although the soda fountain is gone, and the hardware store is still on the corner. Central Market is unchanged except for fancy lighting and new counters, and the village green and the churches have survived."

"Must be a pleasure being there and knowing you will have time to explore it all."

"It is, but I do wish Mother were here too. It's sad to lose her and know that we'd really spent little time together in recent years."

"That is," he answered, "as she wished it. You tried."

"True." There was one of those pauses that was easy but signaled little more to be said. "I guess I'll cook my lamb chops and try to write for a while."

"Well, it's time for me to get back to work here. I'm calling from the theater. Love you, Elise."

"Love you too. Stay safe." And we rang off. The wind was howling by now, and a storm was imminent. The fire was licking up points of flame as the draft became erratic. I refilled my glass and got my PowerBook from the bedroom. Setting it up on the dining table, I pulled one of the Windsor chairs over and sat down to work on divorce for my main characters. This part was difficult for me, but, like any writer, I could draw on moments of anger and construct words around them. I had heard enough painful accounts from others that I presumed I could carry it off. Writing is hard work. You have wonderful ideas while in the bath or on a walk, and then you sit in front of your keyboard in confounded silence, the blank page little more than an accusation.

I thought of Jerry Damione and our few years as lovers. So long ago and how angry I was when we parted! Perhaps that was what divorce felt like, the knowing there would be no reward for time invested; the difficulty in recalling good feelings; the cessation of any wish to plan; the raging anger at the other person and the gaping void ahead.

Drawing on long-buried emotions, I imbued my characters with rage and hopelessness. It was two hours before I stopped writing. I went to pour an extra splash of Scotch into my glass and slip the lamb chops under the broiler. The rain was a heavy drumming on the roof.

I remembered that Mother used to keep cigarettes in the freezer for her occasional pleasure, and there they were in the back. I felt a sense of well being, of accomplishment, when the front door banged open, and the wild weather blew a wet Alex ahead of it.

"Good Lord," I said. "You're a soggy sight. Is this part of your pleasant evening walk?"

"Not pleasant by any standard, but I said I'd stop by, and here I am."

"Well, you make it sound like a grim obligation, and you're dripping all over the place. Back up, take off your slicker and go stand by the fire. I'm cooking my dinner."

He removed his yellow oilskin raincoat and hat, hanging them by the door, came into the kitchen and headed for the cabinet with the glasses. He took one, filled it with ice and poured himself a scotch. "Better," he said, going into the other room. "Bring your meal out. Want another drink?"

"Maybe later," I said. "I'll be there in a minute, when these are done."

I took a puff of the cigarette and set it in the ashtray while I made salad. Putting the chops and the salad on a plate, I carried it and the ashtray back into the living room. Alex was leafing through a copy of *Vanity Fair.*

"I think I like Madonna," he said. "She's like those mirrors in a fun house; she makes people see themselves."

"I never thought much about her. I'm afraid I miss a lot of pop culture these days." I sat in a chair near the fire. Alex took a sip of his drink and looked at me.

"Go on. Sounds a lot like intellectual posturing."

"Well, I didn't mean it to. In fact I resent that comment. I'm not above what's popular, but I have to make choices."

"So, go on."

"Well, there's not a whole lot more. I guess what I was trying to say is that I reached a point in my life where I had to cut distractions. You can either fall prey to whatever comes your way or decide what you'll allow to take up your time."

"I think I've lost the ability to do that, if I ever had it." He laughed.

"Okay. So, pop culture, the latest news, stuff like that is seductive, and you think you're actually learning something, but you're not, not really. And," I waved my hand in the air, "I'm not saying it's wrong. What Madonna does, to Madonna, her agent, her family, her friends, has meaning. For me, though, it informs my life and writing in no constructive way."

"Surely as a writer, you must draw on all sorts of experience and knowledge. What seems peripheral one day might be useful another."

"Well," I was struggling here. "I think if its context were related to what attracts me, it would inform my understanding. Of course I write mostly using what I know and experience in addition to research, and I want to include what attracts me. If I need pop culture for context, I can always investigate. That's different from including it in my daily life as a contingency, as you suggest."

He bent forward, putting his drink on the table and leaned back, his eyes twinkling. "So do you find me attractive? Could you write about me?"

I stared at him, shocked. "What's that supposed to mean?" He grinned at my reaction. "Are you trying to come on to me? If so, you're barking up the wrong lady."

He didn't reply, but sat there smugly smiling, his hands folded behind his head.

Finally dropping his hands, he said, "Okay. Sorry. I'll be serious. Let me try my own version. There was a time when my enthusiasm and curiosity was totally centered on healing, better medicine, in other words, research."

Relieved that we'd brushed aside the awkward flash, I asked, "And then?"

"Then copious money from a top practice in an upscale market, a wife who basks in what it produces — those things came my way. I took what success dished out, and man, was it seductive!"

I didn't want to sound preachy, but it was clear to me where he was going. "And perhaps now you're waiting for a road block, an event that leaves you with no responsibility for the decisions and pushes you where you think you want to go without anyone blaming you?"

He picked up his glass up and took a long drink. "Yes."

"So, this whole journey into medicine started with healing, making the world better — we'll call it altruism. Is that fair?"

"I suppose it is."

I took a deep breath and forged on. "I have a theory on that. Taken on its surface, altruism wears thin, becomes unsustainable. There are unselfish angels among us, few and far between. For most of us, like you, rewards tend to come in material and powerful ways and become addictions. Looking back, we feel we've betrayed the purity of our original intent."

"I think you're right."

"Well if properly understood, altruism is selfish."

He waved his hand impatiently. "Get on with it."

"Have you ever noticed that happy people are nice to be around?"

"Of course, what are you driving at?"

"Alex, it's simple. If everyone around you is doing well, you too prosper. If you're part of a community that takes care of its own and builds solid relationships, you're in a better place than if you have to fight for every morsel you eat and fear others. It looks like altruism, and the benefit accrues to the group, yes, but also to the individual. Generosity then springs from a sense of well-being, and well-being springs from a sense of security, physical and emotional." I leaned back. "Of course that's my view of it."

"Why can't I be both: successful and altruistic?"

"You can do anything you want. Finding out what that is, is the challenge, but I sense you've taken off on the highway to success and turned a blind eye to the less obvious byways of research — efforts that have few guarantees of attainment and material rewards."

"Elise, this is all a bit much. Likely you're right on all points. Equally likely, I don't have the courage any more to experiment, to meddle with uncertainties. I lead an expensive life, boys in private education, a wife who to say the least, likes the status quo, and me, who also is not averse to the good life."

"That's a formula built on optimism and laziness. To break out, you've got to be the one to push the rock from the cave and confront the light and shadows."

"Yes, I know." He smiled at me. "But, as you say, I'm an optimist and lazy to boot. Do you mind if I get another drink?"

"Of course not," I answered, finding to my surprise that I was rather enjoying the conversation. When he returned, he said, "Are you saying that there is a sure way out of tedium that also provides a comfortable life?"

"Oh, for God's sake you're not bored, merely restless. Most men seem to identify themselves by what they do, not who they are. Any steps you take now could have a negative impact, but it takes determination to make change."

"Sounds patronizing, I must say. Are women superior in that regard?"

"No, not superior; different," I replied, refusing to engage in hackneyed arguments about the sexes. "What would you say if I asked you who you are?"

He scratched his head and thought a moment. "Well, I'm a doctor who is weary, who's been listening to complaints often better cured with home remedies from people who can afford me as a substitute for emotional fulfillment, a way of getting attention. I'm a guy who thinks he wants to go back into research. I'm a father. I'm a husband."

"Stop! Those are all roles. Who are you?"

"Well, then, I'm a frustrated poet, painter, nomad, a poor sap who finds himself trapped by his own need to command respect." He paused again. "Well, Elise, good question. Who am I?"

"How would I know, Alex? Ask Anne. Ask your friends. I'm not advocating you stare at what I am sure is a most alluring navel, or that you spend hours going over the litany of your successes and failures, if indeed you've allowed yourself any failures. But possibly re-examining how you see yourself, along with what might satisfy you, could help."

He shifted around in his chair and looked at me. "I am attached to success, Elise. Am I willing to risk losing it?"

"Why? I mean why so attached?"

"At one time I needed to prove to my stepfather that I wasn't worthless. He believed I was, so perversely I fucked up everything he wanted me to do. I did the hippie bit. I smoked pot. I never made the soccer team. I couldn't wait to get out of Denver. I even left halfway through Harvard Med School and lived in California."

"So is he pleased now?"

"I don't know and don't care. I haven't spoken to him in years."

"So there's no reward from that quarter for your efforts? Then what's holding you back except inertia?"

"Anne's been there to see it, a sort of surrogate for my father.

Fortunately, after the California episode, Harvard took me back, although reluctantly. My first practice was back in San Francisco. That's where I met Anne, ten years younger. Her dad was a big-deal investment banker. She struck me as beautiful, spoiled, headstrong, desirable, made me want conventional things. We were married within three months, and by then I was so locked into breathless achievement that I never looked back. Anne continued work at an art gallery until 1977 when Edward was born, and then in 1979 Drew came along. In 1980, I had the chance to join this practice in Boston, so we moved here."

"Forgive me, Alex, but in a way this is getting uncomfortable," I said.

"How so?"

"I don't feel right; it's all kind of intimate, and Anne sits at home, while we . . ."

"While we what?" He grinned. "I'm trying to be neighborly." He took a gulp of his drink and then added, "The sole reason you could feel any discomfort is that you find me attractive. Am I right?"

"What a preposterous thing to say!" I burst out. "Not only preposterous, but insufferably vain. Really, Alex, I think you should go home now. Well, finish your drink first."

"You're right, I've not finished my drink, and I'm not leaving."

I realized he was a bit tipsy and trying to be funny. But he was also taking things to a dizzying level, and I wanted him out of there. I had to admit that he was attractive in a lean, swarthy way, but the idea of entertaining anything but a casual friendship with him, even though he had known and loved Mother, was beyond question.

There was an uncomfortable silence. "Sorry," he finally said. "Long day — a lot on my mind. Drink's gone to my head, whatever. Anyway, while I sit for a few more neighborly minutes and finish my drink, tell me more about yourself, your writing for instance, then we'll be even."

I smiled thinly, stymied. "No, not now. Maybe another time. Please go."

He stood. "Sorry again. Mucked it up, didn't I? I'll go, but don't hold this against me; I can be quite the gentleman."

He walked unevenly to the kitchen and put his glass in the sink. I waited by the door, holding it open to the cold night. The rain had stopped, so he pulled his slicker and hat off the hook and slung it over his arm. Turning as he went through the door, he said, "There will be better times, Elise. Friends. That's what we'll be, friends forever." He reached out and ran his finger down my cheek and left. I closed the door softly and leaned against the frame for a few moments before loading my plate and our glasses into the dishwasher and turning the lights out.

Chapter Thirteen

Disturbances

Friday offered a continuing gray cold rain slapping sideways at the gradually lightening windows. I felt fully energized and wrote for three hours at the dining room table, my feet in socks and sheepskin slippers, my fingers hammering away on the keyboard. Characters were in full bloom, fracturing lives. The more the wind roared, the faster I wrote. At eight thirty, I made coffee and went to draw a bath. The phone rang. It was Adelaide Black.

"Good morning, Elise. Are you comfortable over there?"

"Yes, indeed," I answered. "I've been up for hours writing. What a dreary day it is!"

"Well, light a fire and enjoy it," said Adelaide. "The reason I am calling is to say I've invited a few other people for this evening: the Creightons and a man called Arthur Schlemmer. Alex and Anne Creighton were good friends to your mother, and I know you will love Arthur. He and your father go way back. Never married. He's a writer too."

"Oh, I know," I said. "I remember Mother and Dad mentioning him. I've read nearly everything he's written, and what fun it will be to meet him! Thank you."

"We'll see you six thirty-ish. Do you want me to ask the Creightons to bring you?"

"No, Adelaide. I'd rather come on my own. But thanks."

The house was cold, and I ran a bath watching the steam rise. Soon I would have to dig into the long job of sorting out Mother's belongings. While understanding her restrictions, I was resentful that Suzanne wasn't with me. I thought the best way to go about the chore was to make piles around the house and get boxes later. I'd make a list of the furniture and objects and go over it with Suzanne on the phone.

Once warmly dressed, I worked in closets, emptied bureau drawers, sorted silver and china, and made list after list. Mother's LPs — from Mozart to Ella Fitzgerald and Bobby Short — were my companions through the chore of disassembling the long life of a mother I half knew. I learned much about her that day. There were thirty-seven shoe polishing cloths from hotels around the world and shoes unworn, still in their original boxes. For a frugal and unadorned woman, I found this baffling. Journals were tucked in drawers around the house, entries with different start dates and a few months recorded before they ended. Wrapped presents with no tags on them sat on the hall closet shelf, presumably for the person who for whom she had not bought one but who arrived with an offering. I do the same thing.

Glancing at the line of photograph albums on the closet shelf, I thought I remembered leaving one of them out before heading for Hartford. I looked around me, but it wasn't on the dining room table where I thought I'd put it. Going back to the closet, I found it was in its original chronological order. Later, I had the same unsettling feeling when I found the scarves in Mother's closet shifted and the red ones no longer on the bottom as I remembered. These tiny incongruities could be easily explained by the chaos of the days we'd all been together there. Penny might have done both things during the afternoon Suzanne left. I then remembered that Alex had kept a key until I returned from dropping Penny off. He'd left it for me when he delivered the wine and cheese, but of course that was absurd. He'd had a key for ages. *Why would he be going through Mother's closets now? Odd and highly unlikely.*

Her sketchpads were in one drawer, and I took an hour off while eating a sandwich at midday to look at them. They reached back into our childhood, rough drawings of my father, my sister, and me, various animals who had warmed our lives, and always the sea.

At four o'clock I gave up and made a cup of tea. While I was waiting for the water to boil, I washed up my lunch dishes and came upon an envelope in the cupboard as I was putting them away. It said "Elise" on it. It made me feel odd, a hand from the grave touching my cheek, a mother's voice saying what? I set it aside. I would read it later, after I had come back from the Blacks. Knowing I would see the Creightons this evening reminded me of the conversation with Alex the night before. His remark about finding him attractive had changed the tone, had me speculating on what kind of man he really was. Of course he was good-looking and obviously bright, but his behavior was troubling to say the least. Even if it was merely an attempt at light humor, it wasn't funny.

Chapter Fourteen

Dinner at the Blacks

The Creightons were in the living room when I arrived at the Blacks. Alex followed Adelaide into the hall to greet me, and I noticed Anne standing in the doorway. She looked lovely, dressed in a purple silk shirt and black trousers. Her red hair was fluffed up around her flawless face, and she wore jewelry that was nothing short of spectacular — Schlumberger if my guess was any good.

She came toward me. "What a dreadful time this must be for you," a deepening of her voice and furrowing of her brow emphasizing her concern. "I hope you don't mind my husband dropping by to check on your comfort last night. He was so terribly fond of Elizabeth that it's sort of a habit with him when he takes his little nighttime walks." I smiled back and said, "No, it was a nice thing to do, neighborly. I am pleased to know that you two are nearby."

Dick Black called from the living room. "Are you ever going to come in and say hello, Elise?" I tossed my coat on the hall bench and went in.

He was seated, as he had been since I was a child, in a sheet-covered chair by the fire. In fact, every piece of furniture was covered with sheets, because Dick Black was an amalgamation of barnyard dust, clay from his sculptures, and tobacco from his pipe. The sheets served a second purpose, as demonstrated by five spaniels scattered in soft comfort. I leaned over and kissed Dick on the cheek, reveling in the familiar smells that surrounded him. He wasn't unwashed, simply a distillation of the life he loved so well. Blessed with lifetime trust income, Dick was busy from dawn to evening on his property, mucking out the stalls of his beloved horses, feeding pigs, working on his now famous small sculptures of horses in his barn studio, or contemplating it all wreathed in smoke from the private tobacco mixture that he drove to Boston once a month to purchase. He used to keep a package of cigarettes in his studio for us to feed to the goats. Phillip Morris I think they were. I remember him teaching me to do this on a day I had been sent home from school, punished for being part of a group that put a bully into a metal garbage can.

In the opposing chair, also by the fire, was Arthur Schlemmer, a great bear of a man with sagging jaws and a wooly cap of gray hair. His eyes were bright, almost black, close together and clear, two sentinels peering over a large, beaked nose.

"I'm Arthur Schlemmer," he said, standing up. I liked him the more for that.

"It's nice to meet you," I answered. "I admire your work enormously. You must do endless research."

"I do. And I'm flattered you've read anything I've written. I can also claim to have enjoyed your books. An imaginative and insightful approach to the ceaseless quandary of being human."

"I have misgivings about my take on it as well as an increasingly jaded view of human nature," I laughed.

He smiled. "I'm sure Shakespeare had the same reservations."

"Well, that certainly puts me in exalted, if undeserved, company," I replied.

"Move one of the dogs and sit. What would you like to drink?" asked Adelaide.

"Scotch and water, please. I can get it."

"No, I will," said Alex and went over to the bar. He brought it over to me, and then said, "Dick has offered to show us his new litter of pigs. Do you feel like going back out in the cold, Elise?"

I took a welcome and large sip, grateful the scotch was floating on the top. "Oh, absolutely. I may even take one home. I've always wanted a pig for a pet."

"Oh, really?" said Anne, sitting on the edge of the paw-stained sheet covering the sofa. "What ever would you do with a pig, Elise?"

I looked at her. "Pigs are intelligent animals, easy to housebreak, sweet and affectionate. I've read about a number of people who have them as pets. They're apparently great fun."

"Wouldn't the hooves hurt the floors?" she asked.

"Perhaps they could wear little booties," I answered and took another large portion of my drink. "Let's go," I said to Dick. I turned to Arthur. "Are you coming?"

"Absolutely wouldn't miss it," he said.

"Absolutely would," said Adelaide, deep in the corner of the sofa with knitting on her lap. As far back as I remember Adelaide had been knitting large, shapeless garments for her three sons.

We went out into the hall to gather our coats. "Are you coming, Anne?" I called.

"I'll keep Adelaide company," she called back. Adelaide was the last person on earth who needed company. My attention shifted to Arthur.

"Well, off to the pigs," I said.

He smiled and took my arm. "Tell me, Elise, could the novelist named

Arthur in your last book have been me?"

We filed through the Dutch door, and Dick slammed it successfully after several tries. Crunching down the dirt driveway sprinkled with remnants of gravel, I sniffed the piney air. These woods had always held magic for me. My childhood was connected to the paths, the stone fireplace in the middle of the woods where we children slept with Dick on summer nights, the ponies we rode who invariably rolled in the stream, the saw mill he kept running far behind the house, and his silent and strong sons who were always there when we ran into trouble. They had been older than I, but there was a primitive comfort about them that made me feel secure.

"Dick," asked Arthur, "Did you ever get the commission to do Antigone's sculpture? I thought you weren't taking on any new projects." He turned to me by way of explanation. "The last Derby winner."

Dick said, "Yes. I'm working on the model now. Couldn't resist."

"Where did you go to make the sketches?"

"Baltimore. Hell of a journey; plane delayed and all. Nice place, though. Servants tripping over each other and the mare set up better than the Ritz. Everything but a masseur."

"Is the sculpture for them or a museum?"

"Them. They've had every winner done for generations. Big room with lighted cases, velvet shelves. Impressive. I suppose I should be flattered."

Then there was silence. As I think Kurt Vonnegut said, the big show was in Dick's head, so we trudged on in the stillness. When we reached the barns, we continued down a steep slope to the back where the pigpen, a fenced off shelter, lay. Dick opened the door. Inside was a sow with a group of tiny pink babies lurching erratically or nursing at her teats. I went in and knelt down on the dirt. The sow looked up and then laid her head wearily down again. I picked up one of the piglets, and the sow grunted but stayed still. Alex came and knelt beside me, reaching out to touch the piglet which was nestling itself into my arms. He put his hand on my head and rose. "Fine looking animals," he said.

Dick grunted in response to Alex's remark, "They are." Dick and Arthur were in the corner discussing rebuilding the shed.

We filed out into the night. Dick showed us his studio and the figure of Antigone that was in the clay stages but would end up in bronze. Sketches of the mare were pinned on the wall above his workbench. The figure was delicate, beautiful work, perhaps sixteen inches in length. Dick was the best there was, but he used to take only one or two commissions a year. Apparently he had now tried to retire to no avail.

The smell of the studio roused old memories — the smoky odor from the potbelly stove in the corner; the earthiness of wet clay; and Dick's pipe resting in a stained alabaster ashtray on the bench. A few half-empty coffee mugs rested on old *New York Times* crossword puzzles. I smiled. Happy memories.

Tramping back up the driveway, Arthur said to me, "Would you honor me by having dinner one night this week? I think we might find a great deal to discuss."

"I'd enjoy that enormously," I answered. Alex kicked a stone that was lying in the road, and it landed ahead of us. When we reached it, he kicked it again, this time hard, and it flew off into the woods where we heard it hit a tree.

"Hey, Dick," said Arthur, "maybe you don't need to raise pigs any more. They're working on cloning at the University of Edinburgh, sheep I think."

"Read about it and hope that's the last of it. Positively horrible." replied Dick.

The indoor warmth was welcome as we returned, and the smell of roasting beef greeted us. Katharine, the housekeeper who had been with the Blacks over thirty years, was standing in the hall.

"Well, well, Elise. If you aren't a sight for sore old eyes!" And she gave me a hug. Katharine had shrunk. I know things appear smaller when we get older, but she was clearly shriveled. I hugged her gently, afraid of crushing her brittle bones. "Yorkshire pudding, like you always enjoyed it," she said.

Anne looked up as we came into the living room. She was chewing a cracker and cheese, so she wiggled her fingers in the air and bobbed her head from side to side. Adelaide was knitting around a cat curled up in her lap. Dick went over to the fire and poked it, making the flames kick up, putting on another log before sitting in his chair again. Arthur poured himself another scotch and returned to his chair opposite Dick. "Guess the peace agreement in Bosnia will hold," he said. "And how about 'The Million Man March'?"

"Sure weren't a million men there." scoffed Dick.

"Well, I hope the Republican landslide in Congress is a prediction of election results in a year," added Alex. "Gingrich better get moving with his *Contract with America*. If they drag their heels now, it'll be Ross Perot who rides in on a white horse and gives the election to the damned Democrats."

"There are many issues converging," said Arthur. "It's going to be hard for anyone to downplay them and make hollow promises. You've got health care, crime, education . . ."

Dick snorted. "There will always be the same insoluble issues tied to hyperbole and nonsense at election time."

"Yes, but the problem is also the information we get. The press has become an arena for superstars. It doesn't report; it opines."

"Dinner," called Katharine from the hall.

The meal lived up to the aroma, and we ate and chatted. Anne was charming, and a surprisingly keen mind directed her animated comments. I hadn't expected that from the little I'd seen and heard, but I should have. Alex would take a lot of work, and she had clearly put in time staying attractive and well informed. I left early, having confirmed dinner for the next night with Arthur.

The air was crisp and cold and the sky sprinkled with stars. Taking a quick glance upward at Castor and Pollux in the night sky, I climbed into my Honda and bumped down the lane, past the barns and out onto the main road. It was with gratitude for old friends that I pulled into Mother's drive. The house was silent and welcoming, warm and softly glowing as I entered. I poured a glass of water and sat down at my computer. A whole chapter had formed in my head during the evening and was waiting to break into words. Time evaporated.

Chapter Fifteen

Over the Last Fence

I couldn't stop writing that night. At eleven o'clock, I heard the crunch of footsteps on the drive, and knocking on the door announced Alex. *Who else could it be? Good Lord, this has to stop.* My breathing was uneven, and I wanted to run, but I wasn't sure whether it was towards the door or out the back into the safety of the starry night.

I got up and pulled the door in. Wordlessly he entered, looked at me for a moment, and finally asked, "Okay?"

"Okay if you've brought me a pig," I answered trying to lighten the mood and slow my heartbeat.

"I haven't, but if it would help our relationship, I'll get one tomorrow from the lab at Harvard."

"We don't have a relationship," I said.

"We will though."

"Question: what makes you so sure that's possible?"

He shrugged. "Has to be." Then he smiled, and took off his coat and threw it over a chair at the dining table where I had been writing. "Look, Elise, I need help, and although I don't want to, I have to unload a few private matters on you." He turned and went to the kitchen. "But first, a nightcap. Scotch for you?"

"I guess so; however you can't stay long. It's late."

"I know, but we need to talk."

"Do you walk every night; even in the winter?" I called after him.

"Yes, often. It's my thinking time. Can't sleep. I love it out there alone with the sound of the surf, and the stars and the moon to talk to." He came back into the room and pointed at the sofa by the window to the beach.

"Let's sit over there." I got up and followed him, all the while realizing how familiar with this house he was.

I could go through the whole agonized conversation again, but let me furnish the bare bones. Alex left at three in the morning.

The upshot is that he was at a medical conference in Switzerland two years before we met. There he met a scientist from Russia who realized that the failure of certain drugs to treat Alzheimer's disease was due, not necessarily to the drugs themselves, but to delivery systems, the way drugs reach the blood stream. Alex explained that Alzheimer's was an area of medicine that fascinated him and that he had been doing research into it on the side while practicing as an internist in Boston. He had even published a few articles in *JAMA* (*Journal of the American Medical Association*) on the subject, which is why the scientist had sought him out.

The man, Roald, worked for a Russian company and had recently discovered what became of research through secretive channels. He claimed that the minute they decided a promising treatment or cure was ready to move to clinical trials, people were selected from among the poor and indigent and used as guinea pigs, many dying as dosages and tolerances were worked out. Of course these people were paid well, told the trial was harmless and signed release forms before trial. Thus therapies could move rapidly through the system to approval stage. Once officially approved, they sold the research to one of a loosely knit group of small international pharmaceutical companies that met informally once a year in what passed for a medical conference and was held in an out of the way place. Alex said Roald had no idea whether the government was aware of any of this or not. For his part, Roald was locked into the company until he could leave the country. He had signed a non-disclosure agreement and had seen what happened to two other researchers who tried to leave.

"Strange fellow," Alex interjected in his lengthy narrative, "Size of a major appliance with atrocious breath."

Why was Alex telling me all this? Because Roald had brought with him and given to Alex research, with the hope that Alex could move it into honest channels with no human lives endangered. The potential for money would allow Roald and his family of four to move to the United States through channels already established.

I was transfixed by the enormity of what he was saying. "So what have you done with it?" I asked.

He looked down at his shoes. "Nothing."

"Nothing? Why on earth not?"

He raised his head and turned to look at me. "Because I was fired up and ready to go when I came home, and the first thing I did was discuss it with your mother. She said she'd think about it, and after having conversations with a few of your father's old business connections — she wouldn't say who — she convinced me that the whole thing was too dangerous to touch for a number of diplomatic reasons that actually made sense."

"Was part of it danger of jeopardizing your career?"

"Yes, of course. One option would be to approach a pharmaceutical company and hope for the best. But, you can see what a bunch of research papers with not even official approvals from a country like that would require here in terms of getting FDA approval. And furthermore, what the hell would I be doing with those? The other option was to pretend it was my research, and there would be a dozen ways to poke holes in that claim."

"Did you ever try to get in touch with Ronald or whatever his name was?"

"Roald. And yes, but he wasn't at the laboratory he told me about, and even though I used pretty shrewd people to track him, I came up with nothing."

"Where are the papers now?" I finally asked.

"That's the thing, why I'm telling you this. I don't know. Your mother made me give them to her for safekeeping, said she'd hide them, so I wouldn't be tempted, but would give them back if I could come up with an ethical way to handle it."

"I see," I said, realizing that the displacement of the scarves and the photograph album was not my imagination. "So, when I left, you came in here and started searching."

"I did." He pursed his lips. "Look, I'm sorry, I had no right to come snooping in here, which is why I left the key for you. I've had it for years, a sort of safety precaution in case your mother wanted the house looked after in her absence or if, God forbid, she fell or hurt herself."

"Okay, I understand."

"But," he went on, "having given you the key, I now fall on your mercy and ask you to help me look. I want those papers."

"Why suddenly now?"

"Because there's a possible way to use them that's come up, and also, because your mother is gone, and soon everything here will be too." He swept his arm in an arc and softly dropped his hand on my knee, leaning towards me.

"Please, Elise."

I rose abruptly and walked towards the kitchen. "I need another drink. If you hang around much longer, I may become a dipso! You seem to be nothing but trouble."

He followed me. "Thanks for the compliment, Elise. I remember saying you are like your dear mother. I take it back."

I swung around and picked up a pad of paper from the kitchen counter and hurled it at him. It hit the side of his face and fell on the floor behind him. Staring at me, he reached up and touched his cheek coming away with blood on his hand where an edge had grazed the skin. I was appalled. "Oh, God, I'm sorry, Alex. Really. I mean . . . " I handed him a paper towel.

He mopped at his face, ran the towel under water, and cleaned his face again. The towel was wet and pale pink drops ran down the side of his face onto his white shirt collar.

"You done?" he finally asked.

"Yes," I said, but it came out like a squeak.

We stood there transfixed, staring at each other, at a complete loss as to the next move. What actually happened next still astonishes me. Alex, took two steps towards me, held out his arms and pulled me into them. I laid my head on his shoulder and broke into shaking sobs, unable to stop. I don't know how long we stood like that, but I do remember his stroking my head and murmuring the way one does with a hysterical child. I have no idea what he actually said. I do know it felt good to hold him, to feel his warmth against me. And then we were kissing, releasing knots in my heart and mind. Alex led me back to the sofa. There was dim light there, and we sat together, murmuring, touching, and holding each other. It was an island of peace at the end of many confusing and conflicted days since he had called with news of Mother's illness. We had both loved her, and now here we were, sharing what? I had no idea.

Chapter Sixteen

Suzanne Knows

With Alex gone and the next day in progress, I called Suzanne, read her my lists and asked her opinion. She said, "What's wrong, Lixie? You sound brisk and efficient, not your typical chatty self."

"It's awkward going through this alone," I said in as matter-of-fact a tone as I could muster, trying to deflect sisterly poking. As usual she wasn't deterred.

"I know I left you with the work of sorting out, but that's not the issue here is it? You sound tense. Is that doctor bothering you?"

"Of course not. Don't be silly."

"I'm lots of things, Lixie, and you've probably pointed each one out over the years, but I'm not silly. Something is bothering you."

"Please, Suzanne. This is enough of a strain. In a few days I go back to Baltimore. I have things to do there, but I want to make decisions before I do. Later I'll come back and list the house and get rid of or ship this stuff out. Help me."

She sighed and gave up. "OK, read me the list again."

We worked through Mother's possessions, taking the few things we ourselves wanted and assigning others to our children. "I haven't finished going through the desk, and there are diaries around. What do you think we should do with those? It doesn't seem right to read them."

"I'd like to," said Suzanne. "She wouldn't have left them there if there was anything awful in them."

"What about Dad's letters to her?"

"You should probably burn those."

"Also, there is a handful of letters in a box in the attic. I don't recognize the writing, but I haven't looked at them either," I said.

"It's up to you. Probably see what they are."

"OK," I said. "I almost forgot. We'll need to deal with the paintings. There must be twenty or more here in her studio behind the garage."

"A museum or the gallery. Ask Davis; he'll have discussed them with Mother. I think each of us would like one. You and I have a couple, but the children don't. Would it be too much trouble to photograph them and send pictures to me?"

"No, I guess not. I'll do that tomorrow, and then I'll be able to get the rest done when I get back."

She paused. "Oh, and Lixie, was there any jewelry? Is it there? Dad's? Mother's?"

I'd not thought of this. "Why, no, now that you mention it. I'll look around, but I think I've pretty much covered the house."

"Well do look again."

I paused and then blurted out, "Suzanne, you're right, Alex is a problem."

"I thought so. Oh, baby, don't get involved, if that's where it's headed. He's peculiar. I don't know what it is, darling, but he bothers me."

I paused. "He's not peculiar; he's different."

"Please be careful; this is too fast for anything meaningful to have developed, I know, but you're vulnerable. Your marriage is tedious — well my word; you'd say it differently — but you remember how hurt you were over Jerry. We both know I've been no angel through the years, especially when Phillip was obsessed with that gum-chewing pregnant secretary, and we came close to divorce."

"Wow," I said, "you never mentioned that before. When did it happen?"

"A few years after we were married. It seemed so silly at the time; he kept making me have her and her husband over for dinner. I couldn't take it seriously — she was so NOT his type, which I think is what allowed us to move on. But I have to admit it changed my attitude towards our marriage. Call it trust out the window."

She paused and then went on. "When you're young, trust is vital, but even in its absence, there can be resilience and optimism, the ability to push on. You're fifty, even though you don't look it. Being older makes it worse; it goes deeper, hurts more." I heard her take a deep breath. "How far has it gone?"

"Not really anywhere," I said. "Let's drop it."

"Well, I'm glad you're going home soon. It'll give you time to think. What are you doing in Baltimore?"

"Meeting with my agent over the book. Also, I promised Anthony I'd be there for Helene's surprise party. He's having a dinner dance at the club for her."

"Well, fun, and it will do you good to be back among friends. Is Karl coming home for it?"

"No. You know what he's like when he's staging an opera. Nothing gets in his way. Anyway, he hates parties."

"Better yet. You can go and have a good time. I've always been nice about Karl, but darling, he truly isn't fun."

"Look, you've made your point *ad nauseum*. Enough! He's a lot of other things that are lovable, and I'm used to him."

"Well, baby sister, stay sane, and call me when you get home. Meanwhile, watch your step with Alex. It's not possible for you to know him well right now."

"Thanks. I'll call you tomorrow or Thursday. Love you."

"Love you too. Bye."

I looked at the phone for a long time. There is no substitute for sisters, even difficult ones.

Chapter Seventeen

Elizabeth's Letter

Later, I remembered Mother's letter and retrieved it. With the dregs from the coffee pot in my cup, I sat at the dining room table, pushing the scattered pages of my manuscript out of the way.

Dearest Elise,

You won't find this until I have gone. I'm leaving it for you, as I'm sure Suzanne will leave you with the drudgery, and you'll be the one to find it. You need to tell her what I've written. She's busy and hates this sort of thing. (When Suzanne was little and there was work, she would disappear. I often found her curled asleep behind the furnace on an old blanket.)

I'm afraid of what you both may find out later, so I need to explain. I've left a will — Davis Hopkins has probably showed it to you by now. Pretty simple. What's not obvious is a sum of money that we distributed over the years that could surface in discussions. You have a right to know why we did it.

What on earth is going on here? I thought, pausing to take a sip of the now cold coffee. Anticipating something alarming, I got up and wandered around the room before continuing.

After the war, your father did not come home immediately. Then in 1947, he was part of the occupation troops in Italy that were sent to the Free Territory of Trieste along the Morgan Line between Italy and Yugoslavia. We were apart a long time, and he had an affair with a young woman over there. Later I learned that he thought she moved back to Venice and put the whole matter down to a wartime romance –– a common enough occurrence — and never mentioned it. Naturally when it came to light, I was hurt. Our friend Arthur Schlemmer helped me understand the traumas of wartime and resulting relationships — lonely, frightened men looking for comfort.

Years after he came home, the young woman wrote your father, saying that she had tuberculosis and the prognosis was bad. There was a baby, a boy. She had written to an aunt in Chicago and hoped to send the child there, as she could no longer care for him. The letter was signed with her nickname, Lili. She gave the aunt's name and address, adding that she hoped your father would help in whatever way he could.

He did say she came from a good family — he didn't think she'd lie. Given the timing, it was obvious the baby was his. She wouldn't have written him otherwise. The aunt was elderly and didn't want to take on a child, so she called your father. Once he explained it all to me, I didn't behave well. Here I had your father back from the war, and we had two little girls. I didn't want another child, especially one who'd remind me of what had gone on in Italy.

In the end Dad hired Davis Hopkins to get in touch with the aunt and to provide for the boy. We never knew what happened next except for Davis's assurance of a satisfactory adoption. We didn't want to know more. Over the years your father made contributions to a trust Davis set up. Fortunately we had plenty and found the money no hardship.

There. I've done it. So, if, in going over the will this crops up, you will understand. Your father left me a lifetime trust, but there might be some reckoning at the time of my death. I don't know.

This'll be a shock to you and Suzanne. The boy could be anywhere by now, but likely he was adopted by someone in Italy and never came over here. The fact that you have a half brother somewhere in the world may make you want to find him. You could upset a lot of people that way. Do be careful.

Believe, please, that Dad and I had a happy life together and know too we loved you both. After your father died, I focused on my painting, as you know. When I got cancer, I became more obsessed. You'll sort out the remaining canvases, but definitely I want you to have the one of you in the garden at our old house. I painted it before your father came home from the war and saw you for the first time. For Suzanne, the one of her sailboat in the harbor. Davis Hopkins will know the best way to deal with that estate-wise. My gallery can take the rest.

And, please see that Alex Creighton next door gets the envelope and the package from the shelf in the back of the coat closet as soon as possible. That's really important. Don't let him go all legal and dutiful about the contents; he can be maddeningly rigid when it comes to ethics, but he's been a good and loyal friend.

The pain is bad, and I'm ready to go. One of these days I shall.

May my love for you and Suzanne and all your wonderful children be with you always. You are a splendid reward for an old lady's lifetime.

Your Mother

I wasn't shocked by the revelations as much as intrigued. It was like my mother to have dealt with Dad's infidelity and resulting child in a pragmatic fashion, doing what she felt was right and moving forward with her life. In fact, it might have had a liberating facet to it, allowing her the guilt-free flight to Zurich to study and her subsequent submersion in her art. Certainly, it hadn't seemed to overshadow her life with our father in any critical way. Perhaps that was due, in some part, to his complete return to her.

She was right about one thing. I was curious. She left no clues, apparently had none to offer, and Davis Hopkins in his legal capacity would be unlikely to disclose whatever he might know of the whole issue. I shrugged and returned the letter to its envelope.

Chapter Eighteen

Visits

I put the letter in my suitcase. I couldn't absorb it then. While I was standing facing the bureau, studying my face in the mirror and wondering what my stepbrother might look like, I heard a sharp tapping at the door. I went quickly. Anne was standing on the stoop, the sun sparking copper lights off her hair.

"Hello, Elise," she smiled. "I haven't been a good neighbor, and so I brought fresh banana bread for you."

Startled, I opened the door wider. "Why, thank you," I managed. "Kind of you. Come in. I was about to eat a sandwich for lunch, can I make you one?"

"Oh, no thanks," she said, moving across the living room, glancing from side to side. "I had lunch with friends and was on my way home." She noticed the piles of belongings around the room. "You've been busy. A horrid chore I imagine."

"Not really," I said. "Mother had a good and long life. I'm sad she had to suffer pain at the end, but I expect most of us will in one way or another."

Anne gave a mock shudder. "Oh, I do hope not. I hope I die in my sleep or go in an explosion and not feel a thing." She turned to face me looking serious. "Elise, I'd like to talk with you. That is, if I'm not interrupting anything."

Truly, I couldn't deal with both of them unloading unwanted information on me, and in light of my recent debacle with Alex, I was embarrassed as well. I gestured towards the kitchen. "Not at all. A cup of coffee or a Coke?"

"No, I'm fine," she said, going to the sofa by the back window where Alex and I had so recently complicated our relationship. "I need your help," she said, arranging herself elegantly, one long leg over the other, blue Belgian shoes piped in white casting their subtle shadow on the small oriental carpet. "What I mean," she continued, "is that I'd like to talk something over with you."

"Yes?" I said awkwardly. "I'm happy to put off work for a while."

"Well then, I want to mention a few things about Alex."

I thought I would not be able to endure this. Could this be a confrontation, and if her sense of decorum prevented that, then at least a gentle threat? What did she know of last night except that she may have heard Alex creep in late?

She shifted and gazed out to sea. "You need to understand, Elise, how close your mother and Alex were, how much he misses her. I'm afraid he will try to simply substitute you, and you will get hurt." She turned to look at me. Her green eyes held none of the recriminations I had anticipated. "Alex is a complicated and not happy man," she continued. "It may seem odd, what I'm going to say, but I realize that Alex has been over here talking to you as he would have to your mother. So, to summarize, our marriage has satisfied all of the trappings he so badly wanted, but I personally have never been able to lay his ghosts to rest. Your mother could. So you need to be careful about being used as a substitute." Her hands were working now, gently pinching at the wool of her slacks.

She cleared her throat and went on. "I was dazzled by him when we met. He was handsome, intelligent, had a promising career, and he pleased my parents no end. I was young." She bowed her head. "I wouldn't marry Alex now."

I was touched and relieved at the turn the conversation had taken. This was, after all, a discontented woman.

Anne again looked at me, this time into my eyes. Her expression was bitter and brave and challenging. "You see, Elise, Alex and I have minimal contact. I look out for his house, his welfare, his social life, and in return I lead a comfortable life. No, more than comfortable, luxurious. I do not love Alex now. I do not hate Alex. In good ways we are friends and allies. His affairs hurt once, but they no longer do. In fact, I have had several of my own." Bright tears were teetering on the edge of her beautiful eyes. "It is such a waste," she said, reaching in her handbag for a Kleenex.

I finally found my voice. "Anne, I'm sorry."

"Don't be," she said quickly. "I'm not that unhappy, and I shouldn't have gone on this way. What I really intended was to warn you, not as a potential casualty of my husband's charms, but as your mother's daughter."

"Anne, I appreciate your concern. Really I do. And I'm certain Alex doesn't see me as a surrogate for Mother. In fact I'm afraid I've been the reverse, rude at times."

She raised her eyebrows and smiled. "Really?"

"I feel rather bad about it."

She thought a moment. "Well, don't. He can be a bit overpowering, and with all you have to deal with right now . . ."

"No," I interrupted, "there's no excuse, and I'll try to make amends. Anyway, it sounds as though you have a pretty realistic view of your life."

"I do, and as I said, and I may have come off as more unhappy than I am. It's a good life, living here, having lots of friends, plenty to do. The flirtations, the affairs, well, they no longer bother me. I'm rich, attractive, and can do pretty much as I please."

"An open marriage?" I ventured.

"You could call it that. Alex has had many women, most particularly one named Sheila who worked for him. She started as a research assistant when he was doing early genetic research and she was fresh out of Harvard Medical School. She's the daughter of Raymond Ziegler, the industrialist from Pittsburgh. She's now married to Scott Bigelow and lives here in Hopwood. They come to the house often. The affair ended years ago, and she and I have become friends."

I couldn't help asking, "Why have you never considered divorce?"

"Because, above all, I am a Catholic. I will never divorce, and Alex knows that."

I wished she would leave, but instead she settled farther back on the cushion. "I think I would like that Coke now," she said.

I rose and went into the kitchen and opened the refrigerator to see what my children had left behind. "There's no Coke," I called, "only one ginger ale."

"That's good," she said. I popped off the cap and filled a glass with ice and took both to her.

"Anne," I said, "Do go on."

"Well, what I noticed was the rapidity with which Alex started coming back over here to see you on his way to or from his little beach walks. It occurred to me that he couldn't have gotten to know or trust you that quickly, so the answer must lie in some odd sort of transference from your mother to you as a confidant. You see, your mother was in every sense a friend and even a surrogate mother to him. He adored her. I'm sure much about Alex that even I do not know or understand was known by your mother and died with your mother. I was always glad he had her. By then I was not even resentful that I was not the one he turned to, because the empty spaces he created with his withdrawal from my life have long since been filled with friends, interests, and yes, even lovers. You must think it odd in a way that I would cling to a tired marriage out of religious duty and still think it all right to be unfaithful."

"In fact I do," I answered. "Can you live with the one and not the other?"

"Perhaps." She gave a short laugh. "Catholicism is a complicated web of faith, guilt, and duty. Alex and I both had autocratic fathers with high expectations of us. Psychologically we are still afraid of disappointing them, a childhood vestige I've never explored with any success. I do know he was what I needed once, a sable coat to cover my naked loneliness. The result of course is that he turned me into a passive housewife, an enthusiastic soccer coach and a joiner of clubs and charity work." She sighed. "I had such fire once."

I imagined their young love, their beautiful bodies entwined, their hopes and the births of their sons. It was all sad, and right then I wanted to go back to my own comfortable existence; to Karl and his kindly remoteness; to the lovely city house in Baltimore; to the sunshine streaming in through the upstairs balcony window where I had my desk and bookshelves; to all that was familiar. These uncharted waters were becoming too murky to fathom.

Anne reached out and patted my hand. "Elise, you are a beautiful and intelligent woman. Under other circumstances, I would have wanted to be your friend. I still do, but it's awkward." She paused and looked out the window. "I too was fond of your mother. She was good to our boys and to me. This little chat is my way of clearing the air and letting you know I'm not the nitwit you may have thought me." She looked at me and smiled.

She left me with an admiration I had not anticipated. I smiled weakly, the whole silly tangle touching me like clammy fingers.

When she left, I felt like a frightened animal, and like one, I had a surge of energy and rushed to the beach for a walk, my sandwich half eaten. The day was warmer with a brilliant gloss of the whitest light. I ran a long way down the beach. Finally exhausted, I moved back from the shore to a protected dune where the sun had heated the dry sand. I curled into its warmth and wrapped my arms around my knees and squinted at the calm sea. The yellow Labrador appeared, running towards me. He stopped, tail wagging and a yellow tennis ball in his mouth. I made a clucking sound, and he came up to me, dropping the ball and nuzzling my face as I reached out and scratched his ears. We sat there a long time. I flopped back against the dune, and he lay down and concentrated on chewing the ball. My mind was blank, unable to absorb new challenges. The heat on my face from the sun was a blessing. I lay there a long while.

Chapter Nineteen

Arthur Schlemmer Again

By the time I felt ready to rouse myself, the sun was sinking. There was a warm patch along my thigh where my friend, the Labrador, was curled up next to me. He stirred as I did, and I reached over and stroked his head. "Hey you," I said. "Where did you come from?" I sat up and looked at his collar, but there were no tags. He felt thin as I rubbed my hand over his body. *Curious.*

As I trotted towards home, the dog once again followed me. It occurred to me that I might have to try to find the owner. And then, with a rush of horror, I also realized I was due at Arthur Schlemmer's for dinner and had no idea what time it was. Entering the house in haste, the dog behind me, I glanced at the grandfather clock in the corner but of course it had not been wound in days. I tried the kitchen, and the stove clock read five thirty. Relief swept over me. I let the dog out the back door.

With minimal time for a quick change of clothes from my still limited wardrobe, I chose silk slacks and a white cashmere turtleneck sweater, adding a pair of earrings and pearl necklace. I did cursory artwork on my face and hair. The sun was setting over the sea, and I watched through the bedroom window as it did its final dramatic drop, a never-ending source of mystery and beauty, from blinding glow to diffused glimmer to rapidly lengthening shadows to semi-darkness.

Arthur was waiting with a pitcher of martinis when I arrived. He had bought fresh shrimp and arranged them on a chipped Majolica plate with a blue Pyrex custard cup holding cocktail sauce.

"I think it's a bit cold to sit outdoors, although I hate to give it up," he said as I came into his low-ceilinged living room. A fire was blazing in the brick fireplace. His house was an old village Cape Ann set behind a white picket fence three doors from the library. "I do feel cold," I said, drawing up to the fire. "I fell asleep in a sand dune today."

"Well, that's an unusual thing to do, but make yourself comfortable. My housekeeper left us beef stew, so I won't be running back and forth to the kitchen. We can chat right here."

He sank into a large wing chair beside the fire. I moved to the opposing chair, upholstered in red and green plaid. The whole room was intensely masculine, assembled rather than decorated, full of bright colors, piles of books everywhere, and an old fashioned typewriter on a card table in the corner. "What led you to sleep on the beach in the middle of autumn, if I might ask?"

"Actually, I was upset and took a walk. The sun was warm, and I sat down for a while in a sheltered dune and leaned back. I had a stray dog with me, a yellow lab who curled up alongside me."

"That would be Lefty," Arthur said. "He belongs to the Whitmans at the end of the beach, in that brown shingle house. He spends his life picking up new friends."

"That's a relief. I felt guilty abandoning him."

"Don't," Arthur chuckled. "More than likely he's been through three new people by now and had food as well. What were you upset by, or am I being a prying old man?"

"Oh, I guess a lot of new people and information yet to be absorbed." I paused. "Or rejected," I finished.

"If I can help you with anything . . ." He rose to poke at the fire. "What I mean, Elise, is that although you have recently met me, I did know your parents pretty well and have lived around these parts a long, long time."

I was glad he was taking the conversation in this direction, even though what really upset me was Alex and the ensnaring emotions. The strange story of my parents and the little boy naturally added even more confusion, so I simply forged on. "This is personal, Arthur, yes, to do with my parents."

"Ummm," he muttered and then lapsed into lighting his pipe. I could hear the wind picking up outside, and a branch was scratching at the window beside the fireplace. The room was silent except for the soft puffing of Arthur stoking his pipe and a whistling noise made by the fire. "Elise, if it's somehow come to light that . . ."

"What sort of thing are you referring to?" I asked perhaps too hastily.

"There were things Jack told me — your mother did too — that I think could give you trouble if you, I mean, if you were to come across them." He stopped again.

"Arthur, if you know anything, anything about our family that will help me understand a letter I've read from my mother, I would really appreciate your telling me. What she had to say made no sense at all. I mean it made sense, but why she would tell me now, after her death, is beyond me."

"Can you be a little clearer?"

"I don't know," I said. "My guess is that you may know about a child who figured in my father's war experience.

"Ah, yes, that. I suspect she was in part unburdening herself. Maybe she was afraid you'd find out while working out the will and wanted you to have the whole story. I really don't know."

I sighed with relief, happy to find that there was at least one person around with whom I could discuss unexpectedly having a half brother. I forgot I had recently met Arthur and didn't know much about him except through his books. In a way it was his books that gave me the confidence to go on. They were stories describing decent people with lives like those of us privileged enough to live comfortably but without ostentation — people believing in a time-tested set of rules, people whose problems and tragedies were confronted in codified ways hard to fathom outside that culture. Arthur would understand.

"Arthur, how could this have happened and none of us have any idea?"

"Most of us are incredibly incurious about our parents. That's how. Youth is self-centered, and children don't think their parents could possibly have any life outside being Mother and Father. Now, of course, in your mother's case, she made it clear she had another life. However, even knowing that, I'm sure you felt that her art impinged in no way on your relationship with her. In other words, her art was as predictable as her attitude towards you, your sister, and your father, an area that she reserved for herself in an unthreatening compartment of her life."

"True," I said. "But being faced with a relative, a young man that lives somewhere with a life of his own, is, I don't know, intriguing and disorienting." I paused and took a deep breath. "Arthur, how do you know all this?"

He cleared his throat and took a sip of his martini. "Your father, Jack, and I were very close. We both served in the army, although I was in a different division and a few years younger. It gave us a tie. It's hard to explain to anyone who hasn't been through that kind of hell; that's why people who have experienced extremes of horror feel a bond. We were supposed to come back from the war and pick up our lives, families, girlfriends where we left them, and, I might add, a lot of compromise was asked of those that remained at home. Suzanne was three when Jack was drafted, and your mother discovered she was pregnant with you after he left. That was in 1944 at the time Paris was liberated, and the Germans mercifully disobeyed Hitler's order to burn the city.

"Most of us never shared what we saw or experienced. Your father and I ran into each other one evening at the Ritz bar in Boston after work and got talking. Your father was working for the bank, and I was doing research on a new book. From there we went on to become close friends." The fire snapped and flung a spark out onto the floor. Arthur got up and kicked it back and stood, one arm on the mantle.

"Your father was a good man, dutiful, honest, kind, witty, but loathe to open up to most people. He adored your mother, but you can't imagine what it's like being away from home, knowing that any moment you can die. Danger heightens every sense, and the need for human closeness is elevated;

sex is part of it. While in Trieste, he became attracted to a beautiful young girl who had lost most of her family. It was a short affair, as he described it. Later he had an accident, a broken leg, and was sent home, I suppose he thought little more about it."

"But it wasn't over," I said. "Why didn't they make the little boy part of our family? Oh, I know what my mother felt at the time — from the letter — but they could have gotten over that and pretended they were adopting a war orphan. I mean it seems cruel to have handed the whole thing over to Davis and walk away."

"They could have got away with it, but remember the boy still had a mother. Presumably she died sometime after she wrote, since no one ever heard from her again. Even had it been practical, your mother couldn't bear the thought. I'm sure you can understand both points of view. Jack was agonized over it, and of course the natural male pride in having a son played a part. I'm sure I was the only one he ever talked to about it. I tried to help, and I must admit I got upset with your mother at the time."

I gazed into the fire. "Arthur," I finally said, "Do you think it would be awful if I tried to find him?"

"Yes and no. Part of me says, why upset everyone now? And part of me knows that if I were you, I'd certainly be tempted to find my brother. But given all of Europe and America, and knowing no associations, names and such, I think it an impossible task."

"Mother says in the letter that she never knew where he was or the mother's name, except for the signature — Lili. Davis might know, of course; he helped settle everything."

"Davis is a pompous ass, if you don't mind my saying so, but his ethics as a lawyer are sound. I doubt he'd open up to you. If he felt it were his professional duty to keep you in the dark, you couldn't count on any misgivings."

"I can ask," I countered.

"You can ask."

"Arthur. You know."

His eyes twinkled. "I wondered when you'd leap on that possibility. Well, in fact, I don't. It wasn't and isn't my business." He quickly refilled the martini pitcher; poured us another, and settled again. I stared at the fire.

"At the time," he started, "as your mother probably told you, there was the relative in Chicago. She obviously didn't want the child and couldn't wait to get the whole thing settled. Davis went up there, and I don't know what happened, because after that Jack said no more, and I didn't pry. Even if I knew the girl's real name, I don't think it would help."

"Do you know the name of the relative in Chicago?"

"No, I don't, and she's probably very old or dead by now. Davis Hopkins likely does, but he won't tell you."

"I'm due to go back to Baltimore tomorrow to see my agent and go to a party, and then I'll come back. But, I need time to think about this, this and a lot else. Life has gotten complicated." I laughed. "And I used to think it was comfortingly dull."

"Let's have supper," said Arthur, heaving out of the chair and heading for the hall. "Come on. You can watch me perform the culinary miracle of getting stew out of the oven."

I followed him into a surprisingly large kitchen fitted out with modest appliances. There was a pine table by a window, and I pulled out a chair and sat down while he busied himself retrieving food from the oven.

He reached for a bottle of wine on the counter and opened it. "Want to switch? This is one of my better wines."

"Sure," I said, pushing my martini away. "Arthur, do you have a cigarette?"

"In that drawer in front of you, there should be a package. I get the mood when I'm too lazy to fill and light my pipe."

I found a half-full pack of Benson & Hedges and an old Zippo lighter and lit one. He came round and gave me an ashtray. "So, what else is on your mind?" he asked easily.

I hesitated. Other people's moral dilemmas were one thing, even if they were my parents. It was another to discuss my own.

Sensing my hesitation, he said, "If you don't want to talk about it, don't. I only thought it might help."

"It might," I decided. "Anne Creighton came over today."

"Anne Creighton? Well, there's a puzzler," he chuckled. "She's a surprise, isn't she? That crowd they run in is so…" He hesitated, "so shallow, but they're successful and rolling in money."

"What do you think of her?" I asked.

"Well, what gossip I know obviously affects what I think of her, since our personal contact is limited to a wave in public spaces and a few words at parties. Aside from her reputation for fancying the gents, she's well-informed, polished, and in the swim of an active social life."

"So, she has a reputation?"

"Well, I'm not a prude or anything like, but she has been involved with a few locals, including the son of the carpenter who did their kitchen. The father, Peter, also a carpenter, talks and felt no compunction about discussing his son's love life. I've known him since we were boys. Old fishing family, has been around for generations. Portuguese. Peter, the father, was a wild one back then, and his son's no different. Good looking fellow but up to all sorts of mischief."

"What if her behavior was linked to her husband's infidelities?" I asked. "At least that's the impression I got."

"She talked about her affairs?"

"Yes, I was startled too. It was in the context of Alex and his relationship with Mother and how he seems to have transferred his habit of coming to the house to me."

"Jealous?"

"Not exactly. Observant certainly. I gather their marriage is pretty much of a shell."

"And does he?"

"Does he what?"

"Come to the house, Elise," Arthur said as he put down a cooking spoon and turned to look at me.

"Yes." I took a last pull on the cigarette and put it out. "Yes, he has been doing that."

"Watch out, Elise. Watch out."

This made me cross. "Arthur, explain yourself."

He started stirring the stew again and chuckled. "You're giving yourself away."

"Arthur, I barely know you, and here I am talking away like an old chum. Let's get off the subject."

"If you want. But we do have a lot in common, so it's not surprising we should pick up like old friends. After all, your parents were close companions of mine for many years. And I guess you don't know this: your friend Potter Parker is also a friend of mine."

"Wow. That's news. How do you know him?"

"He was a student of mine at Williams College."

"Small world," I said lamely. "Anyway, forgive my rudeness."

"So?"

"So. Yes, Alex has been around. I was pretty bad-mannered at first, but as a matter of fact, he's okay."

"You can't not like Alex," said Arthur. "He's charming, brilliant, informed, original, and absolutely unfathomable. What woman wouldn't, and hasn't, I might add, have her head turned by him? For years it was that Sheila Bigelow, his one-time research assistant." He paused. "However, having said that, I don't quite trust the man. It's a vague feeling, nothing specific."

"What do you mean?"

He reached up for two soup plates on a shelf to his left and placed them on the counter. Then he pulled a loaf of French bread from the oven below. He cleared his throat and looked at me. "Elise, there are men like me and your father. The way we were brought up stuck with us. Good old boys in baggy tweeds or flannels, if you will, but gentlemen. Right schools, right clubs, wives from the latest debutante crowd, stories to tell, golf to play, fishing to do, trust funds or careers to pursue. We were comfortable, open, knowable for all that we might make mistakes or do things we weren't always proud of. Alex is not like that. It's like he appeared from nowhere, enigmatic at that deeper level where guys like me make assumptions about each other. Hard to explain."

"Well, from what I gather, he came from a perfectly decent family in Denver. Ambitious father who was head of a bank — went to good schools, actually Harvard like my father."

"I know, I know," said Arthur. "Maybe we Bostonians don't trust anyone from west of Dedham."

"Arthur, that doesn't do you justice. Shame."

We ate a rich beef stew, bread and a tasteless salad in cheerful comfort. Arthur scattered crumbs down his shirt front and reminisced about his youth, summers in Northeast Harbor, Maine, travels in Thailand and China, and his quirky frustrations with writing, a complaint hardly unique among writers. "I work out the plots beforehand, but then I'll have a dream that is intriguing. So then I have to weigh the merits of each approach, and the dreams usually win. The exercise turns out surprisingly well," he said.

"That's one I've never heard," I replied.

Original minds like Ayn Rand came into the conversation, as did Georgia O'Keeffe and Aaron Copeland — creativity in general, including reporting versus fiction — Ernie Pyle and Noel Barber. By the time the candles had dripped to nubs and the wine was gone, it was midnight.

"I have be off early, Arthur. I need to go," I said. "It's been a wonderful evening."

"When do you get back?" he asked.

"I'm not sure. I have to iron out details on the book, get the bills paid, all that. But, I'm getting attached to this place."

He let me out the door and gave me a hug. "Until next week or whenever," he said. "We'll solve a few more problems over another dinner then."

He watched out the door as I got into my car, backed it up and turned onto the main road. It was a dark night, but I felt warmed by the conversation and Arthur's kindness and friendship. When I pulled up at Mother's house, I saw the outline of Alex in the shadow of the doorway. My heart started pounding; I wasn't ready to tackle last night's odd turn; couldn't decide how to tactfully frame it as anomaly; or whether I wanted to.

Switching off the engine and lights, I came around the car and called to him. "Have you been here long?"

He came forward in the dark; I couldn't see his face. "A minute or two. I'm psychic. Where were you?"

"You heard Arthur ask me for dinner the other night. That's where I was." He came up and slid an arm around my waist.

"Please, not out here," I said.

Chapter Twenty

David is Sick

I didn't turn the lights on at first but carefully went through the house closing curtains. When I did turn them on, Alex was coming out of the kitchen with two glasses. He smiled in a jubilant way.

"Have I got news for you!"

"What?"

"It's what I referred to before — an opportunity to use the research. Couldn't talk about it earlier, but I got an offer from a pharmaceutical company in England. It's one I can't refuse. The money is amazing, but more than that, I'll finally have a chance to work on development of the drug delivery system for Alzheimer's."

"It seems strange that there's been little progress with something that's become so prevalent," I remarked.

"It's not new," said Alex. "It's been since around the early nineteen hundreds but wasn't really accepted as a disease of its own until the neurological boom in the seventies. This is a dream, what I've wanted for years." He stopped and looked at me. "But, as you know, I need those papers to do it."

"Alex, that's wonderful. Have you told Anne?"

"Not yet. She'll be unhappy, to say the least. She loves it here."

"When do they want you to start?"

"January."

"So soon?"

We sat down at the dining table, and he handed me my drink. "Yes, that soon Elise, I'm going to do it anyway, but if I had Roald's research, I could go in a direction that logically leads to his conclusions, and no one need be the wiser about the origin. Don't you see? Can we search the house again?"

"Of course I see, but is that honest? Shouldn't you try again to locate him before going ahead? I mean you said this would help his family move to America. Isn't that part of the deal you made?"

He folded his hands on the table and looked down at them. "Well, yes, but I'm sure any renewed efforts to find him will lead to the same blind alleys. What's the point of wasting all that time? He had my card and could have contacted me. He didn't."

I thought about it. It still sounded unethical. "Didn't you say it was all written in Russian?"

"Yes. I can get a translator. He told me most of it, so I know where I'm headed in terms of the practical application of his ideas."

"I would be the third person to know the research isn't yours. You do realize that?"

"Three? Ah, yes, well, your mother wouldn't have told anyone. That leaves Roald and you."

"It does."

"And will you out me?" He grinned at me.

"Well I don't fancy being grilled by a foreign spy who is intent on proving this is purloined research."

"Elise, for God's sake. It was given to me, signed over, and no one would know it had ever been in this house."

"Even so."

"Even so what? It's mine, not yours. What are you saying?" He leaned back and looked at me. "You do know where it is."

"No, actually, I don't. But this whole thing makes me nervous. Okay, if I find it and give it to you, then I'm out of it?"

"Please. Find it, and we'll never speak of it again. You go your way; I go mine. Deal?"

The ship's bell rang at the door. We looked at each other in alarm. "Anne?" I asked.

I went to the door. She had a raincoat hastily thrown over a nightgown and rushed in, her red hair untidy.

"Alex," Anne shouted. "Come right away. David's cold is worse, and he just coughed up some blood. He came in and woke me, and I couldn't find you. I was frightened, so I called Sheila. She's with him now." She came across the room and grabbed his hand and tugged at him. I thought of Sheila being there and what Arthur and Anne had both said about their relationship.

Alex put down his drink and looked at me. "God, I hate this. I mean being a doctor and afraid to treat my own family for fear I'll be wrong." He rose and followed Anne's hasty retreat, leaving the door open. I watched them run up the lane. Slowly closing the door, I went back to the table, anxious for David and at the same time disturbed by the conversation. In the kitchen, I found Mother's cigarettes and lit one, knowing I wouldn't sleep, at least not right away.

I decided to pack for the morning and went to the bedroom. Pulling my suitcase from under the bed, I noticed Mother's letter, remembering her request that I give Alex a letter and package. I found both on the back shelf of the coat closet where she said they would be. The envelope, like mine, was blue and said, in her fine handwriting, 'Alex'. The package was a large manila envelope bulked out by a heavy square box inside. It was sealed, so curious as I was, I thought better of opening it, so set them on the dining room table and went back to the bedroom.

After midnight the phone rang. "This is a mess, Elise," said Alex. "We're on our way to Boston. I'll feel better if we get him to Emergency at Mass General. We'll let you know how it goes later. Think we might spend the night at a hotel. If you see lights, it's because Sheila went back to feed the cat. We forgot to do it before we left."

"Thanks for letting me know. I'm leaving early in the morning," I said, then added, "I hope with all my heart David is fine."

"Give me your mobile phone number."

I gave it to him. "Oh, Alex, I forgot to mention a few things Mother wanted you to have; they're on the dining room table, and I'll leave the key under the doormat. She wanted you to get them right away, but I'm sure it's not the research papers, as it's an envelope and a bulky package, like there's a box in there."

"Thanks." There was a pause, and I could hear him breathing over the phone. "Elise?"

"Yes?"

"You know if you leave me the key . . ."

"I realize, and I don't want to hear about it if you have a look around."

We said goodnight, and I finished packing and managed to fall into an immediate and deep sleep. My night was full of dreams, large numbers of people leaping from level to level of what looked like a huge stage set built of old timbers. I stood in the center, and a light shone in the distance, and a man appeared in a pool of light. Every fiber of me wanted him to see me, but I couldn't talk and couldn't move. He spotted me, and a sinister smile spread on his face. "I've been looking for you," he said menacingly and walked towards me. I seldom have dreams as vivid, and I knew the drive home would be spent in part by trying to drive a wedge into the meaning. Much of my life had been an effort to smooth over rough patches, restore peace, but lately since my troubled encounter with Alex, I had an increasing need to confront issues with honesty and less meek civility.

I awoke sweating and thirsty and went to the kitchen and poured a glass of ice water. It was five thirty. Wide awake, the idea of taking off right then appealed. I could stop for coffee on the way. Closing up the house, I left the key under the mat, climbed into the Honda and eased out the driveway.

Chapter Twenty-one

Sheila Mentioned

The morning was crisp and cold as I turned onto the main road and sped along Atlantic Avenue towards the highway.

The journey went easily, but my mind ground away still trying to make sense of the haunting dream, the feeling of implied threat. I pulled up in front of our house in time for late lunch. I'd thought to restart the newspapers, so the Sunday *New York Times* along with the *Baltimore Sun* were on the doorstep. The house smelled familiar and comforting. I threw the newspapers on the front hall table and carried my suitcase upstairs. There had been no word from Alex, and I hoped nothing horrible had happened to David. Not knowing where to reach him, I answered the few messages there were: one from my agent listing the papers we had to sign giving the paperback rights for an earlier book to a British publishing company and to discuss the possibility of a film and another call from Anthony checking that I had made it home in time for his surprise party for Helene that night. I had told my agent, Arnell, I would meet with her on Tuesday.

After unpacking I hunted for what to wear that evening. Shopping had never been a priority, but thanks to Suzanne's profligate buying habits and subsequent boredom with her purchases, I had a collection of clothes from which to choose.

I chose black satin pants and an aquamarine and black silk jacket, both of which my dressmaker had fitted for me. Laying the clothes out on Karl's bed, I went back down to the front vestibule, which was littered with mail, and carried it to my desk in the window of the upstairs hall. The world settled back into recognizable shapes, and Alex and our odd meeting receded into the shadows. Sun streamed past damask curtains, and dust motes played in its rays.

Around four-thirty, Alex called. "Sorry I didn't call sooner," he said. "We've had a hell of a time here. The upshot is that David has an infection and nothing worse. It's being treated with antibiotics. He'll be in the hospital until tomorrow, and then we can go home. I stayed in town. Anne came in, and we'll stay here again tonight. I'm working now, and she's with David."

"How are his spirits?" I asked

"He's a little trooper," Alex said with pride. "Never lost his sense of humor. He asked if we could collect the blood and sell it to the hospital for transfusions. Told me we might as well make money out of the deal."

"Will Sheila continue coming over?"

"Why do you ask?"

"Curious. You said she was feeding the cat."

"Elise, I detect something unbecoming in your question," said Alex. "Is there something about Sheila that bothers you?"

"Nothing much. Just a few rumors."

"And what would those be?"

"That she was your mistress for years."

"So," he said, not laughing, "you've been checking up on me."

"No, Alex, I haven't," I said firmly. "Just stuff that got dropped in the course of conversations."

"With Arthur?"

"It might have been, I don't really remember," I lied, not wanting to get Arthur or Anne in trouble.

"Arthur does not like me," said Alex. "Never has. Can't put my finger on it, but I think it has a good deal to do with my lack of shapeless tweeds, Back Bay relatives, and pipe ash on my moth-eaten sweater."

"Oh, Alex, let's get off the subject. It doesn't matter a bit," I said impatiently.

"Good," he muttered. "Anyway, I'll let you know if I find the research when I get home."

"'Don't," I replied.

Chapter Twenty-two

Potter Parker is Sly

The Valley Country Club, in an outlying suburb of Baltimore, resembled a burst of fireflies from strings of tiny white lights hung from the ceiling. Margaret and Jimmy Marshall picked me up at seven thirty, and Helene was due to make her entrance with Anthony at eight thirty. He'd told her she was to celebrate her fiftieth birthday with him, her parents, and their children at the club. Since Anthony was known for his tightfistedness, downplaying Helene's important birthday wouldn't surprise her. Whispering and clinking of ice were the only sounds after someone shouted the alarm and turned off the lights. "Here they come!"

Presently, the door squeaked open, and lights went on in a blinding flash. "Surprise," everyone yelled, and Helene blinked, dropped her jaw, and put her hands over her face. "Oh no," she shouted and rounded on Anthony who was grinning from ear to ear. "You bastard," she said and wrapped her arms around him.

Everyone pressed in close as Helene detached herself and recognized one after the other of old friends, relatives, people from home and people who had flown a long way to be there. I found tears in my eyes. It was a great homage to a lovely friend. Helene Filmore and I had known each other since meeting at camp one summer when we were twelve, resuming our friendship after I moved to Baltimore.

Laughter and the swell of conversation rippled through the room as people greeted her, moved to the bar for a drink, and settled into small groups.

I found myself alone for a moment and had the luxury of surveying the whole scene. These people were dear to me. I had known most of them for over two decades. We had given birth at the same times, nursed our children through infectious diseases, taught them to ride, swim, play golf and tennis, and laughed and cried with each other. At that moment Alex was a gauzy memory, and even Mother's death seemed part of another life.

A voice behind me said, "Elise, you look positively beautiful. Boston must have rarified air." I turned and gave Potter Parker a hug. Potter was the perennial bachelor around town, rich, debonair, and seemingly without interest in marriage. We had speculated, but no one had ever concluded that he was or was not gay. He shuffled between his flat in Paris, his house in Antigua, and his farm here in the hunt country. Unlike his neighbors, horses were not his thing. His art collection was world renowned, and at one time he had been director of an important art gallery in Baltimore. He was always good company, a dear friend, irreverent, witty, and decorative.

"Thank you," I said to him. "Those are words we need at our age."

"Let me refill your glass; your usual scotch?" he asked and headed for the bar without waiting for an answer. Other friends joined me, and we caught up on news, Helene's surprise, and presently Potter returned. He took my elbow and steered me towards the terrace. "Come, my princess, where we can hear each other," he said. "I gather the eminent Karl is absent as usual." We went through French doors to a dark, glassed-in porch and saw a sky that was every bit as twinkling as the little lights on the ceiling of the clubhouse. "How was Boston and your mother's funeral?" he asked.

"It went off well — simple, outdoors, with relatives and friends around. She would have enjoyed it," I answered.

He took a sip of his martini and scratched his head. "Arthur Schlemmer called last night."

I hoped he didn't hear my sharp intake of breath. "Yes, I found out that you know him."

"Arthur and I have been friends since he taught me World Literature at Williams. We've worked on articles together for various magazines. He's a fine fellow, visits me in Paris at least once every few years, and in deference to him, I crawl through elegant restaurants positively drenched in garlic and wine."

"I had dinner with him last night and enjoyed it. He was a great friend of my parents, but I had never met him before."

"So he said. He was full of compliments." Potter studied my face for a moment. "In fact, what he said was rather cryptic."

"What was that?"

"He said, to keep you in Baltimore for a while. What does that mean, if I'm not prying?"

"Well, Potter, if I say you are prying, then you will suspect the worst; and if I say you are not, then I will have to pretend to guess what he means."

"I thought," said Potter, "that he meant that you were unduly upset by your mother's death, but we've established from your glowing looks that that's not true. So," he drew a deep breath, "I shall have to conclude that you're up to mischief."

I was glad it was dark. "Truly, I can't imagine what he was going on about. Perhaps he thought I was left with too much responsibility for clearing out Mother's house. Suzanne retreated early, and I have been sorting and packing since. Yes," I added, "that's probably what he means. He was being kindhearted and wishing me a rest, I'm sure."

Potter laughed and poked me in the shoulder, "Okay, Elise, I wasn't born on Monday, and I don't believe you. We'll leave it at that, since you deal in fiction and are too good at it for me to pluck out the truth right now. I wanted to let you know that if you are having any knotty little problems, we can have one of our old chats, perhaps over dinner later this week. Please remember Uncle Potter who has admired you lo these many years," and he wrapped an arm around my shoulders and led me back into the room.

People filed into dinner. Potter and I went over to the seating chart and found our tables. He snapped his fingers, "Damn, I'm not the lucky one tonight; Charlie Hendricks most certainly is, though. I'll deliver you."

Charlie, round, beaming, the eternal dose of good cheer, waited at the table along with six of our other friends. He gave me a hug. "Good grief, Elise, what's happened to you? You look glorious; must be love."

"Oh, Charlie, you've guessed," I laughed. "But he's married and so famous that I dare not mention his name or you'll have it all over the room."

Across the table was my other close friend, Louise Blyfield. I slipped through the milling guests to give her a hug. "Did you get my message, Elise?"

"Yes, but I knew I'd see you tonight, and I had a punishment of mail and bills."

"So can you come for dinner Tuesday?" Tuesday was the day I was going to Washington, and I'd planned to leave from there to drive to Boston. Given my relief to be home and my ambivalent feelings about returning to Hopwood, I decided to postpone the return until Wednesday.

"Sure, I'd love to. I probably ought to get back to Boston and finish the job, but I do think a respite will be nice. Anyway, I don't know how long it'll take to finalize the negotiations with the publishers." I went back around the table, and we sat down. On the other side of me was Henry Clay, a crabby old fellow reputed to be the source of funding for more than one of the local start-up technology companies. He had made millions. Certainly his new house spoke of a windfall. And his wife, Alice, also wearisome, had taken on a new flounce along with large, noisy jewelry.

I nodded to him. "Good evening, Henry. Nice to see you."

He graced me with what passed for a smile — little more than a widening of lips with no change in his eyes. "Heard your mother died. Too bad. Hope it doesn't trouble you too much."

"Well, Henry, I'm able to carry it off okay. Thanks."

The tinkling of a fork on a wine glass silenced the room, and Anthony stood and made an amusing and affectionate toast to Helene. Many toasts ensued, and it was one-thirty in the morning when I arrived home.

"Potter, I'd invite you in for a drink, but I'm afraid you might take it the wrong way," I teased.

"Oh, indeed I would," he laughed. "Look, I'm tired too, Elise," he added, "and wild horses can't keep me from dashing home to bed." He leaned over, flipped my door open, and gave me a peck on the cheek.

I locked the door and removed my shoes, feeling the cool tile of the vestibule on my swollen feet. I had danced most of the evening between amusing conversations. It had been a wonderful party, and the warmth generated by being with my old friends carried me upstairs. Doing routine ablutions, even remembering to floss my teeth, I fell into bed, and slept like an innocent until nine the next morning.

Chapter Twenty-three

A Happy Surprise

When I awoke, the sun was already high. Pulling the heavy yellow curtains aside, I watched taxis, trucks, and pedestrians on the street below. I thought of the generations that had watched from this very window, seeing horse-drawn milk carts and hearing peddlers hawking their wares on cobbled, narrow streets. The glass panes were old, and the rippled glass made impressionistic art of the city view.

Crossing the room, I noticed a wedding picture of Karl and me — how young we looked, blank faces on which life would write its story. Karl was smiling his closed charming smile, the perfect groom. I looked like a dazed teenager, which of course I was, so unaware of what I was doing, knowing everyone approved and sure it would make me happy. It had for many years. Karl and I were a team, good friends, not the sort of uncomfortable couple that left tension in the air. We loved our children and respected each other. What more could anyone want? And yet suddenly I wanted much more.

The phone rang. I padded across the oriental carpet and sat on the bed, picking up the receiver. "Hello."

"Elise?" said my agent.

"Oh, good morning, Arnell. How are you?"

"Terrific. Just checking to see if tomorrow is still okay for you? Can you get here at nine instead of later? I think you're going to enjoy this meeting. The folks from the studio are going to join us too, so we can hammer out the movie option at the same time."

"I knew you were going to explore that; you mean it's a real possibility?"

"Cloud Nine Studios out of New York definitely wants to option the book for eighteen months." Arnell laughed.

"This is wonderful, Arnell. Lots of lovely money I hope."

"Never a great deal, so don't get your hopes up. Worst case, if they don't go ahead, the option money is ours to keep, but don't count on it being a fortune. Encouraging thing is they're talking big star names. You could be famous, Elise," she teased."

"Oh, please. That's not me. I'll send my sister, Suzanne, for interviews."

"Don't think so," said Arnell. "You'll do fine."

My mind raced, but of course, I was getting ahead of myself. Nothing was decided, and no contracts signed. Cutting conjecture short and finishing with Arnell, I made the bed and tidied the bedroom.

With CDs playing, I sat at my desk most of the day, writing letters, paying the rest of the bills, and making notes of ideas I had for the new book. The time slipped along in ease and contentment — alone at last and able to string disparate thoughts together.

In the evening I poured a drink and cobbled together dinner from pasta and a can of sauce. It was ghastly, but I didn't have the will to either shop or go to a restaurant. I got a few chapters done, not really inspired, laid out clothes for the meeting the next day and went to bed early, easing my mental tangle with a volume of Dorothy Parker's spicy poems that was on the bedside table.

Chapter Twenty-four

Meeting in Washington

Tuesday I arrived at Arnell's office in Washington a little before nine. There had been fierce storms in Carroll County, northwest of Baltimore, but I missed the worst by driving south. I was glad of an early start, as the traffic in the nation's capital was horrendous. It took nearly twenty minutes to find a garage without a "FULL" sign.

The first time I visited Arnell, she told me to "push the button to heaven." This of course meant the top floor. The office space was small and exquisitely decorated with French street scene paintings, antiques and carpets flowered and scrolled in soft pastels. As soon as I checked in with the receptionist, Arnell flowed out from the back in her usual cloud of silks.

"Darling," she crooned, "You look too divine. Boston must agree with you." She wrapped me in her aromatic, ample body and led me toward her office. "They're not here yet," she whispered, "so let's get ourselves a cup of tea and prepare."

Settling at a round table by the window a few minutes later, Arnell said, "Now, Elise. We are not going to jump at the first offer. Leave it to me. I'll do the negotiating. Harry, our lawyer, will join us, so we can leave the final details to him. If there's anything you don't like, now is the time to bring it up."

The meeting lasted several hours. It seemed a short time ago that I had finally sold my first piece, and now I had reached a point where I had to give up control over the process. Arnell and Harry laid out my options, and I felt we arrived at a good place regarding the possibilities. They would handle it all going forward.

As I left the building to retrieve my car, I had a pang of loneliness. The contract looked fair on the face of it, but I had heard so many stories of writers getting far less than they anticipated by not understanding the small print. I wished I had taken the step of having another lawyer review everything. I did reason that Arnell had done so well for me in the past that I could trust her judgment now. It would have been nice to have a celebratory moment with a friend, but when I thought of calling anyone in the Washington area, I found I wasn't truly in the mood, so I headed for the garage and joined the slow snake of traffic out of Washington.

Many of my high moments professionally had been celebrated alone. Similarly, Karl had usually been out of town when the children had a crisis. In fact, I mused, mine had been an isolated life in many ways, given Karl's and my easy acceptance of separation and individual responsibilities. Perhaps that was why I kept thinking of Alex. Not that I wanted to, but because it was an emotional distraction, bringing on as it did a mixture of irritation and conjecture. Who was he, really? Why was he being persistent? He could have come clean about the research papers and been done with it, but he seemed to be pursuing more than that, trying to forge a bond that I didn't understand. Perhaps it was I who wanted more? Suddenly I wanted to cry from frustration. I wished Karl were home right now to dispel my fretfulness and make this an occasion for rejoicing. Tears squeezed out of my eyes and tickled my cheeks. I brushed them aside as I headed onto the exit ramp towards Baltimore. The eternal critic inside my head told me to stop being foolish and self-pitying. I blew my nose and turned on the radio.

There was traffic everywhere, but I eventually found a parking spot in front of the house. The house had its calming effect, and I gave in to the familiar. Circling the living room, picking up photographs of the children, fingering objects, Copenhagen figurines, silver ashtrays, carvings, I finally came to rest by the telephone. There were several messages, one from Arnell restating her delight and saying congratulations once again. There was also a message from Louise reminding me that dinner that night was at seven thirty and saying Potter Parker had heard about the small gathering, invited himself, and would pick me up at seven. A tweak of anticipation lifted my spirits.

Realizing I had not locked the car, I went back out, and as I was on the sidewalk heard my mobile phone ring from where I had left it in the hall. When I got back and retrieved it from my purse, there was a message from Alex.

> *I wanted to let you know David is showing huge improvement and can go home tomorrow. What a damned relief. It's horrid having a kid in danger. I hope your meeting went well, whatever is happening. Can't wait to hear. Anne has gone back to Hopwood, so I'll be in the hospital with David this evening. I'll try to call later, assuming you're not out with some attractive guy tonight. Bye.*

I retrieved a cigarette from my hiding place in the kitchen drawer and put on a CD of Orff's *Carmina Burana*, which despite its turbulent drama, always sooths me. The phone rang. It was Karl.

"Hi, darling," he said.

"Hello to you too. Wait a minute, let me turn the music down." I flipped the CD player off and picked up the phone again. "How's it going?"

"Not so good. We're wrangling over details and getting on each other's nerves. However, there is progress overall. How about you? You had a meeting this week with the agent, didn't you?"

"Yes, today as a matter of fact. It went well. Arnell had everything pinned down — as much as she can so far. Looks like the book is being optioned, not that it always turns out well, but anyway, it's pretty exciting."

"Elise, that's wonderful. Congratulations."

"I'll have to take a back seat once the movie moguls take over, if they ever do. But, yes, it's exciting to have finally arrived so to speak. Gratifying if it actually happens, which is a big *if*, as I said."

"And what are you doing to celebrate?"

I chuckled. "Going out to Louise and Latimer's. Potter is my date."

"Sounds nice," said Karl. "Wish I were with you, but that's not going to happen for a while."

"Oh, that's okay," I said, perhaps too cheerfully. "I'm fully occupied and have to return to Boston to finish up."

"Do you mind?"

"Not in the least. I love it there, as you know. And Mother's friends have been warm and welcoming; I feel right at home."

"Good," he answered. "How's Penny's ankle?"

"Better. Gosh, it's a mere three months until her baby is born. I heard from Matthew in today's post, a long letter. He loves his job but is not as enthusiastic about Cincinnati. I detect a note of eastern snobbery there. Oh, and Evan found a flat in Paris. He's already moved there and has studio space with two other sculptors. Enid goes next week for good."

"I know, I called her on Sunday. She sounds excited. Well, Elise, I must get back to the group. We're going out for a short break and a cup of coffee. Take care, and congratulations again on the good news. Give Latimer and Louise my best."

"I will Karl. I'll call when I get back to Boston. Love you."

"Me too," he said and hung up.

It was easy and civilized, I reflected, a perfectly scripted relationship. In a similar vein, our lovemaking, so passionate that first year, had also fallen into a companionable and affectionate event. Karl's ardor was reserved for his work. Mine had been redirected to my writing, but what had been satisfactory a few weeks before now loomed as vaguely wanting and annoying.

Chapter Twenty-five

The Blyfields

Potter picked me up promptly at seven, and Louise and Latimer were waiting with smoked salmon hors d'oeuvres and drinks when we arrived.

"So, have you taken up residence in Hopwood?" asked Latimer.

"No, but there is more to do, so I'm heading back tomorrow for the duration." I took salmon from the platter. "Actually, it's kind of an expedition down the years for me to be there. I've been having a good time."

Potter glanced over at me. "What kind of good time, my dear?"

I gave him a frown. *What had Arthur said?* "What the hell kind of good time do you think, Potter? I need to remind you my mother recently died, and I'm cleaning out her house."

"Oh, get off it, Elise," said Potter. "Only joking."

"Now, children," interjected Louise. "I will not tolerate arguments tonight."

"Change of subject," said Latimer. "We've decided to move."

"What? And leave this place? What about the horses?" asked Potter.

Louise smiled. "It's time to switch gears. The kids are grown; the dogs are dead; the horses are work and we want to travel. We've found a terrific place in Roland Park, smaller, easy to lock up and leave."

"And," said Latimer, "we have tickets for a three-month trip to Europe and Asia; going to bang around the world for a while."

"But when are you moving?" I asked.

"As soon as we can get this place sold. The trip is next May, so we ought to be able to do it all by then."

"Wow!" I said. "This is sudden. Well, you shouldn't have a problem selling this. There are people out there who might want the horses too."

"Hard for me to part with them," said Louise, "but I think I'm ready."

Dinner was wild duck from Lattimer's freezer-full of hunting bounty, rice, and peas. Lots to catch up on, including Potter's new book on Asian art, and finally it was time to go.

In the car, with the heater running full tilt, I turned to Potter. "What kind of comment was that, my friend?"

"Oh, I was testing you. You see, I've known you too long. Bet Louise and Helene will be on your case soon. You're different, Elise. Can't exactly say how, maybe more perky? Death in the family clearly doesn't account for it." He winked at me.

"Perky? Ugh. If Arthur said more than you've let on, then out with it, because whatever he's imagining is beyond me."

"No, I told you what he said; well most of it. Anyway, drop it for now. You know of course that any fun you might have would be cheered on by all of us."

Potter dropped me off around eleven, and I went directly to bed.

At midnight, the phone rang. I rolled over and managed to say "Hello" into the phone.

"Sorry to call so late, but I had to eat after I left the hospital," said Alex.

"It's okay. I wasn't totally asleep. How's David?"

"Doing well. So, you didn't go out with that handsome man after all?"

"Oh, I did. Divine. In fact he's here in bed with me. Snores; that's his one drawback." I giggled — *I must have had too much wine at the Blyfield's.* Immediately regretting the lapse, I told him about the meeting with Arnell and how I was afraid it wouldn't come to fruition. We discussed my doubts and feelings, and in the end Alex made me feel calmer and more positive. "Thank you," I said.

"You know, I do want the best for you. Even if you won't acknowledge it, I am your friend."

"But you won't even be here in a few months. You'll be in England."

Alex laughed. "Yes, and we'll probably never talk again. There are no phones in that primitive land. Ah, the tragedy of life."

"Don't tease me."

"Can't you envision us as two old fools, hobbling along using metal walkers, maybe on the beach at Brighton, in our nineties and finally my dreams coming true — a clandestine assignation?"

"Both on walkers," I said and laughed, then paused. "Alex, about the other night. I don't want you to get the wrong impression."

"I don't think I did."

"What do you mean by that?"

"Is that a gratuitous question, or are you entirely naïve?"

"Seriously," I said. "We were both upset. Those things happen."

"They do, and then something else happens. Next chapter. Can't wait to find out, can you?"

"I think it's time for me to say goodnight and hang up," I answered.

"Okay. You do that. When are you coming back?"

"Tomorrow; stopping on the way to see Penny."

"I've got an idea."

"Somehow that makes me uncomfortable," I said.

"What? My having an idea?"

"Yes."

"Well, here it is. I'm planning to stay in town; I have a breakfast meeting on Thursday morning. Why don't you come straight to The Ritz, and we can have dinner together. You can go on to Hopwood in the morning? I mean, wouldn't it be nice to get to know each other in neutral surroundings? Enjoy the evening?"

I thought for a second. *Really, what would be the harm? It might even be fun.* "Okay, I'll do it. I can call tomorrow and get a reservation."

"No," he said, "I'll take care of it. Check in, and I'll be along around six-thirty."

We hung up. I lay back on the pillow and sighed. *What on earth am I thinking?*

Chapter Twenty-six

On the Road Again

I packed early on Wednesday and had breakfast around five-thirty. Having promised Penny I would stop for lunch in Connecticut, I had a long trip ahead of me and wanted to make a few phone calls first.

Reaching Enid in England as she was leaving for lunch, I found her finishing up the last of organizing for the move to Paris.

"Oh, Mom, I'm excited. The flat Evan found has a little park across the street. He called, and the painters are finished. Isn't it a stroke of luck? I've always longed to live in Paris. My French is rusty, but it'll pick up quickly. How are you?"

"Terrific, darling." And I told her about the meeting with Arnell, our friends in Baltimore, and my chores in Hopwood. "I'll be going back today, so we can think of each other traveling this week. Does Evan like Paris?"

"He's in absolute heaven. His brother Thaddeus lives there, has for eons; has a wife and a couple of rug rats, an eight-year-old boy and a ten-year-old girl, so Evan has been playing *l'oncle* for a few days and seeing the sights with the kids. Hope he doesn't get any ideas," she laughed.

"I hope he does," I answered. "I adore being a grandmother."

"Well, at least you don't look like one."

Surprised at this compliment from my beautiful daughter, I said, "Why, thank you, my dear. I'm overwhelmed."

"Are you, at that? I should probably tell you how lovely you are more often. Really, Mum, I guess I take it for granted that you know."

"Enid, when will you learn that everyone beats up on themselves? Here I am, thinking you one of the most beautiful and talented girls alive, and you could probably come back with all sorts of flaws you see in an Enid I don't even know."

"Well," laughed Enid, "for one, my legs are too short, and two, my bottom teeth are crooked, and three, my feet are too wide, and four . . ."

"Stop!" I said, laughing too. "Your short legs, wide feet, and crooked teeth come from me, so don't let's get depressed about minor details."

We hung up on a happy note, and I carefully put the scrap of paper on which I had scribbled her new address and phone number inside my address book.

I then called Matthew, who'd had a postcard from his cousin Will saying he had definitely re-enrolled in medical school. Will had either found himself or given up looking, and I was pleased for Suzanne that he was going back to medicine.

"Is he starting in January as he planned?"

"Yes. Until then, he's going to work at a posh restaurant collecting tips against future poverty."

"Good, good news," I mused. "And how's the reporting?"

"My assignments aren't exactly crucial to the world yet, but they're fun. Mostly I've been covering court news and doing a few business interviews, and Cincinnati has grown on me. Good music all over town. I've been going to performances at the Cincinnati Conservatory of Music, part of the university, and even met a few of the kids who are studying opera. Nice people."

"Oh, good. You sounded pretty glum at first."

"I was. As I said, it's an old boys' town. From a sartorial point of view, wearing a red tie is as exciting as it gets. Your friends, the Cowpers, introduced me to their kids. I've been to their club and even played a little golf. I'm terrible, so I don't think I'll be invited again, but it's made me want to learn."

"Hard to picture," I said to my chronically impatient son.

After a few more pleasantries, we hung up.

Last, I called Penny to confirm lunch, then turned the key in our front door, retrieved my Honda, and pulled out into traffic. I felt a surge of excitement, being on my own, making plans for only me, watching the world whir by and singing songs along with the radio. Stopping to get a present for Fiona was my single pressing errand for the whole day, a day that would culminate in being with Alex.

Mother's death and the ensuing days alone at her house had interrupted the pattern of life I'd imposed on myself: Karl's meals when he was around, birthday and Christmas presents for the children, friends, volunteer work, all of it of equal importance to my writing. A lot of precious time got wasted anticipating the next interruption, paralyzed by my inability to sustain a more rigorous work schedule. This time was for me, I thought with a rising excitement and also a vestige of panic. Could I live up to it? Could I devote myself to a more prolific output, to more discipline? Would the work be good if I did?

By the time I turned off the highway and was in West Hartford, it was after one. I had spent the trip on a gerbil wheel of thoughts. I pulled into Penny and Christopher's driveway, shut off the engine and put the present for Fiona in my purse. The door of the house banged open and Fiona rushed out. "Gran, Gran, come on. I made you a peanut butter sandwich." She reached the car and, clutching my hand, hauled me towards the house. "And guess what? Libby is over for a play date. We're doing dress up with Mummy's nightgowns. I'm a queen. Do you like my crown?"

"It's beautiful, darling," I said, admiring the newspaper approximation Penny had obviously made. "What is your name?"

"Queen Elizabeth, like the real Queen of England. Mummy told me. You really should curtsey before you speak to me." She thought a moment. "But," she said, swinging around to face me with her eyes wide, "you've already spoken to me. I guess it's okay since you're my Gran."

I laughed. Fiona seldom drew breath between sentences.

"I shall bow later if you wish, ma'am."

"It's okay, Gran."

"Do queens accept humble gifts from grans?" I asked

Fiona giggled. "You're silly, Gran. Of course queens accept gifts. 'Specially from Grans. They're the best kind."

"Well, then," I said as we went through the door and towards the kitchen, where I found Penny on the floor mopping up spilled fruit juice. She looked up and smiled.

"Hi, Mom, in my usual position. It's getting harder, and I'm sure little what's-its-name objects every time I do this." She shifted back on her haunches and wrapped her arms around her knees. "It's great to see you. Wow, you look great. What's up?"

"Nothing much. Floating up and down the East Coast with no responsibilities at all."

"Tell me," said Penny.

"I did," I answered, and we both laughed.

Penny, still on the floor, said, "I can't complain. You've already done all this, haven't you?"

I pulled out one of the kitchen chairs and sat at the table. Fiona came over, and said, "So where is it?"

"Where's what?" I teased.

"My present."

"Oh, dear! Did I lose it?" I asked, shuffling the contents of my purse.

"Oh, Gran," she said, reaching past my hand and finding the package, "you're teasing me."

Her eyes grew wide when she saw the necklace made of cast metal animals. "I love it! It is fit for a queen," she giggled and ran off to show it to her friend.

Sun streamed in and I could smell the heady nectar of fresh peaches in a brown bowl on the table. Penny had a mason jar full of daisies beside them, and beside that, in disarray, sat days of tumbled mail. The scene was a poignant reminder of the little efforts we make to beat mounting chaos into submission and arrive ready for the next step, the next day. For me, there were only a few really important items on the agenda now, and being with Fiona and Penny in a sunny kitchen in Connecticut was one of them.

Interestingly, Karl was another. Remote as he was, he remained a towering figure in my life. I wondered, then, where Alex fit in. Certainly, he had my attention, but I knew little about him, not his parents, his childhood, nothing.

Chapter Twenty-seven

The Ritz

Peanut butter sandwiches are not a preference of mine, but in deference to Fiona, I did my best.

"Gran, you didn't finish your sandwich," she complained.

"I know; I'm not hungry. It was the best sandwich I've ever had, and you're a great cook."

I don't think she believed me, but after giving me one of her severe looks, complete with hands on hips, she trotted off to get a book and hurried back to crawl onto my lap while her friend sat on the floor at my feet. I settled in and read about three little boys who got lost in the woods. Penny cleared the dishes, and by the time she finished, the fictional boys had been rescued and were being severely tongue-lashed by worried parents. It was time for me to leave.

"So maybe I'll give you a call tonight to see that you've arrived safely," said Penny, handing me an apple with a wink. "Sorry about the peanut butter," she said. "You'll be hungry on the way."

I hadn't thought of her calling me later. "Ah," I started. "I'll call you when I get there. I may go out to dinner later. Yes, that's a good idea." I never had to dissimulate with my children, and this did not feel good.

Penny and Fiona came out with me, and the last I saw of them in the rearview mirror was Fiona in her mother's arms and her little friend peeking out from the door.

When I pulled up to the Tremont Street entrance of The Ritz, evening was crawling into the city, and the lights on the hotel looked cheerful and welcoming. I registered and went up to a room decorated in blue and yellow with fresh flowers and a basket of fruit on a table. Going to the window, I glimpsed people below walking, peering into galleries and shops, rushing along and hailing cabs — a mild October night in one of my favorite cities.

It was nearly six, and Alex was due in a half hour. I changed clothes and brushed my hair, but by seven-fifteen he had not arrived. Restless, I retrieved my carefully packed flask of scotch, made a drink and switched on the evening news. Another half hour passed, and I paced around the room. I didn't want to call him, so grabbing my key and coat I went down to the street to have a walk and a smoke. As I returned, I saw him rush in the door. He headed immediately for the elevator. I ran after him, but the door closed as I got there. I dashed into the next car and exited as he was knocking on the door of my room.

"I'm over here," I laughed, going towards him.

"Oh, Elise." He came towards me with his arms outstretched. "So sorry to be late. Last appointment was . . ." By then we had reached each other and I didn't hear the rest of the sentence if there was one, as I was buried in his overcoat.

I expected to feel awkward being with him in unfamiliar surroundings, but there was none of that. Here we were, alone, away from ties, and we had the whole of the evening ahead of us. Entering my room, Alex threw his overcoat on the bed, put his briefcase by the bureau, and noticed my half-empty drink. "Ah, you are a wonder. Can you pour me one? I'll go next door to my room and wash up, then I'll knock over there," he said, pointing to a door between the rooms. And picking up his briefcase, he disappeared out the door.

In a few moments I heard a knock on the door. I let him in, and he picked up his drink, noticing my flask beside it. "You can use room service you know. You didn't have to bring your own."

"Once a frugal New Englander, always one," I smiled. He looked harried and rumpled from the day as he stretched out on one of the chairs. "Heaven help me, I've looked forward to this, Elise."

"Me too," I said, "but it's been a busy time, and I'm glad I went home. Helene's party was a success, and it was fun seeing my friends and catching up. Sort of a re-grounding."

"Did you see your friend Peter or Phil or whatever his name is?"

"Yes, oddly he's a friend of Arthur's."

"Interesting. Have he and Arthur been gossiping about you?"

"I wouldn't put it that way, but he made a remark, like maybe Arthur had said more than I know. But Arthur doesn't know anything, because there wasn't much to know except that you'd been stopping by from time to time. And my friend's name is Potter."

"Is he cute?"

"Oh, for pity's sake, Alex. Yes, as a matter of fact he is madly good looking, urbane, a bachelor and positively brilliant. He's writing a book on Asian art."

"Ah," Alex breathed and then took a sip of his drink. "The plot thickens. She's gorgeous, married, and scores of men are after her. What an amazing woman!"

"Alex, look at me. I've known Potter forever. We're close friends, which is the extent of what he seems to want from a woman. It's more likely that he and Arthur are lovers than he and I. Got the picture?"

"I do," he said rising and going to the window. With his back to me, he asked, "Tell me, do you really regret our amorous little hiatus the other night?"

"I don't know. If I'm honest, it felt right at the time, but now? What I'm saying is I don't want it to lead anywhere except perhaps to a growing friendship. We were both upset."

He turned around and gazed at me. "Well, my dear, that's not what I want at all. If I'm honest, I haven't gotten you out of my mind since, and I'm finding it damnably annoying."

"Alex, be realistic; we hardly know each other."

"Has that ever had anything to do with attraction? I mean attraction is why people get to know each other better. They don't make an effort to become familiar over time and then realize there's an attraction. Well, not in my experience."

"You should know," I shot at him and then regretted it.

His eyes narrowed. "Why the hell *should* I know? More Arthur information? That man is a menace, a gossipy old fool."

"There's always talk in a small town. It was vague innuendo. I already told you that. And about Sheila. You know that too. Nothing more, I guess."

"You guess?"

"I mean there was nothing more, really." I said feebly.

"Come here," he said, holding out his arms.

"No. I told you this is not headed in that direction."

"Well then, I'll have to come there." He took four steps and scooped me into his arms.

I looked up at him. "Alex, please . . ." But, by then he had brought his mouth down on mine, and God help me, I couldn't, didn't want to pull away. We kissed, a long hungry expression of uncomplicated longing. Breaking away, he smiled and looked down. "You look amazing. Is that new?"

"Yes," I said, running my hand down the front of a black and white dress I had bought with Louise and Helene. "Too bad curly hair isn't in style, or I'd be right up to date."

"I think you look like an angel. Anyway, I've made reservations at L'Espalier, up on Boylston, dinner at eight-thirty, so, while I'd like to throw you on the bed here and now and attack you, we'd better think of going."

"Wow, you don't settle for halfway, do you? First this," I said, waving my arm to encompass the large room, "and now L'Espalier."

"Don't worry; it's because I'm planning to seduce you and then murder you after you've assigned your royalties to me."

"Fat chance! They're for my children — in all probability at least a thousand dollars." I put my hand over my mouth. "Oops, I've got to call

Penny. I told her I would when I got here so she wouldn't worry. I do hope she hasn't tried Mother's house."

I placed the call and watched Alex pick up my hairbrush and run it through his hair, stooping to see himself in the mirror.

Penny answered. "Hi, darling," I said. "I'm safe and sound but going out to dinner right away."

"It took long enough," my daughter replied.

"I know. Well, actually I got here earlier and forgot to call. But here I am, and all is well. I loved being with you two, and give my love to Christopher."

"I will. I'd talk longer, but you know what dinnertime is around here. I'm trying to set the table, and Christopher has blueprints spread over it. Have a good time. Bye."

"Bye," I answered.

Chapter Twenty-eight

L'Espalier

L'Espalier was in a townhouse, and when we entered the restaurant, the maître d' nodded at Alex, "Good evening Dr. Creighton. Mr. McClelland will want to know you're here; I'm sure he'll come by your table. This way, please."

When we were seated at a corner table, Alex ordered two whiskies for us and laid his napkin in his lap. "So. Here we are. Anything new on the book, the movie, whatever?"

"No, and anyway tell me how David is doing."

"Ah, it's as if nothing happened. He's fine. The big news actually is that Drew got on the honor roll. First time. Bodes well for college."

"That's terrific. Has he any idea where he wants to go?"

"Poor fellow, he wants to be a doctor like his father and thinks McGill in Canada is a good choice, as indeed it is. But, and this is a hurdle that I'm fighting. He wants to take a year off after graduation to travel, mostly wants to go to Japan."

"Why not?"

"Oh, I think it's a thing they get in their heads. Gives us the usual arguments like gap-year before settling down. I don't know, but in my opinion it's better to forge ahead and get education out of the way and then take a year if it seems right. I guess I'm afraid he'll lose momentum given his tendency to try anything whenever the spirit moves him."

"I'm not forgetting you told me you did exactly that," I said.

He smiled at me. "Yes, yes of course. Sins of the father. But, I'm not sure he won't get sidetracked and give up on the idea."

"And if he does? It is his life after all, as it was yours."

I think we were both surprised at the ease with which we had lapsed into the ordinary, the comfort that steered our conversation.

"Now you," he said. "I want to know if you got a good deal. *Gone Crazy* isn't it?"

"Yes, and, I think I did. Arnell is precise and has always done a good job for me. Their lawyer was there. You've seen films and come away saying it was nothing like the book. But I'm getting ahead of myself, conjecturing, because I really don't understand it all, and as I've said before, film rights don't always pan out."

I wanted to get off the subject. I hadn't settled my own feelings about it yet. "Speaking of films, have you seen *Braveheart*?" Karl and I had seen it in the early fall.

"Yes. Splashy epic, and it's interesting to see Mel Gibson dip his toe in as a director. Good subject to pick, since hardly anybody knows who the hell William Wallace was or even if he existed. One flaw I saw was Wallace's dying cry for freedom. In 1300, I don't think personal freedom was in the headlines."

"Well, it might not have been on the scale that we take for granted today," I said, "but given my belief that human nature has never changed, it can't have been absent among the oppressed."

"You're probably right," Alex answered.

The waiter set down our drinks. I took a sip, smiled in appreciation and said, "I may be simplifying things, but isn't the ideal outcome in the tradeoff between security and personal freedom? I mean security means giving up a few liberties for the common good."

"Interesting thought. So, if a group of thugs gets into control through bloodshed, then later they offer a status quo that protects the essentials, like food and shelter, will people choose that over the possibility of deprivation and punishment resulting from insurrection?" asked Alex

"Probably in the short term. Look at Hitler's appeal," I said. "As I understand it, there was a horrible depression, and he promised a way out of it. So, early in the thirties, thanks largely to rearmament, German employment rose, manufacturing increased and the standard of living went up. Germany, having been stripped of its powers by the Treaty of Versailles, rose again. The insidiousness of his policies was not even guessed at until later, and by then it was too late."

Alex took my hand. "Such a lively brain!" I looked at his fingers, long and thin, springing from a well-muscled hand. "Where did you get that ring?" I asked.

"Ah, that. It was my real mother's family crest. The ring originally belonged to her father. My stepfather gave it me when I was small."

"Tell me about your mother."

"Well, I know virtually nothing. She apparently died young, a widow, having lost my real father during the war. So, according to the story my nursemaid, Mamie, told me, I was adopted by the couple I grew up knowing as Father and Mother. They'd been married six years without any children, and I gather it was my stepmother who really wanted a baby. I don't know how it worked, but there I was in Denver anyway."

He waved at the waiter, pointing to our drinks. The waiter hurried off.

"Do you want to talk about it, or shall we get off the subject?" I asked.

"No, no, it's okay." He took a deep breath. "So these two became my parents for all intents and purposes. As I think I told you, my father was an unsympathetic man, and I don't think he and my stepmother were happy together. I remember loud arguments. I loved her. She read to me a lot and played games. Then she died of leukemia, and I was left with my nursemaid, Mamie. My father wasn't around much and took little or no interest in me."

"Go on."

"After my stepmother died — I was eight by then — Father, as he chose to be called, remarried, the widow of a friend of his. Emily is a sweet woman in many ways but drifts along in her own world and certainly wasn't inclined to take on a stepson in any real way. They had a son of their own within six months of marrying. That was my stepbrother, Terry, and from the day he was born, Father clearly favored him — his own son instead of a kid of unknown parentage. Later I could see that Terry was being groomed to take over the bank. He was a nasty piece of work from the beginning."

"Goodness, what a lonely little boy you must have been!"

"Not really, kids get used to what they have, and I was lucky. Mamie loved me and gave me a belief in my abilities. It was really Mamie who brought me up. She was from Scotland and a strict disciplinarian but kind too. She died last year, and I went out to the funeral. Terry didn't even come. Father showed up but left right after the service without speaking to me, and I've had no contact with him or my stepmother since then. I have an idea Terry's in Washington now. I heard the bank went down with the savings and loan crisis ten years ago. So, there you have it."

"So your step parents are still alive?"

"Yes. Well, I haven't heard anything to the contrary, so I expect they are."

We looked up. The waiter was taking our empty glasses and replacing them. "Would you like to order now?" he asked, offering large menus. "Mr. McClelland isn't here tonight or he'd certainly want to see you," he added. Frank McClelland was the famous chef and proprietor of L'Espalier.

"Well, give him my best regards," said Alex looking up. "What do you recommend tonight?"

"We have fresh Dover sole. I would definitely say that's the best thing."

Without consulting me, Alex nodded. "That's it. Perfect. And," he added, "let's have a white Burgundy; I'll leave the selection up to you."

When we were alone again, I asked Alex about the letter and package Mother had left for him and if he had been in the house and found them. He said he had.

"I went in while you were gone. It felt good to be there even though you weren't. I found them where you said."

"And, did you find the other thing you were looking for?" I asked.

"Yes."

I didn't want to pry further, and he didn't pursue the subject but moved on to O. J. Simpson's trial. Simpson had been found not guilty of double murder for the deaths of his former wife Nicole Simpson and Ronald Goldman. We agreed it was an unexpected outcome when everything had seemed to point to his guilt.

Chapter Twenty-nine

Oops

As we left the restaurant, Alex asked, "Are you up for a hike? It's a little over a mile and a half."

Being a warm evening for October, I said yes, so we set off, feeling content after a superb dinner. It had rained while we were inside, so the pavements gleamed under the lights, and the air smelled of damp leaves. As we were passing under a canopy, a couple emerged. The woman pulled away from her companion and ran over to us.

"Alex. Lovely to see you." She glanced over at me. "Out for an evening of fun?"

"You could say that. Hello, Jill." Her companion, an older man, stepped up beside her, and Alex and Jill made introductions. "Jill is a patient of mine," he said to me by way of explanation.

"I am," she said to me, "and you are privileged to be with such a wonderful doctor. He diagnosed my silent migraines when no one else could. He's a marvel." And she tapped him on the arm and winked at him. "Now, don't be modest, Alex, you are. The best there is."

He smiled. "Well, thank you. I'm glad it worked out."

Looking uncomfortable, he took my elbow, and pushed me along the pavement. "We'd best be off. Meeting a group up the street."

She stepped back. "Well, good to see you," she said and turned to her friend. We were halfway along the block by then.

"You weren't exactly pleasant," I said.

"She's an annoying flirt and a friend of Anne's," he replied.

"Ah," I sighed. "So there goes our privacy, right?"

"Not necessarily, but it's probable."

"And the cover story?"

He didn't answer for a while. When he did, I could see he had worked it out. "You called from Baltimore and said you were meeting with the bank people in Boston, and they needed a copy of the death certificate to release funds from Elizabeth's bank account to pay the bills. I told you I'd meet you there with a certificate, and since we were both spending the night in Boston, I took you to dinner like the gentleman I am not reputed to be."

"Barely plausible," I said."

"Oh forget it," he answered, "I don't care. We can say we had dinner together and refuse to say more. People will judge no matter what you do; be as outrageous as you wish and endure the rumors. They don't usually get the facts straight anyway."

He took my hand again, and we walked briskly towards the Ritz, lost in our own thoughts. Alex bought a newspaper in the lobby. "Let's sit for a while before turning in," he offered, so we went up to his room.

"Didn't you bring a change of clothes?" I asked when we were in the room, realizing he had no suitcase with him.

"My important briefcase full of medical files," he chuckled, picking it off the floor and opening it. It had a change of shirt, tie, underwear and his Dopp kit in it.

"Well, I hope the work won't keep you up too late."

"I think I can manage to get through it by midnight," he laughed.

Both of us were suffering sudden shyness. After sitting down near the window, I said, "What time do you need to get going for your meeting in the morning?"

"Should be up by around six-thirty."

"Then we ought to say goodnight soon."

"Probably, but I'm enjoying this."

We chatted on for a while, and then I rose. "I'm sleepy, Alex. Time to call it a day."

"Okay," he said coming over to me. "One more hug." He lifted my chin and we kissed, softly at first, and then he became insistent. I broke away and headed for the door between our rooms. He didn't follow.

Chapter Thirty

The Long Night

Once in bed, I was fully awake. I heard the wind picking up outside and the whirr of tires on the street below. A man shouted, but I couldn't make out what he said. The heat kicked on with a soft whisper, and I tried turning over onto my stomach. I think I finally dozed off only to wake again with the frightening sense of someone in the room. I lay still, listening.

There was an unmistakable scuffling along the carpet, and suddenly Alex was climbing in beside me. "I couldn't sleep," he said.

I sat up. "Well for God's sake, you scared me half to death," I replied. "What on earth do you think you're doing?"

"It isn't obvious?" he chuckled.

"Alex, get out. I mean it. Go!"

He wrapped his arms around me and snuggled in deeper. "Oh, Elise, it's so cozy right here. You aren't cruel are you? Don't you like this?"

Undoubtedly I did, and who was I fooling anyway? By now I was more than a little attracted to this charming fool with the black hair, olive skin, and blue eyes. That he was unlike anyone I had ever known was one thing. That he was weaving himself into my life in an increasingly interesting manner was another.

I reached over and took his hand and sighed as he moved it to my breast. This was the *yes* he needed, and he pulled me closer. We lay quietly listening to each other's breath, anticipating making love, being together, but unsure how to move forward.

"What now?" he asked. "You've got to want this. You once accused me of not wanting to take responsibility for the changes I craved in my life; waiting for something to happen that made change unavoidable. I don't want you blaming me later."

"I do blame you. You're relentless."

"And you're a victim? If that's so, then I can leave now," he replied.

I sat up. "Alex, you wouldn't dare!"

With one motion he pushed me down and rolled on top of me. He was laughing. "All you have to do is say *no*, and I'm gone. Say *no*."

In his condition at that moment I had my doubts that any refusal would change anything. At a point it becomes futile to argue with an erection, and I didn't try. We made tentative love, probing, kissing, and fueled by the deep loneliness we sensed in each other, we propelled our desires into a tumultuous future I couldn't possibly have anticipated.

We were sweaty and exhausted when Alex finally said, "Let's take a shower."

He went into the bathroom and turned on the taps. By the time I got there, he was under the water and steam was filling the bathroom. I flipped on the fan and pulled the shower curtain. And there we were, naked, together. He held out his arms and folded me into them, the hot water beating down on our heads and shoulders. We stood that way for a long time absorbing the sensation of our bodies touching, our hearts beating and the warmth.

I wasn't about to talk sense into him this time. I touched him; he pushed me against the tile wall. I lifted my leg onto the tub's edge, and there we were, joined and lost in luxury.

When it was over, we washed each other, exploring the curves, and then I reached for the bottle of shampoo, and we scrubbed each other's heads.

"Ow," shouted Alex. "You're rough."

"You have no idea how rough I can get."

"Show me, but not right now. I'm rinsing and getting out. Come to bed."

He was gone in a flash. I rinsed my hair and used conditioner. When I got out, I wrapped myself in the hotel bathrobe and used the hair dryer in an attempt to tame the wet curls. I put lotion all over me and went into the bedroom. One dim light was on by the bed, and Alex had turned the radio to classical music. He was on his back under the covers with his hands cradling his head.

"Come to me." I slipped in beside him. "Ah," he breathed deeply, "you smell like a rose."

"Man-made fragrance," I retorted. "Ritz lotion."

"No matter, it's intoxicating. I take that back, it's you who are intoxicating." He rose up on one elbow and looked at me. "You know, I honestly don't remember ever feeling so complete before. Never. It's like I can't get enough of you, and each time, I come away hungry for more."

We looked at each other for a long time, our eyes saying what we did not want to diminish by hackneyed words.

Finally, Alex said, "Let's run away, leave it all, dash the complications. They'd get over it, and when they did, we'd reappear and be there for our kids."

"Ah, those kids, and yours are younger than mine, not yet out of the nest. Do you really think you could do that to them?"

"People do it all the time. Fall in love. Break up marriages. The kids survive it." He lay back on the pillow.

"Survive, yes." I said. "Go on with their lives, yes. But in every case they are changed by the experience. I don't know if I could face that. Marriages can collapse under their own weight, but when the breakup is caused by a third person, the kids will hate and blame that person. It's an awful position to be in. And besides, planning on the basis of one romp is premature, don't you think?"

"That was just a romp?" he asked. "I don't think so, and anyway it's the same thing either way, Elise. No outsider can break up a good marriage. And any random reason is enough to break up a bad one." He thought for a moment and said, "Time. We need time. Something will change."

Alex turned out the light and we curled together and slept deeply. Early in the morning I heard him stirring and saw his outline against streetlights filtering through the gauzy curtain.

"Alex?"

"Hey, my snoring little pig," he said.

"Oh, dear. I'm sorry. Did I wake you?"

"No, by now you know my habits at night. I couldn't sleep. If I had, I wouldn't have heard you. Your snore sounds like little pebbles rolling in a jar, not too loud."

I pulled the comforter off the bed and wrapped it around me and went to the window to stand beside him.

"What were you thinking?"

"About the letter your mother left me. I haven't told you."

"No," I replied.

He put his arm around me and led me back to the bed. "Let's get warm."

He was quiet for a while. "Well," he began. "It's a puzzle. She said you would already know, that she'd left you a letter with the same information.

"She did."

"So we both now know about a little Italian boy for whom your father arranged financial support, apparently his kid from the war. She also said she gathered the child had been adopted by a family near Venice where the girl was from. She wanted me to know, because she never liked Davis Hopkins and was afraid he'd upset you during settling the estate. She must have reasoned that if you heard from her first, I could be there for you in case you made a decision to try and find him, to make you see sense."

"I've been thinking a lot about that too." I paused. "Alex, I do want to find him. He'd be near my age by now, wouldn't he?"

"I guess, give a year or two. Why do you want to find him?"

"Curiosity. Wouldn't you?"

"We've got no clues, and I can't see what possible good it would do," he said. I liked the way he used the word *we.*

"Well, Arthur knew about it but said he had no idea what actually happened to the boy. Now, from Mother's letter, I do know the parents died."

"Maybe Davis knows it all. He'd have to be in on the story to have made the arrangements. However, I wouldn't trust anything he says," said Alex.

"I know you wouldn't. But there must be ways to trace the boy. I could ask Davis for help," I said and then added, "but no, that wouldn't work either; he was sworn to secrecy."

"He has to know at least whom he dealt with, where the money was sent. Now that your mother is gone, he might be persuaded to open up."

I thought for a minute. "I know why I'm curious, but why does it bother you?"

He sat up in bed. "Bother isn't the right word. It's that it concerns you, and if you want to start burrowing into the whole affair, I want you to be sensible." He looked back at me. "Look, Elise, it's so long ago, and what's the point of upsetting a lot of people and maybe reshaping that man's whole idea of who he is? It's likely he's had a great life, probably married with his own kids by now, lapping up pasta and Chianti and happy. You'd mess that up, and no one would thank you for it; you can be certain of that."

He lay back down and reached for me. I lay in his arms, willing morning away, wanting time to stop, but of course time is merely a concept.

Chapter Thirty-one

Back to Work

With the sun making bright bars across the floor, I looked over, but Alex was gone, and the door between our rooms was shut. Of course! He had an early meeting, and looking at my watch I saw that it was nearly eight-thirty. I got up and noticed a note on the bedside table. It was written on a prescription slip.

Best night of my life. Really! I think I'm in love. Alex

I tidied up my belongings and packed for the short trip to Hopwood, putting the bottle of rose lotion in my travel kit with a sentimental rub of my thumb on its side. I called down to the desk for my car to be brought around.

Once on the road, I felt a rush of happiness and a degree of terror. My family came back into focus, as did the remainder of the job I had to do. This time I would call a Realtor, finish boxing up loose items and distributing the art, the furniture, and the other remnants of my mother's life. I realized I didn't have a camera with me to photograph the paintings so the children could choose what they wanted. Maybe Alex had one. If not, I'd buy a cheap model.

Little details kept my mind churning until I drove along the shore road and to the house. I unloaded the car. The day lay ahead.

I called Arthur to tell him I was back, and we arranged another dinner at his house on Saturday. I also called Adelaide Black, and she said her middle son, Jeffrey, was home for the week, so why didn't I come for dinner that night. I said I'd be happy to have the company. Jeffrey was a little older than I, and I hadn't seen him since we were young. I gathered that he was teaching economics at UCLA, and his wife had died of leukemia in her late thirties. There were a few children, but I didn't know how many.

My third call was to Davis Hopkins.

"Davis," I said when the pleasantries were over, "I'm calling because I want to go ahead and list the house this week or next, and I wonder if everything is in order for me to do so."

"Why don't you come in and we can go over the will and deal with the rest. I've told you and Suzanne the bulk of what's in it, but it's best to review it. I've mailed her a copy."

"Okay. I've got a few things to do here; how about early afternoon?"

"Fine. Two o'clock?"

We said goodbye, and I unpacked. I'd brought fresh clothes.

Alex and I had pretty well combed the possibilities of Dad's mystery son, and I realized now that I had been entertaining a selfish view of the whole tangle. I ought to follow advice and leave well enough alone. This really had nothing to do with me.

At two o'clock I arrived in Hingham at Davis's law offices, housed in a yellow clapboard building with white trim and near the center of town. *Hopkins, Stacey and Brigham* read the brass plate to the right of the front door. I walked in. The receptionist greeted me and went off to find Davis while I sat on a prim Queen Anne style settee.

"Hullo, Elise," came Davis's booming voice. "Come back this way." I followed him to a corner office overlooking a hillside with gardens now dormant for the winter, a few orange and white chrysanthemums soldiering on.

I sat in a leather chair in front of his desk while he settled himself, wondering idly if there was a company dedicated to making leather furniture for lawyers' offices with little elves tapping in the brass studs that ran along the seams. He finally looked up after shuffling folders around and handed me copies of my mother and father's wills.

"Okay. It's all here. Let's start with the wills. It's simple. After expenses and taxes, everything from your mother and now the remainder of your father's trust goes to you and Suzanne after a few bequests for the grandchildren, ten thousand dollars each and one other. No surprises there."

He smiled, showing a glittering set of small bleached teeth, like kernels of white corn in his ruddy face. "The trust means that it doesn't need to be probated. I'll open a bank account for you to draw on and a few other things, so wait before you list the house. Anyway there are appraisals to do to satisfy the tax people and set a price. The proceeds of course go directly to the two of you. As executors, you and Suzanne can submit the expenses of winding down her property to me for tax purposes. You can pay bills and expenses directly, but do keep careful records. I'll have money transferred, as you need it. Furniture and paintings have to be bought from the estate. Clear so far?"

"I guess it will have to be," I joked. He didn't smile.

"Davis, do you know where her jewelry is? Dad's too? Not in the house."

"Not mentioned, and I don't want to know about it. Let's assume she has already given it away. I'm sure you'll figure it out in time."

I started to rise. "Well, I guess that's it."

"Sit, sit. One more thing," Davis said, flapping his hand downward. He cleared his throat.

"This is a little tricky," he continued. "I know your mother mentioned leaving you a letter concerning a certain matter. I have administered your parents' affairs a long time. Since none of the past will be a secret to you anymore, I want to discuss an issue that has bothered me."

"Yes, I know about it, Davis. But if there is any further light you can shed on the whereabouts of this man, I would be most grateful."

"Well, the point here was that the child would for all intents and purposes disappear, and that is the case. He was well provided for, and I have reason to believe it went well with him. That's really the end of the story, and I would warn you that your parents had no intention of you or Suzanne ever looking for him. Your mother's purpose in letting you in on the matter was clear. She didn't want anything to crop up now that would surprise you both. And that was wise. The other thing I want to mention is that your father left a bequest for the boy."

"Well, how will you get it to him, if you don't know where he is?"

"I don't. It will go into the account kept by a New York lawyer that we have used over the years. You will see that and would have wondered. Since your mother was living on the proceeds from the trust, which were paid out to her monthly, she didn't know about the bequest, as your father stipulated that the transfer shouldn't take place until after she died."

He cleared his throat and gave me one of his unctuous smiles. "As I have said, and I persist, I do not know his location. He could now be anywhere, and only those lawyers would know. And, being sworn to secrecy, I am certainly not going to divulge the name of that firm and have you pester them to no avail."

"Is that all?" I asked stiffly.

"No, there is one other thing, a small concern really. In your father's possession, at least at one time, was a miniature painting, enamel on copper, given to him by the boy's mother during the war. I gathered from your father that it actually had significant artistic value, was a valuable family heirloom. I asked, and your mother said she never found it when he passed on. I'm sure she assumed I'd mention it to you anyway, in case. She wanted you to know the story, so to speak, so there would be no confusion. So," he cleared his throat, "if in going over possessions, you were to come across the object, I will expect you to deliver it to me for proper distribution. He wanted the boy to have it, so I gave him the lawyer's address to send it to. I don't know if he ever did it, so that's why I'm concerned it might still be at the house. Your mother may have overlooked it."

"I see," I said.

"Also, Alex Creighton — I assume you have met him, since he was at the funeral and lives next door."

I confirmed this. "Well then, the truth is we don't know a lot about him except that your mother developed a certain fondness for him, and they became close."

"That's apparently true," I answered, waiting.

"What I'm suggesting here is that she may have told him if there was a miniature, and although it's an outside chance, he might know where it is."

"If he does . . ." I started to answer but then thought better of it. "What I mean is, he might, but I don't know." I stopped. "Why don't you ask him?"

He pushed the folders aside, placed his clasped hands on the desk, and leaned towards me. "Elise, let me candid about this. I don't trust the man. He waltzed into Hopwood fifteen years ago with his wife and two sons — there's been another since then — built this bloody great house, and, to be frank, the crowd they run around with is different from what we're used to. Asking him anything, in my opinion, wouldn't guarantee a reliable answer."

I didn't want to make this easy for him, but neither did I want to look defensive and give myself away. "So, tell me why you say their crowd is, as you say, different."

"In a word, fast. He was originally blackballed from the golf club but has managed to get in since. He applied the first year he got here, and of course no one knew who he was and, frankly, rushing your fences that way looks pushy. My dear, you know how people in Hopwood would react to that! I have to admit he's since proved himself a prominent physician in Boston and managed to get into St. Botolph, which is not easy."

"I've heard of it," I said.

"Yes, old club," he said. "Actually, as I've heard it, it was named after an eighth century abbot of a monastery in the fens of East Anglia, England. The town took his name, and then the name was later corrupted to Boston." He stopped and shook his head sadly. "They even take women there, since 1988. But I digress."

He paused. "I know I'm being indiscreet here, and I hope you realize that this conversation needs to stay within these walls. Right now, I'm speaking to you as a friend. I think that although your mother's choice of companions was up to her, you should be wary of this pair. Your mother was old when she met Alex Creighton, and I'm afraid he turned her head. You know how old women get — positively silly. He's a good looking chap, and he could have flattered her into trusting him."

His pomposity was becoming insufferable, and I said, "Oh, my stars, then there's no telling what he may know or have run off with, is there?"

"Exactly, my point," Davis replied, his brow drawing down. He sat back and folded his arms on the desk, immune to any irony.

"I see." I stood. "So, if that's all, I'll be going. Thanks, Davis. I'll keep a lookout for the little enamel and will ask Dr. Creighton if the occasion arises."

He rose from behind his desk and came around, holding out his hand. I shook it. It was damp.

"We'll be in touch," he said, patting my arm and holding the door for me.

The brisk air felt good after the wooly atmosphere Davis invoked. I understood Mother's antipathy towards him; really nothing one could put a finger on, more an overall irritation, like the onset of hives. I decided to buy a camera and headed towards the center of Hingham.

Chapter Thirty-two

The Move is Real

Dinner at the Blacks pitched me back into Hopwood, an existence beginning to take deeper root. Jeffrey Black, Adelaide and Dick's son, was much as I remembered him: quiet, sardonic, built like his father but professorial — tweed jacket, khaki trousers and loafers. He too smoked a pipe. His girlfriend was a surprise, a girl I had known at Sarah Lawrence. Thus, Sarah Lindy and I had a good deal in common. She was a tall woman, vivacious and expansive, and Jeffrey had met her at a ranch in Nevada where he had taken his children for a vacation.

Sarah dominated the conversation with descriptions of a trip to Peru. Dick puffed away, one hand on his pipe and the other stroking the head of a spaniel sitting at his feet. Occasionally he picked up his scotch and took a sip. Adelaide knitted away, her arm flying out occasionally to pull more wool from the canvas needlework bag at her feet. During one of Sarah's pauses, Adelaide asked me how I had found Baltimore. I told her about the surprise party, and soon it was time for dinner.

It was a comfortable evening, and as we got up from the table, I yawned. "I'm sorry," I apologized, "but it's been a long day with the drive yesterday and then a meeting with Davis this afternoon. I'm afraid I need my bed." I picked up my coat from the settee in the front hall and left, bumping once again down the pitted lane and through the farmyard to the main road.

Lights were on in the house when I arrived, and opening the front door I saw Alex on the sofa, feet stretched out on the table front of him, asleep with a pile of papers on his lap. He sat up, blinking, as I closed the door. "Hi."

"Hi back," I said. "Should you be here?"

He got up and came over to me, and we hugged. "Of course I *should* be here. The question is whether it's a good idea."

"Well is it?"

"Do I detect a scrap of conflict here?" he tipped his head to one side, a coy look on his face, and said in a falsetto voice, "Oh, Alex, about the other night, I don't want you to get the wrong idea."

I bowed my head, a giggle bursting from my mouth. "You're impossible."

"I beg to differ. I'm entirely possible, and here, and absolutely longing for one little kiss."

I obliged, and then Alex added, "To satisfy your puritanical misgivings,

Anne is in Boston at her annual book club dinner, bunch of women from around here. David is spending the night in Hingham with a friend from school. So," he said, tapping my nose, "are we satisfied?"

"We are," I answered, pulling off my coat and hanging it by the door. "And have we poured me a drink?"

"No, but we are on our way to do that." He headed over to the kitchen.

When we were settled, he asked me about my day, and I described the conversation with Davis.

"As I thought," he finally said. "And no, I know nothing about any little enamel. In fact this whole thing about a half brother is as much a surprise to me as it is to you. Your mother never mentioned any of it."

"I thought not," I said. Then I remembered the package that mother had left along with the letter. "Alex, by the way, what was in the package Mother left?"

"The jewelry, his and hers," he answered. "Sorry, meant to tell you before but forgot. It's all there. I'll keep it for now, and you and Suzanne can go over it whenever you want. If anyone asks, you can say she gave it to you and Suzanne a long time ago. She was obviously dodging the tax people. Can't say I totally approve, but I'm turning a blind eye."

I was relieved. "And how was your day?" We were sounding like an old married couple.

"Same old stuff, except I had a call from Wilding Pharmaceutical, and it's set for the second week in January. They have a flat in London I can use, furnished, making it an easy move for the time being. I still have no idea what Anne wants to do. From the way the Wilding people are talking, this assignment could last up to three years. Whether she'll want to make a total move for that short a time, I don't know. I seriously doubt it, but it wouldn't hurt David to go to school there for a while. The other two boys are settled and can spend vacations with us. But, as I said, I doubt if she'll want to do it."

It was becoming real, and the future loomed as a cipher. We'd of course have to enjoy the now and then decide whether to make a clean break, neutralizing the remnants of passion as best we could. "And what is to become of us?"

"There is no us," he said, gently holding my chin so I had to look at him. "We simply are, I don't know what, but real, enduring."

"Sweet," I answered, "but you do, of course, realize there are practical details to this if we're not to simply brush it all aside and take a step backwards."

"I do. I do," he sighed. He looked over his shoulder, out the back window to the darkened dunes. "Elise, we'll work it out. I promise. Let's get through this tangle of your mother's estate and my move first. But," he added, "rest assured we will be part of each other's lives. At least from my point of view, I want us to have a future, whatever it may look like."

I leaned against him, and we held each other for a long time, and then moving in unison, we shed our clothes, pulled the afghan over us and made love. After a while, we heard a car coming down the lane. "That'll be Anne getting home," he said, leaning sideways and groping around the floor for his clothes. I looked up in alarm, but he waved his hand in the air.

"No worries, she'll head for bed."

We got dressed quickly, and Alex slipped out the back door. "I'll take a detour and plod in from the beach," he smiled. "See you tomorrow," and he disappeared into the breezy darkness.

Chapter Thirty-three

Anne's Book Club

The next morning, as I was finishing breakfast, the bell by the front door clanged. I opened it to Anne being blown around by wind and driving rain. "Oh dear," I exclaimed. "Get in here quickly. What awful weather!"

She stepped in and removed her hat, shaking out her hair. "It is horrid," she said, hanging up her raincoat.

"Come, have a cup of coffee."

She followed me into the kitchen, and I filled both of our cups and headed for the table in the living room. Once we were settled, she looked at me. "This is a bit awkward, Elise. Not in the way you might imagine from our last conversation, but because I hesitate to take advantage of your being here to ask a favor."

I couldn't imagine where this was going, so I waited.

"Well," she began. "Last night I went into Boston. We have an annual dinner for our book club."

"Ah," I said.

"Anyway, my friend Jill Brown said she had run into you and Alex on the street in Boston, but of course she didn't know who you were, so she asked." Here she looked down at her hands. "I'm not going there," she said looking up. "Suffice it to say, I told her who I thought he might have been with, and she leapt on it. You are not unknown."

"I suppose not, although it still comes as a surprise." I paused, "Anne, Alex met me in Boston because I had to go to the bank and needed . . ."

"Stop," she said, "I'm sure there was a good reason." She took a breath and rushed on, "Jill wanted to know more, and I told her you were now clearing out your mother's house. So," she continued, "she told everyone around our table, and the upshot is that the group wants you to speak at our next meeting about your writing and your career."

"Aha," I said. I was stumped for an answer. "I don't know . . ."

"Look," said Anne. "I'll understand if you don't want to do it. It's not for another few weeks, and you might not even be around then," she added brightly. *Hopefully?*

I thought for a moment. Where would I be in a month? I wasn't planning to be home until shortly before Thanksgiving when Penny and her family were coming. "Let's say that I'll do it as a favor to you, but let me ask you this: if I have to leave, could you get a replacement at short notice?"

"Oh, that's not a problem. We don't always have speakers, and we do have a book we are reading, *Men are from Mars, Women are from Venus* by John Gray. So, we'll discuss that."

"Oh, that's fine then. Tell them I'll be there if I can. Where and when?"

"The next meeting is on November thirteenth, a Monday luncheon, at the Hopwood Golf Club. I can take you, but you know where it is."

I nodded. There was a pause. "More coffee?" I offered.

"Yes, that would be nice."

"Do you mind if I have a smoke?"

"Not at all," she said. "I'll have one with you. Alex would disapprove, wouldn't he?"

"Probably," I said vaguely. "I don't know," I added.

When we had lighted our cigarettes, I said, "Describe the book your club is reading. I haven't read anything but the reviews."

"Generally it's about how men and women view the give and take in a relationship, asserts that the perceptions are different. Men, for instance, solve problems, while women usually want to talk about them and don't understand men's silence while they work out solutions. That sort of thing."

"Do you find it rings true?" I asked, remembering Alex's complaint when we'd first met about today's euphemisms for what he considered ordinary parts of life: 'parenting' for bringing up children, for instance.

"Yes, I think I do. I'm not sure I understand men. Chronologically I'm the product of what happened in the late sixties and early seventies, when women broke out and claimed a larger role. That happened by the time I was twenty. I was brought up in a convent school, so being with boys wasn't a part of daily life, and that's important. I didn't have brothers either. Men have always been another race to me, people who were supposed to have a role, different interests, but not people like us."

I didn't share her inability to understand men. "So, where do you think that left you?" I asked.

"Oh, I was determined to carry on the fight for women. Now I think it didn't serve me in any constructive way, and God has given me three sons as His answer." She smiled.

I reflected, as she sat there, that she was beautiful.

"I went to Derby Academy in Hingham," I said. "Boys and girls. Maybe that made a difference. Boys and men have always been in my life, mostly as friends, so I guess I take it for granted that all of us, men and women, have had to play roles by virtue of biology, moral codes and societal demands, but underneath there are many of the same fears, excitements, sense of helplessness or power, and always the gnawing feeling there is more to understand than we are given to do."

Anne smiled, but I realized this conversation was going nowhere. She might not understand what I was trying to say, but also she simply might not want to explore the subject. It was, after all, ludicrous for us to be moving into friendship when recent developments aimed wide of that target.

Into the silence, Anne said, "I need to be getting on with my day. Lots to do." And she rose from the table, snuffing out her cigarette. I walked to the door with her and helped her on with her raincoat.

"Thanks Elise for saying yes, and thank you too for letting me clear the air last week," she said and left. I watched her stride down the path to the lane and disappear around the corner.

At that moment I was jealous of her ability to watch Alex every morning, see him brushing his teeth, wandering about in his pajamas, ordinary things. I didn't even know if he habitually wore pajamas. And the irony was that she could see all that and not appreciate it, living as they did with the facade of a marriage they had perpetuated long after the reason for it had withered away. Or, did I know that either, for sure? Anne simply served to confuse me more.

Chapter Thirty-four

Rush to Boston

Alex called. "I'm in a hurry right now, but can you meet me in Boston around five? I told Anne I've got a meeting and am staying in town. Not untrue at the time, but it got cancelled. I'll stay at a friend's apartment. He's in Switzerland." He gave me the address and said he'd be waiting for me. I said yes and started to add that he shouldn't worry if I was late due to traffic, but he'd already ended the call.

Immediately the phone rang again. Suzanne said, "Hey, little sis. I'm in a hurry, but I wanted to know how things are going." *Is everyone in a hurry but me?*

"Fine," I told her." I started to describe the meeting with Davis.

"Yes, I got the copy of the will; I know you'll do fine," she interrupted. "I'm really sorry not to be there to help, but this is impossible. Chaos at this end. One of the minor actresses has gotten deathly sick, and we have to replace her. Fortunately, we haven't started the actual part where she comes in, but it's still a delay."

"I understand," I lied.

"That's perfect, perfect. Oh, I forgot, where is Mother's jewelry?"

"Alex has it. He's going to keep it until the tax people are through."

"Oh, dear Dr. Creighton. Being a big, big help is he?"

"Suzanne," I began sternly, but she interrupted me.

"Gotta go. I'll call later this week." And she too was gone.

Karl was the only one who hadn't called in the midst of a flurry, so I decided to call him and was surprised to reach him.

"Oh, hello darling," he said. "I was going to phone. We've had an early meeting here in the hotel, and I was getting ready to meet a few of the cast for lunch and then work this afternoon. How's it going?"

I mentioned the appointment with Davis, omitting the information about my stepbrother. It wasn't the right time to go into the whole long story.

"Sounds good. Are you getting any writing done?"

"A little. The longer I delay, the more the plot for the book comes into focus, so it's not so bad."

"Well, fine. Penny said it's definite that they will be with us for Thanksgiving. Not much longer for it to be three of them, is it?"

"No, a few months. Exciting," I answered. "How is your work coming along?"

"Oh, the usual fits and starts, but no, that's not right. It's actually going surprisingly well now. I'm pleased."

"Nice. Any other news?" I asked.

"I ran into an old friend from Austria. We had dinner and caught up. Good time. You should meet him. We went to school together. He studied voice and is now teaching at the university there. Here to see a daughter at college."

'Well, that sounds pleasant, Karl. I had dinner with the Blacks again last night. Jeffrey, their middle son was there with his new girlfriend, an old friend of mine by chance. Pleasant evening."

"Okay. So. Yes, all is well. I'll call in a few days. Stay safe, and I love you."

"Me too," and I hung up and heaved a great sigh. My phone life was a marathon.

I put on Mother's old slicker and hat and opened the front door. The rain had stopped, leaving a foggy atmosphere, and the wind had died. I walked out the lane and up to the main road to see if there was mail, not expecting anything forwarded from Baltimore to be there yet. Bills were still coming in for Mother, and I needed to organize and pay them when Davis got a checkbook to me.

A few late leaves were blowing off the trees and collecting in swirls on the lawn. Birds darted from branch to branch. Barely visible cars whooshed by in the mist, and otherwise it was quiet, like walking in a tunnel of cotton wool. I looked up, and there was a brightness overhead, promising clearing as the day wore on.

Mail was the usual flyers, pleas for donations, a bill from the telephone company, and then a big square envelope from Penny mailed directly to Mother's address. I stopped to open it, and inside were three drawings Fiona had done for me, squiggles of rainbow colors depicting stick figures running across the pages. A note on foolscap from Penny informed me, "Fiona insisted I mail these to you. She said it would make you happy even though Nan had died. I'm sure she's right. Thinking of you, love, Penny."

As I walked back up the lane, Anne's Jeep came towards me. I stepped onto the grass as she went by. She waved. I waved.

The phone was ringing again as I opened the door. I put the mail on the table and picked it up. "Hello," said my friend Helene, calling from Baltimore. "I was thinking about you."

"Oh, wow, lovely to hear your voice. Yes, things are progressing. Lots to do, to think about. It's nice here though."

"Good. We're missing you already. Dinner at Potter's last night. Boring, boring. He invited a bunch of academic types who are contributing to his book on Asian art. That, my dear, is all, and I mean all, they kicked around. On and on. I mean it's an interesting subject, of course, and I simply adore Asian art, but I wonder if the analysis doesn't go beyond what the artist intended. Context, I mean the scene during the time the art was created, is of course important, but the rest of it? Gad, total psychobabble. But I'm slogging on the way they did, and I really called to see how you are."

"I'm fine, Helene, fine, waiting on legal stuff, and then I can move ahead, arrange for the sale of the house and all. People here are nice. I'm beginning to wonder if any of my old friends are still around — it'd be fun to catch up with them."

"Of course you must. You can't sit pondering chores and writing all the time. You need a social life. After all, you're going to be there a while. By the way, did you consider keeping the house?"

"You know, I did. Suzanne of course is rooted to the West Coast, but yes, I did consider it. Seeing the old town, well it was a temptation. Then I realized my life now is down there, with you and everything else."

"Probably a good decision. I'd be bereft without you."

"Really?" I laughed.

"Oh, there's news," said Helene. "Henry and Alice Clay are getting a divorce."

"Wait. Henry and Alice? They've been married for eons."

"I know, but the scuttlebutt is that he has a girlfriend."

"Well, she's such a stick, I must say I don't blame him. But then, he's no bargain either, although rich. Who's the woman?"

"No one knows. Probably his secretary. Isn't that what they do at our age?"

"Yes, but a divorce? That's rash."

"Yes, it is of course, but once the old fools discover their peckers have a second life, they think they're young again and ready to make a fresh start. Concern about Alice is definitely misplaced. She'll do fine, keep the house and anything else she can lay her hands on."

I laughed. "Well it is one of the ways our generation of women learned to make a living, right?"

"Some of us went on from typing to find other ways," said Helene. "Like you. Who would have thought that the nice little girl who moved here from New England could have written a book like you have? Pretty racy, if I do say so."

"Thank you. I hope you assume the scenes were drawn from my own experience."

"Well, if not exactly, Elise, at least I credit you with above average powers of observation and imagination." She paused. "Well, were they?"

"I'll never tell," I laughed.

"If they were, then you're a chameleon indeed, leading a double life right under our noses. Would Karl have noticed?"

"That's my husband."

"Oh, Elise, get real. We've talked this way about our husbands for years. Why so touchy now?"

"Oh, I don't know," I said softening. "Sort of hit a raw nerve."

"Which means you agree," laughed Helene.

"Helene, I've got to go. I'm supposed to get into Boston by five, and I've lots to do here."

"Why Boston?" said Helene, who let nothing slip past her.

"Legal stuff," I hedged. "Boring. Take care, and give Anthony my love."

She let it go. "Will do. Love you, mean it," she chirped and hung up.

After a quick lunch of tomato soup and a grilled cheese sandwich, I packed a few things into an old canvas bag of Mother's, pulled another mystery novel off her shelf and settled down for a nap. Nothing was going to get done that day after all.

Chapter Thirty-five

A New Level of Fun

The address Alex gave me was near Newbury Street in a high-rise building. I found a parking spot and retrieved the canvas bag, locked the car, and headed back towards the park. Shifting the bag from my right hand to my left, I dropped my purse. While leaning over to retrieve it, I heard, "Darling, whatever are you doing here? I thought you were back in Baltimore." And there was my friend Kristina, coming along the sidewalk with her two Pekingese. At the same moment Alex came out of the building towards me.

"Oh, Kristina," I shouted, trying to look pleased to see her. "What a lovely surprise!" By then Alex was taking my bag from me.

"And is this the husband I've never met?" She stepped back and boldly looked Alex over, exclaiming, "Quite divine, darling." I introduced them, avoiding using Alex's name.

He took her hand. "Nice to meet you, Kristina. Elise has talked about you." *What?* Maybe I had mentioned her to him, but I didn't think so.

"I'm sure you two have important things to do, but if you can, I'd adore it if you'd come up for a drink." She pouted, "Now, don't say no and disappoint a bored and lonely woman. Carter is off in Washington at some arcane international meeting."

"Carter was ambassador to France a few years back," I filled in.

"Oh, that was the life," exclaimed Kristina, throwing one hand up in the air and gazing at the sky. "Glamor, lovely parties, fascinating people, Majorca in the summer and skiing at St. Moritz in the winter. I loved it."

Alex took my arm, "Kristina, it's been nice meeting you, but I'm afraid we'll have to decline. We're due out for dinner shortly. Perhaps another time."

"Oh dear," she said. "I know, I know, places to go, people to meet. Well, I'll toddle home and pour a martini, flip on the news, and spend a tedious evening with my doggies for company." She looked down at her feet where the two Pekingese were circling on their leashes.

"Off to Brunei next week to write another travel article. The National United Party is legal again. Have to smuggle in my gin." She moved past us, waving in the air. "Ciao, darlings," and she disappeared around a corner, one dog ahead and one pulling back to sniff a wet patch on the sidewalk.

"Whew!" said Alex as he steered me towards the lobby. "I'm exhausted."

I laughed. "Shrewder than she makes out," I said.

The elevator had brass doors and a mahogany interior with moss green carpeting. Alex turned a key in one of the slots, and we rose quickly to the tenth floor where the doors opened directly into the hallway of a large apartment. He put my bag on the floor by a pier table and led me into the living room.

"This is outstanding," I said to Alex. Yellow walls with white woodwork greeted us as we entered a vast living room with celadon green silk curtains, patterned upholstered couches, and Louis XV side chairs. "Can we stay for a week?"

A tall woman in a crisp green uniform and white apron appeared from what I surmised was the dining room. "Dinner is ready on the warming tray, Dr. Creighton. Dessert in the fridge. If you don't need anything else, I'll be off. Tomorrow's my day off, so if you'd rinse the plates and glasses and put them in the dishwasher, I'd appreciate it. Leave the casserole to soak." She nodded at me and smiled. "Good evening to both of you," and she went out the way she had come.

A platter of cheeses and crackers stood on a table. "Wow," I said, after I heard the back door slam. "Your friend doesn't rely on food stamps."

Alex laughed. "No, but he did come from a mining family in Appalachia. Extraordinary story. Worked for a hardware store after school and came up with a new kind of nail that could be hammered in but would hold like a screw. Moved to East Boston, and he and his cousin started a company with the help of venture capitalists who believed in the idea. Made a fortune. Then he went into finance and doubled his money. Never went to college. Major interest these days is teaching entrepreneurship to the poor. Goes all over the world."

"Why is he in Switzerland now? That's not exactly a third world country."

"Talking to his bankers, and then he's off to Africa. Now, would you like a drink?"

"Indeed," I said.

"Ah, there is something we've forgotten," he said and came and put his arms around me, leaning down for what ended up being a kiss of rising heat. I stepped back and looked up at him. "You don't go in for subtle advances."

"I thought that sort of dreariness was behind us." He stepped back. "Okay, what'll it be? The usual scotch or champagne for a change?"

"No champers; gives me a headache. Scotch will do. Thanks."

When we had settled on a couch, I brought up Anne's visit and the book talk. He groaned. "It's okay," I said. "We had a perfectly benign chat. Anyway, I said I would. Her friend Jill mentioned meeting us in town, so this might dispel speculation."

"I'm sure you'll carry it off, but it's cheeky of her to ask. Jill's a troublemaker, as I told you when she accosted me." He took a large swallow of his scotch. "Mmmm. Good. You should have seen her in my office when she was complaining of headaches. Here I am examining her eyes, and she reaches up and strokes my cheek and then runs her fingers along my neck. Creepy."

"What did you do?"

"I took her hand and placed it firmly in her lap and told her to be still."

"Did that stop her?"

"No. She gave me a card with her mobile phone number on it as she left. She was proud of having the phone and said that any time I'd like to have drinks after work to call her. The card is now in the shadowy cycle of garbage disposal."

I giggled. "You are cute, you know. Even I think so, so any time you'd like to fool around after work, please call me."

"Elise, the scotch is going to your head," he said reaching for my glass.

"I don't think that's where it went, but anyway pour me another, and we'll trace where it goes — research of course, Doctor."

He took my glass and put it on the table, his side motion knocking an alabaster ashtray onto the floor, where it rolled to a stop, unharmed. "Good idea, but it can only be carried out if you lie on your back, so I can get a full view. Part of the examination, of course." I lay back, and after fumbling with belt buckle and pantyhose, we unleashed the frenzy of desire that had built during our short hours apart. "Oh, Elise," he said, finally sitting up. "That was lovely."

I looked at him. "Thank you, Dr. Creighton, and for your part, you do look funny in a shirt, socks and shoes. Isn't there something missing?"

He looked down at his lap, and smiled. "Yes, definitely a tired little fellow."

"Not what I meant," I said, "but yes, he is."

We dressed, and I went in search of a guest bathroom to repair a thoroughly disheveled me.

Dinner was casserole of chicken in wine sauce followed by French pastries laid out on a silver tray. I selected a napoleon, and Alex took an éclair. We had wandered into the subject of his medical research, and I did a great deal of listening while trying to sort the gist of it from the medical terms and various hypotheses. Laying his napkin back on the table, he looked at me. "I hope this doesn't bore you."

"Of course, not," I answered. "I'm trying to understand and probably not making a very good job of it — inebriated gatekeepers guarding my brain."

"Let's go in the living room. Bring your wine; we'll do the dishes later."

When we had set our glasses down on the table in front of the couch, Alex went back into the dining room to get the bottle of wine and then sat beside me. "Okay, I have been thinking about your erstwhile half brother in terms of mixed families, adoptions and the like. So, I started focusing on my life and my own stepbrother, Terry; I mean where he is and what he's like. Either he's the same self-centered bastard he always was, or he's changed."

"Do you really want to find him? I thought you hated him."

"In a way, but it's more idle curiosity than any real longing for family, I can assure you."

"Have you tried?"

"Yes, I thought he was in Washington from something Mamie said before she died, but I couldn't find his name anywhere in the area. I did the usual Internet search and then had a lawyer friend do a more thorough search. Apparently, he did live there for a while, in Alexandria actually, but no one can get any further."

"So, no Terry anywhere?"

"No Terry anywhere, at least in this country. Tried obituaries too. Nothing."

We each took a sip of wine. I could hear a clock ticking from the direction of the hallway and the whisper of traffic below. Alex reached for my hand.

We sat for a few minutes. I roused myself and looked at him. "Alex, Mother really didn't tell you anything about a miniature painting? It's not there with the jewelry, is it? I mean did you check it carefully?"

"Well, no, now that you ask. I mean I didn't empty the envelope except to get a sense of what it contains and look at the note. Figured it was none of my business."

"It could be quite small," I said, leaning back and resting my head on the cushions behind me.

"Come here," he said, holding out his arms.

After falling asleep on the sofa, it was three in the morning before we got to the dishes. Cold and cramped, we roused ourselves, did the washing up, had a cup of tea and fell shivering into a bed in the corner bedroom, under a huge down comforter.

Chapter Thirty-six

Catching Up

On Saturday, Alex had no plans for the morning, so we ate a leisurely breakfast in the apartment. He called Anne and said he'd be home in time for a late lunch. She said not to worry; she was having lunch with friends and then playing bridge. David wouldn't be home until supper, so with relief we packed up, put our bags in my car and set out to visit the John Singer Sargent paintings at the Fine Arts Museum. No matter how many times I walk into that room hung with his luminous and large canvases, I am awed. We wandered in silence, glancing at each other from time to time and then proceeded to visit other rooms, sharing opinions and thoughts. Around eleven, Alex said, "I think it's time you set off. Take me to my car, and I'll follow later."

Soon I was on my way back to Hopwood. The happiness of the last hours was a wisp of memory as my thoughts turned to more practical matters. There was still more to do, and at the end of it? Well, there would be Thanksgiving with my family, and then the future became murky. It would be no time until Alex was off to England.

I stopped at Central Market before going back to the house. It was a clear and warmish day, and I met Arthur coming out, dressed in a light sweater.

"Morning, Elise," he called. "Spring in October. Nice to see you back."

"Indeed," I answered.

"You promised to have dinner with me, you know, and I have a thought. Let me take you to Keenan's for lobster."

"What a tempting idea!" I said.

"Good, I'll pick you up at five-thirty," and he was on his way down the sidewalk holding a large bag of groceries, a bunch of bananas sticking out the top. I watched him from behind and noticed his right foot had a pronounced outward cant, as if he were walking two directions at once. I smiled and went into the market. Clarence was behind the meat counter, and I went over to say hello.

"Well, it looks like you've taken up residence here," he said. "Be staying for long?"

"A few weeks anyway. I'd like to see if any of my old chums from the past are still around. Tom Hawkins maybe?"

"No, he married and moved away, out west I think. Joan Sullivan is here though. Married Sherman Banks and had a bunch of kids. She runs that fancy dress shop over by the harbor. You two were close, weren't you? Always getting into scrapes as I remember."

I laughed. "You've a long memory, Clarence."

"Not much else to do around here these days but remember," he said.

"Well, now for the present, I'd love a pound of that good smoked bacon and a half-pound of ground round."

"Coming right up," he said, and headed for the meat locker in back.

I gathered up a few other things, and Clarence came back with my packages. "See you around," he said, and turning he waved across the store. "Mornin', Mrs. Davis."

I decided to stop at Joan's dress shop on the way home.

She was there: small, lively, red haired with a galaxy of freckles. "Well as I live and breathe," she laughed. "If it isn't Elise. You are a sight for the weary. What brings you here? Ah, yes now I remember. Your Ma died didn't she? Heard about it. Sorry."

"Thanks. She was pretty sick at the end."

"Yes, that's a tough one. The sickness I mean. It'll get us all for sure. My Ma went with breast cancer." She paused to put money in the cash register. "Hold on a minute. You eaten lunch? I know it's late, but I'm starved."

"No, I haven't. We, I had a late breakfast."

"We? I? You got your kids here?"

"No, just me."

"Well never mind. I'll get my assistant to take over for a while, and we can have a good old talk." She disappeared into a back room and emerged in a few minutes with a tan overcoat. "Let's go. Annie's?"

"Sounds good," I said and led her to my car. We drove the short distance, Joan chatting away about changes to Hopwood. "And look there at that house — Benji Merrill moved back here after making a fortune on Wall Street. Did you ever? It's got a pool and tennis court in the back. We call it the Taj. You'd think he might be too high and mighty now for the likes of me, but underneath he's the same old guy. Any time of day you can see pretty flashy cars parked in front. Remember? He used to have such bad acne that us girls wouldn't get near him. Ugh."

No, Joan hadn't changed; Irish to the bone. We settled ourselves in a booth and ordered hot dogs and fries. "So," she began, "tell me all. You're married of course, nice gent with a good income, I expect. Kids?"

"Yes three, two girls and a boy, and you?"

"Four girls. Imagine, four girls and me the town tomboy. Hardly knew what to do with them." She laughed. "All that damned stuff: hairdryers, ribbons, giggles and good heavens, the whining. What a group! Good girls though, married now and settled down, good husbands except one, and she's married to a drunk, a real loser he is. She says she loves him. Bah. Love can't be that blind, now can it? He's a mechanic, that is when he can make it to work."

"And your husband?" I asked.

"Ex-husband. My luck. Got him through college, me working as a waitress, and he had a good career as a CPA. Did everyone's taxes around here. Thought we'd hit good times: nice house, couple of cars, trips now and then. Then he drifted into the mid-forties and started feeling his oats, so to speak; more like his nuts; took off with one of his clients. Came back too, wanting me to forgive him and all that shit. No, says I. No way. Made your bed, now lie in it. So, he trots back to her, and now they have a kid, five or six he'd be. Oh, well, I make a good living with the store. And, my nights and Sundays are my own. I like it that way."

"You've had a busy time," I said. "Makes my life look pretty boring by comparison. My husband is a set designer for opera, gone a lot of the time. I write, and my latest book is a success; maybe going to be a movie. I'm writing another."

"My, my," said Joan, "And aren't I in the presence? Guess I did read about you in one article or another a while back. Wondered how you were and if you had changed. And your kids; oh, yes, you told me, two girls and a boy. Where are they?"

I started to reel off the short form of family activities, but by then our lunch arrived, and we quietly applied mustard and catsup to our hamburgers. "Funny, isn't it," said Joan, chewing. "Our lives came out the way they started. I mean me still a townie and you a famous writer. Don't mean it like sour grapes or anything. It's the way it was and is. What's surprising is that you and I were such good friends as little girls. Started in public school here and even went on after you were hauled out and sent to Derby Academy. We had good times, didn't we?" She looked up at me, smiling.

"We did," I said. "We really did. Remember the time you stole the neighbor's cat, and we hid it in your basement until the owners posted a reward?" She started giggling.

"Yeah, that was a riot. My parents kept telling me they heard a cat meowing, and I told them they were hearing things, probably the furnace going bad. With six of us in the house, that was the easy part. The lid blew off when your mother found the empty cat food cans in the garbage and started asking questions. I'll never forget having to apologize after we'd looked like such heroines finding the cat and getting the reward."

"Unbearable," I said.

We looked at each other and smiled. "This is good," said Joan. "How long you gonna be here? We got to get some more time in."

"Oh, a few weeks anyway. I don't really have to get home until shortly before Thanksgiving. Anyone else from our old crowd still around?"

"Not many. Most of them had sense enough to get out. Of course Benji's here. Then there's Martha. We'll figure something out, supper at my place maybe."

After more reminiscing, I dropped her off and headed back to the house.

Chapter Thirty-seven

Lobster at Keenan's

At Keenan's that evening, I looked up, knowing what a mess I was. Arthur was grinning at me.

"This is the first lobster I've had since I came back here. Oh, Arthur, it's such a treat." I wiped dripping butter off my chin.

"Me? I can take them or leave them after all these years, but it does my old heart good to see you enjoying your dinner. You look like a kid, Elise."

"I'm so hungry I think I'll have dessert too. Okay? I'm not trashing your savings?"

"No, no. My former so-called financial advisor did that single-handedly. These young fellows have no idea about conservative investments. He thought that if he delivered a nice income, that was the end of his duty to me. I miss your father, indeed I do."

"But wouldn't that be the point? I mean giving you a nice income?"

"Well, yes, but if you take, say, a hundred thousand dollars and invest it in funds that pay a good income and the underlying value shrinks at an alarming rate, then all you're doing is delivering your client's own money to him minus an advisory fee that gets charged whether or not the client loses money. Granted the fee declines with the value, but the client still has to pay taxes on the income. At least that's what happened to me before I caught on."

"You have no recourse?" I asked and took a big gulp of wine.

"Oh, sure, you can take it to court, but you'll get nowhere. When you start with them, they hand you pages and pages of agreement forms, and if you're naive, which I am where money is concerned, you sign them when you should have taken them home and read the fine print about submitting to arbitration and other gobbledygook. It's a nice racket, and I'm sure there are good ones out there, but I haven't found anyone since your dad died. They tell you to wait; the market always has ups and downs, and eventually the shares will go up again. Well, I'm done waiting for that. I'm in a few bonds and mostly cash instruments."

"Is it enough? No, no, don't answer that. It's none of my business."

"Yes, it's enough. I don't live in high style, and the books actually bring in nice royalties, even after all these years."

"I hope I can accomplish that," I said. "I've barely started really, and I have a friend in Baltimore who's been handling what I've earned. She does a good job and seems to know what conservative means. Karl handles our other investing, and I pay bills out of our joint account. It works."

Arthur cleared his throat and looked at me. "Elise, is everything all right between you and Karl? I mean, I have no right to ask, and don't answer me if you don't want to. But I got the impression that our friendly doctor has been breathing down your neck and that you aren't running away."

I put my napkin on the table and looked out at the harbor, light blending into night, a few boats at anchor faintly visible as shore lights reflected off their hulls. I didn't know what to say to him or how far to trust him after Potter reported the phone call they'd had. I looked back at him.

"Yes, of course, everything's fine. We both go our own ways and enjoy being pretty independent, but we're . . ." I paused here. "I guess I'd say we're compatible and comfortable."

Arthur chuckled. "Well, comfortable can lead you into a lot of trouble, my girl. Ask me."

Glad to change the focus, I said, "And what should I ask you?"

He looked embarrassed, an alien state for the Arthur I had known so far. He cleared his throat and took a sip of wine. "Let's go back here. Potter said you were dodgy when he told you he and I had spoken. I'm sure that also came as a surprise to you, I mean Potter and I knowing each other and knowing each other well enough to talk about you."

"Yes," I answered, straightening my back. "In fact I found it strange and a little offensive, if you must know."

"There was a time," Arthur continued, "when I wasn't the crumpled old man you see before you. In fact," he grinned, "I was damned attractive and yes, comfortable — a teaching job I loved, life in a lovely New England town, good friends."

"I'm sure you were, still are, I mean." Where this was going I wasn't sure, but I was beginning to get an inkling. "Are you trying to tell me that you and Potter…?"

"Alas, I am. He was a kid, and I was a professor at Williams. I'm not proud of the whole affair, but it happened and in fact went on for many years. Happily for both of us, we have remained friends ever since. The world has not been good to people like us, so of course we've kept under the radar. I hope things are changing, and it looks as though they are, but the shame and humiliation surrounding the possibility of getting caught back then was terrifying."

I took a deep breath and saw with new understanding how hard it must have been for two well-brought-up men to feel that kind of affection for each other. Even now, people made jokes, although the language used shifted in the sixties and seventies. However, it was slow to catch on with those who had grown up in the fifties, and certainly civil law had not yet moved towards legitimizing unions in any meaningful way.

"This comes as a shock?" asked Arthur.

"Yes and no," I began. "I guess that with Potter the conjecture has always been there. But he's discreet and so interesting and amusing that no one really cares. I mean he's a joy to have around, but if you mean did anyone suspect, I'd say yes."

"And me?"

"No, no, not you. I'd never have suspected."

"Well, there you are." He relaxed and smiled. "Now, back to being comfortable, since I am a prying old fellow. When you describe life as *comfortable*, as you do with you and Karl, it can mean easy coasting until something comes along to upset the old apple cart. And I am asserting that an attractive and mysterious fellow such as our Dr. Creighton could be the very person to tip the pippins into the road, in fact may have done so already." He stared at me. *What to say? Anything would give me away. Protest? No good. Agree? Still bad.*

"Okay, Arthur. I don't know where you're going here. I mean are you doing this out of concern for me or to amuse yourself and report back to Potter?"

"Elise, cynicism doesn't suit you. I admit I'm curious, but I will also say that, out of friendship for both your parents, I do care for your general welfare, and I think Dr. Creighton cares nothing for that. He is a lady's man. That's the long and short of it. His long affair with Sheila Bigelow attests to that, and I suspect there have been others. When a marriage is as obviously barren as his and Anne's, it's like a virus; it moves into the larger community and infects those with low immunity. And, I am guessing that yours is low."

I could feel tears welling up, a weakness that made me angry. "Arthur, let me say this once. If one shred of your active imagination reaches Potter or anyone in Baltimore, I'll kill you with my bare hands."

He raised his arms in mock horror and laughed. "Ah, I see the spirit of your mother shining through. Calm down; I may be obnoxious, but I am also the epitome of discretion." He then spread his veined old hands wide on the tablecloth and said, "Look, Elise, all I'm saying is watch out. Be good to yourself. Don't toss away years of a good marriage on the kind of attraction that is apt to happen at your age unless there's nothing left for you at home. I know it's a dilemma, because if you don't proceed, you will always wonder about what could have been. That can be a kind of hell too. T. S. Eliot said it so well in The Quartets; Burnt Norton I think it was.

Footfalls echo in the memory

Down the passage we did not take

Towards the door we never opened

Into the rose garden. My words echo

Thus, in your mind.

"In other words,“ he continued, "in one's late forties and early fifties, we begin to be afraid we will plod along missing wonderful adventures, leave a void in our lives that we'll regret. The leap can be thrilling, but it's not what life is made of in the long run. You want something to go back to when it's over. These things can be handled in ways that make them possible and pleasurable, but Americans always botch it up with confessional excesses. That is selfish and leaves others with the burden. If you're intent on going forward with this, if there is a *this*, then please be sophisticated."

I thought back to Jerry and how I had indeed botched it, knew it was Karl's maturity and discretion that had saved us, not my own. I nodded. "Okay, I've got the message. Now, can we change the subject?"

Chapter Thirty-eight

Listing the House

The following Friday morning I woke with the sun streaming in the window. The week had been cold. A little snow had fallen, and I'd managed to clean up a great deal of the house and send photographs of Mother's art to everyone.

The day looked as though we might have a reprieve from the chill. Alex had decided at the last minute to attend a medical conference in Chicago and would arrive home that night. I couldn't put off a gathering Joan had arranged, but hoped he'd come over later. He had called every evening to report interesting tidbits and mention a few connections he was making involving his new post in London. He'd met a doctor involved in research at the London Hospital Medical College, which was merging with St. Bartholomew's Hospital, and felt that through him he would have access to important information on the local medical scene and its major players.

"Davis Hopkins has cleared the way to put the house on the market," I told him on Thursday night.

"That'll be good, get you moving forward before you have to leave for Thanksgiving. I don't know how we'll manage if it sells too fast, but we'll figure it out I'm sure. By the way, now that most of the legal stuff is under way, and I'm sure the IRS is satisfied with their share, I'll bring over the jewelry when I get back."

"Ah," I answered, "Please do. I have to photograph it and go through dividing it up with Suzanne."

"Not necessary," said Alex. "I forgot to mention before that your mother left a list in the package saying who is to get what. I did glance at that. It's for you and Suzanne, and then you two can figure out any other family you want to include, especially with your father's cuff links, studs, tie clips, watch and the rest. She didn't discuss those."

Before we hung up, he added, "One more thing. Terry has reappeared in my life."

"Oh? Good Lord, how did that happen?"

"Strange. He called my office out of the blue. I called him back, and he said 'Hi brother,' as if these years had never passed. I was dumbstruck."

"Where is he?"

"Living in Nicaragua of all places. Running a bed and breakfast. Said he'd be in New York the end of December and would I meet him. He's also planning to visit my father and stepmother then."

"And?"

"I said I would. What was I supposed to do? Tell him to get lost? I suppose I could have, but what the hell, I'm curious."

"So you'll go?"

"Sure."

For a while we talked about ourselves, the upcoming separation, how much we missed each other and the foolish talk that passes for conversation between new lovers.

"Oh," I said at the end. "I'm going to Joan Sullivan's. Kind of a reunion with a few of the kids I grew up with here. What time does your plane get it?"

"Around seven. I'll look for lights and try to come over after you get home. Bye for now."

"Hurry," I said.

Karl had called on Wednesday with more news of the opera, which was coming along well save for a few ego flares. He said he'd be home around November twentieth in time for Thanksgiving with Penny, Christopher, and Fiona. Had I ordered a turkey?

"Yes," I answered, "and this has been such a hectic time that I'm having the club cook it."

"My, my," he laughed, "my New England girl is losing her frugality. Well, good for you."

I changed the subject. Truth was I had lost interest in most things domestic of late. "Penny's improved and navigating without a limp, and Enid called from Paris. After three days she's ecstatic with the apartment and being with Evan again. She takes up her new post on Monday but has already been in the offices of Bradley and Clark and pronounced them elegant."

I added that Matthew meanwhile was parlaying his connections at the Conservatory in Cincinnati into a cobbled together group of graduate students who met for jam sessions. He'd bought a new guitar. I told all of this to Karl until his replies ebbed to a series of *ah's*. We ran through the litany of patter long honed as a preamble to ending a conversation.

Suzanne was silent these days, her last conversation leaving me in no doubt as to her unavailability for the foreseeable future. She was sure I'd handle everything well, and bye for now.

One glance at the clock, and I leapt out of bed. I had an hour until the Realtor was due. I was happy to find a friend from my past to do the job: Toby Smith, whom Joan said married Benji's sister Mary Merrill,. They'd be at the party tonight. Somehow the prospect of reuniting with my childhood friends didn't look as enticing as it had when Joan and I had first arranged it.

I was missing Alex and wanted the evening to speed by until I saw him again. I knew I had glided into this affair, and that complications were beginning to surface. I didn't care. Not then.

As it turned out, the house was worth more than we had thought, and I signed the papers. Toby would fax them to Suzanne for her signature. He didn't object to my staying on but warned me I'd have to get out when there were showings. "Buyers hate to have the owners around when they look; can't talk freely about how they'd paint, move walls and such."

"I understand," I said, gazing at him. "Toby, you haven't changed at all. I mean where are the wrinkles? And your hair is still blond. Amazing."

He smiled, pleased. "And I'd say the same for you, except you've let a few grey strands take up residence; ought to dye it like the other women do."

"Can't be bothered," I grimaced, "takes too much time and care. Old is old, and personally, I think trying to fake it makes people look silly."

He left after taking photographs. "Well, see you tonight. Mary's looking forward to it. 'Til then." And he slammed the door after him.

With the whole day ahead and most of the work done, I decided to get back to writing in earnest. I gathered up the sheets lying on the dining table and did a quick review and then fired up the computer.

Writing is a lonely business, and there are days when you want to scream. This was one of them. With the wisps of *Gone Crazy* fading from my subconscious, I was deeply into new characters and scenes. It was a good story, but I couldn't get a sentence down. Finally, pacing around the room, pouring another cup of coffee and going outdoors to have a smoke and look at the beach didn't get me any closer, so I sat down and dove into the middle to see if I could make my way in either direction. It worked, and soon I was back at early chapters and humming along.

The phone rang — Helene. "What the hell are you doing still up there? When are you coming home?"

"I'll probably get there the week before Thanksgiving. Karl comes in around the twentieth."

"But that's ages off. What are you doing that takes so long?"

"Well, I'm pretty well at the end of clearing out. I've listed the house, and frankly, this is a great place to write. I love it here."

"You can write at home. You always have. Come on, Elise, what's keeping you there? I miss you like the blazes. So does Louise. We can't gossip properly without you; we get positively tongue-tied."

"Now, now, I'm sure you two do fine. Speaking of which, what's going on with the Clays? I mean Henry and Alice seemed so perfect together, both pompous and tight assed. I can't imagine them getting divorced after all these years."

"Well, as I told you before, Henry's running off. We didn't know with whom when I talked to you before, but it's come out that the woman works in Washington. She's assistant to a lobbyist, and he met her when she went to see him about joining forces with a couple of other companies that have an interest in getting a bill passed on tariffs. She's his age, I gather, but it's really serious, and he plans to marry her. Don't guess it's a pregnancy though, not in her fifties."

"Appalling," I laughed. "Can you imagine going to bed with Henry? What a thought. His breath for starters." I paused. "How is Alice taking it?"

"She's 'taking' it all right," laughed Helene, "Taking the house, taking the Mercedes, and taking a fat settlement. Seems pleased as punch right now. Angry of course, but maybe it's a relief to her, who knows?"

"Would be to me if I had to face him over coffee every morning. Whew, Helene, we really are bitchy."

There was a silence on the other end of the line. "Elise, down to business. What, or who, is keeping you there? Are you up to no good? Come on, you can tell Aunt Helene."

"There's nothing to tell." I thought a moment, and then said, "Really, it's fun being here. I've run into old friends of Mother's who have taken me in, and tonight I'm going to a party where my chums from childhood will be; well, those that are still around. I guess I'm enjoying tripping through the past. It's good."

"Well, if that's all it is, then fine. I sensed a wee bit of evasiveness the last time we talked, and I guess I jumped to conclusions. Truly, it's easy to get carried away at our age, and if you don't mind my saying so, you and Karl —"

"I do mind your saying so. Let's leave it with what I told you. Okay?"

"For now. But don't count on me not to nag."

"No, I'd never ask the impossible," I laughed, and we clicked off.

Chapter Thirty-nine

The Party's Over

The party at Joan's jettisoned me into an odd mixture of reconstructed past and unfamiliar present. Joan set out a supper of fried chicken, mashed potatoes, bean salad, and a huge chocolate cake served on paper plates. Benji Merrill and his Southern wife, May Bell, arrived first. He sauntered in wearing khakis, a pink shirt covered by a white cashmere sweater and Gucci loafers, his wife trailing behind him in a cloud of perfume and shoulder-length blonde hair, bearing a bottle of white wine.

"Well, if it isn't naughty little Elise. Why didn't you call us immediately?" Benji shook my hand. "You look wonderful. I'm so sorry about your mother." He stepped aside and pulled May Bell forward. "Elise, May Bell, my wife."

"Well, honey," she said, "I've heard about you. Benji says you're a famous author; reads the *New York Times* book reviews every week, he does." She giggled, looking up at him with a smile. "Reads the reviews, but not the books, right, sweetie?"

"That's not entirely accurate, darling," he answered. "I read a lot, but it's mostly business stuff. Running a hedge fund is not exactly conducive to relaxation, now is it?"

May Bell winked at me. "Now, Benji, don't get defensive, honey. I was teasing. Of course you're busy, but as for relaxation, we do manage to have our little moments, now don't we?"

Apparently, these two conversed in questions. I looked at Benji. He wasn't bad looking these days, all traces of his youthful acne gone, dark hair slicked straight back, thin and tall. "You look pretty good yourself, Benji," I ventured.

May Bell lunged forward holding out the bottle of wine. "And this is for dear Joanie. Isn't she the angel to pull this together, and look at that scrumptious food!" She looked over at Joan. "Now, don't tell me you cooked all of that by your little bitty self." She turned to me. "Imagine, so clever, running that fabulous dress shop and then being able to do this. We all shop there, such lovely things."

I glanced at Joan and could hardly contain myself while watching the smile congeal on her face. "Sure I cooked it," she said.

Looking relieved, she glanced at the door opening, and in came Benji's sister Mary with Toby Smith, my Realtor. Martha Weinstein was behind them with her boyfriend, and there were a few others I had not met before. Soon we were breaking into small groups and chatting, wine flowing freely and Joan passing cheese and crackers around. I moved on after talking to Martha's boyfriend for a while and listening to the struggles of running a golf club.

"Elise," called May Bell, patting the sofa next to her. "Come sit by me." I did as I was told. "Now," she said as I settled, "you must have met your neighbors, Dr. and Mrs. Creighton."

"I have," I admitted. "Very nice people, friends of my mother's."

"I know that," she said. "We're good friends. But tell me, isn't he too divine?"

I reached for my wine and took a large sip, or dose, as might be. "He's certainly been welcoming to me, and so has she."

"Well, I should hope so. Now, Anne," she started, settling back into the cushions, "she's gotten herself what you might want to call a rep-u-ta-tion around these parts. Hear she came on to the insurance agent that arrived to look at the damage on her car when she was hit last year. You get my meaning?"

Having heard enough of this gossip, I decided to play dumb and said, "No, I don't get your meaning at all. She's been nice to me."

"It's old news, of course," she said, running her finger around in circles on the cushion beside her. "I don't guess he's been the angel himself, but who could blame him?" She paused and took a deep breath, and noting my stony silence, brightened up. "I guess we'll forget that. Tell me about your books."

I'm hopeless when discussing my writing and always end up making it sound dull, so I got up. "Another time." I smiled down at her and went over to Martha.

The party broke up after dinner with promises of phone calls and comments on how good it was to get together after so long. I stayed and helped Joan clean up.

Up to her elbows in sudsy water, Joan looked up at me. "Well, was I wrong about May Bell?"

"On target. She's amazing. I have lots of Southern friends, and I love the metaphoric language, but she's a sugar-coated busybody."

"She's actually smart, but who cares? Can't wade through the rest of it to get there."

"You know, Joan, Benji is a surprise, quite the sophisticate."

"Yes, he's come a long way, and when push comes to shove, he can be sweet." She handed me a salad bowl to dry. "He helped me a lot with advice on money during my divorce. I'm grateful for that."

"Was it awful?"

"Awful. But I'm glad it's over and that man is out of my life. Looking back, he was never easy to live with. Critical, jealous and sour tempered."

When we had restored her house to neatness, I gave her a hug. "Thanks for doing this. It was fun. I'll call you, and we can get together again. I'm going back before Thanksgiving, but there's plenty of time."

Alex arrived shortly after I arrived back to Mother's. We held each other as the ground slipped away under us, and time compressed into warmth and longing. "Ah," he said, holding me away from him, "I've missed you my darling, really, really missed you."

"And I you. You look tired."

"I am. When you go to one of those conferences, people end up wanting to go out after dinner. It's a good time to talk shop and make new connections. Late nights, but that's the part I like best." He went into the kitchen. "Come on, sit. How was the party?"

"Fun. Well fun in a way. I'm not sure I have much in common with most of them anymore, except Joan. We were such good friends growing up that being with her is like old times. She's a comfortable, easy person."

"I don't know her that well," he said, moving towards the sofa at the end of the room, two drinks in his hands. "The Merrills, we see them fairly often; they're part of the group here that runs around together. He's nice, but . . ."

"But," I filled in, "that woman! Oh, Alex, what gushy bitchiness!"

"Actually, she can be funny. But, yes, she's a vicious gossip."

"I discovered that right away."

"Meaning?'

"Well, she launched right into you and Anne, mainly Anne's rep-u-ta-tion," I said, mimicking May Bell. "I had barely met her when she started to insinuate and try to get me interested. I held her off, though."

"Good girl. Small town." He took a sip of his drink and looked at me. "The way I see it is that there is one group here comprised of the old guard, people who have been here a long time. Most of those are your parents' generation, and their kids have largely moved away. Not true of the townspeople; there are many generations of those here including the Portuguese fishing families who moved here from the Azores and a lot of people of Irish descent. And then there are the newcomers like us. People have discovered this town and started coming here, as Anne and I did. We're from all over the country — golf club members, a partying group, professionals who mostly work in and around Boston with a few local exceptions, like Benji, who works from home, and Martha Weinstein's boyfriend. They're the ones I guess you'd call the private school group of who have come back here."

I had heard much of this from Arthur, but it was interesting hearing Alex's take on it. I thought a moment. "When Suzanne and I were little, we went to public school here before being sent to Derby, so our friends came from both groups, like Joan. I certainly feel closer to Joan than to Benji."

"Oh, Benji's a good guy really, can be insufferably pompous but has a good heart."

"That's what Joan said. He was a big help to her during her divorce."

Alex got up. "Come here and give me a hug. I really am whacked and need to sleep." After a few moments of being close, he pulled away. "I'm busy tomorrow night, big party Anne's gotten us committed to, in Cambridge, so it'll be another late one. I'll call you tomorrow."

And with that he was gone.

Chapter Forty

Jewelry

By noon on Saturday, I still had not heard from Alex and was getting anxious. For one thing, I wanted to see the jewelry he had promised to bring over, and secondly, he had been remote the previous night and then not called as he had said he would. As I was eating a sandwich around one I heard footsteps and the door opened.

"Hello. You here?"

"Over here," I said, getting up.

He hung up his jacket and held out his arms. The phone rang. It was Suzanne.

"Hey, little sis. How's it going?"

"Oh, hi, Suzanne," I said glancing at Alex with a grimace.

"You busy?" she asked.

"Well, I've got a visitor right now; can I call you back?"

"Uh oh, I bet I know who it is, the lovely doctor?"

"Yes, as a matter of fact, he's brought over Mother and Dad's jewelry," I answered, noting the large brown envelope in Alex's hand.

"Oh, good. Photographs for me?"

"No, apparently Mother left a list specifying what to whom. I'll send you a copy."

"Well, wasn't she organized? That's fine."

"Dad's stuff is not listed, so we'll have to make decisions there. I'll send photos of those things. Now, Suzanne, I really have to go." Alex was grinning at my frustration.

"The film is coming along really well," she went on. I sighed; there was never a way to talk if she was busy or to shut her off if she wanted to talk.

"That's good."

"Yes, I'm amazed, not a temper tantrum in sight. Everyone is getting on beautifully. They love working with me. A bunch of us went out last night . . ."

"Suzanne, I have to go now."

"Oh, yes. Well, go to your doctor. Enjoy. Talk to you another time when you're not too madly busy for your sister."

Guilt? Ah, Suzanne has a way of making everything about her. "I'll call you," I said.

"Better not. Schedules, you know. Later. Bye." And she was gone.

I hung up the phone and looked at Alex.

"Persistent, isn't she?" he said.

"I suppose that's the word." And I went over to him and we held each other for a moment. Desire lit the air around us, and it was a long time until anything intelligible was said. Later I went to clean up. Alex was asleep. I covered him with the afghan and took my plate to the kitchen. He slept through my banging on the computer keys and finally made a few grunts and opened his eyes.

"You left me."

"I did. You were snoring."

"Me?"

"You."

"Wait a minute, what time is it? David has a soccer game at four."

"It's only three. Do you want a sandwich?"

He sighed. "Not really, I had a late breakfast." He dressed quickly and reached for the envelope. "Well, here is what your mother gave me."

"I'll look at it later," I said and set the envelope beside my computer. "Right now, I want to know about Terry and a lot else."

"Like what?"

"Well, we haven't discussed England, and I don't know if Anne is going with you or what's happening. Also I know I've already asked you, but are you absolutely sure Mother never mentioned that little enamel painting on copper? I thought you might remember her mentioning it. Davis reasoned that since she trusted you, she could have said something."

"Why the hell didn't he ask me?"

"I don't know."

"Look, as I've told you several times, I don't know anything about it. Tell the jackass that." He paused a moment. "Actually, you know full well that I didn't pick through the jewelry. Maybe it's there. You can look for yourself."

I decided not to pursue it and waited.

"Okay," he finally said, "Let's deal with my long lost stepbrother. I don't know any more than what I told you the other night. He found me, and I did say I'd meet him in New York in the middle of the week between Christmas and New Year's. Puzzling, but as I said, I'm curious."

"I don't blame you. I'd be curious too."

I went to get a glass of water. "You want one too?"

"Sure," he called after me.

"So," I said, coming back into the room, "Terry might have something he wants to tell you."

"I can't imagine what there is to tell; I already know the bones of the story. I remember one day when Mamie was clearly angry at the way Father was treating me, she let something drop about favoring Terry over me. When I asked her, that's when she said that since I was adopted and Terry was Father's 'real' son, she thought he wasn't being fair." He paused and looked at the ceiling. Finally, he added, "Of course I knew I was adopted. Father told me after he gave me the ring, but the full impact of Father's indifference to me after Terry was born hit me at that point. I really began to resent and hate them both after that."

"Do you have no idea who your real parents were?"

"None at all."

"Have you ever tried to find out?"

"Yes, once when I was in college, I asked my stepfather. He got upset and said that he had no idea, and why would I care. Wasn't he good enough for me? Hadn't he done everything for me a child could want? I didn't begin to know where to look, so I let it go."

"Okay, now tell me about England."

"Ah," he sighed. "Anne and I have gone back and forth on that one. One day she wants to come, and the next she doesn't. I think she's leaning towards staying put here. She has a lot going on that she'd miss, and while I think David would benefit from a change of scene and education, she's in favor of not disrupting him." He took a long drink of water and set the glass down. "It isn't as though I'll be around much anyway. And since neither of us knows anyone over there, she'd be at sea most of the time. I think we've settled on the fact that at least initially she'll stay here, and we'll try to have a family holiday in England over the boys' spring breaks, if they coincide at all, June if not. But," he added, "she could always change her mind."

"How do you feel about that?"

"Oh, me? I'm good with her staying here, prefer it. I'm going to be busy as hell, and it isn't as if Anne and I are dependent on each other for company. It doesn't work that way now and wouldn't work any better over there, I'm sure. I will miss David, though."

I looked down at my hands gripping each other in my lap. "And us?" My voice came out in an unfamiliar squeak, and I looked up and smiled apologetically.

"Oh, please, Elise. Stop that! You know about us." He reached for my hand. "Well, don't you?"

"At times, I don't. It's happened so fast, and my world is upside down and crazy right now. I can't stop my mind from whirling except when I'm writing. I can focus then."

"Darling girl, they say that God created the world in seven days; we're hardly that adept even though we've had longer."

I laughed. "And all that without superhuman powers."

After he was gone, I opened the envelope and laid the little boxes and bags on the kitchen counter. Opening them one by one, I marveled at the beauty of the pieces, realizing that Mother had seldom worn jewelry. Most of the dazzling array I had never seen. Father's watch, studs, and cuff links were there too, along with pins from various clubs and long-ago sports teams. I set each object aside as I sorted them per Mother's list and found no enamel painting, not that I had really expected to.

I went to find my new camera to photograph Dad's jewelry. Around three-thirty I heard the Creightons' car go down the lane.

Chapter Forty-one

The Grass Harp

Joan called around four. "Doing anything tonight?" she asked.

"Not really," I answered. "What do you have in mind?"

"Well, *The Grass Harp* is playing in Hingham. You know, the Truman Capote story; Walter Matthau and Piper Laurie are in it. Sissy Spacek too. Want to go? Starts at six thirty."

"Sure I do. Want me to pick you up?"

"No, I'm still at the store. I'll come from here to your place, and perhaps we can get a bite to eat afterwards. There's a new seafood shack not far from Hingham Harbor."

I realized I had been in a bleak mood after hearing the Creightons leave, and the distraction was welcome. By the time I changed my clothes, I heard Joan's car roll down the drive.

Once underway, she said, "So, did you enjoy seeing everyone on Friday? Bet you can't wait to see May Bell again."

"She's a dose, but I think there's a good deal of intelligence buried in that blonde head. Or maybe it's cunning."

"She's smart all right. Benji seems to adore her, and he's really no fool."

"Where did he meet her?"

"Actually, he picked her up on a flight to London, seated next to her. She was married at the time, a childhood sweetheart gone bad kind of marriage. I guess the boyfriend never overcame his origins — small town Georgia I think — and May Bell wanted a jet-propelled upswing from hers. Benji offered that."

"Is this Benji's first marriage?"

"Yes. He lived with an actress in New York early on. I don't really know what happened there. She was pretty well known, Laura Thompson."

"Ah, I've actually seen her in a play. Very talented. Hmmm. Interesting. So, no kids?"

"Oh, yes. They have one; Benji and May Bell I mean. A girl. She's at school, Farmington, wants to be a vet."

Joan pulled up at a red light and glanced over at me. "Can I ask you something?"

"Well sure. What is it?"

"As you know, Hopwood is a small town. Stuff gets around, and I overheard Judy Cole in the store the other day saying to a friend that her sister, Jill Brown, had run into you and Alex Creighton one evening on the street in Boston. That right?"

I looked away. The harbor was on our right, and I could see reflections in the water. The light turned green, and she moved the car forward. "Yes, that's right."

"Didn't think you knew them, but I guess being neighbors of your mother's and all, it's natural. But what were you doing in Boston with him?"

"Now, Joan," I tried to laugh, but it came out as a sort of snort. "Don't go jumping to conclusions. I had to get another copy of the death certificate. Alex met me to give me that, and we had dinner afterwards. Simple. He was Mother's doctor, and he's nice."

"Oh, he's nice. Ask Sheila Bigelow how nice he is."

I had regained a modicum of composure by then. "And who is she?"

"Sheila? Sheila had a long-standing affair with Alex. Everyone knows that. I think it's in the past now, but really, Elise, I'd watch out for him. Neither he nor his wife is exactly the stay-at-home type. Who am I to talk, but they are trouble with a capital 'T' I'd say, both of them. He's kind of cute, yes. But I'm warning you."

"Well, thanks for the warning. So far, he's been helpful with what I've had to do here and, for that matter, so has Anne."

By now we were parking in front of the theatre, and I hoped I had settled the matter to her satisfaction. She said nothing more, and dinner and the drive home consisted of reviewing the film and a nostalgic cruise through more shreds of our shared past.

Chapter Forty-two

Anne and Alex

I spent the next week in earnest, finishing up what had to be done. Packers came in to ship what the family wanted, and later the gallery arrived with a van to pick up remaining art works. Activity accelerated with the first showings Toby had of the house. The furniture was down to a minimum, but the place was still livable. The rest would go later. Alex often came over in the late evening, and we walked in the cold, made love when and where we felt it was safe, and talked a great deal, slipping into a more ordinary foundation of friendship under the fire of our attraction, which still burned bright.

Anne actually joined us the last Friday evening I was there, coming over to tell Alex of an urgent phone call concerning one of his patients. She found us sitting by the window sipping drinks. She asked Alex to fix her a scotch and sat in a chair facing the sofa, while Alex went to the kitchen to make the required phone call.

"I'm really whipped," she said, stretching out her feet and kicking off her shoes. She looked at me. "You do remember you're due at book club on Monday?"

"Of course," I replied. "I've decided to leave next Friday and drive home. I should be done here for the moment. I'm still not sure what you want me to say."

"Well, generally what it's like to write; I mean in your case. For each writer, I think it must be different. A little bit about your background, where the ideas for the books came from, you know, that sort of thing. Stuff a group of avid readers wants to hear."

Alex came back into the room, carrying Anne's drink and placing it on the table beside her. "It's okay. One of the partners is taking care of it. I'm not on duty, but they thought I ought to know."

The phone rang again , and I went to the kitchen. "Elise," said Arthur in his gruff voice. "Sorry to call so late, but I have an idea you'll be leaving soon, and I want to see you before you go." I could hear Anne and Alex talking in the living room, quietly. "Oh, hello, Arthur. No, it's not too late. Anne and Alex are here having a drink, and yes, I'm leaving next Friday."

"Anne and Alex?"

"Yes," I said in as breezy a manner as I could. Maybe Arthur would be diverted from any more conjecture when we met. "And I'd love to see you, but much as I'd like to offer a meal here, it's impossible. I've totally dismantled the place, and I'm living in survival mode."

"Then supper here, simple of course. Wednesday?"

I laughed. "My calendar isn't exactly full, so Wednesday it is. Thanks, Arthur. See you then."

"Arthur," I said, by way of explanation, as I went back in the living room.

Alex grimaced but said nothing. Anne said, "We were discussing tomorrow. David is going to be part of the Veteran's Day parade, the Boy Scout's float. Would you like to go with us? Parking will be a mess, and we're better off in one car."

I glanced at Alex and then away quickly. Anne smiled. I was obviously uncomfortable but realized she was actually making an effort to normalize relationships before I left. I would become another brief interlude in the continuum of their relationship. For me, it would be a way of going along with the script and publicly declaring that ours was merely a friendly threesome, the Creightons having stepped in at a difficult time in my life. It wasn't a bad idea after all, and I said, "Yes, I'd like that." Nearly everyone in Hopwood would be there. It had always been the kind of town that turned out for parades.

Predictably, attendance the next day was huge, from babies and the elderly being wheeled to others on canes or walkers with the rest of the self-propelled population milling about. As planned, I drove into town with the Creightons, and we parked by the village green, walking from there. It was a beautiful if cold morning. Joan was standing with Benji and May Bell, and we all chatted. Joan raised one eyebrow at me and then looked away with a smile. After meeting a few other people along the way, we joined the crowd in front of St. Stephen's Church. We could hear a band approaching, and float after float came along ending with fire engines. It was a long parade, and people clapped when they saw friends and relatives on floats. David Creighton was standing erect with the Boy Scouts and refused to acknowledge his parents or anyone else.

On the way back to the car, Anne stopped and spoke with a woman who looked vaguely familiar and then introduced me. "Elise, this is Jill Brown; you remember meeting her in Boston when you and Alex had dinner?"

"Yes, I do," I said, shaking her hand.

"I didn't know then who you were," said Jill to me while gazing up at Alex. "We're thrilled you'll be speaking to the book club on Monday. Such a piece of luck that you were here; I love your writing."

"Why, thank you," I answered. "I'm looking forward to it, but I'm not sure what I can add to what sounds like a group of serious readers."

"I assure you there will be a lot of questions. We're all wannabe authors, and a few of us have actually tried a few pieces, so I guess we're always curious how it actually gets done. Such perseverance! I'm sure I haven't the patience. Don't you agree, Alex?"

Alex mumbled something unintelligible and started to move on. Anne said a quick goodbye to Jill and caught up to Alex. "That was rude," she said.

Alex looked at her and said, "I don't like her. She's a bore."

"Well," said Anne, smiling at me. "I guess that puts it in a nutshell."

When we arrived home Anne said, "Would you like to join us for lunch?"

I was certainly curious about their house and tempted, but I thought I'd had enough of this charade and begged off, pleading the need to catch up on writing. "But thanks for the ride. I enjoyed the parade, and tell David I thought him very dignified and handsome."

Alex backed their car out, and they disappeared along the lane and up their drive. I let out a huge breath that I had been figuratively holding throughout the morning.

Chapter Forty-three

Book Club

Taking a break on Saturday after the parade, I had lunch with Joan and drove along the coast afterwards, stopping at a few shops along the way, buying nothing, a welcome respite.

In the evening, Alex stopped by after supper, and we walked along the beach. He was subdued.

"You're quiet tonight," I ventured as we came back over the dune and into the diffused light from the house.

"Yes."

"Something wrong?"

"Not wrong," he said, taking my hand. "Just a lot to think about." He pulled me to him. "I'm going to miss you."

"And I you," I said, looking up at him. I stepped away. "Alex, do you think we can hold onto this? There are so many things that can fracture it."

"Elise, have faith." He looked down at the sand. "It's an odd thing to say, but I've never really been in love before. I don't know how to handle the loss of control."

"What do you mean? What about when you first met Anne? And Sheila? Others? You know, we're not teenagers; there is a history."

He began making circles in the sand with his foot. "Yes, of course there was attraction, excitement, the challenge, all that. I don't know how to say this, except that it was about me, not them." He looked up. "With you I want to know what you think, what you feel, your opinion. That's new. When I'm at work or listening to the news or anything, I think, 'what would Elise say about this?'"

He looked boyish, confused and utterly sweet at that moment. We left it with a long embrace. I didn't know what to say; I was overwhelmed. In retrospect, I see that I felt a burden shift to me. This was more than a mutual rush of adrenaline and excitement. Did I feel the same certainty? I had thought so. But now, now that he was actually counting on me to reciprocate with the depth of his own commitment? It was daunting. Part of me wanted to run; part of me wanted to go the whole length into the light and shadows of an enduring relationship.

We made quiet and deeply satisfying love that evening, and then he was gone. I didn't see him all day Sunday, and Monday dawned with the book talk to face.

When I got to the golf club, I followed a cardboard sign that indicated that the meeting was in the smaller of two dining rooms. Women were scattered about, and the high bird-like sound that comes from a female gathering greeted me. Anne rose and came towards me. "Good morning, Elise," she said, taking my arm. "Let me introduce you." And one by one, I met the well-dressed, well-groomed women. Smiling faces, flawless makeup, erect bearing in all shapes and sizes. I knew no one there except Anne and her friend Jill.

One woman handed me a cup of coffee, another passed little cakes. I smiled and made polite sounds. A sturdy dark-haired woman got up and announced, "Time to call the meeting to order, ladies." And the room quieted. "This is Elise von Sturnheim; I'm sure you're familiar with her books. She's here to share her writing experience and answer any questions you might have. Elise, it's an honor to have you here."

Smiling at them, I walked to the front of the room. "And it's an honor to be asked here," I answered, glancing at Anne. "My thanks to Anne Creighton for doing so."

Slips of paper were passed around. "Now, ladies," said the chairperson, "write your questions down, and after a brief talk by Mrs. von Sturnheim, I'm sure she will be happy to answer them." She nodded at me.

"Well," I began, "Ernest Hemingway is reputed to have said that writing is easy; you simply sit at a typewriter and bleed."

There was a ripple of laughter. "That sums up the process. I don't want to make myself sound like a heroine, but it's a long and tedious climb at the end of which you have no idea whether the result is good or embarrassing. Many people think they have a book in them, and likely they do. But most of us are not willing to put in the lonely hours it takes to write word after word to tell a story or relate history, write a play or a poem, and then go over the work again and again making edits. One bad review and years of work can go down the drain. One good book followed by two bad ones, and your career is done for a while if not forever. What was it that Jonathan Swift said about criticism?

> *That was excellently observed, say I, when I read a passage in an author, where his opinion agrees with mine. When we differ, there I pronounce him to be mistaken. You never please them all, and ultimately, I believe, it is readers like you and word-of-mouth that eventually determines a book's popularity. Like any other creative endeavor, there has to be a drive that overwhelms all other considerations."*

I rambled on, outlining the various stages I had gone through between research and writing, fact checking and inspiration and then looked around the room, adding that the exercise of doing character studies, visiting locations featured in the book, and doing an outline is a worthwhile discipline. "I guess that's all I have to say in general terms about writing. Questions?"

I took the notes from the chairperson. "Ah, here's one: *Where do you get your ideas?* Well, it's a funny thing, but an idea can come out of sitting in an airport or getting your teeth cleaned. It doesn't matter. You see a whole story unfolding from a comment or seeing a scene laid out in front of you. The point is that this one idea burgeons because it resonates with your own perceptions. You may envision a quirky plotline, but ultimately it's your own thoughts, experience, and importantly your ability to observe and portray others that fleshes out the story."

And so it went. I answered twelve questions as best I could, and then it was over. Everyone clapped. I smiled my way through the ensuing luncheon and finally and gratefully escaped into the bright November day.

Chapter Forty-four

Arthur's Again

On Wednesday I went to Arthur's for supper. Once settled, he asked me what I had been doing.

"The predictable," I answered. "Monday I spoke at Anne Creighton's book club."

He shuddered. "Was it awful?"

"Not too bad. They were an appreciative lot actually."

"Where do they meet?"

"The golf club."

"As one would expect." He sat back and took a puff from his pipe. "You know, Elise, it's funny. There's a whole layer of life that goes on in this town that I never see or hear. In the old days, one knew everyone. There was a sort of mutual regard. I remember Milton O'Riley who owned the Ford dealership in town. Every Christmas Eve he sold trees, and I would pick up your father, and we'd go downtown. No one put up or decorated trees before Christmas Eve back then. No big commercial hoop-de-la. So, there we'd be, men only, and old Milt would bring out the whiskey, and we'd roll home to our families in high spirits to set the trees up and please the kiddies. Having none of my own, I usually ended up at my brother's house in Hingham as the uncle who read *The Night Before Christmas*."

"That really takes me back," I said, remembering my mother sniffing as Dad came in with the tree. "'Into the whiskey again, Jack,'" she'd say. "And he'd let our a chortle, and we'd get on with trimming the tree."

"If you wanted rowdy behavior," added Arthur, "we could provide it. Like the time the five of us loaded a spinet onto the back of Dick Black's truck and drove around town with Dick playing rag time and the rest of us singing." He chuckled. "Your mother danced a jig.

"And," he continued, "I remember the time that Mrs. Milne, who was always the first to get any new fangled thing, bought a pressure cooker, and everyone got busy drinking martinis and forgot it. A whole ham went up the spout and onto the ceiling! I was the one cleaning it up on a stepladder. She had servants, but it was Thursday, and they were all on their day off."

"The picture of you on the ladder with ham dripping down is hilarious," I offered.

"Yes, but back to the book talk. The ladies there? Do you feel any affinity with them?"

"As you might expect, I've never been one to seek out large groups of women, and I didn't really know any of them except Anne and her friend Jill. If I'm to be perfectly candid, then no, they weren't the sort of women that my friends are. I don't know; they're probably nice."

"I know. I know. I'm being a fuddy duddy yet again. And it's hard to put one's finger on the difference, but there is one. I keep asking myself what it is. Maybe it lies in the values. For one thing, they're a lot showier than we were, are. They wear their money like a badge. We did our best to hide it, if we had it at all. We grew up knowing the rules."

"They're rules you can't teach anyone and are probably going the way of the dinosaur," I offered. "What's even more complicated is that those rules are both class and geography. I noticed this with my friend Joan Sullivan; there's a lot of common ground in the way we look at people and life. That seems to be New England; nothing to do with class. It's the stuff that seeps in over years, like my mother sniffing at anyone who used *The Joy of Cooking* instead of Fanny Farmer's *Boston Cooking School* recipes, or having any other vacuum cleaner than an Electrolux. Odd but rooted there in the subconscious."

Arthur switched the conversation. "No more fussing about long lost brothers?"

"No, I really haven't had time to think about it, and somehow it has become less important. I mean no one stays married forever without upsets along the way. People aren't monogamous to the extent we'd like to believe. And I keep remembering how long Dad was away from home, away in an awful war."

"All true," he said. "It was awful, too awful to talk about. And any comfort, any scrap of normal human contact, was welcome." He paused "And has Dr. Creighton continued to visit you?"

I felt myself blushing. I turned my head and looked into the fire. "Yes, from time to time."

"I told you once to be cautious, and I'll say it again."

"You do keep on about it, Arthur. But why? It's clear you don't really know him."

"It's vague. One keeps asking who he really is. Oh, I suppose it's grossly unfair, and again, I'm being a repetitive old fool."

I smiled at him. "You really are, Arthur. These are things I have to work out, but rest assured I will."

"I said I'm sorry. Look, let's eat our dinner, and I'll try to make it up to you with the fabulous dessert I bought at the bakery."

"I'm sorry too, Arthur. I know you mean well. Things are in a muddle.

I'll be fine once I get home this week and see my family before having to come back and wind up here."

After that, we had a pleasant enough dinner, and I left right afterwards. Arthur gave me a big hug as I went out the door. "Call when you get back. Please."

"I will," I said.

Alex was waiting when I got back to Mother's house. His first words were, "I've got to go out of town again. The managing director of Wilding is making a pitch to investors in New York and wants me there. I couldn't very well refuse."

I sat down. "Of course not. You must go. Anyway, I'm leaving on Friday, and then it will be family time, and there's not really any reason to come back here until the closing, when the house sells. Then it's over. I can't keep hopping up here; no reason to." I stared at him.

"I know. Let me get you a drink."

I waited. I was exhausted, tired of the whirlwind in my mind, disturbed by the gossip around Alex and Anne and wondering how and if Alex and I would move forward. *Were we a moment in time, a flare in a dark night likely to fade with the coming dawn, the dawn of reality?*

We moved to the sofa and for a long time held each other in silence. Finally, Alex said, "This has been a wonderful time for me, Elise, the best ever."

"You sound as if the final curtain is flying across the stage, the lights coming up, and we are in the silence before the audience reacts," I added.

"No, no. That's not it. It's that things will have to change, take a new course. I'll be gone in a little over a month, and you'll be caught up in a tornado of activity working on your book, the film, and winding up your mother's estate. Unless we pack tonight and simply run off together and leave all that behind, there's no way around it, is there?"

I put my hands over my face, despair washing over me. "No, there's no way around it. I couldn't run off, especially on my family. No, I'd never do that, even for you."

He pulled my hands down and made me look at him. "Look, Elise, I love you, and I can't see a way around the course both of our lives are taking. I can't give up the dream of a lifetime. I've been gnawing away at Alzheimer's for decades. This is my chance. You have your commitments. We'd end up hating each other for what we gave up when we settled down and took a look at the wreckage."

"I know."

We didn't make love that night. I think we were both feeling fragile. We simply sat on the sofa for a while, holding each other, both too distracted to do more. Alex kissed me goodnight around midnight. He would be gone early in the morning, the start of a long separation. Sad and confused, I went to bed.

In the remaining days, I wound up immediate arrangements. I had lunch again with Joan, this time with Benji, and did a lot of writing. On the last evening, Alex called.

"First of all," Alex said, "the meeting was a huge success. The investors were mainly interested in Wilding's research, what's in the pipeline, so that's why I was trotted out as an example of the caliber of project they take on. They were impressed, and I'm led to believe that a good chunk of the cash they plan to throw our way will go into my research. Wilding is a privately owned company, so investments like this are a real bonus."

"Well, exciting," I said pausing. "Alex, I know we agreed not to mention it, but is part of what you're offering the research the doctor gave you?"

"Yes."

"And how . . ."

"Don't ask, please. I've cleared it. That's all you need to know."

So, Alex's life looked promising and full of future interest. I was pleased for him. "When will you be home?"

"Late Friday. I know you'll be gone by morning, but I'll call in the evening if I can and the next morning if I can't."

"I'll miss you," I said.

"I love you, Elise. Stay cheerful. There is much to be thankful for and much to come."

Chapter Forty-five

Baltimore

On Friday, I packed my few belongings, checked everything in the house, threw out food, and then remembered the box of letters from the attic. I hadn't looked at it so decided to take it with me to Baltimore. On Friday morning, after labeling a few cartons in the garage and making phone calls, it was later than planned when I finally got on the road.

There is no simple way to describe the interlude around Thanksgiving. Arriving home, I called Louise and Helene, my two best friends. We met for lunch downtown on Saturday at a new Italian restaurant on the harbor. After catching up on the local gossip, Helene zeroed in on me.

"Okay, among friends, Elise, what's going on? Tell."

"There's nothing," I replied, looking from one intent face to the other. I laughed; they looked comical. "Stop it, you two. I have no idea what you're driving at," but I could feel the heat rising up my face. "I've been in Hopwood, packing, sorting, writing and seeing friends from an eternity ago. Surely not anything you want to hear about at length."

Helene looked at Louise and skewed her mouth to one side, closing her eyes. Louise smiled at me and then said to Helene. "Leave it alone, babe. She'll tell us when she wants to."

"Well," said Helene, "stand warned that we're both riddled with suspicion. You've always been clear as crystal, so take your time. Now," she said brightening, "Potter is having a dinner tomorrow night. I've told him you're home, so he'll be calling you."

"Well, I'm still not sure when Karl is arriving, but probably not until Monday or Tuesday. Penny, Christopher, and Fiona are due on Wednesday. Yes, that would be fun. A little festivity before I have to figure out Thursday's meal."

"Ah," sighed Louise, "we're beached this year. My daughter and family were to come here, and then her husband found out he was on weekend call. We're thinking of going to the club for our turkey."

"Oh for goodness sake, Louise, you and Latimer come to us," I said. "We'd love it. More people, fewer leftovers. Turkey sandwiches and then turkey soup and then turkey what?" I said.

Helene added that she and Anthony would have loved to have them, but they were going to New Jersey to their son's house.

After lunch we roamed art galleries and dispersed. I had a small pile of bills so settled into deskwork while listening to music. Potter had left a message about the dinner the next evening while I was out, and I called to let him know I'd be there.

The next evening, I was first to arrive at Potter's, and he showed me the dining room table, elegantly set for ten with Herend china and Baccarat crystal. Pale pink roses and daisies were mounded in a Steuben bowl in the middle. I glanced at the place cards and found a couple of names I didn't know. "Oh, Steven and Andrew, yes, they're from the Albright Knox Museum in Buffalo," said Potter. "Steven is a curator, and his partner Andrew is a courier who accompanies artworks around the world, to and from museums. They're staying here."

"It's beautiful," I smiled, glancing around the room, "but then your house is always stylish."

An antique sideboard had a heavily embossed silver tea service on it, and large Asian scrolls lined the pale blue walls.

I heard a clatter on the staircase, and both houseguests appeared, freshly dressed and showered, their hair still wet. Potter made introductions, and we filed into the living room to get cocktails. Soon others filtered in, and the decibel level increased as conversations accelerated. A maid in a white apron passed canapés of caviar dolloped with sour cream and lemon zest and little rolls of smoked salmon and cream cheese. "Our fish course," said Potter, coming over to where I stood. "So, when is Karl due in?"

"Monday or Tuesday," I answered. "I haven't heard yet."

"Well, later this evening you and I need to have a little chat. There's a tidbit I think you should be aware of." With that he gave my shoulder a pat and sailed off to talk to Helene and Anthony. Apprehensive, I stared after him. Steven and Andrew were holding forth in the middle of the room on art forgeries, and I drifted over to them.

Presently, dinner was announced. Roast chicken, peas, and souffléd potatoes were passed, wine flowed, and after a huge rum cake was decimated, we were herded back to the living room where coffee and liqueurs awaited. Around eleven, people started to leave, and Potter waved at me and mouthed, "Don't go yet." I stayed until the last of the guests went out the door.

"Well, that went well, didn't it?" he asked, coming back to the living room.

"It was a glorious evening, Potter," said Steven. "Thank you."

"Sumptuous, magnificent," added Andrew.

They were perched on opposite ends of the sofa looking expectant, but Potter said, "If you will excuse Elise and me a moment, I need to talk to her."

They both waved him away. "Don't mind us," said Steven. We went into the adjacent library, and Potter closed the door. "Sit," he commanded. "This is delicate, but since the little wife is always the last to know, I thought I would remedy that."

"What on earth are you talking about?" I asked, flopping into a deep leather chair. "May I smoke?"

"By all means. You want a drink? You may need one."

"No, Potter, please get on with it."

"Well, Andrew," he said waving at the door, "the fellow out there, he brought me a morsel of information that rocked me to the soles of my shapely feet. By way of background, Andrew has a cousin who is a singer with the opera in Denver. They're close, talk every week."

This was making me nervous. "Yes?"

"Well this cousin is a woman, and you're beginning to get the drift here. Yes?"

"Obviously it involves Karl."

"Right. I'll get to the point. The cousin's best friend is also a singer, a mezzo with the opera, and apparently . . ." He stretched out the last word dramatically, rolling his eyes.

"Potter, if you want to tell me something, tell me. Histrionics don't become you."

"Hold on, girl, hold on. I'm doing my best. Anyway, this mezzo and Karl are pretty cozy." He held up both hands in defense, "I have no proof of course, but you know what this sort of gossip is. It seldom arises out of a void, so I thought I'd let you know. According to Andrew, the liaison, if you want to call it that, has been going on for years. It came up when I was reviewing the guest list for tonight with them, so they'd have an idea who they'd be meeting. He asked if you were any relation of Karl's, and of course . . ."

I let my breath out in a loud whoosh. "Wow," was all I could muster. Dear steady, patient Karl. Aloof, remote, mannerly Karl. Karl? It was unthinkable, but as my mind cleared, it did begin to make a certain crazy sort of sense. *How had I missed it? Easy, given our relationship.*

"Well, Potter, I'm going to have to think about this. Do you believe it?"

He shrugged. "I don't disbelieve it, if that makes any sense. I know you two pretty well, never a spat or any marital sparring, simply a long history of serene cohabitation and preoccupation with children."

He looked at me, seriousness furrowing his brow. "Elise, I wouldn't have popped this on you but for the fact that I think — and here I refer to Arthur's phone call and noticeable changes in you, a sort of energy that wasn't there before — something's going on in your life. So," he sighed, "I thought you ought to be forewarned. If you can get distance on this, if might actually work in your favor if you're looking for a break. Of course I'm seriously inferring from unsubstantiated information here." We were silent. I was lost in the vacuum that precedes understanding. Finally, he clapped his hands together. "So, that's it. Either I've wandered in where I clearly don't belong, or I've given you a gift. In either case, you're welcome to blame me for being meddlesome."

We both rose and returned to the living room, but Andrew and Stephen has disappeared. We heard dishwashing noises from the kitchen. I took my leave as well, and Potter gave me a hug by the door. "God speed, Elise. I do love you."

"And I you," I said, going down the steps and out into the night. It was cold with clearly visible stars above the tall old trees. I stood for a moment by the door of my car and looked up. "Oh, Alex," I whispered. "What have we done? What is Karl up to? What will we do?" The restless branches overhead gave no answer.

Chapter Forty-six

Karl Comes Home

I had nearly two days to let Potter's news, or perhaps rumors, take form. *What if?* If I thought of myself as betrayed, who was I to talk? It probably wouldn't make any difference in the overall picture that Karl's affair had gone on for years, while I was lapsing into my own fling; well to be candid, my latest affair. If I dared think of a future around Alex, the improbability of Anne's ever divorcing yawned. And what did I really want out of all this, anyway? That was the hardest question of all.

Karl had provided the bedrock of my life for so long that the possibility of its vanishing gave me a sense of vertigo. I realized that if truth were to emerge, we'd need the inevitable discussion. I couldn't go on conjecturing, or I would provide enough angst to sabotage our marriage anyway. If Karl was indeed in love with someone else, then the question I must ask myself was if I was ready to live alone. And, if Karl corroborated the rumor, wouldn't I have to confront my own infidelity? Would there be anything left for the two of us, or for that matter for Alex and me?

Alex called on Sunday, for the last time. We agreed to each rent a post office box and write in the absence of risky phone calls. We had both signed on to America Online, but email seemed too public, sitting as it did on a computer laid somewhere in the house.

"Hey, how are things going?" he asked.

"Fine," I said. I couldn't reveal what Potter had said; it was too enormous, so I told him about the dinner. "And you?"

"Aside from missing you to distraction, all is well. Anne's definitely not going to London. She said she might reconsider during the summer if I could really find a good school for David. Anyway, as I've told her, I'll be busy as hell trying to get going in the new job, which is true. Any chance of your coming over?"

"Yes," I said, "a good chance now that Enid's in Paris. I'd love to have a few days in London with you. I could actually do research there for a couple of chapters in the new book."

"I'd like to have a few lifetimes anywhere with you," he replied.

"Don't tempt me, you old roué."

"Now who's old, you cradle-robber?" He laughed.

"Not funny. Not at all," I said.

"It is. It's sidesplitting. I've never fallen for an older woman before. I like it."

We talked about his meeting Terry in New York and the exact date he'd be leaving for England and hung up with the sweet and loving words to which I was becoming accustomed.

It was a rough two days, moderately ameliorated by preparations for Thanksgiving — buying gifts for Penny, Christopher and Fiona, cooking pies and vegetables and getting flowers for the table. I heard from Karl that he would fly in Monday evening, and that moment in many ways came too soon.

I drove to the airport through the early evening traffic and was waiting when Karl's plane landed. He emerged at the end of the line, lugging a heavily scuffed briefcase, his raincoat slung over his shoulder, a grin on his face. He waved. I waved back, and soon I was enveloped in his hug. I fell into step beside him, and he looked down at me. "You're a sight for tired old eyes," he said.

Baggage collected, we drove out of the airport area. He was all good cheer and chatter about the opera, the bumpy plane ride and other news. As I navigated the highway traffic, I nodded, asking suitable questions. I wanted him to chatter on. I was in no mood to converse, so when he asked me about events during his absence, my replies were condensed. I soon realized this would never do, so as we neared the city, I went into longer descriptions.

"And have you had time to prepare for Penny's arrival and get food for the feast?"

"Oh, yes. The turkey needs to be picked up from the club Wednesday afternoon, but everything else is ready."

"Are you going back up there?"

"Not immediately, later for the closing whenever the house sells. Otherwise, I don't know. Nothing planned right now. And you?"

"Oh, yes," he said. "I'll have to go back out for a couple of weeks after Thanksgiving and perhaps several times again in the new year. We've done a lot, but I'm not finished by a long stretch."

That was a relief. The future weeks were unknown territory in my mind, and I didn't look forward to them. "I thought I might try to take some time to visit Enid in Paris as soon as she's settled," I ventured. "Could do research in England on the new book too."

"Good. Be a treat for you," he answered. "You've had a lot thrown at you. A break would be a nice respite."

"So you wouldn't want to come?"

"Ah, it isn't that I don't want to. You know that. It's that I can't get away right now. Maybe by spring, but you go ahead. I think you should."

My heart lifted. I could go to London after Alex got settled and then go on to Paris. A little spot of brightness loomed on the horizon, but meanwhile we would have to slog through some pretty unpleasant business, unless I was willing to pretend nothing was wrong and drift along. Could I do that, with this knot of new doubt that Potter's information had produced? I didn't know.

When we got home, I went to the kitchen to get us a late supper while Karl went upstairs to unpack. There was a thump in the front hall when he tossed down his laundry, and I heard the shower running. I went out to the hall and picked up his clothes and tossed them down to the basement. I would deal with laundry tomorrow.

We ate in the kitchen, hamburgers and a salad. I told Karl about our friends and Henry and Alice Clay's divorce. "And I've asked Louise and Latimer to join us for Thanksgiving," I added. "They were going to be alone. I hope that's okay with you."

"Fine, fine. The more the merrier. How's Latimer's knee?"

"He's probably not going to need an operation. For the moment it seems better."

"I'll give him a call." He smiled at me, his dark eyes catching the light under his long lashes. He was still a handsome man at sixty-five in a large compact way.

And so it went, as we slipped back into the familiar routine of domestic chores, dish washing, closing up the house for the night and idle chatter. Karl was in bed in his pajamas when I came out of the bathroom. Grey chest hair curled out of the open neck where a button was missing. He put his book down and turned out the light beside him. Slipping down in the bed, he said, "I'm really tired, Elise. Come here." I went over and kissed him quickly and walked to my bed. He smelled of toothpaste and was asleep before I had settled.

I tried to read *The New Yorker* for a while, skipped to the cartoons, and then sat staring at the painting on the wall opposite. It was a scene of Trafalgar Square in the rain we had bought on our first trip to England, done by a now well-known Spanish artist. Under the grey, typically English skies, a sort of yellow light shone, giving it a mysterious quality I had always loved. A rush of courage came over me, and I knew that I would not only get through this tangle but could also do it with the patience and kindness it deserved. I looked over at Karl, deeply asleep with his mouth open and a bubbling kind of snore punctuating his breathing.

I don't know you, I thought. The firewall around his feelings was impermeable. Even his hand, curled around a corner of the pillow looked unfamiliar.

Chapter Forty-seven

Hot Breakfast

In apology for my wayward thoughts the previous night, I cooked Karl's favorite breakfast: bacon, scrambled eggs on toast, and fresh orange juice. He came down in khakis and a blue shirt, looking fresh and rested. I was still in my bathrobe, surfacing from a tornado of conflicting thoughts during the night.

"Good morning," I twittered as brightly as I could.

"And to you too. Sleep well?"

"Not really, but you look rested."

"Definitely better, thank you. I needed that. Thanks for letting me sleep in this morning, and what is this? Breakfast for a king."

I had already eaten yogurt and with a cup of coffee beside me, I busied myself at the sink. Karl picked up the newspaper and sat down. I could hear him chewing and drinking behind me, the papers rustling as he turned the pages.

"So," he said, "it looks like the stock market took another dive. Well, we'll live through this one too."

"Is it bad?" I asked.

"Not good, but we have a lot in fixed income, so no worries, at least for a while. I think I've still got a job."

I poured him another cup of coffee and went to the table and sat across from him. "I had a message from Penny. They'll be here around five tomorrow."

"Good. Be nice to see them all. Her foot still better?"

"Lots better, thank goodness."

I picked up the arts section of the paper and started reading. He went back to the business section, and only the hum of the refrigerator, punctuated by an occasional car horn, broke the silence.

Finally Karl looked up. "You're quiet this morning."

"I'm not exactly the life of the party in the morning; you know that. Anyway, I've had a lot on my mind with one thing and another. Busy weeks."

"I'm sure," he said. "But you always handle things well, my girl. I never have to worry."

It's true, you don't, I thought.

He stood up. "Well, I'd best be off."

"Off?"

"Oh, didn't I mention it? I told Latimer I'd play squash this morning. Between his knee and my old body, it ought to be slow and short. I'm sorry, Elise; was there something you needed me to do?"

"Not really. Is Latimer's knee really good enough to play?"

"Must be," he said and leaned over and gave me a kiss on the top of my head and left the kitchen. Presently, I heard the front door slam and his car start up.

I felt let down and resentful. Then I became angry. None of this was going well, at least for me. I missed Alex. My feelings were raw. I wanted things to be reasonable between Karl and me, and I could see more starkly than ever how he had managed to carry off his part of our marriage cheerfully all these years. A new thought appeared. Wasn't this exactly what Alex had done with Anne? *Would life with him, were it possible, be any different after the glow of romance wore off, as it inevitably does?* I shuddered at the prospect. Since neither of these men was likely to change, I had to.

I checked the food in the refrigerator for the next evening and for Thanksgiving, making sure I had everything. I wished I didn't have to carry multiple lists in my head, that Karl would take a part of that burden, but that was an old grievance. Karl had been raised in a culture where men didn't consider household management part of their purview, and both of us were of a generation that gave that perspective residual support. The young, often with two people working full time, were better at sharing child rearing and domestic life. My writing wasn't considered work. It was what I did to fill the time, now that the children were gone.

I went upstairs to get dressed and wrap the presents for Penny's family. That accomplished, I left to check the post office and found an envelope from Alex.

> *Dearest Elise,*
>
> *Not a lot of news at this end. I have to tell you, this letter writing is a bore, especially for a doctor who's never learned to write legibly. I got so used to your being nearby and to our easy conversations (well, after a cantankerous while) that this feels like work.*
>
> *Alas. Sigh. Anyway, I had a grand time today shepherding David's class around the Isabella Stewart Gardner Museum. What a strange place that is, and how those pictures survive in that exposed atmosphere, I can't imagine! But they do, and the kids more or less responded. I went prepared with a few stories about Isabella and background on the artworks stolen five years ago. They were amazed by the fact that the*

thieves had been able to make off with so much, even cutting paintings out of their frames. After a while, though, they got restless and started tussling and asking when we could eat. We got back onto the bus and ate our boxed lunches and then walked to the Museum of Fine Arts. More culture than they could absorb, I'm afraid, but all in all a good day.

On a more serious note, I heard from the people at Wilding Pharma today and am enclosing the pictures they sent of the new digs. The place looks nice, and I can't wait to entertain a certain lady there and perhaps even seduce her. What do you think of that? Sorry for the quality of the pics, but I Xeroxed them onto regular sheets of paper. Had to keep the originals to show Anne.

Anne said the feedback this week from your talk at her book club was glowing, and they rushed out to buy your book. Don't people always say that? I'm a cynic, but I'm tired of people saying what they think one wants to hear and not coming clean with their own thoughts and opinions. After all, that's more interesting and can be done in a perfectly civil way — one of the things I love about you. You have an original take on people and situations. And, you aren't (don't seem?) particularly concerned with people's reactions. You don't go around trying to be liked. But you are likable, of course. I am muddling this aren't I?

As the time approaches for meeting Terry, I get apprehensive. As you know, we were never close, and I always felt he was a liar: complaining there were missing things from his room and then hiding them under my bed for Father to find. But, I guess I'll go and see what he's like now. Imagine his taking off for Nicaragua. Do you think he was in trouble with the law? Wouldn't surprise me.

Any chance of your getting to New York while I'm there? I arrive on December 27th and leave on the 30th (another damned party Anne has gotten us into at the club for New Year's Eve). I'm sure I won't be with Terry every minute, and I hoped you might find a reason to be there. If not, I'll go home whenever we're finished with whatever evolves.

So, this is it for now. Want to get this in the mail early. Think of us holding each other, loving each other, and laughing at silly things together. Keep those thoughts close to you heart. You are always in mine.

Alex

I couldn't help smiling and wanted to keep the letter to reread but didn't know what to do with it. I finally decided to put it in the glove compartment where I kept the registration and insurance cards — couldn't remember anyone ever having a reason to go in there. I picked up the dry cleaning and a case of our favorite wine and went home.

Around one, Karl came back. "I'm home," he boomed.

This is supposed to make the little wife's day? I mused. What I actually said was, "How was the game? Have you had lunch?"

Clearly, we had to talk. I couldn't stand this.

I made us both tuna sandwiches, and we ate in the kitchen. "We didn't finish the game," said Karl. "Latimer's knee started acting up. He really shouldn't have been playing at all. We had a beer, and I came home. Potter was there and said he enjoyed seeing you at his dinner."

"It was nice. He had two houseguests from Buffalo, and of course the food was divine as usual."

"He says he's going to Japan in the spring to do more research on the Asian art book."

"Oh, really? He didn't mention that. Interesting."

"Indeed. And now, I have work to do, a couple of hours worth, and phone calls to make." With that he ambled off to what had been a maid's room off the kitchen that we had turned into an office for him.

I cleared away his and my dishes and stacked them in the dishwasher, washed up a few things, cleaned the counters and dried my hands. I could hear Karl on the phone.

Chapter Forty-eight

A Pigeon Takes Flight

In the late afternoon, I decided to take a walk. Keeping up a warming pace, I came to a little park and sat on a bench, watching people go by who were huddled in warm coats, walking dogs, watching children play. It occurred to me that I was running along on emotional reaction and winging it. I would never do this to the characters in a novel, so why do it to myself?

A few questions came up. First of all, why was I so angry with Karl? Had I really thought that I could do whatever I wanted and expect him to be a reliable resort if all else fell apart? Hadn't he done that once already? Had I underestimated his understanding of the situation, in fact misjudged his ability to feel anything at all? I had to answer *probably*.

If he was having an affair, in fact had been having one for years, who was I to complain? Wasn't it his consistency in our marriage that gave me permission to do whatever I wanted within the reasonable bounds of decency? Everything in my nature rebelled at this tacit understanding of the priorities by which Karl lived: home, family, civility, at the center, with any deviation from that not part of what we shared. Objectively, it was rigid, but I now needed to reconsider it.

In his European past, as I knew, lurked a deeply imbedded double standard as well as a more sophisticated view of marriage's vagaries. I'd often thought about the primitive instinct of a man wanting to know from whence came the children he sheltered and fed and thus the need to keep his woman to himself, whatever else he might do with his desires. However, modern life had provided solutions in the form of contraceptives, bringing with them more moral latitude for both sexes concerning fidelity. Would he understand my having an affair now, this late in life? Would he even want to know? I thought about my mother and father and their ability to weather life's vicissitudes and stay together.

Like magical blocks, it fell into a construct that began to make sense. What good would it do for Karl and me to wallow through confessions, recriminations, and thus be forced into decisions we might regret? To part would require the possibility that one of us was ready to divorce. Any good outcome was improbable. And, Lord help me, Alex was doing exactly the same thing as Karl. Look at how Anne was dealing with it. And what about our friends? Did I have even a vague understanding of what lay beneath the surface of their lives? A few seemed happy enough, others argued all the time.

I'd seen many of the outwardly happy ones part.

The possibility of two people living together year after year with no change in their interests and attitudes flew up in the air with a whoosh at the same time one of the pigeons wandering around the park took off into the blue sky. I watched it go and felt a certain peace settle on me. Yes, it was I who needed to change, to grow up. It was a miracle that my long-ago affair with Jerry had taught me nothing except that I had been lucky to come home safely after playing where I shouldn't.

I got up and walked on, stopping to buy a pack of cigarettes. I enjoyed a smoke as I ambled along the Baltimore streets, feeling calmer and seeing more, much as Alex's silent forced march through Central Park had made me do. This had to be about what I wanted, was willing to do, and my career. Yes, I could now call it a career and stop trying to downplay it as nothing important. It was important, and I would enjoy it, enjoy Karl, enjoy my family, enjoy my friends, and yes, enjoy Alex, giving each a place in my life with space for myself. I was not exactly the be-all and end-all for any of them, was I? Why should any of them be that for me? They too had lives to live, as I had one, one where over-reliance on others for happiness was misplaced.

When I got back, Karl was watching television in the living room, absorbed in an old movie starring Cary Grant. "Hi," I shouted from the hall.

"Hello," he answered, muting the television. "Have a good walk?"

"Excellent," I said, coming into the living room and taking off my coat. "It's cold and beautiful. Are you through work?"

"Yes. Couldn't get anyone on the phone except Carlos. Most of them went home for the holiday, anyway. It'll have to wait."

"Well, I'm going to have a quick lie-down and read for a while. Then I thought it might be nice if we went out for dinner. There'll be enough cooking ahead, and I'm longing for fish. How about that new restaurant down by the harbor, Barney's or a name like that?"

He smiled at me. "And here I've thought you were fretting. Well, enough of that; I'd love to go out for dinner. Shall I make reservations?"

"Do. I'll see you in an hour or so."

I heard the television go back on as I mounted the stairs.

Around six, I came back down, having had a longer nap than anticipated. Karl was already in a blazer and green tie, sipping a glass of bourbon. I hadn't even heard him come up to change. He got up from the sofa.

"You look lovely, Elise," he said. "Can I get you a drink? Reservations are for six-forty five. They didn't have any for later."

"Well, thanks, but I'd rather fix my own."

He chuckled. "When will I learn?"

"When will you learn?"

Chapter Forty-nine

Complication

The restaurant was noisy and full, but Karl had managed a table in a secluded corner, and once settled into the banquette, the noise was bearable. The young were in full force, leaning on the bar, talking animatedly, waving wine glasses at others across the room, and wandering around. Most of the women had short pixie-styled hair, and suits were in short supply among the men — Bill Gates's trendsetting casual attire.

The waiter who filled our water glasses and asked for drink orders brought a large white menu with a raised gold crab at the top. While waiting we perused the short list and murmured over the choices. Karl settled on lemon sole and parsley carrots; I felt like more robust flavor and ordered crab cakes.

"So," said Karl when the drinks arrived. Looking around, he added, "This is nice. Good idea."

"It's got a decent reputation and appears to be a success," I ventured.

Karl paused, took a sip of his bourbon, and looked at me. "There's something I want to say, more like a confession I might add."

I shuddered. At the same time as I had come to the conclusion that I could handle the status quo with finesse, was Karl going to upset equilibrium by divulging his infidelity?

"Yes?"

"Well, this is difficult. As you know I'm not prone to wading into emotional shallows, but I'll get to the point. Fact is, I don't think I've been a very good husband to you."

I started to protest, holding my hand up in a dismissive gesture.

"No, no," he interrupted, "Let me finish."

"Okay." This threatened to be worse that I anticipated.

"I think I've been so absorbed in my work that I've neglected you over recent years. I haven't been around a lot, and when I have, I've lived in a bubble of my own thoughts without regard for you or what you might want."

Again, I started to equivocate. "Karl, I too . . ."

"Please, Elise," he said. I stopped.

"What I'm trying to say is that I'd like to be better, be there for you more. Maybe a trip. Or at least we could go out for dinner more often or plan a visit to a museum, a play, a film — the two of us. I know you've created a busy life for yourself, but having reflected on it, I think it was because you partially wanted to fill the time when I wasn't around. I realize your work has taken on a life of its own, and now you have obligations too, but couldn't we try to claw our way to more, I don't know, sharing our lives on a deeper level? We're very separate people now, and I think it wasn't always that way." He waited and then added. "Maybe it was, maybe it's the way I've always been without realizing it."

I wasn't aware I'd been holding my breath, but I let it out slowly, quietly. Knowing Karl as I did, this was a huge gesture on his part, and I didn't want to cheapen it with palliative words and clichés. But what to say? The idea of romantic travel, or 'date nights' as the young now called them, horrified me. I felt trapped. I put my head in my hands and thought for a moment. Looking up, I said, "Karl, thank you. I appreciate how you feel and more than that, your saying it."

"And?"

I smiled at him. "I don't know what to say."

"But you will?"

"I will."

The waiter came over. Karl ordered second drinks, probably more than we needed on top of what we'd had at home, but right then I didn't care. He looked at me and said, "Elise, you still want the crab cakes?"

"Yes." He ordered our dinner.

I sat back. "Okay, my turn. From my point of view, our marriage has been, I don't know the words exactly, but I think mutually independent will have to suffice. You were older than I and had a career forming. I was a kid, dazzled by your sophistication and probably in love with the idea of being married, especially to a man unlike like the rowdy college boys I'd been around for years." I paused. "I'm not saying this right, am I?"

"Go on."

"I'm leaving out what I thought of you personally, aren't I? To be honest, I think I was too young to really consider you more as a person and less as a symbol if that makes sense. I certainly admired and liked you a lot. But youth is self-centered, and our generation was deeply into roles. I would be the wife; you would be the husband; and we'd live happily ever after."

He looked at me. "I don't think I'm exempt from that perspective, the role-playing I mean."

"Well, there we are. You see, I took it for granted that your work and your position as husband were a given, even a priority. I took care of domestic details, had a few jobs with no eye to advancement, enough to tide us over in rough patches. And we had babies, part of the script, and on we went, lives filled with our own concerns and our joint love of the kids."

"And now?" he asked.

"Now? Well, now we are in that trough known as the empty nest, with the focus off our children and on our own lives. I guess the question of where we go with that is valid and not unique."

"And," he said, "we find ourselves locked into compelling careers and quite liking the results, the success. Right?"

"Right."

"So do we go on that way?" he asked. "Nothing would change, be new, except that now it has been discussed, it might at least constitute a tacit agreement that this the way we want it, and we both know it." He waited. "Elise?"

I'd never seen Karl this way, was bewildered. He was uncertain and needy. Karl, always the resolute and determined man, let distractions fall around him like scraps of torn paper while I tidied up in his wake. It was not that Karl looking at me now. Certainly I had expected none of this, confessions and recriminations maybe, but not inquiry into how our own marriage could be rescued or at least understood.

"I think," I started, "that what you are asking is not a shift back to what once was and could be again but more than that, a complete change."

"Perhaps."

"Perhaps, or yes?"

I waited. It was hard to admit but I was clinging to the status quo of amiability and habitual alliance as the foundation, or permission, to pursue my own selfish and emergent affair with Alex. If Karl wanted my company more and not less, then what? It would not be possible to maintain intimacy with both of them at once. It was unthinkable and repugnant.

Dinner arrived, and with the waiter's departure, Karl said, "Let's set this aside for the moment. It needs time." He cleared his throat. "Now, tell me how things stand in Hopwood. Oh, and I'll pick up the turkey tomorrow for you, and then the kids arrive for a few days."

And so, with relief for both of us, we lapsed into the familiar for the remainder of dinner and a dessert of blueberry pie.

That night Karl made love to me. It would have been churlish and a total repudiation of possibility to refuse him. I counted breaths, distracted, not by Alex specifically but certainly by happy nights and wind blowing off the sea, analogous to counting sheep while we went through the familiar routine, and finally it was over. Karl slept, and I turned on the light and read for a while before falling into uneasy sleep myself.

Chapter Fifty

Arrival

The next day was full of activity: fetching the turkey from the club, setting the table for that evening, and making up fresh beds for Penny, Christopher, and Fiona. Karl and I walked up the hill to a small café for lunch. It was a cloudy and cold day, with the skies threatening.

"I hope it doesn't rain or snow before they get here," I said while we waited for coffee after lunch.

He reached over and patted my hand. "Stop worrying. They'll be fine."

"We should have a nap this afternoon. It'll be nonstop once they're here."

"We should," he agreed.

We stopped by a few local shops and then meandered home. At close to six they arrived, beeping the horn to alert us. Fiona jumped out of the backseat and ran up the steps, shouting, "Gran, Pops, we're here."

Karl caught her in his arms and said, "I can see that, Fiona. And my, my how heavy you've become! I think you've been working on growing."

She looked up at him adoringly, "I have to. I'm going to have a baby."

He looked over at Penny who was heaving herself out of the front seat of their Saab. "I can see that too," he laughed and embraced her with his free arm as she came up the steps. I hugged them both and waved at Christopher as he was yanking bags out of the trunk of the car. We left the door open for him and spilled into the front hall. Fiona, released from her grandfather's arms, ran up the stairs. "Where do I sleep? Can I sleep with you Pops?"

Karl smiled at me. He came alive when the children were with us, a usually absent jolliness emanating from him. I went out to put meat loaf in the oven and potatoes on to boil. I could hear Penny and Christopher moving around upstairs in the guest room and Fiona bouncing on the small cot we had set up for her in the corner of their room. The water started running, and I supposed Fiona was getting a scrub and then climbing into her pajamas before they came down.

Karl came out to the kitchen and handed me a drink. "Purely medicinal," he said.

"Oh, thank you." I took a quick sip before attacking string beans laid out on the chopping board. "Mmm, that does taste good."

He looked around the kitchen. "Any dessert tonight?"

"Certainly not Sacher Torte, but chocolate cake anyway. You'll get your fill tomorrow too, with pumpkin and mince pies."

"I'd rather the Sacher Torte of course," he said. "But chocolate cake sounds good too. Of course Americans don't really know how to make pastries and cake. Now when I was a boy . . ."

"Karl," I cut in, laughing, "I've heard it before."

He grunted. "I really dislike pumpkin pie."

"I know that too, and if you ask me again why Americans put a revolting vegetable in a pastry, I'll scream. You like the mince, and there will be plenty of hard sauce and ice cream to go with it, so I think you'll survive."

Christopher came into the kitchen, and I went over and hugged him. "You've gotten thinner than ever," I exclaimed. "We'll have to feed you up while you're here."

"Big muscles though," he said, flexing his right arm. "I've been working out at the gym." He glanced over at my drink. "Any of that for a weary chauffeur?"

Karl said, "Follow me. I think I know where there's a drop left." And they disappeared into the dining room.

"Wait," I called. "Take the cheese and crackers with you." Christopher came back, and I handed him a plate with Brie and rice wafers.

I heard Penny come down with Fiona and then Karl's low voice intoning, "This is the way the ladies ride."

When I entered the living room, Fiona was happily bouncing on Karl's knee, and Penny was pouring herself a ginger ale. She looked up and saw me.

"It'll be nice to have a glass of wine again. I can't wait for this baby to be born; I'm huge."

"Did you find out what it's going to be?"

"Yes, I finally succumbed. It's a boy, a big one at that."

Fiona swiveled around on her grandfather's lap. "A boy. A boy! A boy! I'm going to have a boy."

"Any names?"

"We can't decide between David and Alexander," said Christopher. "We don't want easy nicknames, so either way, he'll be called David or Alexander."

"David Karl," said Penny.

"Alexander George," said Christopher.

"Danny Dee" shouted Fiona, glancing at me. "That's the name of my teddy bear." She cocked her head and thought a moment. "Or Willie Woo. That's the name of my other teddy bear. He's the black one. Danny Dee is brown." She hopped off of Karl's lap and ran upstairs. We heard a crash on the floor, and presently she reappeared dragging the two bears.

"What fell?" asked Penny.

"The suitcase. Shoes came out," she grinned and brought me the bears.

"They're lovely," I said, patting each in turn. Penny sighed.

Dinner conversation was punctuated by Fiona's chatter, and shortly afterwards she was packed off to bed. Christopher went up to hear her prayers and tuck her in. Penny said she was ready to turn in herself, hugged us both, and went up too. Karl and I looked at each other and let out a simultaneous sigh.

"I don't think I could do it over again," I said. He agreed, and we went out to clear the table and do dishes.

After dinner we ventured out for a walk but rushed home, as it started to rain large cold drops. Karl was asleep before I had even brushed my teeth. I lay back on the pillows and thought about Alex, wondering what he might be doing right that minute. His and Anne's boys would be home by now. Had their time been as family-oriented as ours or had they gone out? Had he settled into the old routine contentedly? He felt far away right then, and I hadn't had a moment to answer his letter. Where had those wonderful days and nights gone? They had receded into another part of my mind as domesticity and Karl's presence had settled around me, first like a too-tight sweater and then gradually becoming a comfortable old slipper. Peculiar, when Alex's and my ardor was all consuming a few days before.

I felt restless so got up and retrieved the box of Mother's letters. Quiet so as not to wake Karl, I climbed back into bed and took one out. The postmark was from Nova Scotia, July 10, 1936, and I couldn't imagine whom it might be from. It would have been three years before Dad and Mother married.

Dearest Elizabeth,

We finally made it here. Stormy trip, and the boat nearly capsized several times, but we're all fine, and Mr. Latham is a super captain. Tired and wet. We're staying with a family in a house right on the ocean, and it's really beautiful here. We had mackerel for dinner with corn and peas. The Joneses (that's the family) have a daughter your age, and she's going to show us around tomorrow. From what I can tell, it's a small fishing village, so I don't expect we'll be pub-crawling or seeing any shows. (That's supposed to be funny, by the way). One of the guys got seasick the last day, but I expect he'll be all right by tomorrow. Mr. Jones had homemade beer for us, and it wasn't bad. We'll be here for a week, sailing during the day and coming in at night. We can swim and relax, but I hear the water is really cold.

I'm glad your final grades from Dorchester were good. Are you still set on going to The School of the Museum of Fine Arts? I was wondering if it might not be better to go to a regular college first, but maybe not, and besides, it's probably too late to apply anyway. You've got lots of talent, so I guess you've made the right choice. As you know I love it at Princeton, but we both know I'm more of a studier than you'll ever be, and the professors are top drawer. I wonder if, now you've graduated from school, your parents will let you come to Princeton for a party weekend? That would really be fun for us both. Next year bicker starts, and we'll know who makes the cuts for clubs and who doesn't. I gather it's a real grind, the whole process. You have to sit in your room and wait for them to call on you. I'll probably get blackballed by all of them and end up a hundred percenter. Do you think that's possible? Am I that peculiar? (Don't answer, that's supposed to be funny too.)

I knew "hundred per-centers" were boys chosen by no one and later scattered discreetly among the clubs. Everyone knew who they were regardless. I kept reading.

I do have my heart set on Ivy Club, super guys. Maybe my standing with the Mermen will get me through. I still can't get over our victory at Annapolis with us winning in all but the breaststroke. Amazing.

I miss you, you funny little thing. My friends still tease me about robbing the cradle and seeing a schoolgirl. Well, you can't really call it dating, can you? Not with your parents hovering around like bullmastiffs. Next year'll be different with you grown up and out of school. We can neck whenever we want and not jump at every creaking board, because you'll be allowed to really go out! Yippee.

Sorry that there's nowhere you can write to me as we'll be moving around, but I'll keep writing you when I can. Can't wait to see you in August.

This is all for now. I love you,

Peter

This was obviously one of Mother's old boyfriends. Why had she kept the letters? What had happened to this Peter? I put the letter back into the box, set the box on the floor, and turned out the light.

Chapter Fifty-one

Thanksgiving

We greeted Thanksgiving Day witha laden table. Latimer and Louise arrived around three, and we ate at four.

Before dinner, we had a treasure hunt for Fiona in the back garden with pictorial clues hidden in flowerpots and tucked between boards in the fence. When she found her prize, a battery-powered duck driving an MG, I brought out the other the presents I had bought, a bottle of single malt scotch for Christopher and a bottle of *Ma Griffe* perfume for Penny, one she had always loved. The day flew by with the predictable result of Fiona getting cranky and whiney at the end from too much sugar and excitement. We hugged Latimer and Louise goodbye around six-thirty and did dishes while Penny and Christopher took Fiona out for a walk.

Around seven-thirty, Karl poured us a drink and we collapsed in the living room. When Penny and Christopher came in, I waved towards the kitchen.

"Leftovers in the icebox, pies on the counter. Help yourselves. I couldn't eat another thing."

We chatted for a while, and then Karl read Fiona *The Tale of the Flopsy Bunnies* by Beatrix Potter. It was an old copy of Enid's, heavily fingered and strewn with crayon marks. By the time Karl was through reading, Fiona was asleep, and Christopher carried her up to bed.

"Nice day," murmured Penny, stretching her legs out. "I like the Blyfields. She's funny; comes off as cool, but she isn't at all. In fact she has a really dry sense of humor."

"She does," I agreed. "What time do you plan to take off tomorrow?"

"We thought late morning. There may be a lot of traffic, and I want to get home by supper time."

"Then pack in the morning, and we'll take you out to brunch. You can take off after that."

"Well, thanks. That's perfect." She yawned.

After they went up to bed, Karl and I decided we were hungry after all and made turkey sandwiches and went back to the living room to read. Presently, he looked up and said, "Well, that's it for me. I'm off. Coming?"

"No, I think I'll read a while longer."

He patted me on the top of the head and went up. I could hear the floor creaking as he moved about. When all was quiet, I went to the kitchen and retrieved a small pad of paper from the drawer near the phone. I wrote, telling Alex about Thanksgiving, the children, and a few funny things Fiona had said. I finished it with a few thoughts.

I miss you, dear one, but you seem far away and our time together a hallucination, a lovely one mind you, but still ephemeral. It's hard to patch my two lives together and make sense of the whole. I guess I'm more deeply into futures and outcomes than I anticipated, and there is little for us in that respect. I looked around at my family tonight, Karl reading to Fiona, Penny and Christopher sitting across from me on the sofa, the fire burning low, and I thought how could I even consider upsetting this? It's precious and fragile. Did you do the same thing with your boys around you? One moment I want to run away with you, and the next I realize neither of us has the right to such heartless selfishness.

Tuesday night Karl and I went out to dinner, and he surprised me by talking about our marriage and how he feels he's neglected me and doesn't want to in the future. That's timing for you, isn't it? When I thought the way it's always been was the norm! I feel guilty and destructive. Now what?

I know it would help if we could talk through this, but of course that's impossible. I'd try to find a reason to come back there, but I've done what can be done right now. Of course when the house sells, I will do a final look-over, sign papers and that sort of thing, but I don't know when that will be. Perhaps, depending on when Karl goes back to Denver, I'll try to come up to New York when you said — the week you're there between Christmas and New Year's to see Terry. Shopping would be an obvious reason, although I'm not known for my preoccupation in that regard. Alas, we'll think of something. Don't you have a meeting in Washington? Joke.

For now, it's letters when I can grab a quiet time and ferry them out of the house. Really, Alex, I do hate being plunged into this kind of subterfuge. But I'm a grown woman and should have known it would come to this, so I'll stop whining.

Take good care of your sweet self.

All love, Elise

I still wasn't ready to tell Alex about what Potter had said, the rumor of Karl's affair, since it had a flimsy basis. Too, there was more than a vestige of loyalty to Karl. Nothing rational at work here, but I knew Alex might see it as an opening.

I folded the letter and tiptoed out to the hall. I would have to find an envelope in my desk tomorrow. Right now I didn't want to risk waking anyone. I found my keys on the front hall table and, opening the door, stepped out into the cold. Clouds were scudding along in front of the moon. I opened my car door and put the letter where Alex's was hidden and came quickly back into the house. After taking our plates to the kitchen and cleaning up, I locked up for the night and went upstairs. Karl was snoring, but tired as I was, I hoped I could coast through it, but it was midnight before I fell asleep.

Chapter Fifty-two

And Then What?

Penny and family left after brunch the next day, amid hugs, several trips back into the house to retrieve forgotten items and Fiona waving a Kleenex out the car window. We watched them disappear into traffic at the corner and returned to the house. Karl went straight to his office and came out fifteen minutes later. I was reading the morning paper and sipping a glass of water.

"Damn!"

"What's the matter?"

"Nothing, absolutely damned nothing, is getting done in my absence."

"It is a holiday week with the weekend is coming up. They probably need a rest."

"All well and good," he said, "but they had Monday through Wednesday to finish up with what they promised to do. Nothing done however. I'm afraid I'll have to go back out sooner than I thought." He looked down at me. "Elise, I had hoped that we . . ." He stopped.

I looked up. "What?"

"Well, I hoped we might have time together. You know. What I was talking about at dinner the other night."

He looked awkward. Poor Karl. He was wandering into unfamiliar territory. "Karl, it's okay," I said, getting up and giving him a hug. "We've lived this way for years. I'm used to it. And, I appreciate what you're saying. I do. Right now, you've got to do what's necessary for the opera, and I have lots of work ahead with the old book and now the new one. It's not so bad."

He didn't say anything.

"Well, it isn't, is it?" I prompted.

He smiled. "No, it isn't. Think of the couples our age that haven't got the interests we have, who drift along. Golf, bridge, parties." He patted my back. "Anyway, I guess I'll fly out on Monday and hope to be home a week or so before Christmas. Maybe sooner. We should be pretty well done with the preliminary work by then."

"Good." I brightened up and took my cup to the sink. "What's on for today or what's left of it?"

"I'll do work after lunch, and then I think I'll go to the club and see if I can dig up another gentle game of squash. Work off Thanksgiving dinner, you know."

"Oh, I forgot," I said. "Helene called. They're back from New Jersey and want to get together tomorrow night, dinner at their house. Okay?"

"That's fine," said Karl. "Anyone else?"

"I think her sister, Carol, is in again from Charleston. She was here for the birthday in October. I don't know if she's invited anyone else, but she said it would be simple, a steak on the grill or the like. I think we're all overfed right now."

"Steak doesn't sound like famine," Karl observed.

"No."

Karl disappeared into his office. I stripped the beds upstairs and started the wash going. After Karl left for the club, I retrieved an envelope from my desk and addressed it to Alex's box number and went to the post office. There was nothing in my post box, so I mailed the letter and went to pick up a few groceries at my favorite market in Roland Park. Potter was bent over one of the shelves, eyeing an array of preserves. He looked up. "Well, hello there. Good Thanksgiving?"

"Wonderful," I said. "The kids were here."

"Ah. I went to my brother's house. My sister was in from LA with two of her kids and one grandchild. Nothing like a family gathering to bring up the old insecurities," he laughed.

"That's right," I said. "You were the baby of the group, persecuted I'm sure."

"Oh, yes. Lots of pranks and teasing. My sister is a tyrant, spoiled and self-centered."

"Well that sounds like a harmonious holiday," I said.

He was holding a jar of marmalade. He looked at it, then at me. "Why can't they get decent marmalade here? This stuff is too sweet."

"Make your own," I answered.

"Make my own? You have to be joking."

"No, really, it's easy. And good."

"Well, forget it. By the way, are you going to Helene's tomorrow?"

"Yes," I answered, "as a matter of fact we are."

"Gather her sister is in from Charleston towing another new boyfriend, an antiques dealer I think. Where she finds these characters, I can't imagine. Remember the last one? A dentist or maybe a dermatologist, can't remember."

"He was a photographer, you ninny," I laughed. There was little more to say in the middle of a busy store, so I turned to go into the next aisle.

He touched my arm. "Elise, I do want to apologize. I think I was completely out of order passing along rumors the other night. I thought you ought to know, but afterwards I realized that in all likelihood they could be baseless. You know how people are."

"I know how people are, Potter," I said. "Don't worry about it. Karl and I are fine, and I've decided to simply ignore the whole thing. There's no reason to bring it up."

"Good girl," he said, patting my arm, and with a smile and a wave, he headed off. "See you tomorrow."

Karl and I decided to go out to a bistro within walking distance for dinner. I couldn't face cooking another morsel, and we fancied a break.

Around midnight the phone rang. It was Christopher.

"Penny is having contractions. A neighbor is here, and I'm taking her to the hospital. With the baby not due until the middle of January, this is not good."

I roused myself out of a deep sleep. "Do you want me to come up?" I asked.

"No, stay put. I'll call you from the hospital once we get her checked out." And he hung up.

Karl was awake, and I explained to him. "I should go maybe," I ventured.

"No, do what Christopher says. Wait until he calls."

Of course we couldn't sleep, so we went down to the kitchen and made a cup of tea. I grabbed a coat and went out to the cold garden to have a smoke. Karl came out and joined me, a jacket thrown over his pajamas. I glanced at him. "Will we hear the phone out here?"

"I left the door open. You shouldn't be doing that," he said, looking at my cigarette.

"Oh, Karl, stop. If you don't like it, go back in."

He paced around a while and then disappeared back into the house. The sky was dark, no stars. I could hear a few leaves stirring in the corners. Then something rustled in one of the little flowerbeds, probably an animal or small bird. It went on for a while and then stopped. I put the cigarette in a tin can I kept out there and went in. As I got into bed, the phone rang.

"Hi," said a more cheerful-sounding Christopher. "All is well. The doc said it's what they call Braxton Hicks, a false alarm, contractions that mean nothing. She's fine."

"Oh, good," I said. "Go home and get some sleep. I'm so relieved."

We got ourselves back to bed, and after tossing around, fell asleep.

Chapter Fifty-three

Change of Plans

On Monday, I drove Karl to the airport. Helene and Anthony's dinner had been seven of us. It was the usual cheerful group until Helene made a scene over Anthony's overcooking the steaks, and no amount of our glossing over their leathery texture as we sawed away stopped the glaring and pouting until Potter said, "Stop it, you two. Must we regress to the sandbox in the middle of a pleasant evening?" We left around ten.

When I returned from the airport, the phone was ringing. I dropped my keys on the hall table and rushed into the living room to get it. It was Arnell.

"Hey, sweets," she crowed. "I've just gotten off the phone with Frank Moore, and he was hoping you could make it to New York this week to go over plot changes. They've decided to option and want to go ahead. You do remember him, the one from Cloud Nine Studios?"

"Of course I remember. When was he thinking?"

"Wednesday or Thursday."

"Sure, I can take the train up on Wednesday. I'll stay at the River Club. My sister's husband is a member and can arrange it for me."

"Okay, I'll tell him." She paused. "Elise, you do know this might be a frustrating business, don't you?"

"Yes, I'm aware. As long as they keep partly to the story line, I'll try not to be a brat about it. This is exciting news actually."

"Should be. Henry, our lawyer, is winding up negotiations, and we'll have something for your approval when you get back. As you realize, we're all agreed in theory, so work can go ahead."

"What will they call it?"

"That I don't know," answered Arnell.

"Ah, yes. I'm prepared. Think I can get a starring role?"

Arnell laughed. "You'd be good, but you're going to have to start writing about women of a certain age instead of beautiful, headstrong young things if you want a role." She paused. "On second thought, perhaps I could put in a good word for you as the waitress at the hotel."

"Thanks," I said. "You've got a big heart."

Arnell rang off with the promise to call back to let me know final meeting times.

The house was dishearteningly quiet after being filled with family, and I was restless. I needed a voice, anyone to distract me, so I called Helene.

"I wanted to thank you for Saturday night. It was great."

"Except for Anthony's ruining expensive steaks," she snorted.

"Oh, get off it. It was good, and the evening was fun. I liked your sister's boyfriend."

"Oh, well," said Helene, "there'll be another one next month. He's no Robert Redford, but yes, he was interesting. One of her better ones."

"Has she left?"

"Yes, they drove off this morning, headed to New York for theater and shopping and then on to tour New England to look for antiques for his shop."

"I've got to go up to New York this week, meetings with people involved in the film."

"If I'd known that . . ."

I stopped her. "No, I don't want to do anything special while I'm there except to get this done and come home."

"Doing anything for dinner tonight? I assume Karl got on the plane this afternoon."

"No, I'm not, and yes, he did."

"Why don't you join us? It'll be the three of us, and guess what? Beef stew. Nothing else to do with the steak leftovers except sell them to the shoe repair place."

"Now, now," I laughed. "Yes, I'd love to. I'm feeling restless after all the activity around here. That'd be lovely."

I called Penny after that to see how she was faring. "I'm fine," she said. "Tempest in a teapot, but it could have been serious, so we didn't want to fool around."

"You did what you should have," I said. "What did Fiona think of the ruckus?"

"She was simply excited that the baby would get here sooner. We tried not to scare her. When I came home, she asked me if I'd left him at the hospital. I had that big old down coat on. So, when I took it off, she eyed my stomach and started sulking."

"She misses nothing," I said. "Hey, it was a delight having you here. We loved it."

"We did too. Dad looks great. He's lost a little weight, and he seemed to be in good spirits."

"He is. But he wasn't pleased with progress, so I packed him on to a plane this afternoon to go back."

"Wonderful, Mum. Aren't you pleased with what you two have

accomplished?"

"Of course, but for my part, I am forewarned that authors have a frustrating time seeing their work sliced and diced by screen writers, and it has come to that. I promised Arnell not to be a brat."

"That's great news, but I wouldn't count on your keeping your promise," said Penny.

As soon as we were done, it was near time to go to Helene and Anthony's. I wished there were an easy way to get hold of Alex and tell him I was going to be in New York and also that he could now call me at home if he wanted. He would have left the office by now, and I didn't dare try his mobile phone in case he was already home. Maybe tomorrow I'd call his office and hope to catch him. Short notice, but if he could get away, it would be a chance to see him and face up to my ambivalence.

I changed quickly into slacks and a heavy sweater and headed out to Helene and Anthony's house.

Chapter Fifty-four

On To New York

At eleven the next day, I tried Alex's office. Alex's secretary answered, with "Who's calling?" I told her it was Mrs. von Sturnheim calling about details concerning Mrs. McKenna. She informed me that Dr. Creighton was out of town and offered to relay a message when he called in. I thanked her and hung up.

I rifled through clothes and tossed them onto Karl's bed, ones that were mildly sophisticated: black trousers, a red wool jacket and a pretty Hermes scarf the kids had given me for my last birthday. A little gold jewelry and I should be okay. If by chance Alex could meet me, then I'd take clothes for the evening as well. Otherwise I'd eat dinner at the River Club and take a train home early Thursday.

Idly, I picked up the box of letters from under my side of the bed and sat down to leaf through a few more. I read about Peter's further adventures on his sailing trip, and it was obvious from the tone of the letters that he and my mother were deeply in love. As I pulled out one yellowed envelope from near the end, a newspaper clipping from the Boston Herald fell on the floor. I picked it up, carefully unfolding the fragile page. It was dated August 15, 1936.

> *During heavy seas, the "Molly Carter", a sailboat captained by Foster Latham of Quincy, Massachusetts, a professor at Harvard, and his crew of undergraduates from Harvard, Princeton and Dartmouth, capsized. It was a number of hours before a nearby ship, summoned by the desperate ship-to-shore call placed by Mr. Latham, was able to reach the "Molly Carter". Missing from the rescued sailors were Mr. Latham, Peter Janssen (Princeton 1939) and James Lipscomb (Dartmouth 1938). They have not yet been found. Families have been notified.*

Pictures of the missing sailors showed Mother's Peter Janssen to be a handsome young man with an open smiling face and thick dark hair parted in the middle. Poor Mother. I looked at the date on the last letter in the box, and it was August 9, 1936. I had to assume that Peter had drowned, and she must have been devastated. I wondered about her marriage to my father and if she'd ever found with him the kind of love that she had for Peter. I put everything back in the box, reluctant to pursue the tragedy further.

The phone rang at two, and it was Alex. "Didn't you get my last letter?" he asked.

"No, I had to take Karl to the airport yesterday and then went out to dinner. I was going to stop by the post office this afternoon."

"Ah, I figured since you called today that it's okay to call you at home. So, Karl went back to Denver?"

"Yes. Things were unraveling in his absence. The reason I called was that I have to go to New York tomorrow to meet the head of Cloud Nine Studios and thought maybe you could come down. By the way, where are you anyway?"

"In New Hampshire. I had to deliver a paper at a conference in Concord and got here early to meet with other speakers, as we're going to share the Q&A session. I'll have to stay through tomorrow and part of Thursday but could get down late Thursday afternoon if you can stay over."

"I can," I answered. "I'd actually love to have free time to poke around a few art galleries. Where would you stay? I'll be at the River Club."

"The easiest would be the Harvard Club. I guess that doesn't allow for a lot of romping around, given that either of us could run into people we know in both places."

I smiled. "You'll work it out, I'm sure. How long can you stay?"

"Until Friday late morning. Drew is coming home from Hotchkiss to have a wisdom tooth pulled on Friday afternoon at four, and I said I'd meet him in Boston and then drive him home for the weekend."

"Not much time."

"I know but won't it be lovely to have the evening and then breakfast together? I miss you horribly." He paused. "Oh, hell, why don't I make a hotel reservation instead? You can go over Thursday, and I'll meet you there. I really don't fancy running into other people you or I know. And of course there is the little matter of wanting to sleep with you."

"Yes, that would be better. Where?"

"Let's say the Elysée. It's at sixty East Fifty-Fourth. Fine place. Named after you," he chuckled. "I should get there around four or five, but I'll call your mobile phone if I can get away earlier. I'll make a reservation in my name and tell them I'm expecting you also."

"Won't that be awkward? I mean who do I say I am?" I asked.

"How about my grandmother?"

"That's just not funny."

"Don't be silly. They know me there; there won't be a problem."

That gave me pause. *How many other women had he taken there?*

"I'll take your word for it," I finally said.

I hung up and felt a lift of spirits, but the situation with Karl was still nagging at me. His change of heart where our marriage was concerned reminded me of the extraordinary antennae we humans have for ties that are slipping away, no matter how subtle the signs.

I had tried to be as normal as possible, but he must have sensed my reserve. Had he been thinking about this a long time? Well, I still had work to do packing and gathering up various papers I would need for the morning so distracted myself with preparations.

Chapter Fifty-five

Down to Business

I emerged from Penn Station to a blustery cold day. Trash from the street was being jettisoned into the air by wind. I brushed my hair from my face, hailed a cab, and we headed north to Cloud Nine Studios on Sixth Avenue. The driver was silent, which was unusual for a New York driver, but lately there were a lot of foreigners, not the familiar chatty men with Brooklyn or New Jersey accents who waved their arms, gesticulated rudely out the window and used car horns in an arcane language.

I was fifteen minutes early, so I took the time to light a cigarette and wander along the avenue, trying to relax. Returning, I found that Cloud Nine had a private elevator to the right of the main two, and during the short ride I tried to compose myself and ready my mind for the next phase of launching *Gone Crazy*. During the ensuing meeting, I realized that the challenges of making a film were huge, and although I had my strictures in writing the book, such things as genre and the unwritten law that romance novels can't have bad endings, these seemed small compared to what a studio faced. Imagination is fully active when reading a book; a film has to visually represent everything in a short amount of time, and if it gets it wrong, fans of the book howl.

At one point I was told they had decided to call it *After Hours* instead of *Gone Crazy*. Catchier."

I asked, "Why?"

Frank Moore tried to explain. "Why? Because *Gone Crazy* has negative connotations and may offend people. Also, being about a psychiatrist's life outside his practice, well, after hours so to speak, it makes sense."

"But what about people who like the book? How will they know the movie is the same story?" I asked. I thought it was a boring name that misrepresented the whole intent of the novel.

"Well, for instance, *Clueless* came out this year based on Jane Austen's *Emma. Blade Runner* was based on *Do Androids Dream of Electric Sheep*? There are others."

Had I not seen the tiny grey print at the bottom of DVDs where the original author's name is usually buried? Did I not by now realize how unimportant I was to the upcoming process? I felt deflated but also realized that what I needed to do was sit back and hope the film got made into a success and that money would follow.

Arnell had also warned me that the film could vastly influence my future books. If it was a success, then book sales would be brisk; if not, well, we knew the risk. She felt confident of Cloud Nine Studios, a newer company and one with a string of box office winners already. Frank Moore and his cousin Andy Moore, both graduates of the University of Southern California, ran it.

"And Lionel Cordovich will be directing the film."

That was a name I recognized and which impressed me. "Why, that's wonderful news," I said.

"I was saving that for last," said Frank. "Thought it might settle any fears you must be having."

We parted on amiable terms, and when I reached the street, my mind was buzzing. I was glad Alex wouldn't arrive until tomorrow; the coming afternoon and evening would be mine alone. I found a cab at Fifty-first Street and crossed town to Fifty-second and the East River where a doorman opened the cab, took my suitcase and led me into the comforting lobby of the River Club.

Coming down the stairs as I was turning to go to the elevator was Sarah Lindy, Jeffrey Black's girlfriend with whom I had reconnected at the Blacks' in October. "Oh, for heaven's sake," she laughed. "We meet again. Whatever are you doing here?"

"Details over my book being turned into a film. And you?"

"My daughter works in advertising, at McCann Erickson, and I'm visiting and seeing the sights. Jeffrey's coming in on Thursday. Will you be around then?"

"Yes," I said, "I'm going home Friday."

"Oh, well, I'm on my own tonight, an office to-do for Linda — that's my daughter — so would you like to meet up for dinner? I was planning to eat here. Jeffrey will be staying here too, so perhaps we can get together tomorrow or Friday."

"Well, I'm not sure," I said, regretting that I had not said I'd be leaving tomorrow, because of course in effect I would. "But dinner tonight would be lovely. Meet in the bar around seven?"

"Perfect," she said, tying a silk scarf over her head and with a wave, propelling herself out the revolving door onto 52nd Street.

Chapter Fifty-six

Dinner with Sarah Lindy

I had a smoked salmon sandwich and a bowl of watercress soup sent up to my room and retrieved John Grisham's *The Rainmaker* from my suitcase. Once under the comforter I settled in for a long read which didn't last. With apologies to Mr. Grisham, who can keep anyone awake, I set the book aside and fell into a deep sleep.

I awoke, groggy and disoriented. After staring at the ceiling for a while and mentally reconnecting, I glanced at the clock. In an hour I would meet Sarah Lindy for dinner and had slept the afternoon away. Heaving myself off the bed, I headed for the bathroom to splash cold water on my face.

Sarah was at a window table in the bar sipping a drink, her hand in a bowl of peanuts when I arrived. She stood, smiling.

"This is fun," she said.

"I agree," I said. The barman came over, the three of us chatted, and I ordered a scotch on the rocks. Past the window lights from a barge as it ground its way inland glinted off the East River.

"So, tell me about your writing, Elise. I remember your interest at college, always writing, poems mostly."

"Oh, yes," I laughed, "and highly sentimental ones at that. I was into my Sara Teasdale phase then and in love with a boy at Brown."

"We could never keep up with your romances," said Sarah. "One a month, but they never lasted, did they? And here you are now married for eons to the same man — so Jeffrey tells me. What's he like?"

"Karl? He's an opera set designer, loves his work, is good at it. He seemed devastatingly glamorous when I met him, older, settled career, foreign. I was swept away."

"And now?"

"Now? I suppose it's like many long marriages; the glitter wears off. A sort of peace and structure that is sustaining take its place. And you? Obviously you married, since you're here to see your daughter. Linda is it?"

"Yes, Linda. And yes I did marry. He was tall, dark, and handsome, as they say, fresh out of Yale and working for a corporation in New York. Such a catch!" And she grimaced. "It wasn't a year before a quote-unquote friend of mine felt obliged to inform me that he was having an affair with a woman at work. I didn't believe her, but then a pattern emerged, the way he behaved when running around. By the third year, I bolted. Linda was a year old then, and I went to work and raised her alone. I really thought I was through with marriage. All these years alone have been surprisingly happy, but then I met Jeffrey when he and I were both staying at the ranch with our kids."

"And are you going to take a chance again?"

"It's heading in that direction."

"Well, he's a solid sort, isn't he?"

"Yes, that, but also a lot of fun. We have a ton of the same interests and tastes, and I'm surprised at how much I enjoy sharing them. His kids are great too, and Linda thinks he's a prince."

"You're lucky," I said. "As you know, I grew up around that family, and they're wonderful, all of them. I had a crush on the youngest one."

"Oh, he's cute, and what a smart wife he has! She runs a big charity for kids in San Francisco, did you know that?"

"No."

And so it went, Sarah and I sharing snatches of our lives, rekindling what had been a fairly close relationship with each other and four other girls, all of us scattered now. I had never been drawn to reunions or made an effort to follow the lives of schoolmates, but Sarah had, and she brought me up to date. After dinner we decided to take a walk. We got our coats and strolled out the door and gazed at the East River for a while.

"Let's go for a drink," said Sarah.

So we reversed direction and wandered out to First Avenue and then north until we came to an open place. It was crowded, and music was playing in a back room. We sat at the bar up front and ordered drinks.

Taking a sip, Sarah said, "You know I think falling in love at our age is harder than when we were young."

"How so?"

"Well, we young didn't usually experience living with another person first — well, not back then. So, having to take the good with the frankly irritating, making compromises came as a surprise. It's this imaginary fluff about happily ever after without knowing what the ever after is. We didn't learn a thing from watching our parents."

"And now?"

She paused and looked around the room. A couple of well-dressed elderly men sat at one table behind us, sipping out of brandy snifters; another elderly man sat with a young girl; and at yet another table six young men and women chattered and gesticulated. Lights were low, and there were travel posters on the walls.

Sarah swiveled around and looked at me again. "And now? Like I said, it's hard. The passion is more intense; the questions are bigger ones mixed in with awareness of one's own shortcomings, including age's alarming effects." She smiled.

I wanted to say, *I know, I know*, but fortunately I kept quiet and let her assume I was drifting along in a happy marriage of long duration. "Who was it?" I started, "who said 'reality leaves a lot to the imagination'? I think John Lennon. In other words, I guess we don't know what's real and what is perception. You know the drill. You're madly in love. It ends. And years later you look at that person and say to yourself, 'What on earth was I thinking?'"

"So love is a disease, a high fever, and when it breaks, then what?" asked Sarah.

"Perhaps you have one of two things: the bitterness or revulsion on one hand or, on the other, a slow drift into friendship. When it doesn't break, then you might have companionship, a deeper kind of love and hopefully mutual respect."

Sarah laughed. "Listen to us. Amateur philosophers. Funny."

I looked at my watch and was surprised to find it was edging on to midnight. I thought about Alex's arrival the next day with rising excitement and dread.

"Time to go to bed, I think."

Sarah nodded. We paid and walked back to The River Club in silence interspersed with a few comments about this shop and that pedestrian, bid each other goodnight, and with a hug as we got off the elevator, went to our rooms.

Chapter Fifty-seven

Alex Arrives

Thursday dawned grey with a look of rain. I planned to shop in the morning for baby things to give Penny for Christmas. I ordered breakfast sent to the room and showered and dressed while waiting, unlocking the door and leaving it ajar for room service. My mobile phone rang; it was Matthew.

"Where are you?" he asked.

"New York; and life in Cincinnati? How's that?"

"Good. Getting to know a few people better, and ah, well, I've sort of got a girlfriend."

"Really?" I answered. "How do you 'sort of' have a girlfriend?"

"Well, she's from an Indian Hill family. That's the high rung of real estate around here. She went to Miss Porter's and Vassar, the shit I swore I'd never go for."

"Doesn't sound like your usual choice." Matthew had spent his teen years avoiding WASPs like mad and taking up with girls with tri-colored hair and nose rings, art students, aspiring literary types, and the like.

"No, except she's stunning, funny and bright, but that's the 'sort of' part. She's so different. Her father is from Sweden. I enjoy talking with him."

"That's a start, Matthew, a good start," I laughed. "Will you be able to come home for Christmas?"

"I don't think so. Juliana — that's her name — and I want to go skiing over the holidays. Maybe Sun Valley. Her sister lives out there, so we'd have a place to stay."

"Is there a mother?"

"No, she deserted years ago to follow a guru to Montana, and Mr. Berglund brought up the two girls, Juliana and her older sister. He has a factory here making plastic tubing; came here to marry the mother and stayed."

"He sounds like quite a man, taking on two girls. Never remarried?"

"Nope."

"You sound as if you're enjoying living there after all. Juliana's influence or a matter of settling in?"

"A little of both. It's actually a great place once you get to know your way around. A lot of the resources of a big city but more accessible. So, yes, it's good."

"That's a relief."

Matthew laughed. "Guess so. Gotta go Mom. Called during a break in a trial I'm covering. Love to Dad."

"I'll tell him. Stay well, Matthew. I love you."

"You too," and he clicked off.

I glanced out the window. The sun looked like it might make a break through the clouds. There was a new shop for baby things on the Upper West Side I wanted to visit — Z'Baby.

It was a few minutes before ten, so I ate and gave up on a shower, gathered up my coat and purse and went out to find a cab. After a few minutes of waiting, the doorman started up the block to First Avenue to hail one, but I called him back. Fifty-second Street dead ends at the East River, off-track for cabs.

"The walk will do me good. I'll get one on the way," I called. I pulled a scarf up over my head and started off.

Z'Baby was more enticing than I had imagined, and a little before noon I lumbered out the door with two large shopping bags. A cab came along, and we sped across town, arriving back at the River Club in record time. As I came in the door, the woman behind the desk said, "Mrs. von Sturnheim, you have a visitor. He's in the library."

"May I leave my packages here?" I asked, puzzled.

Unburdened, I went down the hall to the library and saw Alex and Sarah sitting by the window, chatting comfortably. I drew a breath and went over to them.

Alex smiled as he stood, and looking up, Sarah said, "Your cousin here has been entertaining me with horror stories about mountain climbing in the West. I heard him come in and ask for you. They told him at the desk you'd gone out, so I ordered us coffee, and we've been having a lovely time waiting for you to get back."

My cousin? I looked at Alex, who managed a wink in my direction. "Yes, hello, Elise," and he leaned over and gave me a familial peck on the cheek. "I was hijacked by this attractive lady when I found you were out. Good shopping?"

I cleared my throat, which had nearly closed. "Ah, yes, scads of baby clothes and such. For Penny. My d-daughter." I stammered.

"Charles here seems to have led a most adventurous youth," said Sarah.

"Ah, yes, Charles. Yes, I guess he did," I replied. "It's great to see you again."

"And you too," replied Alex. "I was telling Sarah that I came in to kidnap you and take you to New Jersey. Mother is longing to see you. It's been years, and she thinks you've been avoiding her. I'm so glad you called me when you got into town."

I collapsed into a chair and looked at them both. "You okay?" asked Sarah.

"I'm fine," I managed. "Busy morning." I opened my purse and pulled out a handkerchief and blew my nose.

"Why don't we go gather your things and get to the station?" asked Alex. "Mother's expecting us for a late lunch. She said she'd wait until two to eat."

I stood, and we said our goodbyes to Sarah.

"What a disappointment," said Sarah, "I know Jeffrey would have loved to see you, but another time. When will you be back in Boston?"

"I'm coming up for the closing on Mother's house whenever that occurs. I hope you'll be around then."

"Another time then. I loved our evening last night."

"Me too," I said as Alex and I took our leave and headed for the front hall, where I gathered my packages and went to the elevator with him.

Chapter Fifty-eight

Near Argument

As soon as I closed the door on my room, I rounded on him. "Well, that was a farce!"

Alex laughed and wrapped me in a hug, lifting me off the floor. "Ah, darling, I am glad to see you. Too long."

We kissed and held each other a long while, and I broke away. "We need to get going; I don't want to have to go through that kind of act again," I said, scooping up clothes and throwing them in my suitcase. I tried to consolidate my purchases between my suitcase and one shopping bag, barely making it work. Alex lounged in the chair by the window and watched me.

"How come you got away early?" I said over my shoulder. "Why didn't you let me know?"

"There was supposed to be a meeting this morning, but too many people were leaving early, and it was cancelled. I didn't call because I wanted to surprise you."

"You succeeded." I grimaced and then went on. "Of course it's lovely, but in our position, probably not wise. I mean I wasn't thrilled to see you with Sarah; you know how people talk, and it'd be so easy for her to mention you to Jeffrey and so on."

"And what is she going to say? That your cousin showed up?"

"I don't have a cousin. Mother and Dad were both only children."

"Oh." He paused, his brow furrowing and then asked, "Would Jeffrey know that?"

I was getting irritated and swung around, throwing my hands on my hips. "No, probably not, but his parents sure as hell would if he mentioned it."

"Oh," he said again and looked out the window. I resumed my packing, realizing that the long separation, Karl's about-face, the time with Penny's family, and the gradual digesting of gossip were inflating my critical abilities where Alex was concerned. He stood up and came over behind me, putting his arms around my waist and burying his head in my neck.

"Are you angry with me, little Elise?"

I turned and stepped away. "I am. A little. Everything is moving too fast: your departure, the film, the future." I knew I still wasn't ready to discuss what I'd heard about Karl, since there was a confused tangle of fondness and guilt mixed up in my feelings towards my husband.

"Well, let's get to the departure first," he said, moving back to the chair. "I'm now leaving on January eighth definitely. There is a slight difficulty; the research assistant they lined up for me has taken a job in France. I'll need one right away and have been thinking of taking Sheila with me." He held up his hand as I started to speak.

Sheila? I thought.

"Hold on and try to understand," he continued. "Sheila means nothing to me, and I don't know how many times I have to tell you that. But the fact is, she is the best research assistant anyone could ask for, and we work together like the cogs in a machine."

It was my turn to say, "Oh." Then I asked, "Would she want to go with you?"

"I don't know. But if it were limited to a six-month stint to get me started, then yes, I think she would. The money's good."

"Fine," I said, wanting to avoid the looming quicksand.

I snapped the suitcase shut and picked up my purse and coat. Alex rose and said, "Okay, let's get the show on the road."

He lifted my suitcase, and I took the shopping bag and we left in silence taking the elevator to the lobby where he picked up a small suitcase he had left there. I think we were both shocked at our first impasse, a flare-up that hadn't matured into an argument but was close.

I returned the room key and said my goodbyes. The bill would go to Phillip as the member, and he would let me know what I owed. Luckily the doorman was opening the door of a cab for a woman getting out as we emerged onto 52nd Street, so we hopped in. As we headed south to the Elyseé, Alex reached over and took my hand. We remained silent for the ride.

It didn't take long to check into the hotel, and since Alex wanted to see the *Stieglitz at Lake George* show at MoMA, we headed out immediately and walked east, ambling along and enjoying the bustle of New York, stopping to gaze at various buildings and the occasional shop. At the corner of 53rd and Park, while waiting for the light to change, Alex turned to me.

"That was close, Elise. Don't let's be unhappy in the short time we have. There's little to gain by letting irritations get to us. I love you. That's the fundamental thing here."

I nodded. "You're right of course. I'm being silly. You have a life, I have a life, and it's beginning to look like they won't really blend in any conceivable future, so yes, let's enjoy what we can."

He smiled, and when his face lit up like that, I was helpless to resist him and would have gone to Siberia if he wanted. As it was, I had little interest in the show at MoMA, not being drawn to photography, but I was doing it for him. He grasped my elbow as the light turned green, and we trotted across the street and made it in time. At Lexington we looked for a place to eat a quick lunch and ended up at a deli where we had corned beef sandwiches and split pea soup.

We found the exhibit in the International Council Galleries at MoMA. It comprised ninety-three black-and-white images from 1914 through 1936. To my astonishment, they captivated me with their light and shadow, ranging from Georgia O'Keeffe, her own person rather than the representation of generic woman he often did, to poplars that had been Stieglitz's friends at his summer place for years, many now crabbed and old. There were also *The Equivalents*, sky and cloud pictures with thrilling tonal quality.

"Do you know," said Alex, beside me, "he took over three hundred pictures of O'Keefe? What a love affair that must have been!"

"Mmmmmmmm," I mumbled. "Oh, Alex I'm so glad we did this. I would never have come here on my own, but these are amazing. I certainly have learning to do."

When we had exhausted our capacity for absorption, Alex suggested we head up to the Plaza for tea. After a short walk, that marvelous chateau-like building loomed in front of us, and as we walked towards it, Alex glanced at the fountain in front with the statue of Pomona. Putting his arm around me, he said, "She's got nothing on you, my dear."

"She's got nothing on, period," I laughed.

We went up the front steps and stood, looking. "Shall we do the Palm Court?" asked Alex.

"Oh, I'd love that. Who owns this place since Donald Trump sold it?"

"Fellow from New Hampshire, I think, name of Campbell."

We had tea and pastries, I my favorite napoleon and Alex a raspberry tart. With a surfeit of sweet in us, we decided to walk in the park. The side door delivered us into late afternoon sunshine, and Central Park lay in front of us with a line of Hansom cabs waiting along the opposite curb. We ducked between two of them, stopping to pat a horse on the nose, and started north.

The day had turned warm for November, and bicyclers, runners, nannies or mothers with large English prams or strollers, and dog walkers with four to six dogs on leashes surrounded us. I took a deep breath, a mixture of fresh air with a hint of exhaust along with the hissing sound of buses' air brakes, taxi horns, and the occasional siren in the distance, things you barely hear in the moment but remember later.

"I feel like we could walk forever here, drinking in the beauty, the exhilaration of New York and being together," I said.

"We could. We could go up to a Hundred and Tenth Street and then weave our way back over the whole park. That should take us at least until the end of January, given time to sleep and eat. Cold though."

"You know what I mean, silly. This is perfect, like a good novel one doesn't want to end."

"Why must you eternally jump to transitions and endings? You have to learn to live in the moment, Elise. No one knows what will happen even in the next hour, so it's an awful waste of time to diminish the present."

"I can't help myself," I answered.

"Of course you can; it's a matter of training your mind."

"Maybe it has to do with being a mother and always having to look ahead to prevent harm from coming to one's children."

"Okay, first of all I don't buy that. And second, I want you to close your mouth and open yourself to what is around you. Later, I'm going to ask you what you've seen, heard, and smelled."

I glanced up at him. "You're serious?"

"I am."

"Is this what you do when you're walking on the beach?"

"Yes. It's my way of clearing my head. I stop the voices, the *shoulds* and *whys* and *whens* and simply smell and listen and hear and taste. You'd be surprised what comes of it after a while."

"I don't know how."

"Well, first off, do as I say, Elise, and stop talking."

"Okay."

We walked along for a while, and I couldn't shut my mind down; it rattled along unfettered. Alex. Karl. Mother. Georgia O'Keeffe.

The children. They danced in fragments. Arthur talking about Alex and Anne. Joan talking about Alex and Anne. Potter talking to Arthur. Alex talking about Terry. I wanted to stamp my foot like a child and tell him this was ridiculous. Instead I plodded forward. Alex was gazing around him, up at the trees and then at the low sun's dappled patterns on the leafy ground. I merely walked.

The first thing I heard was the crunching of our feet on the leaves, and that became a cadence: step, crunch, step, crunch. I concentrated on it and began to smell earthy decay and then heard the whirr of a helicopter overhead, a child crying across the grass, a bird in the tree above us hopping from branch to branch, the low hum of traffic on Fifth Avenue, the bark of a dog, the slap, slap of a child's feet at running speed and the sight of its little body flying past. Why, a symphony of sensations was available if one paid attention! I saw Alex glance down at me and quickly look away with a tiny smile.

"Bernie, over here," came a loud cry from under a tree to our right, waking me to the insistent present. I tried again. A church bell rang, *dong, dong,*

dong, dong, dong. Five o'clock. Probably time to go back to the hotel if we were to have dinner at seven. But were we? Alex hadn't said he'd made reservations. *Hush, Elise, stop thinking.*

Quietly, Alex said, "Remember, Elise, none of it has any meaning. It is as it is."

This introduced an intellectual concept that I started to pursue and then stopped myself. Meaning? No, not now. Everything seemed to quiet down for a while, and a light breeze rose, intensifying the smells. We walked on.

Out of nowhere, a bicycle with a young African-American boy on it flew over the lawn and came towards us. I stepped back, and Alex grabbed my arm. Behind the boy was a group of four white boys on bicycles, dressed in grey sweatpants and orange jackets. They were shouting. As the lone boy reached us, the four others came crashing in and hit him broadside, hurling him to the pavement. It was seconds before I realized they had also hit Alex, who was now on the ground beside the boy. The four boys started beating on the other boy with their fists and kicking him. One foot thudded into Alex's side. I screamed.

"Stop! Stop! Help! Somebody help."

Two men came running up behind us, and another man arrived from the lawn. Everyone was shouting, and the four boys got on their bikes and hurtled off to the north. A few mobile phones were out, and soon a police car arrived. I was on the ground beside Alex trying to help him get to his feet, which he did slowly, holding his side, pale and breathing heavily. I put my arm around him and led him to the side and made him sit down on the grass. He was ashen. The young boy was unconscious and bleeding from his mouth, his head resting on a wheel of his bicycle.

Two policemen jumped out of the cruiser and hauled the boy up. Still holding Alex, I shouted, "Be careful of him. They beat him up."

One of the policemen looked over at me, "Kids, lady, nothing but trouble."

"He was attacked," I said.

The policeman walked over to me. "Your husband here, was he attacked too?"

"No," I said. "Not exactly. He was in the way. Aren't you going to go after the four boys who did this? They took off that way," I pointed north.

"Yeah, lady, another car is up ahead," and we heard a siren in the distance.

An EMT van arrived, and they loaded the boy into it, too roughly I thought. Alex was coming around and trying to get up. "Look," I said, pointing to him, "he's hurt too." A crowd had now gathered.

"No," said Alex, "I'm fine, a little bruised," he said struggling to his feet.

It was horrid watching him. I had never seen him anything but in charge, and he now looked weak and helpless. I put my arm around his waist.

"You're sure?" asked the policeman.

"Sure. I'm a doctor, and I am sure."

"Formality's sake, Doctor, let's have your ID and the lady's too."

"Is that necessary?" asked Alex.

"Yeah, it's necessary. Not that anything will come of this. They'll patch the kid up, and he and the other boys will be out on the street in no time doing the same thing. An accident of course. This is in case we need witnesses to prove this kid was actually attacked and not at fault; won't come to that unless the kid starts making claims, which he won't."

Alex groaned and pulled out his wallet. I opened my purse. The officer looked at our IDs then at our hands. "Not your husband?" he asked, looking at me.

"No," I answered, "a friend."

He copied down the information. "Numbers where I can reach you?"

Alex gave his office in Boston, and I gave my home phone. The officer looked us both over again and then nodded. "Take care. Get that looked at," he said over his shoulder to Alex as he headed back to the cruiser.

Chapter Fifty-nine

Evening

"Remember what I said about living in the moment and not anticipating what's next?" asked Alex, when he had showered and gotten into pajamas.

"Yes."

"Did you enjoy our walk?"

"Yes, until . . ."

"Exactly, until. So if you had been anticipating what might happen, good or bad, for the whole time we walked, would you have enjoyed it?"

I smiled. "Point made."

It was the first time I had seen Alex in pajamas. He looked like a little boy, pink from the hot water, dressed in blue stripes and sheepskin slippers, hair slicked down and wet. We had stopped at a liquor store and gotten a bottle of Chivas when we got back to the Elysée. I persuaded him to have dinner in our room and stay quiet. His side still hurt, and taking a deep breath was difficult, but he assured me no ribs were broken.

"Even if I have a cracked rib, there's precious little I can do about it anyway," he told me. He went over to the bureau and tipped the Chivas into a glass.

"You got ice?"

"Over there," I pointed. He took a long sip and smiled.

"I guess unless you can get me morphine, there's also little I can do about you tonight." He touched his side. "It really does hurt."

"You're sure about not having someone look at it?"

"Yes, aside from what the hell I'm doing in New York instead of New Hampshire, I want to see how it is tomorrow. I'll be back in Boston by then and can say I fell in New Hampshire and go to the emergency room at Mass General for an X-ray after Drew's appointment."

I was still doubtful but took his word for it. I poured myself a drink and picked up the room service menu. "Shall we order dinner?"

"We can make decisions, but I do want to have a few drinks and time to talk." He sank into the green love seat by the window.

I skimmed the menu and decided that filet mignon would be my choice. Rare. I don't eat a lot of beef, but after the shock of the accident I wanted robust food. "I'm set with the filet and asparagus hollandaise," I said, handing the menu to him. "And you?"

He handed it back. "Sounds perfect. A baked potato too. I'm starving. And I see they have an orange cake for dessert. Let's indulge, since exercise is clearly out of the question."

"No worries," I said. "It's lovely being here together." I sat in a chair. "Now, I didn't even ask you about the conference. Was it interesting?"

"Better than most. I gave a paper on general advances in Alzheimer's research. There were a few questions and a couple of comments. Then a woman from Seattle gave a talk on the politics of medicine. She was pretty good — stuff like the pharmaceutical industry's penetration into the government; the relative reliability of FDA approvals and other self-interest groups interfering with integrity. It isn't only the pharmaceutical companies, it's places like Monsanto too, all of them lobbying like mad. Legal of course, but insidious." He took a breath and winced. "It was later that a scientist from Switzerland came up to me," he continued, "and asked for a word in private. That was intriguing. He has been following the same line of thinking as I about Alzheimer's. We had a long conversation and are planning to meet up in January in Switzerland at another conference where we're both booked in."

"Where does he work?"

"He's doing molecular biology research at the University of Geneva."

'I'm hoping to go see Enid in Paris around that time."

"Well, good. We can meet up and see that beautiful city together. That's definitely an enticing prospect."

I got up to pour us another drink, and Alex rose too. "This damned thing is really bothering me. I think I'll crawl into bed."

I went over and folded back the spread and turned down the sheets. He lay back on the pillow with a sigh, and we talked for a while longer and then ordered dinner.

When the room bell rang, I opened it to a waiter bearing a table and our dinners warming under silver domes. A bottle of wine stood on the table, and stiff napkins made little tents at each place. I had him wheel the table over to side of Alex's bed, and he pulled a chair from in front of the desk to the other side. I tipped him as he left.

Alex swung his legs over the side of the bed, and we ate gratefully. After our orange cake, Alex slid back under the covers, holding his glass of wine, and I moved the table out to the hallway.

I sat on the end of the bed, and Alex said, "Do you know why I'm doing this, going to England? I mean really why? I want to tell you, Elise." He took a deep breath and cried out.

I jumped up. "Alex, I can go get pain medicine."

"No. Sit down and listen. For too long now I've used other people's misery for gain: esteem, money, social position. I've always loved research, and I'm good at it. Now I want to get to the bottom of a scourge that's leaving people moribund when life experience and wisdom could be their biggest contribution to the world around them, their families, their communities, the time when they influence grandchildren, have leisure to write books or paint or do whatever they have longed to do."

There was a moment of silence. I didn't know what to say. *Noble? Yes. Giving back, so to speak? Yes. The typical mid-life crisis? Maybe.* But I sensed this came from a deeper place.

"There's more," I said.

He grinned at me. "You're perceptive. Okay, I tell you at the risk of sounding like a victim. But, here it is, and I may not say it right. Somewhere back in my miserable youth I felt as if the 'me' I was got hijacked by my autocratic and insensitive stepfather, a man who clearly disliked everything I represented. And too, there was Terry, his real son. What I'm trying to get at is what I became as a result."

"And that was?"

"As you know, as I've already told you. I was sent off to boarding school, St. Dick's in New Hampshire."

"That's where my father went," I chimed in.

"Quite beside the point," he said impatiently. "Terry wasn't raised that way — stayed at home and went to the University of Colorado. Father hadn't gone the Ivy League route either, but, unlike Terry, my grades were high all the way through middle school, and my teachers urged Father to send me east to a good boarding school. With our strained relationship, he must have acquiesced in part to get me out of the house. That's what changed me. I learned how to talk, behave, and think in new ways there and at Harvard. I graduated with a class of young men who were to become *successes*, Father's favorite word. Everyone he met was described as either a success or a failure. What success meant in his case was money, but not money alone, money and power and social standing. So I learned well."

"And you *succeeded*," I said.

"Yes, all the way up to a beautiful wife from a so-called good family, a respected practice in Boston, three sons, and a house right out of a *Sunday Times* architectural supplement. Grand and glorious, any woman I wanted when I wanted her, head waiters who know me; oh, Elise, at some point it started to crumble like a stale cookie, and the rancid smell got to me. And then you came along."

"And what do I have to do with it? I'm another woman who fell for you. Literally."

He smiled. "And gorgeously."

I looked at my hands, now quiet in my lap. He went on.

"Okay, that little boy was shaped and made aware, to paraphrase Rupert Brooke's poem, and he never could convince that stepfather of his worth, get that man's respect. Without that, it was a charade. When I met you, I began to have a notion of what real is. You are real. You were born to the same conventions that were foisted on me, but they are as natural as air to you, whereas for me they were ill-fitting clothes. In a way it's like patterned fabric, the design either printed on or woven in. My printed colors began to peel away as I grew to like and then love you. I actually had to explore what it means to love, and yet with my pretenses, the history of womanizing, and the aura of nouveau riche that Hopwood laid on me, I didn't think I'd ever get it. Hopwood saw I wasn't to the manor born, or more importantly to their preposterously understated version of it, and they were right. I was sure that assessment would turn you against me too."

I watched him. He was sitting forward in bed now, his arms spread sideways, propping him up, his black hair falling across his forehead, a wistful look on his face.

I didn't know what to say so stayed silent. With his blue eyes and skin redolent of tropical sun, he looked exotic. Karl's foreignness had once affected me the same way.

"So," he continued, lying back on the pillow again, "as the facade finally lost meaning, the offer from England came along. Now, while its effect is to actually move away from you, its allure was in the effort to draw closer to you, to be authentic for the first time in my adult life. Can you understand that?"

"I'm trying." This was surely a binding confession on Alex's part. And what about Karl's comparable revelation? Was Sheila really part of the past? And the phantom woman in Karl's opera crew? Anne? She was the real victim if what he was saying was true. Anne was smarter and more feeling than she originally seemed, and I suspected that under the bravado she loved Alex. It would take a thousand acts of self-justification for me to throw my life down and take up one where Alex was paramount. I wasn't sure I had it in me to do.

"Now, before you say anything, Elise, I want you to also know that I hold you to nothing. In a way it's enough for me to love you, to use that feeling to strip away myth and get on with redeeming myself in my own eyes by being the person I now think I can be and doing the work I want to do. In a strange way, I think Anne understands that."

"I think she must," I said quietly.

He looked at me, surprised. "You like Anne, don't you?"

"Yes, Alex, I do. And I think she loves you."

"And Karl? Does he love you?"

"Yes, I think he does."

"Tell me," said Alex.

So I repeated the part I had described earlier in my letter to him — Karl's wanting more from our marriage, omitting the gossip Potter had imparted. Judging from Karl's new attitude, it was unlikely that it mattered, even if at one time it had, but what it might mean to Alex in terms of permission I wasn't ready to address.

When I had finished, Alex said, "So there we are. Obviously, we're not going to run off to a deserted island. We can create our own islands of escape when we can, in the midst of tolerable marital languor instead of in isolation watching each other's teeth decay without a dentist at hand." He smiled at me, but I couldn't return the gesture.

"Perhaps. It's not only Karl and Anne, but also six wonderful children. And truthfully, are our marriages so very bad?"

"Elise, be real. The problem is that I know I'm unhappily married; you are discovering that unremarkable little nugget of truth and facing the compromise and, yes subterfuge, necessary to endure it. The fact that Karl is good, or kind, or whatever doesn't enter into it. It merely serves to tempt you to sacrifice your feelings because you feel sorry for him. Pity is never a good foundation for friendship or love; it always backfires."

"I don't know, Alex, I don't know. I hate the deception. I'm not good at that." I got up and leaned over and kissed him. "Right now, my friend, you need to sleep."

He rolled over, threw his pillow on the floor, and within minutes he was asleep. I watched him, and he looked like the fledgling boy he had described.

Chapter Sixty

Back to Baltimore

As the train clattered south, I tried to read the *New York Times*, an op-ed piece by Richard Rhodes about family values and welfare, but my mind was jumping from one emotional island to another. Alex's ribs were no less painful in the morning, so we had a quiet breakfast in the hotel restaurant, and then he left for his flight back to Boston and I went to Penn Station. He promised he would go to the hospital and get an X-ray after meeting Drew. We'd talk in the evening.

I leaned my head back against the seat and sighed. I realized we had come to a different place in our relationship: closer, less frenzied, more loving, and certainly more aware of our ties and binding obligations.

December arrived that day and with it the prospect of Christmas; Alex's meeting with his stepbrother, Terry; and finally in January Penny's baby and Alex's departure for England, with or without Sheila. Toby, our Realtor, had called as I was leaving the hotel with the news that the house had sold that morning, an all-cash deal, so I had to be in Boston the following Wednesday for the closing. I would check on the house, but being empty, I couldn't stay there so arranged to stay at a nearby bed and breakfast for the one night this trip required. I let the Blacks know and planned to have dinner with them the night I arrived. Adelaide said she'd like to include Arthur, which suited me, as I'd have no other chance to see him before dashing back to Baltimore. I hoped to catch a glimpse of Alex, but it didn't sound likely.

I arrived home around five to a ringing phone. I dropped my suitcase in the hall and rushed to answer.

"Hi, darling," said Karl. "Thought I'd check to see that you got home safely and find out how the meeting went. Meant to call last night, but the rehearsals ended up in chaos."

"Oh, Karl. Yes. Hello. The meeting was good. Fun time in New York, as I had dinner with Sarah Lindy who happened to be staying at the River Club too."

"Who?"

"I mentioned her to you a while back. She's the girlfriend of the Black's son, old friends of Mother and Dad's. I also went to college with her. We had a good time."

"Well, that was a bonus. Short trip, what? Got home yesterday?"

I took a moment to think. Of course I had told him my plans, but he wouldn't know about the extra day since he hadn't called.

"Elise? You there?"

"Oh, sorry Karl. Switching to the other ear, so I could get out a Kleenex. Yes, but late."

"Ah. Well, I'd best get back. They're waiting to go out to dinner. Take care, my dear, I'll call again."

I resettled as quickly as I could, throwing clothes into the laundry basket but leaving my suitcase out, as I'd be off again soon.

Downstairs, I mined the freezer for dinner. It was early to bed that night, and I woke to Alex calling the next morning with the news that Terry had changed plans and would be arriving in New York next Friday instead.

"But you'll be home when I come up next week, won't you?"

"Yes. I guess it's best that Terry changed plans," he said, "as fitting him in between Christmas and New Year's along with preparing to leave for England was looking like a hassle."

"Now that you mention it, at least you'll know what he has to say, if anything, sooner."

"Right. Maybe I can get through a trip to New York this time without cracking a rib."

"That was my next question. It was cracked?"

"Yes, cracked, but as I said at the time, there's not a whole lot one can do but let it heal. I did get a pain killer, and maybe I'll use it."

"Good boy," I laughed. "How was Drew?"

"Not much better than his father at pain. I sent him back with a little bleeding from the extractions and a lot of complaints, but he'll be fine. Other than that, his grades have stayed up, which pleases me."

"Well, I can't wait to hear what Terry has to offer. It's mysterious, isn't it?"

"Yes. He might fill in a few ancient gaps in my understanding, but I don't look for any big surprises. The only question is why he would want to reconnect now. There has to be something; it certainly isn't a sentimental gesture."

"No, doesn't sound that way. You've got me curious too."

"What are your plans today?"

"None. I thought I might call Louise and see if I can cadge a dinner off her and Latimer."

"You do have some great sounding friends there. I'd love to meet them, but I expect that's not going to happen any time soon."

"Not likely," I said.

"Well, have fun. I miss you."
"Me too."
"You miss you?"
"Don't be literal. It's tedious."
"Goodnight, darling."
"Goodnight, Alex."

Chapter Sixty-one

Hopwood

The days in Baltimore passed quickly, and suddenly it was time to catch the plane to Boston, rent a car, and drive to Hopwood. I never sleep well before a trip. With gritty eyes and a pain in my neck, I rose to a grey day and threw on a robe. Breakfast was the dregs of a box of corn flakes and canned peaches accompanied at least by good coffee Karl had bought before he left. Feeling restored, I finished packing, showered, made sure the answering machine was on, and as I went out to load my car, the phone started ringing in the house, so I rushed back in. It was Alex.

"You caught me," I said breathlessly.

"I realized I don't know where you're staying."

"Angie's Bed and Breakfast. It's out towards Norwell. I'm having dinner with the Blacks and Arthur."

"And the closing?"

"At Davis's office at nine-thirty tomorrow."

"Then why don't you check out when you go to Hingham, and I'll wait for you there in the Yacht Club parking lot. We can leave your car and at least go off for a few hours and have lunch."

"Sounds perfect. I should be through by eleven."

"Bravo. See you tomorrow."

"Right."

I locked the door and drove to the airport. The flight was smooth, and I picked up the previously reserved car and drove straight to Mother's house. Everything was in order, so I gathered up the keys I would have to turn over the next day and went on to the bed and breakfast. Angie was a tall cheerful woman, and I had a room full of ruffles overlooking a tidy yard in the back. We made arrangements for my early departure, and saying she would have coffee, orange juice and fresh muffins for me, she left.

By now there were only minutes left to change for dinner at the Blacks, so I splashed water on my face, did my best with makeup and a wet comb and went back out again. There were a few snowflakes swirling around, but the sky was clear and full of stars.

Driving along the familiar farm road, I saw lights dimly through the tangle of tree limbs and bare shrubbery surrounding the house. A yellow bug light rife with spider webs cast a hazy glow at the front door. I went in without ringing and heard voices from the living room.

"That you, Elise?" called Adelaide.

"Yes, hello."

"Leave your coat on the bench and come in," shouted Dick.

I did as instructed and rounded the corner to the living room. Arthur was sunk into the chair by the fire opposite Dick, and to my shock I saw Anne on the sofa beside Adelaide. Alex was standing by the drinks in the corner, grinning as widely as the proverbial cat — easy to picture canary feathers floating out of his mouth.

I gaped. "Well, what a gathering!"

Adelaide looked up while flinging out her arm to release more yarn from the ball at her feet, not missing a beat in her knitting. "Yes, I thought since you won't be coming back often, we'd ambush you."

"Fix you a drink?" asked Alex, now as impassive as a croupier at a hot craps table.

"Ah, yes, thank you," I answered.

"So what will it be?" he asked as if he had no idea, and with his back to everyone else he cast a wicked wink in my direction.

"Oh, yes, scotch on the rocks, thank you," and I turned my attention to Dick. Walking over I placed a kiss on his cheek and turned and said hello to Arthur.

"You look well, my dear," Arthur said. "I gather you've had an eventful time. Alex here was telling me you were off to negotiate movie rights. How did it turn out?"

I sat down and described the trip to New York and the meeting about the film.

"But what I want to know is what you get out of this," said Dick.

"I'm still sketchy on that. From preliminary talks, the royalties will be good if the movie is; not if it isn't. That simple. But I have a superb agent and lawyer, and I'm sure they'll take good care of me."

"And themselves too," laughed Arthur.

"Jeffrey said you and Sarah ran into each other in New York and had dinner," said Adelaide. I cringed inwardly, but there was nothing further, not a word about my 'cousin'.

"We did. We had a nice evening reminiscing. She's delightful. Jeffrey's lucky."

"So is she," said Dick and went back to scratching the ears of the spaniel on the floor beside him.

I looked at Anne. She was wearing green silk slacks and a purple cashmere sweater. Her diamond ring caught the light as she waved at me.

"Good to see you, Elise. I wish I could say we have lots of news to catch you up on, but Hopwood has provided little of consequence since you left."

"I suppose that's a blessing. Monotony has its benefits," I said.

Alex came over, handed me my drink and sat down in the chair next to Dick, facing me. He told the Blacks and Arthur about his upcoming stint in England.

"Isn't Anne going too?" asked Adelaide.

"No, I can't really leave at such short notice, not with the boys here and David still at home," Anne answered. "I'm going over in June, and we'll decide what to do then. Alex wants David to go to school over there, thinks he'll benefit from a British education."

"Well, that's likely so," said Arthur. "I think it's a great opportunity for you all, a couple of years in England and time to travel Europe too."

"The months until June will be busy for me; it's best for them to come later," said Alex. "I'll be setting up a whole department and getting research started."

"Is this move to research a permanent thing for you, or will you want to come back and pick up your practice?" asked Dick.

"I don't know yet," answered Alex. "It's what I want to do, and when this offer fell out of the sky, well, I couldn't refuse."

"What kind of company is Wilding?" asked Arthur.

"Newish, privately held, but it's made headlines with the kind of research it's turning out. It doesn't actually make the drugs. It gets the patents and sells the licensing to manufacturers. It's also into testing and delivery systems."

"Exciting," said Arthur.

"Alex had a fall during a conference in New Hampshire and cracked a rib," said Anne, shifting the subject. Everyone looked at Alex who made a grimace.

"Good Lord," said Adelaide. "How did you manage that?"

"Stupid," he said, glancing at me then quickly away. "I was running late and tried to vault up a flight of marble steps. They were wet."

"Does it hurt?"

"Yes, surprisingly a lot."

There was a pause. "How's Karl?" asked Adelaide, turning to me.

"Fine. Swamped with the new *Flying Dutchman* production — tempers, resignations, illness, along with signs of progress. At this point it is going smoothly, and they are in rehearsal. Once they're in production, Karl's part is pretty well done, and he can relax but still be on call."

"That's nice," Anne said. "Then you and he can have time together." *Did I detect the slightest note of sarcasm in her voice?*

"I hope so," I said, glancing over at Alex. His finger was stirring ice around in his drink with comical concentration.

There was silence. Breaking it, Dick said, "Moved the pigs."

We turned to him as though he'd proclaimed the arrival of a spaceship. Arthur recovered first. "Ah, yes, good, so where did you put them?"

"Back of the barn still, down lower in a more protected space. Nice big pen. They love it."

"How can you tell they love it?" laughed Adelaide.

"They tell me," said Dick. " Different kind of oink."

The snapping of the fire and the click of Adelaide's knitting needles echoed through the room.

I looked at Arthur. He was watching Alex. Alex was picking at a hangnail on his left hand.

"Arthur," I said. "What are you writing now?"

The conversation picked up a faster pace, and soon it was time for dinner.

Chapter Sixty-two

Closing

At nine-thirty the next morning, I parked the car in Hingham in front of Davis Hopkins's office, my suitcase in the back seat. I checked in the rearview mirror to see if my teeth held any telltale signs of the blueberry muffins Angie had fed me for breakfast. There was a high wind as I made my way up the path, and it caught the door as I opened it. I entered with a crash. Davis was standing in the waiting room with the couple that had bought Mother's house along with their Realtor. He rushed over and closed the door and then made the introductions as we moved into his conference room.

Mr. and Mrs. Collins were in their early forties I guessed, both blonde and dressed in casual clothes.

"Sit," commanded Davis, and when this was accomplished, he pulled a large folder towards him. There was another bang from the door, and Toby, my Realtor, rushed in.

"Sorry I'm late," he gasped. "Got picked up for speeding, wouldn't you know? Damn annoying. I was going five miles over the limit, new cop, intense. Wanted to punch him."

"Bad luck, Toby," I said. "It's okay, I just got here too."

Davis cleared his throat. "Shall we begin?" Since no one answered, he opened the folder. "I have the papers signed by your sister, Elise, so let's get started with the rest."

It went smoothly if slowly, as Mr. Collins was determined to read every word of the documents and asked a lot of questions. Finally, their Realtor departed with her check, and I started to leave with Toby when Davis tapped my arm.

"Elise, a word if you don't mind."

I hung back, and Davis headed for his office. When we were seated, he asked, "I wanted to check with you about the little enamel painting. Any news there?"

"Why, no," I said. "I did ask Dr. Creighton, and he had no idea."

"I guess that's that," he said and then added, "I'm sure if Creighton knew anything about it, he wouldn't say. If he really doesn't know, then it's futile. Maybe your father got it to the boy."

"Maybe," I said.

"Now, now, Elise, best to let sleeping dogs lie," and he smiled his chubby, avuncular smile.

I rose to go. "Will that be all for now?"

"Yes, I'll deposit the Collins's check, and when we finalize the IRS reports and add any sales from the paintings, I'll send the remainder to you and Suzanne after our fee is deducted. As future paintings sell you'll be dealing directly with the gallery."

"Thanks, Davis. I appreciate your help." I fled out the door. Goodness that man made my flesh crawl!

Once back in the car, I made a U-turn and went to the Hingham Yacht Club. True to his word, Alex was parked in the empty lot and walking near the harbor. I got out and caught up with him, my hair flying into my eyes. "Wow," I shouted, "some wind."

He turned and grinned. "Hi there. Everything settled?" He reached for me and we hugged, the wind flapping our coats around us, our hair flying. He put his arm around me, and we leaned against the wind and walked to his car. "Did you lock your car?"

"Yes, sir."

He ruffled my hair and smiled. "Good girl. It's nearly lunch time, so why don't we find a place nearby? It's no good trying to walk in this wind."

"Sounds good. Where?"

"There's a good seafood place along towards the city, if that's what you'd fancy."

"I would. But we'll have to backtrack to get my car."

"Hardly a problem, it's only a few miles away."

The restaurant was off the road by a quarter of a mile, up a lane and in a white clapboard house. It was paneled with pine inside and a big fire was going in the main dining room. "This is perfect," I said, taking off my coat. It wasn't yet noon, so except for a group of four men in the far corner, there was no one there.

We went to a table by the back window and stared out at the leafless trees being twisted and tossed. When the menus arrived, I stared at the array, feeling ravenous. "Everything looks good," I said.

"It is. Betty and Sam Pike, a couple from Hopwood, bought the restaurant a year ago. The food is outstanding. Try the lobster roll. I promise you've never had better."

When we had placed our orders, I asked, "So how do you feel about your meeting with Terry on Friday?"

"Well actually I have news on that score. I got a call from him yesterday. My stepmother, Emily, got in touch with him, and Father had a heart attack on Monday and died yesterday, so he's going straight out for the funeral.

Wanted to know if I'd come too. I wrestled with it for a while and then thought perhaps I should."

"Why? You haven't really seen any of them in years."

"I don't know. I think it might be the right thing to do." He paused. "Anyway, I have a flight booked for tomorrow. I'll meet Terry there, and it's possible it might lay old ghosts to rest."

"I can't imagine what it will prove, but perhaps there's something to learn."

"Yes, information may surface. I'd really love to know where I came from. I've been pretty cavalier, but there's still a part of me that wants completion, a missing link. I'm not sure what that could be though. Father might have told Terry more than he told me. Not likely, but possible."

"You still care?"

"At this point, it's more curiosity. If I never know, it's not a tragedy, merely frustrating."

Our orders came, and we started eating. The lobster roll was as promised, on a soft toasted roll with large chunks of beautiful lobster inside, perfectly seasoned. I rolled my eyes. "Pure heaven," I muttered between bites.

"Told you," said Alex, as he dipped fried clams in tartar sauce.

Taking a long sip of tea, I looked at him. "Alex, this is hard. I don't know when or where we will be able to be together except in snatches. I don't even know when I will have time to work on my new book. And you will be totally absorbed with your work in England soon, so very soon."

He spread his hands on the table and gave me a long look. I stared at his beautiful hands: long, narrow, and covered with a down of dark hair. "I know, Elise. You blew into my life, a woman I wish I had met years ago, one who I wish were the mother of my children. It runs that deep. Obviously I've had relationships; one attracts women by being reasonably good-looking and, probably more significantly, being a doctor. The doctor part adds a veneer of glamour. Don't know why. But, seriously, I never thought I could love anyone in the tender and wildly passionate way I've come to love you. To give that up would amount to a crime against nature."

His headlong dive into our relationship still left my head spinning. It brought with it responsibility on my part, an obligation to define my role, and I knew there was a vestige of ambivalence that tugged at me. Finally I said, "It's clear we can't come up with solutions at the moment. We're both being bounced along in a stream of commitments, and anything we plan now will surely fall apart anyway."

My mobile phone rang. I stared at it."

"Answer it," said Alex.

I did. The voice was unfamiliar and rushed, but I began to make out the horror of what the woman was saying. I listened, made appropriate answers and finally said, "I'll be right there."

Alex looked at me questioningly. I had my hand over my mouth as I listened. Finally, I said, "Okay, who is this, and where can I reach you? Where is he?" I pulled a pen and notebook out of my purse and wrote quickly. When I had clicked off, I turned to Alex.

"Karl's had a stroke."

Chapter Sixty-three

Denver

Alex quickly paid the bill, and we hurried out of the restaurant. "Tell you what," he said, "I'll take you to the airport and arrange for your rental to be picked up. Give me the keys. I assume the papers are in the glove compartment." I nodded. "And give me your ticket to Baltimore," he added.

We stopped in the vestibule of the restaurant, and Alex called his secretary and told her to get a reservation for me on the next flight to Denver, to cancel my flight to Baltimore and see if I could get a refund based on family emergency. "I'll write a doctor's letter for you," he said aside to me.

Soon we were tearing back to the yacht club to retrieve my luggage. His phone rang, and we learned that the next flight was at three forty-three. We should make it. When we had the suitcase in Alex's car, he turned to me.

"I'm so sorry, Elise. No matter what our situation is, this has got to be hell for you."

My throat closed. Images of poor Karl lying helpless in Denver brought tears to my eyes. "It is," I squeaked, then cleared my throat. "It's awful. You can't live with someone for year after year without . . ."

Alex patted my shoulder and shoved me towards the car. "Get in. We've got to rush."

Once on the road, I said, "Not the least of it is our situation — guilt mixed up with panic and feeling horrible for Karl. The woman's name was Alicia Cassini, a friend of Karl's. Apparently there was a rehearsal last night. Karl left to get a cup of coffee, and when he came back he leaned over to talk to her, and the words that come out were completely garbled, gibberish. She called 911, and he's had a mild stroke, TIA I think she said. I'll find out more when I get there. He's still in the emergency room."

"Best place to be," said Alex.

"Good."

I looked out the window. I realized I was twisting my hands, rotating my wedding ring. I stopped. "Alex, what can I expect?"

"No telling. If she's right about it being a TIA, that means transient ischemic attack, and recovery is probable. If not, then symptoms can run the gamut from mild to paralysis of parts of the body. Think positively until you know more."

"He's a lot older than I am."

"I know."

"Sixty-five in March."

"Elise, that's not old these days. Please try to take this one step at a time."

We were quiet for a long time. As we entered the Sumner Tunnel, I realized this might be all Alex and I would have for a long, long time. The strain broke through, and I started crying.

Alex reached over and rubbed my knee. I got out a Kleenex and mopped at my eyes. We drove to the garage and got out. He retrieved my bag.

We walked across to the airport and went to pick up my ticket. "We made good time," he said. "It's barely two. Want a drink, beer, coke, whatever? It's a long flight."

"You know, I'd like that. I also want to pick up a book, a mystery, anything to keep my mind off what's ahead. And I need to call Penny, so she can let the others know."

"Let's do the call and the book first. Then we can relax until you need to go."

Penny was out, and I left a message. I disliked letting her know about her father this way, but given the fact that I would be out of touch for the trip, it was the best I could do. After I found a potentially good book, we went to a bar and settled in.

"God, I feel completely out of touch right now," I said.

"Shock does that — insulation against absorbing the full impact all at once," Alex said. I buried my face in his shoulder and took a deep breath.

"Truly, I'm a wreck, and I must look like one too."

"You do, an unholy mess. Never seen you like this. Quite puts me off."

I tried to smile but couldn't. He was trying to cheer me, but I could think only of Karl. Alex merely put his arm around me and squeezed. We talked for a while; going over how to reach each other, his upcoming trip to Denver and ways the coming days might play out. Alex looked at his watch and said, "The airport was pretty full when we came in. We need to get you going."

He left me with a hug. I started walking and then turned around. He was gone.

I remember little during the flight to Denver. I managed to get through one chapter of the book and fall asleep, which was what I needed right then. Hours later I woke to the announcement we would be landing soon. Looking at the evening sky, I realized it was two hours earlier than at home, so it was around six o'clock. I had called the woman back from Logan and given her the flight time. She said she would meet me and be wearing a red coat.

There were three women in red coats when I entered the airport. Taking a chance on the tall brunette whose coat was more like a cape, I went over to her. "Alicia Cassini?"

"Yes. And you must be Elise. Follow me. Do you have a suitcase?"

"This wheel-on. I was in Boston for one night when you reached me. How is he?"

"Still in critical care being monitored. They took an MRI, and it appears we may be in luck. He's conscious now but still talking nonsense. He doesn't understand what people are saying either, but he recognized me."

"Have you been with him right along? I asked."

"Yes." I lapsed into conjecture. Was this the woman to whom Potter had referred?

We hurried across the airport, and I followed until we emerged into a garage. She led me to an older model green Mercedes. In no time we were speeding out of the area. I looked over at her. She had soft features, was tall but not in any way heavy, probably early fiftyish, attractive.

"Thank you for staying with him," I said.

"Of course I would. I've known Karl for ages; he's been a friend and a huge boost to my career. He's a darling. We all love him."

Alicia drove fast along the highway. She talked about Karl, his work with the opera. "This is such a shock," she said, shaking her head. "He's always been so vibrant, so forceful."

"Funny," I said, "Karl is mostly quiet at home. Another side of him I guess," I added lamely.

We were silent for a while. "What sort of parts do you sing?" I ventured.

"Oh, I'm a mezzo. I don't have a part in *The Flying Dutchman*; I'm coaching the singers. I do that a lot these days." She glanced over at me with a smile. "Age is upon me."

"You don't look it," I said distractedly as I reached in my purse for my mobile phone. "Sorry," I added, "I need to call my daughter."

The phone rang through. "Penny? Oh, I'm so glad I caught you — Yes, I'm in Denver, just landed. A friend of Dad's met me, and we're on the way to the hospital — No, I don't know anything more. He's still in the emergency room. I'll call you when I know what's happening. Did you get hold of Matthew and Enid? — Oh, good. I love you too. Bye."

Alicia was pulling up in front of the hospital. "I'm going to drop you here. I'll be back in a while. I have a few things I have to do like feeding the dog. I live a short distance away, and you're welcome to stay with me."

"That's kind of you," I said as I got out of the car. I started to open the back door to retrieve my suitcase, and she said, "Leave it. I'll put it in the apartment."

Chapter Sixty-four

The Hospital

Following instructions, I found the emergency room. Reception had called ahead, and there was a nurse waiting for me. "Mrs. von Sturnheim? Follow me."

Karl's eyes were closed and his face pale. I took his hand. He stirred, and his eyes fluttered open. He stared at me and recognition slowly animated his eyes. A tiny smile spread his parched lips. He sighed and closed his eyes again. I looked at the nurse.

"We think he's going to be fine," she said. "The doctors now say it was a TIA."

"Can you explain?"

"The doctor will be along in a few minutes. We've called him. He'll do the explaining."

I set my purse and coat on a chair in the corner and pulled another chair up next to the bed and watched Karl, a million scattered thoughts racing through my head. Part of me struggled with the idea of losing him, and memories flooded back of our lives together, the children, laughter, sadness, boredom, and excitement. I was still afloat outside myself, a spectator trying to make logic of the images below me.

I closed my eyes and took deep breaths, willing myself into the present.

The door opened, and a young doctor came in. I stood.

"I'm Dr. Alston," he said, holding out his hand. I shook it, and he patted my shoulder. "Please sit." He put my coat and purse on the floor and pulled up the other chair.

"What exactly is a TIA?" I asked.

"It's a stroke, but mild, transient. With a real stroke the blockage of an artery doesn't move; with a TIA it's temporary. That's what we believe has happened to your husband in his carotid artery. It temporarily affected the part of the brain that processes language. He speaks, and he thinks he's saying words, but they come out wrong, distorted. Patients report afterwards that they thought that the people speaking to them were not speaking clearly either — in other words, they hear from us what we're hearing from them."

"Does it go away?"

"Yes, generally. Now," he took a deep breath, "this does not mean it's not serious. It is. This is a warning, and Karl should see a specialist either here or back in Baltimore. You have Johns Hopkins there, and I suggest you take him home and proceed from there. The doctor may prescribe medications and certain lifestyle and diet changes. He'll also want to do further tests. Right now we're giving him cholesterol medication and aspirin – – they'll want to continue that I'm certain."

"But, can he travel now?"

"We'll see. He's coming around, and the MRI shows that the prognosis is good. Of course we'll keep him here tonight, but by tomorrow or the next day, I think you could make plans to fly home."

Karl stirred again and looked at us. "Elise?" he said.

Dr. Alston smiled. "This is good."

"Hi, darling," I said, leaning over him. He smiled and began to speak. Nothing intelligible came out. I looked at Dr. Alston.

"Give it time," he said.

A nurse came in with a hypodermic. "What is that?" I asked.

"Insulin," she said. "We give it to all older patients. For high blood sugar."

"But he doesn't have high blood sugar."

"We give it to all of them," she persisted.

"Well don't," I shouted. The nurse came closer to Karl's bed. "I said stop," I shouted again.

Dr. Alston put his hand on the nurse's arm. "You heard her, nurse, don't give him the insulin."

The nurse glared at me. "Well, the risk is yours," she said coldly as she marched out the door.

"Right," I said, looking straight at Dr. Alston. "This is absurd."

"Hospital rules."

"I don't get it. What else do they give them routinely?"

"Diets for high blood sugar."

"Really?"

He glanced at his watch. "I'll be back in a couple of hours. Supper will be served shortly. Do you want anything?"

"No, thanks. I'll go to the cafeteria or whatever they have here later."

He left, but in a few minutes he was back in the room with two nurses.

"I see we're moving him to a room now," said Dr. Alston, glancing at his watch again. "I'll come with you."

I picked up my coat and purse and followed him to an elevator as they wheeled Karl through the halls in a different direction. Dr. Alston and I arrived at a small but cheerful room with a view of the city and sky. By the time the nurses wheeled Karl in, he was fully awake.

"Where are we?" he asked clearly. Dr. Alston and I smiled at each other. Dr. Alston explained to Karl that he was well enough to be moved to a room. "Ah, good," said Karl. No muddled speech. Once Karl was comfortably propped up in bed, the doctor and nurses left.

Karl explored the buttons around him and switched on the television that was bolted high on the wall. He glanced at me. "Well, this is an adventure." He switched off the television. "I guess I blacked out."

I explained to him what had happened and how I had gotten the news while in Hopwood signing papers for the house, mentioning Alicia's call.

"Oh, dear, what a bother for you. I'm sorry."

"Karl, what do you mean, 'bother'? This is serious; of course I would come as fast as possible. The doctor thinks everything will be fine, and we'll be able to go home in a couple of days."

"But I don't want to go home. There's still work to do."

"For now, that won't be possible. You need to see a doctor at home, get checked out. Then if everything's okay, you can come back after a couple of weeks. I'm sure Alicia can carry on."

He nodded. Finally, he said, "She's a good friend." He closed his eyes and rested a while. I pulled out my book and started to read, glancing over at him now and then to make sure he was okay. Finally my eyes drooped, and I fell asleep.

The news came on, and I woke to find Karl sitting up and watching. Supper arrived: red Jell-O, white bread, margarine, rice, gray meat, gray string beans, a salad with iceberg lettuce turning yellow at the edges, chocolate cake and a packet of synthetic sweetener. *Supper for a supposed diabetic? Really?*

I had seen a market down the road as we approached the hospital. Tomorrow, if we were still here, I'd get him decent food. I asked the young man who delivered the tray if there was a place where I could get a meal in the building. "Hamburger place on the first floor, great fries," he called over his shoulder as he left. "Lots of people go there and bring food up to the patients."

I set the tray on Karl's bed table and put my hand on his arm. He woke up. "Elise," he said. "I'm glad you came." He was speaking perfectly. My heart lifted.

"Hi there; had a bad scare."

"I remember now. It was like everyone was talking in a different language. I kept speaking to them, the opera people, and they stared at me. Someone must have called an ambulance, and here I am." He smiled ruefully. "I'm sorry to cause everyone trouble. Where is Alicia? She brought you here you said."

"She's gone home to feed her dog. I'll be staying with her."

"Nice," he said. I rolled his supper over to him. He looked at it and then up at me. "Pretty awful, isn't it?"

"It's apparently what they give old people, high blood sugar."

"But I don't have high blood sugar."

"I know. I stopped the damned nurse from giving you insulin."

"That's crazy. Why would they do that?"

"Hard to say," I said. "Now eat what you can. I'll get you better food tomorrow."

He poked around the food on his plate with a plastic fork and ate a little of meat and beans, took a bite of the rice and pushed the tray away. "State prisoners get better than this."

I laughed. "I asked about food for me in the hospital. Apparently they have a hamburger restaurant downstairs. Not exactly a step up, is it?"

He was approaching normal now, if pale. Alicia arrived. "So, how's it going? The nurse in the hall said he's speaking fine."

"Yes, I am," Karl chimed in. "You can talk to me now."

"Wonderful. When can we spring you?"

"Not until tomorrow at least," I said. "The doctor suggested I fly him home and get him to a specialist there."

"Good idea," said Alicia. "You've got the best in Baltimore, what with Johns Hopkins and all."

"But what about the opera?" asked Karl. "I still have work to do."

"Not really," said Alicia. "All the big work is done, and your assistants and I can keep in touch by phone. We don't open for weeks, and you can probably come back before that. Until then, you need to rest and lie low, get over this horror. Sets are a marvel, and the remaining work is mainly in voices and blocking, stuff for the director. Dicky may have a great voice, but he still bumbles around on the stage like a hyena on the prowl. Costumes too. Still waiting on the last of the fabric order."

Karl looked at me. "Alicia has been coaching the singers, like she did at the Met, but she's also the unofficial assistant to the director. At least he acts as if she is." He smiled at Alicia.

"Ummmm," was all she offered.

Around nine, Alicia and I each gave Karl a kiss on the cheek and left the hospital. It was dark, and lights twinkled along the streets as she drove us to her apartment.

"You live out here?" I asked.

"I'm from Denver. My parents are still here, so I keep this little place. Not fancy, but it allows me to be with them and see friends. This time, with the opera being staged here, I stay. You'll be sleeping on the rollout sofa. I hope you don't mind."

"Of course not. You're nice to have me at all."

"Glad to help," she said, as she pulled into a parking space in front of a brick two-story building with a door on either side.

Chapter Sixty-five

Alicia

"I'm on the ground floor, so I have a little garden in back." Alicia was flipping light switches, and I looked around. Red. Red everywhere, like her coat. Even the coffeemaker was red; so was the toaster. Amazing.

She laughed. "I love red."

"Well, that's evident," I said. The only relief was the white slipcovers on the chairs in the living room and the brown of the wooden furniture. The curtains were red with white stripes. My suitcase was on the floor by the sofa. It was blue and looked every bit the interloper it was.

A Yorkshire terrier bounded out of the kitchen and over to me. I gave it a pat, and it backed off barking.

"She's excited, not unfriendly. Give her time. Meanwhile, let's have a drink," she said. "Wine, scotch, gin, whatever you wish."

"I'd love a scotch on the rocks," I said. "Also, I don't want to be a burden, but do you have crackers or nuts? I'm starving."

"I was coming to that. I'll get out nuts, and I've got a frozen pizza and greens for a salad. Is that okay with you? Otherwise we can go around the corner to the little restaurant and get supper."

"No, no," I answered. "The pizza's fine. I do want to take my shoes off and relax."

I sat on the sofa and leaned my head against the back. The dog bounced up beside me. "What's her name?" I asked.

Alicia grimaced. "Aida," she said. "Corny, isn't it?" She went into the kitchen, and Aida settled down by my side. My eyes closed, and the next thing I heard was the tinkle of ice as Alicia set a glass down in front of me.

"Oh, sorry," I said sitting up.

"You must be exhausted. I turned the oven on. We can eat whenever you want." She sat in an armchair across the room. "What were you doing in Boston before you came out here?"

"I went up for the closing on my mother's house."

"Yes, Karl told me you've been pretty busy between finishing up the estate and negotiating over your book. By the way, congratulations on the movie option."

"Yes," I said, "I feel good about that."

"And will you earn a lot on this, if I'm not being too nosy?"

"Hard to say. Mind you, I have a tough and wonderful agent, but deals are deals, and even though I've published before, I'm still considered a second-tier author."

"My brother in Wisconsin writes novels too; same complaints."

"What's his name?"

"Bill Casey." She smiled. "Casey, Cassini. You know opera and the penchant for Italian names."

"I think I've heard of him. Mysteries, right?"

"Right. Unlikely settings like grain mills, industrial feed lots, cattle auctions."

"Well, it's a change from Chicago, LA, or the proverbial sleepy village in the UK."

"Actually, he's got a sizeable following. The plots are good, and he's a master at character development, dreams up eccentric people. You two ought to get together. You'd probably be up all night comparing notes."

A ding went off in the kitchen, and Alicia went to put the pizza in the oven. My phone rang. I looked at the screen. It was Alex.

"Hello. If you'll hold a moment, I'll move from where I am." I went into the kitchen and said to Alicia, so Alex could hear it, "It's my son. I think I'll go out on the porch and have a smoke and talk to him if you don't mind."

"Not at all. There's an ashtray on the little table out there and a chair too."

When I reached the porch, I said to Alex, "Hi, darling. I'm staying with one of the members of the opera company."

"I won't keep you. I'm going to head home. Big medical dinner tonight, tedious, awards, speeches. I wanted to see how Karl is."

"He's doing pretty well, as a matter of fact. The doctors say it was a TIA. You understand all that. It was scary when I got there. His speech was all messed up but resolved itself after a few hours. They're keeping him at least for tonight, maybe more, and then I'll fly home with him and get him to our doctor there."

"Good plan. So, how are you?"

"Wiped out. Confused. Not particularly lucid at the moment. I'm staying with Alicia Cassini, who works with Karl. She's been wonderful; she's the one who took him to the hospital." I paused. "Oh, Alex, I forgot. You come to Denver tomorrow to meet Terry and go to the funeral, don't you?"

"I do. Makes me feel creepy."

I looked up, and Alicia was standing at the open door. She waved. "Just checking. The pizza is about ready, but I'll put it on the warmer. Don't hurry.

Another drink?"

I nodded and handed her my glass and went back to the chair. "Sorry, my nice hostess offering another drink. So, Terry. We'll see."

"I suppose. By the way, we got the car returned to the rental people, and the airlines is refunding the ticket as soon as they get my letter."

"Thanks, Alex. That was really nice of you."

"I am nice." He paused. "Nice to women I sleep with, that is."

"That must cover a full complement of grateful ladies," I answered

"That wasn't nice," he replied.

"Oh, and Alex, I'd better try to call you tomorrow, not the other way around. I'll be pretty tied down. If I don't call, you'll understand. Where will you be staying?"

"I'm renting a car and I've booked into a hotel; call on my mobile phone. Last thing I want to do is stay in that house."

"I don't blame you. Funny thinking of both of being us out here and unable to see each other."

"It is," he said.

"I love you," I said automatically, surprising myself.

"I love you too. Take care, try to rest." He clicked off.

I went into the apartment. Alicia was laying plates on the coffee table in front of the sofa.

"Mind if we catch up on the news?"

"Not at all," I answered. I didn't feel like conversation, and I expected she didn't either. The pizza was good, and the salad had a good vinaigrette dressing.

We watched the news for a while, and then she clicked off the television and together we pulled out the sofa bed. It was already made up, and it was no surprise that it had a red blanket. I helped Alicia with the dishes.

"I thought your son was named Matthew," she said, handing me a towel.

"He is."

"Oh. I thought I heard you say 'Alex' when I came out on the porch."

I turned and looked the other way but recovered quickly. "That? It's a joke we have."

"Oh."

Presently she went around turning out lights and locking the door. "Goodnight, Elise. Get a good sleep. Tomorrow is likely to be busy. Oh, and if you need anything, knock on my door. I put a fresh towel and washcloth in the bathroom."

"I don't know how to thank you for your kindness," I said.

She grinned. "Then don't." She waved and walked down the hall with Aida trotting behind her.

I knew I was tired, but I was too wound up to sleep. An album was lying on the pushed-aside coffee table. Idly I leafed through it, recognizing it was Alicia's career, and the people were performers, taking bows and posing in scenes from various operas. A few programs were stuffed in the back. I saw one photograph with Karl in it. He had his arm around a younger Alicia, and they were looking at each other and smiling. I went slower and found a number more. In each group photo, Karl and Alicia were side by side, either holding hands and gazing at the camera or facing each other.

"Oh, bother." I whispered. "I certainly don't want to think about this now." I went to the bathroom and brushed my teeth, retrieved my book, changed into pajamas, and crawled into bed. In minutes I was asleep.

Chapter Sixty-six

Home with Karl

It's tedious putting on the same clothes day after day, but I did it for two more days. Karl lapsed back into garble for a few moments on Thursday, and the doctor insisted he remain in the hospital for observation.

On Saturday, both Alicia and I overslept, and around nine o'clock we ate a hurried breakfast of orange juice, coffee, and a slice of coffee cake. I packed my bag and was starting to pull sheets off the bed when Alicia came in and said, "Don't strip the bed. We don't know what we'll find at the hospital, and you may be here another night."

I groaned inwardly. All I wanted at that point was to collect Karl, get on a plane and head home. I knew there would be more to it than that, however. *At any rate, I'll put my suitcase in the car,* I thought. His belongings would have to be collected as well if we were indeed going home.

While Alicia drove, I called Penny to update her. I could hear Fiona chattering in the background.

"Who is she talking to?" I asked.

Penny laughed. "Christopher bought her one of those dolls where you pull a string and it talks. She carries on endless conversations with the thing."

I smiled. "Cute. Look, I'll let you know what we're doing later. I'm hoping we will be flying home. Let Enid and Matthew know, will you?"

"Will do." I hung up.

Alicia looked over at me and said, "I noticed my photograph album lying open, and I'm glad you had a peek. I'm sure Karl doesn't keep that stuff, and it must be fun for you to see what he's up to while doing his magic."

"It is," I replied. "Looked like you and he have worked together a long time, been friends."

She smiled. "We go way back. As I mentioned before, he's been a real help with my career from when I was a virtual nobody.

"Nice," I said. There was silence.

Knowing it was unwise, I pressed on. "Alicia, did you and he ever . . .?"

She turned her head and looked at me questioningly. "Elise? Surely you don't mean . . ."

We were not finishing sentences; tension hung between us. I didn't answer.

She said, "Look, I suppose looking at those cozy pictures maybe got you thinking. Is that it?"

"Yes, sort of."

"Let me set you straight then. I adore Karl, as do the rest of us. He's been like a brother or uncle to me, but never more. Please, I'm sorry if you got the wrong idea."

I smiled at her. "No, it's my fault for even asking. It's — well, a weird time right now — I'm being irrational."

She reached out and patted my hand. "Forgotten, okay?"

"Forgotten."

When we got to Karl's room, he was sitting up talking and laughing.

"Good morning," I said.

"Hello," answered Karl. "This is Nurse Jenny. Jenny's an angel."

"We love meeting angels," laughed Alicia. "Hello, Jenny."

Jenny waved at Karl and left the room.

"I suppose I ought to say how are 'we' today," I ventured. Karl laughed.

"We are fine. They say they'll release me this morning. So I guess you can make reservations to go home."

"Oh, that's wonderful," Alicia and I said in unison, then looked at each other and smiled.

"Tell you what," said Alicia to me. "I'll pop around to Karl's hotel and get his things. You have yours. I'll be back here in an hour. Meanwhile you can make reservations, and I'll drive you both to the airport. I think there's an afternoon flight if you can get on it. Karl's taken it before."

"Thanks," said Karl. Alicia glanced at us both and left. I noticed she didn't ask for a key.

"Are you really feeling better?" I asked, nearing the bed and putting my hand on his arm.

"I am. It's as if nothing happened. Sorry, old dear, it must have scared the hell out of you."

"It did."

"Well, I expect we'd better call the airlines and see what we can get. I can't wait to get out of here."

I got to work on my mobile phone. After a good deal of back and forth, we finally had two seats, not together, on a flight to Dulles International. My car was parked there from the flight up to Boston. With that settled, I sat down in a chair by the window.

"Alicia was extraordinarily nice to take me in," I said.

"Oh, her heart's as big as Texas. Did you go out to dinner?"

"We had drinks and a pizza at home on Wednesday. She gets them from a place that produces them uncooked, and you cook it at home. Then we ate at a nearby place Thursday and last night." Karl grunted. I continued, "I paid. It's the least I could do to say thanks."

Karl smiled. "I've had those pizzas," he said. "Lots of them. Pizza is a staple when you've got a crowd rehearsing. We have a little kitchen at the theatre. Yes, lots of pizza."

At that point Dr. Alston knocked and came in. "Well, we're going to get rid of you today," he said with a smile.

"Thank God," said Karl.

Dr. Alston looked at me. "I think you'd be well advised, as I said before, to get him to a doctor at home to double check everything."

"Of course, I plan to."

"Do you have a physician in mind, or do you want me to look up specialists in Baltimore for you?"

"No, we're fine. I'll call our regular doctor for a referral. I'd feel more comfortable with that."

After Dr. Alston had checked Karl over, he said goodbye and left. Karl flipped on the television, and the news came on. As he watched, I leaned back in the chair, listening to droning voices. Before I drifted off, I realized that Alex would be with Terry by now. I wondered drowsily what he might learn.

Alicia arrived later with a suitcase for Karl, along with the nurse, Jenny, who had a plastic bag with Karl's clothing in it. It was noon, and we had to get to the airport by at least one-thirty.

Alicia and I left the room while Jenny helped Karl into his clothes. Presently he appeared in a wheelchair, and we followed him and Jenny to the elevator and down to the back entrance of the hospital. Alicia went to get the car. I patted Karl's head.

"You okay?"

"Fit as a fiddle," he said. "Back to normal, whatever that means."

"Well, you surely weren't anybody's kind of normal a few days ago," I laughed. "And you'd do well to take it seriously. You need to rest and see a doctor when we get back."

Jenny moved away to look for Alicia's car, and Karl looked up at me. "I know; I know. My little Elise, always the watchdog for the family. I do love you, you know. I don't think I've told you that often enough."

As Jenny returned, I leaned over and whispered, "It's okay Karl. Let's get ourselves home."

Chapter Sixty-seven

Finale

We spent a quiet Sunday, with the *New York Times* and the local *Baltimore Sun*. Our doctor said he would phone a referral to a specialist first thing Monday morning. By one o'clock Monday afternoon we were in the waiting room of a Dr. Crowley. The appointment lasted forty-five minutes. Dr. Crowley had by then received the results from Denver, and after checking Karl out, he told us to see how Karl progressed and return in two weeks.

"If it looks as good as it does now, we'll give him a clean bill and send him on his way," he said.

Up to that point, we had eked out meals from the freezer, so we headed off to a supermarket on the way home and picked up a few fresh fruits and vegetables. "I want a big steak," Karl announced.

Mindful of cholesterol, I suggested fish, but he wouldn't be deterred, so we got a large T-bone. The next day I was confident enough to go by myself and do a bigger shopping trip. Pulling into the parking lot, I left the motor running for heat and dialed Alex. He couldn't have called me during this time.

I got him on the first try. "Where are you?" was his first question. I told him. "So it's going well?"

"Yes. I think Karl is going to be fine. He needs time. And now, I'm longing to hear what went on in Denver. You're back home now, aren't you?"

"Yes, and I've a lot to tell you, none of it good." His voice was shaky. He cleared his throat and then was silent.

I fell a chill of foreboding. "What do you mean?"

"I wish I were with you, Elise. This is not easy. In fact, it's disastrous."

"Being with you is not going to be possible for at least a few weeks. Maybe after Karl goes back to Denver. It looks like he will be able to go and finish up after Christmas."

"Then this will have to do. Are you where you can talk for a while?"

"Yes." I switched off the motor.

"Okay. I got into Denver on Thursday and went straight to the house. Emily, my stepmother — you remember? — and Terry were there; it was stiff, but we settled down in the kitchen. Emily's in great physical shape but vague; her mind wanders. Her account of Father's heart attack and subsequent events was fuzzy, but it was clear that she got the gist of it and had in fact been working with Terry to plan the funeral, which was yesterday.

"On Friday," he continued, "Terry insisted we go through Father's things while we had the chance — not leave it up to Emily. She said she wouldn't know what to do with everything anyway. So we pitched in, his desk first. Papers were neatly filed, and at the bottom of one drawer were two envelopes, one for each of us. Terry opened his first, and there were old photographs, school reports, a few letters Terry had written from camp, from college, even from Nicaragua. So, I could see they had kept in touch through the years when I had been out of the picture. There was a really nice family photograph — Father, Emily and Terry — that Terry was especially pleased about, and . . ."

"What was in your envelope?" I interrupted.

Alex paused. "Yes, of course. You can't be interested in what was in Terry's. Sorry."

There was a long silence. "Alex?"

"Yes. Um. Well, here we go. There were letters from Harvard at the time I quit and a photograph of a woman I guess was my real mother, and here's the shocker: there was the enamel miniature from your father. Tucked in the back of the frame was a slip of paper saying 'Ti amo, Lili'"

"Oh, my god," I breathed. Neither of us spoke. I could hear him start to sob at the other end of the line.

Finally, he said, "Oh, Elise, this ends it. I mean how can we go on, knowing what this means?"

There was a throbbing in my head. My mind sailed out of focus, and images of Alex and me during the past weeks spun around.

"Elise, are you there?"

"Yes. I don't know what to say. There's nothing to say. Oh, Alex, how cruel! Why wouldn't he have given it to you when it came?"

"No answers there. Sheer meanness? I wasn't at home at the time, and he forgot later? Doubtful. I don't know. I don't know."

I held my breath. The last days with Karl had taken their toll, and now this. My life was strewn with emotional debris. Later I would wonder if Mother had known the whole extraordinary tale and thus taken a special interest in Alex, maybe to make up for her rejecting him as a child. Right then, though, I was flattened, speechless, and had no energy to cry or rage at the pointlessness of everything. I could hear Alex blowing his nose.

"Alex, I think we'd both better hang up now and try to sort our thoughts out, talk later. I can't think of anything to say." We were silent. "Alex?"

"Yes?"

"I do love you," I said.

"Good thing, Sis" he said bitterly and hung up.

PART TWO, 2010

Chapter Sixty-eight

Brighton Fifteen Years Later

We paused to rest on a bench near the beach, having wandered through the wonderful Royal Pavilion, the seaside fantasy palace of George IV, admiring the art, the gardens, and enjoying tea in the tearoom. The sun was low in the sky, and a brisk wind came off the water. I pulled my scarf tighter around my head.

Alex looked at me, "Well at least we're not infirm or leaning on walkers yet. Oh, Elise what a wonderful sight you are!"

I squeezed his hand. "You don't look so bad yourself. Fifteen years. Imagine it. Do you think we'd have run off together back then if . . ."

He looked out towards the water. "I don't know. There was a lot going on; we were tied to family; I was hell-bent to do my research; Karl had his mini stroke, then another, and then the big one later. I don't think you would have left him, half-paralyzed as he was, do you?"

"No. No, I couldn't have done that," I said. I turned to look at him. "And besides, it does no good to guess; we were both in shock over the enamel miniature. I mean finally figuring out that your father, my father, had sent it to you changed everything for both of us. The viciousness that kept your stepfather from giving it to you is amazing."

"I realized later that when the package came for me," said Alex, "I'd been off at school for years. He had no reason to consider me as anything but completely absent from his life. At some point Father showed Terry a note from your father saying that my mother had given the enamel to him in Italy during the war, and he wanted me to have it. Result was they kept both the painting and the note to spite me. Terry did admit as much to me later.

"As I told you at the time," he continued, "the note said that your father was dying and had reason to believe that I was his son." He must have became upset at some point and wanted to clear the cobwebs. Terry also knew, I guess from my stepfather, that there had been an anonymous trust fund, and all those years Father let me believe he was paying for everything and held it over my head."

"No wonder you were devastated. Yes, it affected you and me, but it also underscored how your family felt about you."

"Devastated is definitely the word. A tiny beautiful enamel miniature and then a note, and the life went out of me."

"Of course we knew Dad's side of it," I said, "from my mother's letter, but finding out it was you was the darkest moment of my life. I thought at the time we might get used to it, move into another kind of relationship and not have to throw away what we had."

"We tried."

"Not a success," I said, smiling ruefully. "You know, Alex, I was also mad as hell at my father, probably unreasonably, but I was."

"I was too. If he had only . . ."

"What?" I asked.

"Oh, I don't know. I suppose it was one of those things that people resolve, or don't, and never think it will affect their children. I kept trying to imagine what I'd do in a similar circumstance. Probably be as honorable as I could and then sweep the whole thing under the rug and get on with life."

"As he did?"

"As he did." He smiled ruefully and lifted my hand. "Nothing has changed, Elise. I still love you."

I smiled at him. It wasn't hard. He was still the handsome, dear man I had parted from fifteen years ago. "Did you ever see Terry again?"

"No, he went back to Nicaragua. There were a few phone calls during the first year, and afterwards I didn't hear another word. I've no idea what became of him. Good riddance. He did try to be decent that time in Denver, he really did, but he can't help being a mean-assed swine. Genetic."

Alex went to England as planned, and I'd known he was taking Sheila with him as his assistant. I was both jealous and confused, knowing there was nothing I could do and that I had no way to find out what was happening. Before he left, Alex and I had met several more times, trying to reach equilibrium amidst our jumbled feelings.

Once, after Christmas when Karl had gone back to Denver, Alex came down to Washington, and I met him there under the pretext of seeing Arnell, my agent. We stayed in separate rooms, and over dinner and too much wine, we decided to go back to my room. The inevitable happened. But, the knowledge that we had the same father overwhelmed us, and finally Alex rolled off the bed and went to a chair. He put his head in his hands, and truly it was a disaster. We were both destroyed, and we parted the next morning having decided that the best way to deal with our turbulent emotions was to cut off contact altogether and not tease ourselves by being together with the looming specter of a tawdry Greek tragedy.

The last thing he said was, "We used to laugh about growing old and meeting on the beach at Brighton leaning on walkers. Let's look forward to that."

After six months passed, Alex called occasionally, since I had assured him I would tell Karl about the uncanny circumstances that had led to our discovery that we were related. That was all I told Karl. Anyway I didn't want to confess to transgressions in order to relieve my conscience with no regard to the effect on him.

I also told Suzanne, and she actually took it in stride while not being able to resist jabbing at my wounds. "Oh, Lixie, I've always believed in keeping things in the family."

Both Karl and Suzanne had been sworn to secrecy, for none of us could see any value in involving the rest of our families in a relationship that was unlikely to significantly affect their lives, even though they now had cousins.

For a long time I lived in a climate of mood swings, sun one day, storms the next. As with most shock and pain, it dulled over time, but I knew I would not stop loving Alex. I also knew that our passion would never dwindle into the mundane and manageable. Best to be apart.

After Karl died of a final stroke in 2001, Alex's phone calls became more frequent, and we shared more of our lives with each other, but our conversations didn't have the sense of possibility, or the charged focus they once had. We were careful to keep the tone casual and cheerful, but it always felt studied, and skirting the proverbial elephant in the room became a tiresome burden. We did however continue to keep in touch sporadically over the months and years.

Alex now had a flat in London and a weekend cottage in Cornwall. Anne never did go over, and eventually she met a banker from Chicago who swept her away. It was still several years before she would give Alex a divorce, but it finally happened, and Anne remarried. Alex did not, but it was axiomatic that he had girlfriends from time to time. Alex was Alex. Any residual love for me wouldn't alter his nature.

I was in England now, waiting for Fiona to arrive. She was living in Spain and working on the restoration of gardens at a large estate outside Barcelona. She would have started college in Vermont, but the offer to do the work she loved best had been too much to resist. It had actually come through Alex, whose friend owned the property. Knowing of Fiona's passion for landscape gardening, he relayed the possibility to me, and I contacted his friend with the result that Fiona had left the day after high school graduation and been there ever since. Possibly she'd go to college eventually.

Fiona and I were going to tour Scotland and go on to visit Enid and Evan in Paris. They remained the same devoted and unmarried couple as ever.

After that Fiona was due back in Spain. I would fly back to London for a few more days with Alex before going home.

What surprised me was how relaxed Alex and I felt with each other now that we were at last together. The depth of our feelings and the shared history made a reunion after fifteen years more natural than I had anticipated. I felt my age at sixty-five but thought Alex had changed little — grey in his hair, radiating wrinkles around his eyes and mouth, but still the fetching devil I remembered, thin as paper and now smartly dressed by a Savile Row tailor. Even his shoes were elegant. "John Lobb," he told me when I admired them. "They keep everyone's last on a shelf, so they don't need to fit you after the first time." I knew these shoes went for nearly a thousand dollars, so I assumed Alex was doing well.

"I was able to retain one of the patents on a delivery system I introduced when I left Wilding, and that's about to pay off." He smiled. "Also, I was paid well there, investments have been good, and then working with another company since has allowed me to cover the boys' college tuitions with plenty to spare." He looked at me, "How are you set for money? Everything okay? I'm sure you'd have said so if it weren't."

"Oh, I'm fine. Not rich, but fine. Karl had a pretty big insurance policy, and the royalties on the books and the movie are considerable. They're suggesting a TV series for my last book. And of course there is Social Security, which as security is decidedly antisocial, but a help."

"Are you working on another book now?"

"Not yet; taking a breather. That last one was over four hundred pages, and I was brain dead afterwards."

"I loved it, as I told you on the phone," he said. "The research was amazing; I never knew about Plains Indians, and you brought it to life is such a natural way. It will be a great series. By the way," he added. "How did you dream up that dreadful character, Albion Humphrey? A true villain and inveterate womanizer."

I grinned. "As to his womanizing, I had a role model."

He jabbed me in the ribs. "Not I, and he wasn't a gentleman. I am."

"Really?" I asked.

"Really. Well, look at my suddenly elevated genealogy for instance. Boston Brahmin, if I'm not mistaken." He got up and stretched. "A walk on the beach? That's how we started gazing into the future wasn't it? I mean has tomorrow escaped you as a coincidence?"

I looked up at him. "Tomorrow? October thirteenth? I don't understand."

"Well then, I'll explain. It will be the date you and I met fifteen years ago."

My hands flew up to my face. "Oh, Alex, I never made the connection. How terrible of me!"

"So," he continued, "today is an anniversary eve of sorts, and I've made reservations at a nice restaurant for dinner, champagne and all."

I started to cry, and once in the throes of this inexplicable emotion, I couldn't stop. Alex sat down and put his arm around me. The years had been long and often lonely since Karl had died, although my friends were supportive, and Potter even took me on three of his research jaunts to Asia. One time Arthur had caught up with us in Singapore, and the three of us went on to Malaysia and then Tokyo. After all the years of their historical relationship, Potter and Arthur made no pretense, and they took me to strange nightclubs where transvestites and assorted flamboyant men gathered.

Arthur, though in his eighties at the time, was full of energy, and we visited shrines, temples, and bought silks and exquisite batiks in shops, so I hadn't been neglected or unhappy really. But as I sobbed on that bench in Brighton, I realized that no one could fill my heart as completely as Alex.

He handed me his handkerchief, and I mopped at the untidy mess my face had become, and hand in hand, we walked on the beach, older but not yet feeble enough for walkers.

Chapter Sixty-nine

Bistro Du Vin

We changed our clothes in our rooms with modesty. Here I was with the connecting door open and Alex wandering in and out, a man whose naked body was once as familiar to me as my own, and I was half hiding behind a closet door as I struggled into a black dress and pulled on pantyhose. I hadn't been sure when Alex told me about adjoining rooms, and now I was even less convinced this was a good idea. As I leaned over to put on a shoe, Alex's hand came around the closet door with a glass of whiskey in it.

"Knock, knock, who's there?" he asked.

I stumbled and fell forward, steadying myself on the wall opposite. I looked down and saw that the heel of my shoe had snapped off. "Oh, Alex, dammit, look what you've done." I shouted.

He came around the door. "Ah, pity. Go barefoot. Such pretty little feet you have, my dear."

"And what big teeth you have."

Surprisingly I hadn't knocked over the drink, so I took it from him and had a large sip. "Mmmm, good. Thanks, I think."

I went to my suitcase and pulled out a pair of black flat shoes. "These will have to do," I said.

"I like you little. Makes me feel all male and protective," he smiled.

"I don't need protecting," I said. "I need a good dinner."

"Well, I'm waiting for you; not the other way around."

"I see. Well, it's not time to go yet, is it?" I asked, glancing at the clock.

"No, come sit by the window. We'll converse in modest phrases."

"That, coming from you, will be a novelty."

I knew we were forcing normalcy with our banter and that a vague unease had arisen in such close quarters. Were we ready to be together again? Could we meet after so much time and be the brother and sister we were, or would old habits and hungers creep upon us? And if so, would shame or a sense of the inevitable take shape?

I leaned forward in my chair. "Alex, I want to ask you something."

"Mmmmmmm?"

"Did Sheila — I mean did you and Sheila; ah, I don't know how to ask what I want to know." Alex burst out laughing. I stared at him. "I don't think it's slightly funny," I said.

"Well it is. You always had a thing about Sheila. If you could have the least, the tiniest, the most subatomic idea of how little regard I have had for her for years from that standpoint, you wouldn't gnaw away at it." He took a deep breath. "So, no, I didn't bed Sheila while she was here. But," and he waved a finger in the air, "make no mistake. She is the best research assistant I have ever had, and I couldn't have gotten the work I wanted to do up and running as fast as I did without her."

We were quiet. I knew I had stepped over a line. I took a drink of scotch. "Can I smoke in here?"

"Probably not, but we can leave now and walk if you wish."

"Yes, good idea."

I got my coat, and we headed for the elevator. The wind had died down, and the sky was clear and starry. I lit a cigarette, and we wandered along, looking at the Regency architecture and making idle comments as we went. In one window well a rose was still in bloom, and Alex took my hand and said, "Like us, isn't it? Still blooming in the cold."

I could feel a lump forming in my throat, but I vowed to ignore it. There were times when it felt hopeless, a trap that fate had created for two people who by now ought to have been able to live and love. I simply smiled at him and tugged his hand, wanting to keep moving, not wishing to see that rose, knowing it would soon be bitten by winter frost.

Alex said, "And you? Did you meet anyone wonderful after Karl died?"

I was caught off guard. There had been one special man I met in Singapore, a musician friend of Potter's. He was French and living in Seattle. We had seen each other off and on for a couple of years, a few weekends in New York and San Francisco and another time in the south of France, longer. "Well, yes in a way, but he wasn't breathtaking. No, not at all, a decent kind of person, fun, interesting, and I got used to him. Yes, he was nice, but in the end it didn't really work out. But if you're talking about love, for sure, no. There's never been anyone like you."

"He the only one?"

"Hell no. But it really doesn't matter does it?" I glanced up at him, "And you? Fifteen years is a long time."

He laughed. "Long enough for me to tell you with complete conviction that English women aren't blighted with American puritanism — present company excepted of course."

"Well, as I said, fifteen years is a long time, and we had sworn off each other. But honestly, Alex, it's never been the same with anyone else. I don't know what prompted me to tell you I was coming over this time, except . . .

"Except," he said, giving my bottom a not gentle pinch, "except that we both know life is moving along, and it would be a waste of what is left to continue denying ourselves what we both want most. Am I right?"

I stopped, looking down at my less than elegant shoes. "Right. It's a hopeless pursuit. There isn't a day I haven't wondered what you were doing, feeling, thinking."

It was then that my life changed. Alex took me in his arms, and my arms flew up and around him. We held each other a long time and then with resignation, we kissed. The years wafted away with the sea breeze, and it was as if time skipped a beat, giving us a small moment, a tiny opening to embrace the present and maybe move into it. With wordless agreement, we drifted into a long and blessed renewal of the heat of what we had once been.

Thoroughly chilled by the time we arrived at the Bistro du Vin, the warmth and smell of food was welcome. They had a table for us in a corner. Alex stopped on the way to greet friends from London and introduced me.

"Tina and David Lowther, this is a friend from America, Elise von Sturnheim." He looked at David. "What are you doing here so far from your usual haunts?"

"Visiting my sister who's abandoned us tonight for a baby shower for her ex-husband's niece. Back to London tomorrow," said Tina.

We did our how-do-you-dos. Tina looked up at me. "Staying long?" she asked.

"A while. I'm meeting my granddaughter and then visiting my daughter in Paris. So, maybe as long as a month, possibly less. Right now, I have time, so plans are loose."

"Elise recently published her sixth book, a four-hundred-page monster on Native Americans. It's wonderful," said Alex.

"How fascinating," said David. "What's the title?"

"*Plains Truth*. It's about the Plains Indians."

"Well, I see we'll have to add to your royalties, or Alex will never forgive us," said Tina, glancing at Alex and winking.

"Damn right," answered Alex. "And by the way, I think I've forgotten my manners and not properly thanked you for the wonderful weekend in Sussex. Although, I also have you to thank for hardly being able to walk for a week; I haven't been on a horse in years."

Tina and David laughed. "Well, we'll do it more often and get you in shape." said David. "What say you two come down next weekend?"

"Oh, I can't," I said. "I'll have my granddaughter with me by then."

"Bring her," said Tina. Alex looked at me.

"I suppose we could. We were planning to head to Scotland, but we have no firm plans or reservations, so, yes, we could."

"Splendid," said David. "Then it's on. Right, Alex?"

Alex's smile was broad and happy. "Right, David, Tina, and thank you yet again."

"You can motor down with us from London or come on your own now that you know the way," offered David.

"I think we'll come on our own, but thanks," said Alex, and he prodded my elbow, pushing me forward.

"See you in Sussex," called Tina.

When we were settled, I asked, "How are your boys doing? I know Drew has followed in your footsteps and is practicing in Los Angeles. I can't remember if you said he was married or not."

"No, he's not, but Edward has one son; wife in advertising; He adores her. David is now, let's see, he's twenty-four, out of Middlebury where he studied Mandarin Chinese and Japanese. He's working at the State Department. As I must have told you, David did come over for the last two years of his schooling and went to Winchester. Fine school. He loved it. Anne wasn't happy, but David was insistent. We had a wonderful time together. I took him to France, Japan, and Denmark on vacations. He's a great kid."

"Do any of them know about us?"

"No. I wanted to tell Anne to get her off my back concerning you, but I didn't. With the wandering we both did, I don't know why she got upset with the idea that I was attracted to you, except I think she sensed that I was actually in love for the first time."

"I told Karl, only the family connection part, and his reaction was simply to find the coincidence amusing and to tip his hat to my father for the fact that he carried through with seeing you got a good education and all. Then of course, he had the second stroke, and later, well you know the rest from our phone calls."

"European absence of puritanism again."

"I guess."

We ordered dinner and I feasted on steak and kidney pudding while Alex had lamb chops. After a dessert of fresh fruit and cheeses and while we were enjoying brandy and coffee, Alex cleared his throat. "Elise, I've thought about this a long time, and I know we probably shouldn't marry, but I also know we're well past the danger of producing idiots, so I'd like to offer you a brotherly present."

With that, he pulled out a small red box from Garrard jewelers. In it was the most beautiful ring I've ever seen, a single square-cut sapphire with small rubies on either side, set in pink gold. I gasped. Precipitous decisions were being forced on me. Given my weak will and strong inclination, it would have been ridiculous to deny our situation. I did put forward an argument, but the sheer onslaught of Alex's convictions made resistance difficult. He had thought about this a long time. My memories had not faded either, but I at no time anticipated a future together.

"Look, Elise," he said, taking my hand and slipping the ring on, "no one knows about our relationship now but Suzanne, and given her off-hand attitude, she poses no threat. No one cares anymore."

I glanced down at the ring sitting on the third finger of my left hand. It was a little large for me and beautiful. "Alex, so what do we do? Are you ever coming back to America?"

"No. I have business interests here. You've met David Lowther. I work for him. Haven't told you about that yet. Exciting stuff." He twisted the ring around on my finger. "We'll have to get this fixed, go into Garrard's when we get back to London and have it sized."

"Alex? Answer me. What do we do now? My whole life is in America."

"Why?"

"Why?" I started to come up with a dozen answers and faltered. *The children? Well they had their own lives, didn't they?* Penny still had the two boys at home. Both Christopher's and her name choices had been used; first, David Karl, now sixteen, and next Alexander George, now fourteen. Matthew had married the girl from Cincinnati, Juliana Berglund, and stayed there as managing editor for a monthly business magazine. They had a daughter. And Enid and Evan were Enid and Evan. My books? Of course I could write anywhere, and transatlantic flights were routine for many people. "Oh, I don't know, Alex, except I'm rooted there — my friends, my children . . ."

"You don't sound any more convinced than you are convincing."

I smiled. "Alex, I don't know anyone over here except one old school friend, and she's dull."

"I do. Scads of people. Wonderful, fun people, and they'll welcome you. And we'll get an enormous flat or maybe a house, and you can have your friends visit whenever you want. I looked at a perfect place with an estate agent last week. It's two houses that a couple put together off Allen Street. It'd be perfect. Has a wonderful walled garden behind it."

"You had this all planned, didn't you?"

"Yes, of course I did. I woke up one day and asked myself what the hell we were doing with our lives. Coasting along randomly year after year until we die, separated by diabolical circumstances and our own misplaced moral rectitude?"

"I guess I had myself convinced we did the right thing and would have to live with the consequences. I built a life of sorts with my friends, writing, and the children. Bearable and often downright enjoyable."

He patted my hand. "Think about it, darling. If you decide no, then we'll go to Garrard's, take the ring back and restore my bank account."

I smacked him on the arm. "Fine. That's not what I call a present, and you said it was brotherly, you liar! I'd like you to find one brother who has ever given his sister a ring like this. Hypocrite."

The waiter came with the bill, and Alex tossed his American Express card inside the folder and handed it back to him. When it was returned for signature, Alex scribbled his name, added a tip, grabbed my arm and said,

"C'mon bitch, let's go fuck."

"Do shut up, Alex. People can hear you." It had sounded thunderous to me, but no heads turned. I looked at him leering down at me and surrendered to a giggle. We left.

Chapter Seventy

Heading into the Wind

We had a few days before Fiona was to arrive. We went back to London the next day, and I moved into Alex's flat at Albany, next to Burlington House in Piccadilly. I was impressed, as Alex must have influential friends to get him into such a place.

"You didn't tell me," I whispered when we pulled up in front. I had been writing letters to a Royal Mail box number so had no idea where he actually lived.

"Don't you know the tradition?" laughed Alex. "We don't speak of Albany."

Albany, omitting the article *the*, is a lovely Georgian building near St. James Park that was turned into residences, originally for single gentlemen who wanted discreet quarters at reasonable cost. No women on the premises, at least until the 1880s. Of course I had heard of the legendary place, but I'd never known anyone who lived there.

It seemed I might see the ghost of Lord Byron rounding the corner, or a favorite of my mother's, Fleur Cowles, welcoming famous guests to dinner. In the settling of Mother's estate, I kept one of Cowles' delightfully whimsical paintings that she had given Mother during a stay in London.

"You actually have a flat here?"

"Well, no, it belongs to a friend who is spending the year in Greece at a teaching hospital. Of course he had to jump through hoops to let me use it, but fortunately I passed muster. It's lovely. And you don't call it a flat; it is a set."

"Oh."

We were standing in the street gazing up at Albany, holding hands like a couple of lovesick teenagers. The night before had turned into the most exciting night of my life. Now, we couldn't stop touching each other.

Alex broke loose. "I'll carry our cases up and then come down and take the car around to the garage." He looked at me seriously. "I have to warn you there's one bedroom and what was a maid's room, now a tiny single bedroom. You're going to have to figure out what to tell Fiona or sleep in a single bed with her."

"I'll figure out what to tell her," I said confidently.

Both of us had our arms loaded, cases, coats, groceries, a huge bunch of roses, and three bottles of wine, as we went up to the set. Alex dumped his lot in the front hall and went back down. I too dropped mine and started to wander around the place: formal, decorative and comfortable. It's often easy to tell from surroundings when people live alone and when they have to share space with others, compromise. This of course had the earmarks of a bachelor, set in his ways, cultured and precise. There was a shelf of poetry books and another of philosophy, a few large modern art books and a number of biographies and novels, a lot of Proust. The carpets and fabrics looked as if David Hicks had sprinkled his faerie dust of patterns on the floors, walls, and furniture in delightful colors; certainly far from being a fusty sort of place, it was ordered and cheerful. I commented on this when Alex returned, slamming the door behind him with a solid whack. He dropped his keys on a marble table in the hall and came in.

"Rumor has it that Hicks kept a set here at one time, so it's no coincidence that these smack of his taste. He probably did up a number of these places."

"This is wonderful," I said, gazing out the window at the roof of a walkway below.

"It is, and I want you to feel totally at home." He joined me at the window. "That's called the Rope Walk; it joins the sets in the other two buildings." He pulled me away from the window and said, "But right now, it's still early afternoon, and I want to get to Garrard's to have that ring taken care of."

"Oh, really? Go right out again?"

"Yes. It's not far, Albemarle Street, and then we'll go to Fortnum and Mason and pick up smoked salmon and whatever else strikes your fancy. You might also enjoy Hatchards, a truly amazing book store."

"Shouldn't we put the cream and vegetables in the refrigerator?"

"Oh, right. You do it." And Alex disappeared into the bedroom. I found a small kitchen and a Lilliputian refrigerator by American standards, and then I heard the toilet flush as I finished with the perishables. "Alex," I said as he came in, "there's only one tiny ice tray in there."

He smiled. "Very British. Americans like ice, lots and lots of it. The British don't."

We walked. It was a sunlit fall day, and I stopped to look into shop windows artfully arranged with jewelry, cashmeres, and paintings. I didn't dare admire anything, as Alex was in a mood to indulge my every whim. I wasn't used to the kind of money he seemed to have, and I understood why Anne was always turned out to perfection. Coming from New England, I was bred in an atmosphere of modestly played-down wealth. The idea of being even the least bit showy about one's circumstances was in the worst possible taste. And yet, there was a seductive power in all that beauty for sale. *He must be making a fortune*, I thought.

What originated as the prospect of two older people reconnecting was now a whirlpool in which I swirled, unable to resist. That Alex was forceful I knew. That I was ambivalent enough after fifteen years to let him make these crucial decisions was a surprise. I wondered whether if I departed right now this would shrink into a ridiculous anomaly and fade into the routine of my life back home.

"Good afternoon, Dr. Creighton," said the Garrard store manager, showing a familiarity that gave me pause.

Alex nodded and then took me by the elbow. "Mr. Thomas, I'd like you to meet my friend, Mrs. Elise von Sturnheim." He held up my hand. "The ring is a mite too large."

"Ah," said Mr. Thomas, "no problem at all. We can have it ready tomorrow afternoon." He nodded at me, throwing out his right hand to direct me to a chair. "Let's get the right size, Mrs. von Sturnheim." I sat, and he slipped several steel rings over my finger until he was satisfied, and then he picked up the ring. "Really a beautiful thing," he said.

"It is," I agreed.

I could see interest in his eyes, but he didn't ask any questions as he summoned a young woman from the back and explained to her what needed to be done. After formal goodbyes, Alex and I left. "He was curious," I giggled.

"Indeed. Would you have begged his credulity by having me pose as a generous brother?"

"Stop it, or I'll grab my passport and go home."

"Shall we walk around for a while?"

"I'd like to walk," I said. "This is a wonderful part of London."

We ambled along, and Alex pointed across the road. "Look, darling, what a coincidence. Ferragamo."

"No, Alex, you've done too much already."

He stepped in front of me and turned around, stopping me. "Elise, there has not been one day in the last fifteen years when I haven't thought about you. Now, I admit I succeeded in convincing you that this would be a relaxed meeting of old friends, a total lie. But, I'm not letting you go. Please let me spoil you."

He looked like a sulky boy, and I laughed. The freedom of being able to look long and hard at that dear face made me dizzy with happiness.

"Anyway," he went on, "I'm not going to be seen again in public with you wearing those frumpy shoes you wore last night." He took a breath and steered me across the street. "So, we go to Ferragamo and get stylish shoes for those pretty little feet. Then we're going to Brown's for tea."

We arrived home laden. Shoes — three pairs; a beige cashmere sweater; *The Hare with the Amber Eyes* by Edmund de Waal from Hatchards; cheeses and an apricot torte from Fortnum and Mason. I unloaded everything on the sitting room floor, sighed deeply, and collapsed in a chair.

"Wow!"

Alex stood by the fireplace and grinned.

Chapter Seventy-one

Out of London

By Friday, we had settled to a routine, if that definition could be applied to two people wildly in love and savoring the lovely treats London had to offer. Alex bought three tickets for the new stage adaptation of *Flashdance* at the Shaftesbury to give Fiona a taste of London theatre. She had called and was delayed with a shipment of new specimen plants and wouldn't be arriving until Tuesday afternoon. She also had to go back to work in a week, so that put an end to touring in Scotland and likely going with her to see Enid.

We had picked up the ring, and it surprised me every time I looked at it with its vivid colors and the warm gold surrounding them.

Most days, Alex went off to the office he shared with David Lowther and with whom he had partnered in investing in a pharmaceutical company in China. Both he and David were on the board and made frequent trips there. They were negotiating to sell Alex's remaining patent to the Chinese company. He was usually back home around two, so we had plenty of time to see art collections and take long walks. I rapidly become addicted to little meat pies and sausages from Fortnum's, so I relished my quiet lunch respites from writing, which I was finally doing again on a computer Alex bought for us to share.

I finally called Enid to tell her what I was doing, who I was with and why, fearing a horrified reaction. Later I was able to get in touch with Penny and Matthew. Surprisingly, each of them was supportive, a huge relief. Of course they had never learned of their relationship to Alex, so the view was that I was having a romp with an old friend, and good for Mum after all these years. I also got hold of Helene and Louise. Helene said she and Anthony were planning to come to London later in the year.

"So if you're still there and as giddy as you sound now, we'll see you. Otherwise, we'll see you back here. The ring sounds ominously permanent however."

I began to do a few housewifely things, shopping for food and planning our dinners, tidying up the set and then settling down to make notes that would flesh out the new book. I had purloined a small mahogany writing table from the bedroom and moved it into the sitting room by the window overlooking the walkway. Alex objected to my moving the sofa around at an angle to accommodate the writing table, and I realized how closely he observed his life, keeping everything organized.

One evening before dinner, as we were having largely iceless drinks of scotch, Alex asked me about my long time taking care of Karl. "I know it was hard for you, but was it awful?"

"Yes and no. Naturally the basics were difficult, but I had a home-care woman come in to bathe him every day, and three days a week she stayed until three, so I could write and periodically get out for lunch with Helene and other friends to keep my sanity. Potter was wonderful, and a number of people came in to see Karl."

"You travelled too, didn't you?"

"Oh, yes. There was also Margaret who worked for Louise's father until he died. She would come and stay if I needed it. She managed him beautifully, because obviously his own frustrations with being able to do little for himself could make him angry. He made a few sounds, and we got to know what they meant. He could also use his left hand, so we rigged a sort of stand, and he was able to write after a while. He kept dropping the pencil and made a kind of roar when that happened. He started composing music, which kept him occupied and as happy as possible."

"Did he ever hear it played?"

"Potter got one of those electronic pianos and left it at the house so he could play for Karl. Karl loved that. He would grunt, which Potter came to recognize meant a pause, and Karl would make notes on the score. Often in the evenings after I had fed him, I read to him." I shook my head. "It was sad, so sad; to even contemplate getting locked inside one's own defective body is a nightmare. He lived it."

"Did you think of me?"

"Every day. But you have to understand. Karl and I had a long-settled marriage until before the stroke when he tried to reach out to me, as you know, but the familiarity, family, and many good memories meant that I knew, really knew without doubt, where my loyalties lay."

"What hell that must have been for you," said Alex, as he got up to get the plate of cheese and crackers from across the room.

"Oh, Alex, much of life is not what we dreamed for ourselves. It happens, and one endures, but beyond the endurance comes a sort of grace and love that suffices. There are little pleasures, even humorous moments, and generosity is grossly underrated as a sustaining support in itself."

He smiled. "One more question. Did you ever resent Karl for keeping you tied to him?"

"Of course I did at times, but his condition was not deliberate, so how could I be angry with him? Little by little I transferred the disappointment to a vague karma over which no one had control. In short, I learned to behave myself, for my own sake and as much for the children's sake." I shook my head. "I don't know, Alex; it's a sort of blur. I guess my memories of Karl are kindly now. I did care for him in a lot of fundamental ways."

So, now it was Friday, and we were due at the Lowthers' for the weekend. I asked Alex what I should bring.

"Do you ride?" he asked.

"Well, I used to, a lot. But I haven't for years. Anyway I don't have the clothes, and I don't want to end up as sore as you apparently were last time."

"Then bring outdoors stuff, sturdy shoes — we did get you a pair — and woolies. It's cold, and the bedrooms can be ferocious. I slept in my overcoat last time."

We packed one duffle and took clothes for evening, in case, on hangers. Alex went down to bring the car around, bumping through the hall with the big canvas bag. I went around the rooms, checking for dripping taps and open windows, and then followed him downstairs.

When we were angling our way out of London in fits and starts, I asked him, "Do you know if anyone else will be there?"

"Have no idea. Tina is pretty social; David is a recluse. So, you never know who will win on any particular occasion. David would rather grow vegetables than friendships. A large turnip is a work of God's glory to him; a party in black tie is to her."

"Do they have children?"

"Two. Mathilde is doing her first year at St. Hilda's at Oxford, and Jeremy works for Credit Suisse in London. She won't be there, I'm sure, but I'm hoping to have her and Fiona meet. They'd enjoy each other. Mathilde was that late baby that everyone dreads and then loves to bits. Jeremy is in his mid-thirties."

"Where are we going?"

"To Horsham in West Sussex. Theirs is a beautiful place with about seventy-five acres. David inherited it from his parents, and it must be worth at least four or five million pounds by now. It's done it up in the casual, elegant way the English have mastered. I expect we'll be staying in the lodge, which is fitted out as a guesthouse, kitchen and all. The original place was built around fifteen hundred, stone and brick."

"Impressive."

"Yes, it is. The interesting thing is that when we Americans revere old houses, we're mostly talking about something a hundred to two hundred years old. It's hard to conceive of a building that's been around five or six hundred years still being lived in.

"How long a drive is it?"

"About an hour and a half on a good day. A lot of Londoners weekend down there, so we're bound to run into traffic. It's not far from Brighton, so some of this should look vaguely familiar to you."

As we drove, Alex filled me in on the details of his and David's business in China.

I interrupted him and asked, "Why can't you practice medicine here?"

"With a lot of paperwork and possibly tests in a specialty or an equivalency test, I might. But, I came over here on a work permit with Wilding to do research for them. That in itself was a pain, for them anyway, having to prove that there was no suitable candidate, not only in the UK but in the whole EU. Fortunately they are big enough to have an immigration department, so I had to do little except provide documents and sign paperwork. That done, when my job with them was over, so too would have been my residency in England, but since I had been here four years by then, I could apply for Indefinite Leave to Remain. That too is a lot of jumping through hoops, and you can't job hunt on a tourist visa, so I had to find another sponsor. David stepped forward at that point. For a long time I was simply an employee of his company and actually earned my keep by looking for acquisitions in the medical field, research and inventions mostly. I was paid a small salary plus a big bonus when deals came through, which happily were a good many. David has built a large conglomerate worldwide."

"So now you're a permanent resident here?"

"Yes."

"What would I do if I decided to stay?"

"*Would* you do?"

I looked out the window as we sped by traffic, thinking. I had slipped into this so fast that part of me was still catching up. Giving up America, proximity to two of my children, my friends, was much to swallow. What about the house in Baltimore? I loved it, even more so since I'd had it to myself; the way the light came in the front in the morning, the shady garden in the back that I had completely redone, the old wood floors, and the wavy window glass. I felt tears welling up and gave a sniff.

Alex reached over and rested his hand on my knee. "I know, sweetheart, it's a lot. Can you think of any alternative? I can't leave now. You can. You can write anywhere." He glanced over at me. "Oh, come on, Elise. We're together at last. I wouldn't have thought this possible a few years ago. Chances are you'll see your children as often as you do now. They don't need you like they once did."

I looked at him, the concern on his face, and make a weak attempt to smile. "I know."

"Then can we jettison the word *would*?"

"I think so."

He sighed.

"So now you've replaced it with *think so*. Not good enough."

I remained quiet, so he went on.

"So, what you *will* do is go through the process to remain here."

It was my turn to sigh.

Chapter Seventy-two

Weekend In Sussex

We drove into Horsham on the A24, and I was anticipating a small, typically English town, but what I saw was a large developed sprawl of commercial enterprises.

"This is big," I said.

"Oh, yes," Alex answered. "It's actually a commuter town, and we could have come down by rail, but I prefer to have a car."

"Why?"

He looked over at me and winked. "In case I get bored, I can leave."

He drove me around, pointing out the sights like the Shelley Fountain, which was fenced off for repairs. "They say it will be finished in 2011," he said. "Cost of over thirty thousand pounds."

"What else is here?"

"Well commercially, that big glass building we saw is the RSA Insurance Company, and Novartis is here, as was Ciba-Geigy, their gastrointestinal and respiratory research centers. The place was once a market town for cattle, sheep, and corn, so it's always been a major center."

"I assume David and Tina don't live here, not with horses."

"No, of course not. They're outside town."

We were silent as Alex maneuvered the streets, and we were soon beyond the town. "Biggest statistic I've heard is that the heaviest hailstone to ever fall, fell here in 1958," he said as soon as we had cleared traffic.

"Quite a distinction," I laughed.

Before long we turned through an open gate set in a high stone wall and were winding along a rutted gravel drive that ran off the main road. A small sign at the entrance read Bedlington-Morton House. We drove past fields with horses, then sheep, and finally went over a stone bridge and up a hill to a rambling brick and stone house. Off to the left was another road leading to a lodge, stables, a greenhouse and outbuildings. As we pulled into the drive, a swirl of Shih Tzus barreled out the front door with Tina after them.

"Welcome." She waved from the front door. "Park around the corner. Leave your luggage in the car; you'll be staying in the lodge. Come in through the back."

Alex grabbed a parcel from the backseat I hadn't noticed before, and plunked it down in my lap. "House present. Take it in with you."

We entered through a stone-floored room rife with boots, green Barbour coats, leashes, and large bags of dog food. Dog bowls were ranged on the floor beside them. The kitchen was huge and modern with light pouring in windows that faced a field and woods behind the house. Tina came through a swinging door, allowing a glimpse of a dining room beyond.

"You're in good time for tea. Follow me."

We went through the dining room, which had dark beams across the ceiling and a fireplace at the end. The wide-board elm floors gleamed. I saw a table set for six, which answered my earlier question about how many were to be here.

As if in response, Tina waved at the table and said, "Blakes are joining us for dinner. They live along the way; nice people if a bit dull, sorry, but it was laid on weeks ago."

David was in the sitting room, a large square room decorated in yellow, green, and white with a white carpet reaching to within a foot of the walls. The ceiling was low, and there were French doors leading to a terrace beyond. I could see a swimming pool, covered now, and a tennis court.

"Good to see you," said David, setting a copy of *Sporting Life* on the table and getting up. "Did you bring rackets? The weather's great, and I thought we might play a few games."

"No," answered Alex.

"No matter," said Tina, "we've masses here, if you're old enough to remember wooden ones with gut stringing." She glanced over at us. "Sit, sit. David, pour them tea." And she passed a plate of little sandwiches, cucumber and watercress, and then said, "Was the drive a terror?"

"Not really," said Alex. "Not bad today."

A door slammed, and the Shih Tzus rushed in. Tina called out. "Jeremy, is that you by chance?"

Their tall blond son poked his head around the door. "Yes, I tried to ring before coming down, but no one answered, so I gave up. Didn't think it'd matter, since I won't be here for dinner anyway."

"Lovely to see you, darling," said Tina getting up. "Come meet Elise von Sturnheim, a friend of Alex."

We said hello, and Jeremy slumped down in a chair. "Hellish drive. Traffic is piling up."

"Guess we missed the worst of it," said Alex.

Jeremy was tall like his father, fair like his mother, his lank hair spilling over his forehead. He was dressed in pleated flannel trousers and an open-necked striped business shirt under a blazer. I could see his tie poking out of a pocket. He glanced at me.

"Over from the States for a visit?"

"Obviously, darling. She's not a spy," said Tina.

"Right," said Jeremy and applied himself to his mobile phone. He looked up again at me. "Jolly good, hope you have a grand time. Old Mum and Dad will take good care of you. Pleasure everywhere around here. Horses, golf, tennis, caviar, whatever strikes your fancy."

"No need for sarcasm, son," said David. He turned to me, "We think Jeremy is leaning too far into socialism at the moment, gap between the rich and poor."

"So," I said to Jeremy, "you work for one of the largest investment banks in the world, and you're a socialist? How does that gibe?"

Jeremy looked interested. "Well, what I do and what I think may appear at opposite poles, but in fact it's hopeless to make changes unless you understand how things work, isn't it?"

The day was darkening, and the door gave a loud crash in the hall. "Jeremy, you didn't close the door all the way," said David.

"Yes. No, I suppose not." And he got up and lumbered out to the hall and slammed it, returning to his seat and facing me. "Look, I'm sure you think me an awful poseur, spouting radical thoughts that I'll grow out of, but that's not really on the mark. I've felt this way since I was a kid. In fact I am in awe of what Julian Assange did in April. It's amazing. I hope they never find him." He grinned. "All those state secrets out in the open, the dirty tricks and lies, ninety-two thousand documents in July alone; I love it."

"It's hard to love the fact that many of those so-called secrets expose people who were covertly helping the United States and could get them killed. Do you believe in no government secrecy?" asked Alex.

"Well, sir, I wouldn't go that far. Of course governments have enemies, always have had, but I think the U.S. and other countries take secrecy and privacy invasion to a level of criminality. If you look at the fiction promulgated about so-called American *exceptionalism* and being a democracy for the people and so on, it's laughable. Civil rights are neither civil nor rights. And look at the torture at Guantanamo; same thing going on in Iraq with the U.S., Britain and others turning a blind eye to it. Thank you, Julian. We here aren't exempt; not at all."

"I can't completely disagree, Jeremy," Alex said. "I also think that the real perpetrators of the 2008 meltdown should be punished, not allowed to go back to the same old tricks, which they are doing post haste."

"You're right, and this is where the gap between the rich and poor comes in. I could go on about that for hours, but the parental yawns are devastating and hurt my tender feelings." He grinned. "Well, I guess I'll go have a bath and change. Got a dinner date."

"Oh, really," said Tina. "Who?"

"Irish girl, waitress at the local pub. Preggers with my kid." He laughed with a wink at me and left the room.

"Need I apologize?" said Tina, grimacing.

"Not on my account," I said. "I think he's a breath of fresh air."

David picked up his magazine and started reading. "Stop it, David, that's rude. We do have guests."

"Alex isn't a guest; he's a fixture."

"Oh, I give up," said Tina. "Anyway, if you two want a rest before dinner, you'd best get down to the lodge and settle in. Drinks at seven for dinner at eight. Mrs. Pitcairn is coming in to cook, so I know it will be good."

We started for the door, and David called after us, "If you see an old fellow wandering around, Elise, don't pay him any mind. Mildly useless really, a real talker, the farm manager so to speak, but we can't get him out of his house due to the odd laws — damned Rent Agriculture Act passed in the seventies. He takes care of the dogs when we're away and feeds and cares for the horses. Decent chap for the most part."

"Where does he live?" I asked.

David put down his magazine and pointed towards the French doors. "If you look out beyond the pool and courts, there's a hillside. There are a couple of old buildings up there and one bigger house. He lives in the house. Wife gone, kids scattered. He has a vegetable patch and raises his own livestock. Muddles through with a pension. We help out from time to time."

"His name?"

"Oh, his name. Yes, it's Caleb Hawkins."

Alex moved towards the door. "Come on, Elise, let's get on to the Lodge. I'd like a short nap before the excitement of the evening."

Tina smiled. "I don't think the Blakes merit the word *excitement*, Alex."

He put his arm around my shoulders as I joined him. "That's good. I have enough to tax me here," he said, looking down at me.

Tina and David looked at each other as if to confirm what they had been thinking. I followed Alex to the door.

Chapter Seventy-three

Calamity

The Blakes came as advertised, a couple in their mid-seventies. Laura Blake was a solid women tucked haphazardly into a tweed skirt, white blouse, and a Fair Isle cardigan at which she plucked as she talked. A cloud of white hair set off her plump pleasant face, pale blue eyes and a set of long teeth. Alistair Blake was thin, intense, and kept saying, "Do shut up, Laura, and let someone else speak."

Alistair's clothing looked as if it had been extracted from a moth-ridden trunk. There were holes in the elbows of his cardigan, and food stains down the front of his flannel shirt. I couldn't for the life of me figure out what they had in common with David and Tina.

The conversation hopped from local agriculture to mention of various scandalous events and opinions of the locals. Everything short of *the way it has always been done* ruffled Laura and elicited Alistair's tut-tuts. As the evening wore on, it became clear that part of the land on which the Lowthers' horses grazed belonged to the Blakes, and their good will meant not having to replace centuries-old hedgerows with new fencing. Not only that, but they were mixed up in all manner of committees and watchdog groups that affected other landowners. This, then, was their entree into neighborhood dining rooms, and it was my guess they made the most of it, for their appetites proved robust.

Jeremy had peeped in on his way out, seen the Blakes and made a hasty exit, waving and shouting, "I'm late. Sorry. Hello everyone and goodbye."

Mrs. Pitcairn lumbered back and forth through the swinging door from the kitchen with a meal of roast lamb, mint sauce, roasted potatoes and peas, the latter happily not the mushy kind widely featured in England. A flan followed for dessert, and while Tina was serving it, the phone rang.

A few moments later, Mrs. Pitcairn popped her head through the swinging door and called David. "Sorry, Mr. Lowther, but the gentleman on the phone says it is urgent."

David got up, and presently we heard him shouting from the other end of the front hall. Tina looked puzzled but carried on with conversation about a new road under consideration. Laura Blake, not surprisingly, had opinions on the issue, so it took a few moments for Alex to notice David frantically beckoning him from the hall. When he did, he rose and excused himself.

"Oh, my dear," said Laura, noticing the two men departing, "I do hope it's nothing serious." I suspected a crisis wouldn't entirely displease her.

Tina soldiered on, and after we were resettled with coffee in the sitting room, David came back in. "Laura and Alistair, I'm afraid I'm going to ask your indulgence. Something important has come up, and we need to deal with it immediately."

"Oh," said Alistair, looking at his wife. "I expect we ought to leave."

"Well, Alistair, I should think that was rather obvious," she sniffed, hefting herself off the sofa and heading for the hall closet. Alistair followed, and with coats finally donned and platitudes murmured, the door closed behind them.

"What the hell is going on?" shouted Tina. "That was rude, David. I know they're dismal, but really."

"Come back into the sitting room you two." He turned and shouted, "Alex, come on in here."

Tina and I looked expectantly at the men. Alex was ashen. David's face was red with anger. He cleared his throat.

"My solicitor," he said by way of explanation. "Seems the Chinese have filed a suit against my firm and Wilding about the patent we've offered them, the one on the product Alex developed at Wilding. You see, Wilding kept two patents on Alex's work and assigned this one to him when his research assignment was over instead of a share in their retirement program."

"How did this surface?" asked Tina.

"Announcement in a major Chinese medical journal. That in turn brought a couple of Russians down on their heads saying that research belonged to them. They said one of their former employees had done the research while working for them. The research disappeared when he went to a conference in 1995. They claim the scientist has not been seen since. All they have to show is a summary of the product, and they probably haven't been able to replicate the research but are pretending they have. The product is unique in its final form, unlike anything out there now, so the Russians could identify it from the Chinese description."

Alex looked at Tina and then me. "I'm completely baffled. It's awful, stupid. The patent I still hold is indeed the delivery system for the type of drugs that would be used if the Wilding tests are positive, which they appear to be. Worth a lot though, as it is also applicable to other sorts of drugs now under final approvals." He paused and put his head between his hands, leaning his elbows on his knees. "Holy shit, David. I'm so sorry. This is like, like . . ."

"Look, Alex," said David, "Stop. I'm not accusing you; Wilding possibly is. Stolen research is serious business. Apparently they've looked into it, and the summary is too close to what we are selling to the Chinese to be a coincidence. As we know, there's nothing else like it out there. The trick however is, since you were the main man, so to speak, on the research, to build a defense showing that yours is original research and tied in no way to what the Russians are claiming belonged to them. He looked up at the ceiling. "Think. We've got to think. Who else was familiar enough with every phase of the research to be able to reconstruct it?"

"Oh, God!" Alex burst out. "Only one person went the whole way through with those experiments. Only one."

"So who?"

"Sheila Bigelow."

I gasped and thought a moment. "Have you kept up with her since she went back to the States? I mean does she know you're working with that specific Chinese company?"

"Yes," he said softly. "Yes, she would know. I told her."

"Who the hell is Sheila Bigelow?" asked Tina.

"She was my research assistant. We worked for years together in Boston too."

And slept together for years as well, I thought. "Sheila Bigelow," I said. Alex glanced over at me and quickly away.

David, managing to keep cool, said, "Okay, that's one possibility. There must be others. First let me ask you this: would Sheila have any reason to betray you? Any rancor or motive to set you up?"

"Unlikely," said Alex in a whisper. "I mean she might have a reason to be angry with me, but it would be completely uncharacteristic of her to get involved in a scheme this monumentally awful. She'd have to have Russian contacts. There's no way."

"Do we want to get into this right now?" asked David.

"No, of course I don't," Alex said, glancing my way. "I'd have presented it in a slightly different light for Elise, but why the hell not do it now?"

Chapter Seventy-four

Sorting it Out

No one spoke for a few minutes. Alex walked towards the chest near the kitchen door and helped himself to a glass of whiskey. He stood with his back to us for a moment and then wheeled around and went to a chair near the fire.

"The beginning." He took a gulp of his drink, coughed, and continued. "I met Sheila years ago when she was working in research at Harvard. She and her husband live in Hopwood, where Anne and I used to. Elise knows that, and Tina, David knows that my marriage was less than ideal. Sheila became my research assistant when I was doing a little work on Alzheimer's. I had an affair with her."

David interrupted, leaning forward. "Is there a short version of this?"

Alex looked surprised. "Well, yes there is, but I was trying to give Tina background so you'd all understand where any urge for revenge might have originated."

"David, do be quiet and let Alex do this his own way," said Tina.

David sat back and tented his fingers under his chin.

"So, where was I?" continued Alex. "Oh, yes, Hopwood. Well, we saw a great deal of the Bigelows along with a group from the golf club."

David cleared his throat, impatience getting the best of him.

"Okay, so as I said, I started an affair with her. Later I broke it off, got bored I guess. She was not pleased, but as the years went by, she and Anne became friends, and everything flattened into the ordinary."

"Okay," said David. "At this point then, when you were asked by Wilding to come over and head up a team, you brought Sheila with you, again as a research assistant."

"Correct. Let me go on," said Alex. "So, she came over with Scott. That's her husband. They rented a flat not far from mine, and Sheila and I spent our days together in a purely professional capacity, and the three of us would go out to the theatre or dinner together. Scott is an architectural historian and was commissioned to do five articles, so after a while he went home for another gig and left Sheila here."

"And," filled in David, "that's where the trouble begins."

"Yes."

"I can guess the rest," said Tina. "So get to the part where she becomes angry at you. I mean after years, with a residual sting from being dropped, she gets you back. What's to be unhappy about?"

"You're making gross assumptions, Tina, if you don't mind my saying so. To go on, an argument started one night over dinner where she maintained that the success of our research could be partially credited to her, and thus she should get part of any future compensation. I finally agreed to pay her if I got anything, which in the end it looks like I should, that is if this whole thing hasn't put an end to our deal with the Chinese."

"What did you offer?" asked David. "I mean was it a flat sum or a percentage or what?"

"We didn't pin it down, but she was content with the concession and trusted me to do the honorable thing."

"She might be intelligent," said Tina, "but it's clear she has no head for business."

"She was in love," I said, quietly. "It makes one do stupid things." Everyone stared at me. I felt myself redden.

Alex rushed on. "This brings us to a point when I heard from Elise that her husband had died after years of her caring for him. He'd had his third and big stroke, and this woman whom I have loved ever since I set eyes on her was free. I knew I had to think clearly about the future, and the thing I wanted most on earth was to have Elise back. We had broken off in 1995 when Karl, her husband, had his first stroke."

He paused and looked at me, his eyes pleading. "Our contact since then has been intermittent but enough to keep up on events in our lives."

"But not this event," I said.

He looked at me again. "No, not this event. I called you when Karl died, but it was clear you were in no frame of mind to think about us in any but the most abstract terms."

He turned to Tina and said, "Elise had another book coming out and was caught up being with family, friends, grandchildren and a full and busy life. I didn't want to intrude and ruin whatever we might eventually salvage from the past. So it was a long while before I could lure her over here, but now here she is, and this is a hell of a welcome."

He turned back to me. "I'm sorry."

I looked at my hands.

David said. "Do go on, Alex. What made this Sheila so angry that we should consider her as a possible source for the leak?"

Alex took a sip and said, "I'm not saying any of this with certainty; it's only a thread of possibility." He looked agonized.

"Yes?" prodded David.

"She was, ah, pregnant. In her late forties and pregnant. She suggested she leave Scott and marry me. My world had possibly opened up, and the last thing I wanted was to be tied to Sheila for the rest of my life and miss any hope of being with Elise on whatever basis." He paused and looked at each of us in turn, and seeing our expressions, held up his hand. "No, no, it wasn't my baby; I never slept with her over here. Turns out she'd been having an affair with one of the junior executives at Wilding. Later she discovered he had a wife in Germany who in the end moved to London."

"Whole thing is appallingly messy," commented Tina, looking at the ceiling.

"Yes, I guess it is," said Alex.

"So, Dr. Creighton arranged an abortion?" asked Tina.

"Tina, let him tell it his own way," said David.

"Well, Tina's right. We went to Switzerland. Clinic there. She was distraught but could see the wisdom of it. She agreed." He looked around at the rest of us. "I said it wasn't mine," he repeated. "Her argument was we could marry and pretend it was. Misguided to say the least, and I certainly didn't want to play the good Samaritan."

"And she has carried a grudge ever since?" asked Tina.

"Yes, possibly. I don't know. She went home pretty soon after that, and I thought we'd cleared the emotional issues, but I got increasingly cross letters over time. I kept up with her, more out of irrational guilt than anything else. We've had the occasional phone call. She wanted to stay up on what I was doing with the remaining patent, because she has a financial interest in it." He sighed deeply. "So, there you have it."

There was silence. "Well," said David finally, "that's one idea. Any others?"

"No. Honestly no. No others."

"Okay, let's deal with the larger question mark. The original research." It was David's turn to look awkward. "I dislike asking you this, but tell me, was it yours?"

Alex appeared to be thinking for a few minutes and then stood up abruptly. "No."

David too stood up, glaring at Alex, and in a pinched voice, said, "Good God, man, what are you saying?"

So the whole story about the Russian scientist and the conference spilled out. Obviously, It had dawned on me where this was going and sitting there suspended in time, I waited in an icy haze. A clock in the hall ticked loudly into the silence that followed.

"David," started Alex, sitting down again. "Hold on. I have a document signed by the scientist releasing his research to me."

David let out a sigh. "Ah. You do? That helps." He thought a moment. "Was it witnessed? I mean if the fellow has disappeared, what good would that signature be if we can't verify it?"

"It was witnessed by two Americans at the conference, and we had it notarized in Switzerland. "I know I can find the witnesses again. One I know is at Berkley."

David resumed his seat and stared at a painting above the fireplace, his balled fist pressing on his mouth. Finally he said, "That helps, but what doesn't help is that you clearly didn't come clean with Wilding and let them vet it before you went ahead."

"It didn't occur to me. I had the release. The research was mine. It was a perfect way to get it out in the open. I did go to them and tell them that I had this pretty well down coming in, and they benefitted enormously from what I learned from that short project to go on with the additional work that they now own. If I could find Roald, I could help him get established in America, but as we know, he's gone — either into hiding or, well I don't want to consider the *or*."

"That gibes with the Russians' story as told to the Chinese," said David. "But they claim the research didn't belong to the scientist; that it belonged to the Russian company where he worked, and there's the rub. Of course they're all up to mischief these days, so we might have a hope of figuring it out. We'll have to meet with our Chinese friends and figure out what to do. Wilding too. Jesus, what a cock up!"

Tina stirred. "Look, let's all get a good night's sleep and leave it until tomorrow. No good babbling on tonight with nothing more to go on."

Our goodnights were uncomfortable but not unfriendly. We were tired and stunned, so presently Alex and I were winding our way along the gravel lane to the lodge in silence.

Chapter Seventy-five

Early Departure

Saturday morning late, Alex and I walked up to the house. We did not go to bed until three, and we shared a drowsy breakfast of Weetabix cereal and coffee left for us at the lodge. I was still reeling, one moment feeling abject fury and the next trying to be supportive.

When we met again, David took the high road about the confusion, keeping the rest of us calm and away from any sort of pondering or blame-laying. After a quick lunch of sandwiches and soup, Tina and I took a walk while David and Alex played tennis. We ambled through fields behind their house and into the woods, the Shih Tzus bouncing along in our wake. We had all decided to cut the weekend short, and Alex and I would be leaving late afternoon. The wind had gone out of our sails, and we wanted to be quiet to either lick or exacerbate wounds.

"It seems a bloody mess," said Tina as we came upon a clearing with a large flat rock in the middle. We sat down in the slanting afternoon sun, which bore a little heat. The dogs curled up at our feet, panting. Up until then we had merely compared notes on our lives, children, food, clothes, and finally books.

"Yes, it does," I answered.

"I mean I don't think for a minute that Alex did anything dishonest." She glanced at me. "You mustn't either. Once the lawyers get into it, it costs, and it gets tangled. Also there is the Sheila part. You can't like that for a minute can you?"

"Well," I said, "I wasn't around at the time, so how can I blame him for whatever he did? From his account, it wasn't much."

"But you do, don't you? Blame him the tiniest bit, I mean."

I smiled at her. I was beginning to like Tina more than a little. "Yes, I do. Sheila has always hovered in Alex's life. But back in ninety-five Alex and I were both married, and what happened then wouldn't win a prize for moral integrity, so I can't behave like a jealous wife."

"But you are."

At this I laughed outright. "Yes. Ouch. Not very cool of me is it?"

"Probably not, but natural I should think."

One of the dogs hopped up with a sharp bark and took off into the woods, and Tina went after her, calling, "Jaybird, Jaybird, get the hell back here."

I heard them thrashing about in the underbrush, and presently Tina returned with the dog under one arm, picking twigs off her coat with her free hand.

"We'd better get going. The men will be wanting tea, and we've got ourselves quite a distance from the house."

We convened over tea at around four and tucked into Mrs. Pitcairn's crumpets, freighted with clotted cream and strawberry preserves. While Tina and I had been walking home, Alex had gone back to the Lodge, taken a shower, and collected our luggage, so we were ready to leave.

I had ample time to think on the ride to London, as Alex was mired in thought, driving at an alarming speed and muttering threats to other drivers. He was however monosyllabic with me, so I was left to roll various aspects of the problem around in my brain like marbles. Nothing clear emerged. It did occur to me that Alex's reaction, if indeed there were murky aspects to any of this, was over the top as compared to David's measured response. The origins of such behavior could be rooted in the relationship with his stepfather, making him wary of failure in any form. When Enid, Mathew, and Penny were growing up, we encouraged them to test their abilities and choices — told them mistakes were a sign of trying. With Alex, it had been the reverse. Humiliation and punishment were his rewards.

We arrived at Albany around six and decided to eat at home, since there was still cold chicken in the refrigerator. Silently we unpacked and later convened in the sitting room for a drink. Alex had laid out Caerphilly cheese and crackers, and I gratefully took a glass of whisky from him.

We looked at each other over the expanse of geometric carpeting. "Hell of a thing," said Alex finally.

"Yes."

"I honestly don't believe that Sheila would ruin her own career to spite me. And," he paused, "in the final analysis, she's not the kind of person to hold a grudge for long. She isn't."

"I wouldn't know," I said.

He looked at me. "Well, then, Elise," he said coolly, "you'll have to take my word for it. She's normally a sunny sort of person, and whatever her moods, she bounces back rapidly."

"If you say so."

"I do."

We were silent for a while. Finally I said, "Alex, I've been thinking."

"Yes?"

"Well, this whole thing has affected us both, hasn't it?"

"Obviously."

I cleared my throat. "Then, with Fiona arriving in a few days, would it be better if I moved to a hotel? I mean with the three of us packed in here and this dark cloud hanging over us, wouldn't it be healthier?"

"No."

I looked at him, startled.

"No?"

"No."

"No explanation. Just no?"

"Elise, that's not a difficult word to understand." He got up and went to the window and then turned to me. "Frankly Elise, I think that's a particularly selfish thing for you to say. Two days ago you were prepared to spend the rest of your life with me, well, pretty sure. You had at least enough conviction to have Fiona stay here with us, and that in itself is a declaration, family-wise. And now, because I've hit a bad patch, you want to scurry away to the relative propriety of a hotel in case it turns out that I'm guilty of passing off research I didn't own for a profit. That way you can keep your distance from the stink?"

"No, Alex, I didn't mean that. Not at all. I do want Fiona to have a good time for the few days she's here, and I don't exactly think the atmosphere around here is conducive to that."

"Who's creating gloom except you with this infernal teetering?" He came over, looming in front of me. "Darling, if you got into trouble, would you expect me to grab a handkerchief and hold it over my nose while I back out the door?"

I looked at my hands. "No."

"Well then?"

"Well then, let's eat," I said. I stood up. He backed off a few steps, put his glass down and then held out his arms. We hugged each other tightly. "I'm sorry," I said. Alex leaned down and kissed me gently, patted me on the back and pushed me towards the kitchen.

Chapter Seventy-six

Equilibrium

We gave ourselves an emotional holiday, dodging demons and enjoying a lazy morning over the *Sunday Times*. Later I called Enid in Paris as she was rushing out with Evan. I told her that plans were still up in the air as far as my visit was concerned and that maybe Fiona would be with me and maybe not.

"Not a problem, Mum, give a day's warning. I know a lot is happening in your life. I've thought it over and am really excited for you. Be sure, though, before you jump for good."

"I will."

We went to a late afternoon piano concert and dinner afterwards at a tiny French bistro, where the owners knew Alex well and hovered, choosing our dinner for us. We walked home in the chilly October evening, holding hands and relaxing under the effects of music, food, and wine.

Fiona was due on Tuesday, so Alex had made plans for dinner on Wednesday by inviting Tina and David, their son Jeremy, another couple named Caroline and Richard Allford and their daughter Roberta. Richard was a good friend of David's, having gone to school with him at Eton.

"Do her good to meet a few young," Alex said. "Having started work in Spain, she might end up deciding not to go back to the States. She could do university here as easily."

"Penny would be heartbroken if she did that."

"Don't be silly. Penny and Christopher would probably be thrilled to have her here with us, or at least near enough if she needed anything. Kids should travel the world today. It's changing so fast that you don't want to raise a bunch of provincial, complacent Americans. As you know I managed to get David over for schooling here, and now he's going to be working in Singapore for the State Department."

"Alex, this could be construed as interfering with my family," I said, smiling at him.

"Ah, yes, it could, and I know how you'd hate having your favorite grandchild nearby."

"Of course that part would be lovely, but I don't want to intrude either. And she's not my favorite. I have no favorites." Alex smiled, then said, "Darling, enticement and interference are two different animals."

Coming from a man who danced perilously close to the dividing line, that was quite a statement, but I forbore making a comment.

When we got back to Albany, I announced that I was cold and tired and wanted a bath. The bathroom had been updated, and the tub was huge. I crawled in gratefully, sinking back into the hot water and closing my eyes. It had been a disorienting couple of days, so I allowed myself to drift. The door banged open and Alex leapt into the tub, water splashing over the sides.

I sat up. "Alex! What the blazes?"

He sank down under the water and came up dripping. "Should be obvious."

I laughed. "Okay, I see what you are doing. Now, what are your plans?"

He leered at me. "Well, first I intend to get clean, or as clean as I can with another body in here, and then I intend to dry you off and take you to my bed and have my way with you."

We were both shivering by the time we crawled under the duvet but soon warmed. Lovemaking for us had taken on a new sort of gentleness combined with a heightened urgency, as if we were in a race to beat off old age. We fell asleep twined around each other and deeply content.

By Monday we settled into an easier acceptance of the strange reality we had chosen and the uncertainty of the future until the mess with Wilding was addressed. Alex went early to the office, and I settled down to research notes and stayed submerged until well after noon. Hungry, I ventured out in a light rain and found a little pub where I ordered a ploughman's lunch and read *The Hare with the Amber Eyes*, which had lain forgotten the past few days. It was after two when I arrived home. I picked up a business magazine that Alex had been reading and curled up on the sofa with it and skimmed the U.S. News, moving on to a few articles on IPOs. Then I spotted an article on cyber-hacking.

I learned that in 2007, Angela Merkel had confronted the Chinese over hacking into her office and other German government ministries. It appeared that the use of military, economic, and corporate hacking with suspected Chinese and Russian roots was commonplace and getting worse, allowing scattered companies to avoid the cost of research and development altogether by simply buying appropriated patents. It wasn't a big leap to find a possible explanation for the Wilding leak. It remained for the company itself to establish that they had been hacked. I prayed that it would and fell promptly asleep on the sofa.

Around six, Alex came in holding a newspaper out to me. "Didn't take long," he announced. I took it from him and read the headlines: "Proprietary Secrets Stolen, Wilding Management Announces." It went on to explore any avenues by which this might have happened, including hacking, the last being "the possible breach of confidentiality by an as yet unidentified former employee."

He slumped down in a chair. "I called Sheila."

I looked at him, waiting. The silence went on.

"Well?" I finally asked.

He sat up and hooked his hands behind his head. "As I suspected. She didn't know a damned thing about it. Nothing. She was stunned."

"You know," I said, "I am actually glad to hear that."

He smiled, "Well that's damned generous of you."

"I mean it."

"Ah. Well, I have to commend you on resisting temptation. You've never asked me if I was telling the truth, what happened between Sheila and me."

"No."

"Why not?"

"I figure it's none of my concern. We were barely in contact at that point."

"But you're still curious, aren't you?"

Control is not normally my strong point, but under certain circumstances I can be steely.

"Not madly," I answered, flicking a wayward curl off my forehead.

"Can I interpret that for the lie it is? Don't fool with me, Elise, I know you'd like to know, and it's worth all your pride not to ask me. Right?"

I looked at the ceiling. "Alex, if you'd like to tell me, then feel free to do so. Otherwise, let's discuss how I get out to Gatwick to meet Fiona tomorrow."

Alex sighed. "Okay, but first. Enter the postman. He has a letter to the president of Wilding. The letter says the drug has been approved by the EMA, the European Medicines Agency, meaning it can be used throughout the European Union, plus Iceland, Liechtenstein, and Norway. Said president comes down to my office and tells me, and I let out a whoop of excitement. He leaves, and I rush in to tell Sheila and the others — including my secretary — who have been part of this years-long effort. We are elated and decide that going out for a drink immediately to celebrate is a must. We do that. We pack into a lift and empty onto the street and start walking."

"Speaking of drinks, Alex, I think I'm going to want one. Shall we pause here?"

With a half smile, Alex rose and did as I asked. When we were settled again, now both on the sofa with a dish of nuts between us, he continued.

"So one thing led to another, and soon we were going from pub to pub, dancing or sitting and talking, grabbing a bite of this here and that there. It got late, and I found a cab, intending to drop Sheila off at her flat and then go home. We were both clearly drunk at the time, needless to say, and we ended up in my flat too drunk to do anything but fool around ineffectually and go to sleep. She was seen leaving the next day by several neighbors, so if she wanted to make up a story later, she'd definitely have witnesses. The rest is history. As you know, she was pregnant at the time. Perfect ruse for cornering me had she wanted to pursue that angle."

A wave of relief crept over me. So, he hadn't had a long-standing relationship with her over here — nothing but a drunken night between two people who have known each other for years. It did ameliorate the heightened resentment I had been feeling.

"Oh my," I whispered.

"So, about Gatwick. I'm planning to be home at two in time to drive out there with you, so don't worry."

Chapter Seventy-seven

News

The mail from the previous day had lain on the hall table all night. Alex picked it up on his way in to breakfast on Tuesday. In it was a large envelope from Anne. There was a smaller manila envelope inside as well as a note from Anne on heavy ivory stationery with her monogram. While reading the note, he sipped his coffee at the tiny table in the kitchen where we often ate and then handed it to me.

Dear Alex,

I had to hear this from David. Never mind, you owe me nothing. I gather you and Elise have gotten together again after all these years. I am grateful I'm not there this time to witness your total absorption in that woman. She seemed so mild compared to your usual flings that I guess I should have seen this was different. Too bad I could never make you happy, but there it is.

I suppose I should be delighted for you. Rest assured I have been happy since I married Max. It's nice being loved for simply being me. Jimmy had his tenth birthday and is becoming a competent pianist.

I intended this to be a letter of congratulations to both of you. Believe it or not, I liked Elise a lot, and I flatter myself she liked me. That must have made things hard for her, but who knows?

The enclosed envelope turned up in the oddest way. An attorney called from New York and said that in winding up your stepfather's estate and getting the balance of your trust to you, he'd overlooked a few things in the file. He couldn't find out where you were but tracked me down through the Hopwood Post Office. Since your parents — step- and otherwise — are dead, he felt it was right that you should have everything he had. I wasn't sure exactly where you are living, since you moved, and I didn't know if the old box number worked — didn't want to risk having this lost, so got your new box number from David.

Anyway, best of luck to both of you. I guess we'll meet at Drew's wedding in April. So like him to stage it in an Irish castle. Have you looked up Castle Leslie on the Internet? Impressive place.

Best to you, Anne

"I guess she really wanted to be supportive but got sidetracked by the past," I said.

"She should have reread it before she sent it. A little editing might have helped," Alex retorted.

"She was angry about the divorce?"

"Yes, in the end she got nasty. Breaking down the old rules of Catholicism was hard for her, but she had become resigned to the futility of staying together. And of course Max was in the picture. Since there wasn't any money to fight about, that part went smoothly. She's loaded. Her father died, and as you know she was an only child."

"The few times she came over to Mother's to talk to me," I said, "she shared that she felt she had failed to keep your interest over the years. Was it love or pride that made her upset, I wonder."

"Probably a little of both. She was young when we married. I was taken with her looks and her streak of independence, which dried up as soon as she became pregnant. She went flat, and being pretty, having a stylish wardrobe, being a mother, and playing with her girlfriends was all she enjoyed. Of course she had feelings, and I wasn't the kindest of husbands, too ambitious and self-promoting."

"We were young," I said, "naively trusting when we married. I think we meant well, but time passes, we grow and become different people. That can mean we end up not really liking each other. But by then we are tied to routine, children, shared habits. Many marriages limp along on that until the end."

"Yes," said Alex. "And if one were to step away from the obligations of that union, one might find a genuine liking for the other person but no love left. That's a tough one. Love forgives. Liking doesn't. You can really like someone but not want to sleep with him or her, share a bathroom, that sort of thing. If forced to do so by contract, the whole thing shrivels, literally." He laughed.

"So a big wedding in Ireland? Tell me about Drew's fiancée."

"As I think I did tell you, he graduated from Hotchkiss, went to McGill, became a doctor, an ENT. He's as crazy as a bedbug. In his office, outside the room where they examine ears, he has a big plaster sculpture of an ear, a large nose for the nose room and an open mouth for the throat room. Funny guy. The fiancée? She's from Canada; he met her while doing his residency up there. She's an actress, TV mostly but determined to get to Broadway. They're hoping to live in New York. He'll have to find a practice there. She has remote Irish ancestry, the Leslie family, related to the Churchills. Castle Leslie is the old family homestead, so to speak, where they're being married. Big pile of a building if you look at the pictures."

"What fun. I'm looking forward to it. I'll have to continue smartening up my wardrobe. Will my family be invited?"

"Oh, yes, I'll see to it. We'll get everyone over. Rent a big place in Ireland for a few days. And by the way, the house I mentioned when you got here, well I've put a bid in on it."

"You what?"

"You'll love it. I'll take you and Fiona to see it tomorrow."

"Then you're not worried about the Wilding thing?"

"Not overly now. Of course I've done a lot of thinking. And David got a call yesterday from his solicitor, and their people are looking for a possible hack into Wilding's computer systems."

I positively grinned. "Alex, I was reading an article in one of your magazines yesterday about the Chinese, Russians and others hacking. You think that's what happened? What about the Russians having the summary report on the research that matches the end results?"

"We don't know yet. They could have as easily written that after they lifted the data from Wilding. Thank goodness the contract for the patent hasn't been signed yet. Anyway everything is on hold right now pending further digging by us and by the Chinese firm. It should all come out well, as I had no part in double-dealing and have the papers assigning the research to me. Should be fine, Elise."

"You didn't tell me."

"I couldn't. I promised to wait to hear from David, which I did while you were still in bed this morning. So . . ."

"Oh, Alex, this is encouraging news."

"So far promising, but we'll wait until we know. Okay?"

I couldn't help feeling that we might soon be free of the issue, and at the same time I was ashamed of my doubts concerning Alex. Had the past gossip, Arthur's antipathy, or Joan's comments as reflective of the town perspective worn at the edges of my attraction to Alex back then? Surely by now, years later, I should be able to trust my own instincts where he was concerned. He had been steady in his love for me, good to his children, and generous in every way I could imagine. I sighed loudly.

"So why the sigh?" asked Alex.

"Oh, nothing. Thinking ahead." I looked up, brightening. "Plans for Fiona? Shall we still try for a few days in Scotland? We've got a week after all."

"We could, maybe over the weekend. I want to see how things play out here. Tonight, let's have a quiet dinner here. Can you pick up chops this morning?" I nodded.

"Then tomorrow," he continued, "I'm taking you to see the house, and we have dinner with the Lowthers and Allfords. You could take Fiona to Selfridges or hit the boutiques on Oxford Street in the morning. Those are the hot spots for the young to buy clothes these days. Also, if you want really lovely things, try Browns on South Molton Street. Then I'll meet you at the Wolseley for lunch before we see the house." He rose, readying to leave.

"Alex," I said. "Don't you want to open the envelope from the lawyer?"

"Nearly forgot," he said lifting it off the table and ripping it open with a butter knife. I took it from him and studied it. There was a smaller envelope inside, and the address was to a woman in Chicago, written in a florid hand. The stamps were Italian. A different hand had written, *Not to be opened unless Alessandro requests it.* I handed everything to Alex.

There were a couple of photographs and two yellowed pieces of paper. Alex unfolded the latter and gasped. "Oh, my god," he stammered. "Oh, shit, shit, shit! Do you know what we've been put through, what your parents were put through? This is awful." He handed the paper to me and picked up the photographs.

I couldn't believe what I was seeing, a birth certificate, Alex's birth certificate, stating that baby Alessandro had been born to Maria and Carlo Michiel, March 27, 1948, in Venice. The second piece of paper was the earlier marriage certificate for the Michiels. So the girl had not gone back to her family after having an affair with my father, but had gotten married to another man. The pictures were of the mother and Alex as a newborn, standing in front of a tall man, presumably Alex's real father. Even barring wishful thinking, there was an uncanny resemblance between the attractive man and Alex, and his mother was beautiful. These must have been sent to the lawyer by the girl's relative at the time of the adoption and then tucked away.

Alex sat down with a thump. We were both silent, sipping coffee and thinking. I could not absorb the awfulness of our pitiful parting and the wasted years we had gone on denying ourselves what we most desired. My hand was shaking as I picked up the thin pieces of paper. We gazed at each other, and I idly wondered if Alex, looking into my eyes was seeing not me but what I saw gazing into his: scenes of our early loving, the humiliating final meeting in Washington, the intervening attempts to build relationships with others — fifteen emotionally hollow years.

Finally he said, "You know, it's hard to believe that my mother could have been a cruel woman, but what she did was awful. I imagine in her desperation, sick as she was, she saw this as a way out for me, using her relative in Chicago to help trick your father into thinking I was his child, his responsibility. My real father must have left her or died. And your father naturally found her story plausible. This fabrication was based on their earlier affair, so he would, wouldn't he?"

"My father was nothing if not honorable, a gentleman through and through," I said.

What it meant in terms of our own lives and those of my parents washed over us both. Finally, Alex said, "I can't fully absorb this right now. I need to leave." It was after ten when he slammed the front door and was gone.

In a daze, I tidied up the kitchen, put the letter, photographs and certificates in Alex's bureau drawer and dressed quickly. I wanted to get makings for dinner from Sainsbury's before he came back to pick me up to go to Gatwick Airport. I left the building, finding a glorious morning, the sky a clear cloudless blue, the air fresh with a soft breeze — England at its best.

It was punishing coming to terms with the missed years of our lives this way — alone, lonely for each other and *doing the right thing*. The waste was a vacuum that turned the past into a churning quagmire. I thought about Suzanne as I walked along, longing to share this turn of events with her soon.

She and Phillip had retired and divided their time between Mexico and Los Angeles. Suzanne continued to be involved in film, now as an agent for scriptwriters. Phillip in retirement was restless and traveled a lot, alternating between golf, hunting, and the occasional board meeting. I realized I had been avoiding the phone call that would surely involve listening to Suzanne's take on my actions, whether cynical or breezy, but now it was a different story, simpler on the surface of it. After Mother's death and the estate settlement, we had drifted apart again. There was little to hold us together temperamentally but the threads of family loyalty that would always guarantee unity in time of need.

Tina Lowther came rushing out of a shop loaded with parcels, and we nearly collided. "Oh, for pity's sake," she cried. "Fancy this. Where are you headed?"

"Glamorous errand to get food for tonight. My granddaughter is flying in from Spain."

"Ah yes, I knew that. We're to meet her tomorrow night."

"That's my understanding," I said.

She looked at me. "Well, the air seems to be clearing on the big horror, doesn't it?"

"So I gather. I hope it stays that way. It's puzzling, and it's impossible Alex could have anything to do with it. I guess you know he called Sheila, and she was astonished."

"So David said. Well, that's off the page then, if of course her word is reliable."

"I think it is," I said.

"Corporate hacking. So creepy, isn't it? I mean if that's what it is."

"It is creepy, but I guess that's the world as it's evolving, one planet full of big and little nations bumping uncomfortably against each other due to the Internet."

"Bound to get worse, I expect." She shook her head and then smiled. "But not today, so I'll get on. Have to meet my ancient mother-in-law for lunch at her flat, miserable old trout that she is."

"That bad?"

"A terror, a fearful snob, keeps firing anyone David hires to help her out." She blew an awkward kiss, hampered by a shopping bag dangling from her arm, and hailed a cab.

Chapter Seventy-eight

Fiona

From the moment Fiona joined us at the airport, it was obvious Alex had her completely charmed. "Your grandmother is stuffy," he said, "but I'll try to see you have a good time."

Fiona laughed. "Alex, Gran may be a lot of things, but stuffy she's not. I can see she's got her hands full putting up with you."

He stopped and swung around, walking backwards. "Me? Fiona! I am the soul of propriety, probity, and discretion."

Fiona giggled. "I'll leave you to your fantasies."

We collected her suitcase and headed into the parking garage. "Oh, damn," said Alex. "I forgot what floor we left the car on."

"Follow me," I said. "Bit senile," I whispered loudly to Fiona.

When she and I turned around, Alex was hobbling along like an old man, grabbing at anything upright to keep balance. Fiona laughed, and we ignored him and headed for the elevator.

While we were waiting for Alex to catch up, Fiona said to me, "Mummy briefed me on your scandalous situation, Gran. I think it's awesome."

"Thanks, darling, I'm very happy."

When we finally located the car, Fiona hopped in the back seat, and Alex put her suitcase in the trunk and came around to open the door for me.

"What's got you in such a good mood?" I asked.

"You'll understand," he said.

"Understand what?" I probed.

"Well, if you must know, I'm planning a wedding, and it's not Drew's. Now get in the car." I grinned at him, abruptly aware of the ramifications of this morning's shock.

That evening was full of chatter. Fiona was thrilled with the work she was doing in Spain and determined to make horticulture a lifetime career. "I've been looking around, trying to find good courses at home."

"Why go home?" asked Alex.

"Alex, slow down," I warned.

"No, Gran, let him speak." Turning to Alex, she said, "What did you have in mind?"

"Well," he started. His look of feigned innocence was comical. "I'm not sure, but I think the University of Edinburgh has a pretty fine program."

"Alex!" I again tried to stop him.

"He's been plotting, hasn't he?" asked Fiona, turning to me.

"It would appear so."

I overcooked the pork chops, so we were reduced to enjoying potatoes and fresh spinach. I'd bought a raspberry tart from Fortnum's for dessert, which was delicious. After dinner, Alex suggested a walk, so we donned overcoats and headed out into the night air. Fiona walked behind us, gazing around. "I've been here once before, when I was fourteen, with Mummy and Dad. It's really a wonderful city, isn't it?"

I looked back at her. She had grown into a lovely young woman, blonde, small, and delicately boned. Her hair was pulled back in a ponytail. After ambling along for a while, Alex headed into a pub.

"Time for a drink," he said.

Alex and I ordered brandies and coffee, and Fiona, after deliberating, ordered a hard cider. The place was full and noisy, so it was an effort to hear each other, but I could tell Fiona was absorbing it all, a little smile playing on her mouth.

"This is great," she shouted. "Thanks, Alex."

"For you, anything," he replied.

"I'll have to remember that when I need a car," she said.

Alex winced. "I can see I'll have to watch what I say."

It was a delight to watch the two of them joking, two of my favorite people on earth. I felt a surge of wellbeing.

When we got back to Albany, Fiona disappeared into her little room off the kitchen to unpack and make phone calls. We bade her goodnight, did the dishes, and went to bed ourselves.

"Was that a proposal back there?" I asked

"You could take it that way," he answered, leaning over and nibbling my ear.

Chapter Seventy-nine

Whirlwind

The next day, Fiona and I left the flat around ten and headed for Selfridges. I had sorted through her clothes and determined that at minimum, she needed something for dinner that night and for the theatre.

"You aren't camping here, darling," I said. "You'll need more than a T-shirt and a baggy sweater."

"Uh-oh," she said. "I didn't bring anything that will do. At work, we wear nothing but work clothes, and if we go out in the evening, it's casual stuff, like I packed."

"Well, we'll remedy the situation, and then we'll see tomorrow."

She was enchanted with everything she saw and finally settled on a Dick Smith dress on sale, and even at that, the price made me blanch.

"Alex said I could buy whatever I wanted," she said. "Did he mean this kind of extravagance?"

"I guess we'll have to take it home and see if he's as good as his word," I said.

Of course that led to new shoes, a small purse and a woolen coat. Laden with parcels, we hurried off to meet Alex for lunch at the Wolseley. Entering the restaurant, which was next to the Ritz. Fiona drew in her breath.

"Wow, Gran, Alex doesn't go in for shabby, does he?"

I looked around. The place was beyond elegant. The maître d' guided us to a table where we saw Alex chatting with Jeremy. They both stood up.

"Met this fellow out on the street, coming out of the Ritz. Asked him to have lunch with us," said Alex, gesturing at Jeremy. Fiona, Jeremy Lowther, and Jeremy, you've met Elise."

Jeremy sat down, and after we were settled, he leaned towards Fiona. "'Fraid you're going to get sick of me. We're supposed to have dinner together tonight as well."

Fiona was up to the task. "Rather depends on you, doesn't it? Are you interesting or dull?"

Jeremy threw his head back and let out a loud laugh. "Touché."

Alex ordered wine, and we spent the next few minutes discussing the impressive menu. Fiona had no doubt about the eggs Benedict. "Tiny breakfast," she said by way of explanation.

That done, Jeremy leaned back and addressing Alex said, "Doesn't take much to get the French excited, does it? I mean what a mess over Sarkozy proposing to raise the retirement age from sixty to sixty-two."

"What's happening?" I asked.

"Oh, well, people, millions of them, are swarming all over the place, blockading roads, closing schools, even violence."

"Is the effect going to be measurable?" asked Alex.

"I can't see how. But with world economies still reeling from the meltdown, things take on magnified importance. But I'm running on." He turned to Fiona. "Where do your interests lie?"

"Horticulture or agriculture, I'm not sure what part of any of it I want. I love beauty and cultivation of that beauty, and I also enjoy botany, earth stuff."

"Hmmm," said Jeremy leaning farther over the table towards her. "So we are talking about raising pretty gardens or erasing world hunger?"

"I don't know. Obviously I wouldn't be an example of my generation if world hunger and other social issues didn't concern me."

"Any thoughts as to what's actually causing world hunger?"

"Ideas, yes." She looked at me and then back at Jeremy. "Is this a quiz or are you patronizing me?"

Jeremy leaned back with another loud chuckle. Alex was observing and smiling. Fiona looked at me again. I wasn't sure whether to applaud or frown so did neither.

"Gran, I'm not trying to be rude. I do have ideas, but this isn't a fair discussion."

"Okay, okay," said Jeremy. "I see I've stepped over the line here. You're obviously not a brainless child."

Fiona was clearly getting irritated. "And if I were, would you satisfy your ego by trying to make a fool of me? That would be cruel, wouldn't it?"

Jeremy smiled in a pacifying way. "I apologize, again. My defense is that it's been a hell of a morning. I've been to a meeting with the most pompous executive I've ever met, in a suite at the Ritz that tops Versailles, and I suspect I was ready to fire back at the next person I met. In fact, Fiona, I'd really welcome the chance to talk at length about world hunger and influence you, if that's possible, in that direction." He looked at her. "Truce?"

"For the moment," said Fiona, holding up her hand as our waiter arrived with lunch. Everyone tucked in, and for a few moments there was silence. I looked at Fiona and then at Jeremy and found him also gazing at Fiona with a puzzled expression. I dearly hoped he wasn't beginning to think of her as a possible conquest, for Jeremy had totaled many such according to Alex. He was decidedly attractive, and I wondered what Fiona was thinking, if anything, as she concentrated her appetite on the Eggs Benedict. The age difference was large, but who was I to make judgments, having fallen for Karl at near the same age. I knew I was getting ahead of myself, but Fiona was an unusually bright child, and I wanted the best for her. That meant a few uncomplicated years to hone her skills.

In rapid succession, we sat back, replete with the good food. Alex looked at his watch. "Dessert anyone?"

"I couldn't," said Fiona. "That was yummy; thank you, Alex."

"Anyone else?" We demurred.

"Then, I think we need to get moving. I told the estate agent we'd meet him at two." Alex beckoned the waiter for the check and said to Jeremy, "We'll see you this evening."

Jeremy rose. "Definitely. Thanks for lunch, Alex." He turned to me. "Good to see you again, Elise." Then he looked at Fiona. "And as for you, my dear, I'm slinking off to my cave to sharpen my weapons and mend my ego."

Fiona laughed and started out of the restaurant ahead of the rest of us. Jeremy caught up with her, and I could see them chatting outside the door while Alex and I put on our coats and collected the morning's purchases. Alex looked at me. "Interesting, what?"

"Not," I replied. "He'd better leave her alone."

Alex chuckled and, taking my elbow, steered me out the door. By then Jeremy had gone, and Alex hailed a cab.

As we drove along, Fiona said to Alex, "I'm afraid Gran and I ran up an atrocious bill at Selfridges. You're going to roar like a lion when you see it."

"I told you to get what you want, didn't I?" answered Alex.

"You did, but there have to be limits."

"For now, none. Later when your grandmother impoverishes me, we'll see."

The house was splendid. Alex had his heart set on it. I had to admit to its charm, but it was broken up into a lot of rooms and floors for two people drifting into old age — or already there depending on the perspective. "This area definitely holds its value," said the estate agent.

Fiona loved it. "I think I'll move in permanently," she said. "Can I have the third floor?"

"On school vacations, and only if you actually go to school after this year," I said, still smarting from what I perceived as a budding distraction from the direction of Jeremy Lowther.

Fiona looked at me, puzzled. "Of course I will," she said.

Alex and the estate agent were on the basement level when Fiona and I went down. There was a study opening out onto a small back garden, and we went out through French doors.

"Alex, this is enchanting," I said.

"This, my darling, will be your bailiwick, the place where great works of literature originate. Look, an escape hatch where you can go to conjure and smoke."

"And do the laundry, I suspect," I answered, having spied a small room off the hall with a washer and dryer.

"Naturally," he said.

When we had inspected every cupboard and room, Alex sent Fiona and me home while he and the agent took a cab back to the agent's office.

"Gran, this is so, so exciting," said Fiona as we entered the flat. "Fancy you landing here in London. Aren't you happy?"

"Yes, I am, but I'm also confused. It's happened with the speed of a rocket, and I don't know what to do with the house in Baltimore and anything else for that matter."

Fiona gave me a hug and said, "I think you'll figure it out, Gran. You always do. Remember, you're the practical one in the family."

"I think I'm in the process of dispelling that notion," I said.

We went to our respective rooms to read and have a nap. Alex must have come in later, but I never heard him. I emerged groggy and disoriented. Alex and Fiona were in the sitting room peering down with intense concentration at a chessboard. Alex looked up.

"Well hello, Miss Sleepyhead."

"I do feel as though I've napped through the entire night. I went into a coma. We've got to get ready for dinner, and oh, I had wanted to call Suzanne today, but there's no time now."

I looked at Fiona. "Did you show Alex the dress?"

"I did. He loves it. I'll go put it on." And she got up and left the room, throwing, "I'll win this round later, Alex," over her shoulder.

After we were dressed, we met in the hall. Fiona had twisted and piled her blonde hair on her head, and the dress with its purple, blue, and yellow blocks of color suited her well.

"Wow," breathed Alex at the effect the beautiful clothes and makeup had rendered.

"You don't look half bad yourself," Fiona remarked, looking us both over. "Gran, you're radiant, and that dress is gorgeous." Alex was dressed in a grey pinstriped suit and sporting a Liberty tie with yellow and red flowers.

So, feeling chic, we left for dinner with the Lowthers and the Allfords.

Chapter Eighty

Roberta Allford

We were the last to arrive at the restaurant. Our large round table was in a niche in the back room. Introductions went around. Richard and Caroline Allford were opposites, she small and dark, he huge by any standards, and what hair he had left was faded blond. Their daughter, Roberta, took after her mother in build but had blond hair bobbed short. She was china-doll pretty with large pale blue eyes. It became apparent after a short time that she and Jeremy had more or less grown up together, their fathers being close friends from schooldays. Her proprietary attitude towards him was assertive once she had seen and met Fiona.

Jeremy stood as we arrived and remained standing while introductions went on. He looked at Fiona with undisguised admiration, but muted his reaction with a continuation of their earlier sparring. "Love the dress, Fiona, colors of a large bruise — becoming."

Glancing at him in surprise and then noting his tie, a wild swirl of reds and greens, she shot back, "Why Jeremy, you've already spilled on your tie."

Everyone laughed in relief, as there had been a momentary silence after Jeremy's ostensibly rude remark.

Roberta, who was sitting on Jeremy's right, laid her hand on his arm and looked at Fiona. "Fiona, you mustn't mind a word he says. He's a tease," and she glanced up at him, smiling. He continued to look at Fiona, who settled herself next to Alex. A place had been left for me between David Lowther and Richard Allford.

With drinks ordered for the three of us, conversation picked up. Caroline Allford, it appeared, was also a writer, children's books that enjoyed great success in England. "The first one is coming out in America in March," she told me. "It's a series about a dragon and an avatar, great heroics, that sort of thing."

"How long have you been writing these?" I asked

"Started ten years ago, but it took five to get anything published. By then I had four of the series done, so when the first one caught on, the rest followed rapidly."

"Bloody children's books nowadays," boomed Richard, "have to have dragons, vampires, or wizards. My day we were satisfied with the antics of Winnie the Pooh and Eeyore."

"I think that's the last book Richard ever read outside of his studies and dental journals," said Caroline.

Richard glanced at her and then burst out laughing. "She's right of course. Always is."

Alex and Fiona were in deep conversation. I caught snatches mentioning studying in Scotland and what the work she was doing in Spain was like. Jeremy and Roberta were chatting animatedly, and the Allfords started telling Tina about a recent trip to St. Petersburg.

David turned to me and in a low voice said, "I guess Alex has caught you up on the latest."

"Well, I think so. He said Wilding was investigating to see if its computers had been hacked."

"You know he called Sheila?"

"Oh, yes I know that. And," I added, "I believe her."

"Oh good." He took a sip of his wine. "Well, before leaving the office . . ." He paused and looked down at his casual clothes. "I didn't have time to change, sorry."

"Don't apologize to me. Alex has had to lead me around by the nose to spruce up my wardrobe," I laughed. "Didn't want to be seen with me looking a prison matron."

"Quite certain you could never have pulled that off," said David gallantly. "Anyway, where was I?"

"You were leaving the office."

"Right. Tell Alex if I don't have a chance to tonight. My solicitor called and said that Wilding has had ITs crawling over their computer systems, and it's apparent that there have been breaches. They're tracing them. How? Don't ask me; I'm a Luddite."

"That's the best news possible. Alex has been keeping a cheerful demeanor, but I can tell he's worried, distracted."

"That part is indeed good news. The money we'll probably lose if we have to back out of the whole deal is not. And if cleared, we'll have to start the process of peddling the patent elsewhere."

"Still, from my point of view, it lets Alex off the hook and clears his name with Wilding. That's big," I said.

David smiled at me and patted my hand, which had been twisting my napkin. "I know. Can't have been easy on you, newly arrived here and throwing your lot in with him in a short span of time."

"No, not easy," I said.

"Funny about that, you know. Alex and I are pretty close, and yet he seldom mentioned you. He had a few girlfriends. I guess you'd expect that.

Tina and I wondered why none of them lasted long. The minute they got marginally serious, he'd drop them. Developed a bit of a reputation that way. Don't go out with Alex Creighton if you want anything permanent — stuff like that. The only one that stuck is a woman I suspect he never had any romantic attachment to, Lady Bromley."

"Oh, who is she?"

"Odd duck really, mannish sort, a poet as well as a playwright."

"Really?"

"I swear. I've seen them together. They chatter like two little birds."

"Seems like an unlikely focus for Alex's attention," I laughed. "Does she live in London?"

"She's here from time to time; stays with her sister who is actually a good friend of ours. That's how we met her. But, most of the time she's in Cornwall near where Alex has his cottage. Tina and I've never been there, and I don't think Alex uses it more than a couple of times a year."

"How old is Lady Bromley?"

"Hard to tell, but definitely old. Steel gray cropped hair, wire-rimmed glasses, full of energy," said David.

"Well, I'll have to ask him."

"Do. Be interesting to see what their relationship amounts to. Tina has been pining to know."

"Why didn't she ask?"

"I don't know; didn't want to pry I guess, start gossip, that sort of thing."

"Really? Sounds unlikely material for gossip when you must have real scandal to discuss from time to time."

"Of course," said David, "if a man comes home and finds his wife *in flagrante delicto*, then of course there's an uproar. We love gossip, so it gets chewed up along with the Stilton and biscuits at cocktail time."

"So how do the more clandestine affairs get handled here?"

"Well," said David, "mind you it's only what I've heard, that in America, if a man (well, most men) has an affair, he would eventually agonize over it and ease his conscience by telling the wife and asking her forgiveness. What good does that do? It sows suspicion and discontent, nothing more."

"I admit I have heard such from my friends."

"Do women do the same?"

"Less likely," I said, smiling at him. "We all have unwritten rules, and breaking those always causes ripples."

"As for unwritten rules, I have three, borrowed from Marella Agnelli, a story I heard: 'sogni, salute, soldi'.

"And that means?"

"Forbidden topics of conversation: dreams, health, and money."

Dinner arrived, and I turned my attention to Richard Allford when the bustle had settled down. He was studying the label on a bottle of wine that had arrived. "Your treat or are you counting on me, Alex? Rather a fine specimen."

"My treat," said Alex.

"Well, thanks," said Richard as he took a sip. "Ah, ambrosia." He looked at me.

"So, you're a new arrival on the scene? Alex an old love or a new one?"

"Old," I said. "He's over sixty."

"Clever. The lady betrays nothing."

"What do you want to know about me?"

"Candidly, I want to know what you earned from that film they made of your book."

"That was years ago, and the short answer is: not much. It did pretty well, but it wasn't a box-office smash."

The evening capered along, and after dessert and coffee, Jeremy stood up. "Come along, ladies, it's time to let London get a glimpse of really beautiful people."

Fiona and Roberta stood up and said polite *good nights.*

"Wait," called Alex. "Fiona, come back here." He was wiggling a key off his key ring. "Take this, and don't wake us when you come in, please. I imagine it won't be for a while."

Fiona dropped the key in her purse, and grinned at him and ran after the other two.

"Ah," whispered Richard in my ear, "we are living in perfect familial harmony, are we?"

He was beginning to irritate me. "We? I hadn't noticed your part in our domestic group. Have you been hiding under the doormat?"

"Ouch, sorry. Didn't mean to be rude."

"Good," I replied, and then we were all ready to leave. We said our goodnights on the sidewalk, and Alex hailed a cab.

Chapter Eighty-one

Jeremy

I heard Fiona tiptoe in around one thirty. I was restless until I heard the door close and then turned over in bed and went to sleep, knowing she was safe.

By the time I woke in the morning, Alex was dressed and in the kitchen, drinking a cup of coffee and stirring eggs on the stove. I wandered in, tying the sash of my bathrobe.

"Any sign of Fiona?"

He looked up, "None. I imagine they did significant carousing last night. Jeremy certainly showed signs of a young man wanting to impress."

"He did, didn't he? It worries me. He's visibly practiced in the art of being electrifying."

"We've been over this already, Elise." He went back to stirring the eggs and then removed the pan from the stove and dished them onto two plates. "Toast is on the table. Sit."

I did. He poured my coffee and sat down. "I think Fiona is able to take care of herself," he said.

"Maybe, but she is young. Eighteen. No matter how wise she is, it's early days for her to get involved."

"Elise. How old were you when you married Karl?"

"That's different. And anyway, I don't want her to marry now. She has to finish her education."

Alex smiled at me. "Where can your mind be this morning? She's been out once with Jeremy, and let's not forget that Roberta was along as well. Hardly a foundation for marriage."

I laughed. "Of course you're right. I'm being an old broody hen. I love her and want the best for her."

"Your mother wanted the best for you too," he said.

Fiona appeared in the doorway. "Good morning. Is there enough coffee for me?"

Alex got up and filled a cup. Handing it to her, he asked, "Anything else? Eggs? Toast?"

"Maybe toast," said Fiona, taking a slice from the plate on the table and pulling out the third chair. "Mmmm, good coffee."

"How was last night?" I asked.

"Great. We went to a nightclub, wandered. They're nice, both of them. I think Roberta is sweet on Jeremy, but he treats her like a kid sister."

I switched topics. "Anything special you'd like to do today? We're going to the theatre tomorrow night to see *Flashdance*."

"Oh, wonderful! I've heard good things about it." She took a sip of coffee. "Today? Well, Jeremy said he'd meet me for lunch and take the afternoon off to go to the Tate Modern and maybe The British Museum if there's time. He also mentioned dinner."

I looked at Alex. "Is Roberta part of the plan?" he asked Fiona.

"Don't think so. She said she is going to Kent. She's a manufacturer's rep for a line of children's clothes. Nice job; she gets to go all over the place."

"Fiona," I started.

Alex interrupted. "Sounds as though you have a full day planned. I have to go to the office, and I know your Gran wants to write, so we'll leave you to your own resources. Let us know if there's anything you need or want to do. You have your mobile phone, and," he added, pulling a card case from his pocket and handing her a card, "here's my office number." Alex got up. "You still have my key to the set, I expect. I've got an extra, so keep it."

"What do you two think of heading for Scotland on Saturday?" I asked. "That was the original plan. We could drive up and come back Monday. At least see Edinburgh."

"Gotta go," said Alex. "We'll talk about it later." He kissed me, gave Fiona a pat on the head, and headed for the hall only to return a second later.

"Forgot to tell you, David called and wants us for dinner tonight. A fellow from the States has arrived with his wife. He's head of a medical instruments company in New Jersey. They've been landed with entertaining them, so . . ."

"I'm supposed to have dinner with Jeremy," said Fiona with the edge of whine in her voice.

"No problem, Tina's made him promise to join us, so there's your dinner," said Alex and headed out again.

Fiona made a face at me. "Doesn't sound much like fun, does it?"

"I don't know," I said. "We've got to help them out, and who knows, the visitors might be agreeable after all." I gazed at her. "You're getting fond of him aren't you?"

She flushed. "Well, he's nice. And entertaining. So, yes, I like him."

"Okay, my darling, do take it slowly. Jeremy appears to have been around."

"Well, I like that about him. The boys at home are, well, boys. Jeremy acts grown up, is interested in more than sports, beer and boasting. He's really keen on environmental issues — making the world a better place."

"All good," I said. "I'm merely saying take it slowly."

She took a deep breath and then nibbled on a crust of toast. "I got it, Gran!" Rising, she added, "I'll go get dressed."

She appeared an hour later looking neatly tailored with one of my scarves around her neck. "Hope you don't mind, I saw it lying on your dresser."

"You minx. No, it's fine. Are you leaving now? It's early for lunch."

"I want to wander around, look at things. Then I'll meet Jeremy." She leaned over to where I had settled by the window with my computer and said, "So, cheerio, as they say."

"Cheerio my love. Have a good time." I sighed as I heard the door slam and went to call Suzanne.

"Hello there, stranger," she said. "You in England or Scotland or wherever you said you were headed?"

"London right now," I said.

"Fiona coming over?"

"She's already here."

"Fun."

"I'm at Albany with Alex."

Silence, and then, "Are you out of your mind?"

"Yes," I answered.

"Well, well. Aren't you well past it for cavorting around?"

"That's clearly insulting, and I don't know what you mean."

"I mean that was fun years ago, but he wasn't ever a person you'd want to go on with forever, especially after . . ."

"That's what I want to tell you if you can be civil." I related the news about Alex's parentage, and Suzanne let out a loud whistle.

"My God, Elise, that's horrible — I mean what that woman did to Dad." She paused a moment and than said, "For you I guess it's good news. So, are you planning to marry the man?"

"Possibly. Suzanne." I said, "You're last one who knows anything about the past. Can you keep it that way?"

Of course." I could hear her yawn. "Look, Elise, I'm going to hang up now. Process this as the young say, and I'll call you back later. Okay?"

We hung up, and I sat for a minute. I hadn't realized that this would affect Suzanne except in her usual offhand acceptance of the vagaries of life. My children were happy for me, but of course they knew nothing of Alex's and my past.

It was an hour before the phone rang. "Okay, sweetie," said Suzanne. "All processed." She cleared her throat. "I want to say that if this is what you and Alex want, then I'm happy for you."

"You mean it?"

"I do. It was a shock, but after what you've been through, anything that gives you pleasure is good enough for me. Alex and I might even learn to tolerate each other."

"Will you visit?"

"You couldn't keep me away!"

So we chatted for another fifteen minutes or so. I hung up feeling relief and actually looking forward to having Suzanne come over.

Chapter Eighty-two

Dinner with the Bachmans

We arrived at Tina and David's flat at seven thirty. It was small compared to their Sussex house, a narrow living room decorated in light-colored silks and heavy cottons. A large portrait of Tina with two Shih Tzus in her lap hung over the mantle, and the gas fire burned brightly.

David ushered us in from the hallway. "Elise, Alex, Fiona, this is Carla and Tom Bachman. They're here from New Jersey on business mixed with pleasure I gather."

"Oh, more pleasure than business I hope," said Carla. She was an indistinct shape under a green-and-white-striped jacket widening to black trousers and shoes that could only be called serviceable.

Tom was tall, bald and ample as well, sporting a rust-colored tweed jacket with leather patches on the elbows. His repp tie was green and purple, a gaffe the English, who cherish their stripes as proof of regimental, school, club or other membership, frown upon as ignorant and similar to Americans sporting Scottish clan tartans.

We all shook hands and exchanged banalities, and the evening promised its share of tedium. Jeremy was not there, and I caught Fiona looking at the doorway expectantly. Tina did not miss it either.

"Jeremy called. A client. He'll be here late," she said. Fiona smiled. Tina arched an eyebrow and glanced over at me. I smiled back.

In the time it took for David to pour drinks and see us comfortable, I studied the Bachmans. They were perfectly at ease. Carla was helping herself to a bowl of olives, chewing energetically and dropping the pits in a little dish. Tom sat expectantly in his chair with a half smile.

"So," said Alex, "Have you been enjoying the sights in London?"

Carla pitched herself forward on the sofa and addressed him. "Indeed we have. I have a terrific guidebook. We travel a lot, you know, so I read up on everything beforehand. That way I can brief Tom on what he's seeing. I mean he's so busy."

Alex beamed at her, "No surprises if you do that." With dread, I noticed his concerned expression.

"I do hate surprises," she agreed. "So time consuming. You should make the most of limited time in any place," and she laughed, a faint stuttering sound. "I admire efficiency enormously," she added and then turned to me. "So where are you from, Elise?"

"I grew up in Massachusetts, and . . ."

"Where in Massachusetts?"

"Hopwood on the South Shore."

"Where did you go to school?"

"Why, Derby Academy and then I . . ."

"Never heard of it. I'm from New Haven, Connecticut. Tom went to Yale. That's where we met. Love at first sight."

"How nice," I said.

I glanced at Tina whose eyes were merry as they peeped out from the top of the hand she had over her mouth. David was impassive, and Alex was watching me for a reaction, which with effort I withheld.

Not missing a beat, Carla turned to Alex, "And you, Alex, where from?"

"My mother was an Italian immigrant," he said. Carla stared at him. Tina turned her head away and coughed, unable to contain herself any longer.

"Oh," said Carla taking a sip of her wine and recovering her composure. "So then, what do you do?"

"When?" asked Alex, leaning slightly forward and flashing his most charming smile.

Fiona was looking from one of us to the other, her face pensive. David was picking at dog hairs on the arm of his chair and holding them up to the light for inspection. Tom was still perched on his chair with the same fixed and pleasant look on his face.

Sensing her lack of progress, Carla waved her hand in the air and asked, "So how do you know each other?"

David flicked the dog hair on the carpet and said, "Rather well." He turned to Tom.

"Interesting business you're in, Tom; I mean making specialized laser instruments. Tell us about it."

As Tom was explaining the intricacies of his business, giving us a respite from Carla, the door in the vestibule slammed and Jeremy came in.

"Hello, everyone," and Jeremy headed for the bar, passing Fiona on the way, leaning over to give her a kiss on the cheek. She looked up at him, over at me and then at the floor. "Late meeting, sorry." He looked around for a chair.

"Darling, get one from the dining room," said Tina.

He went out and dragged a chair over beside me. "Looking glam, Elise," he said.

"Thanks, you don't know how dowdy I can look."

"Don't believe it," and he looked over at Carla. "Hello, I'm Jeremy, the wayward son of the house."

"I'm Carla," she beamed at him, then waved her hand in Tom's direction. "And this here's my better half, Tom."

Amen, I thought.

"So what kind of client kept you, Jeremy?" asked Carla. "What do you do? Are you in business or finance?"

"As to the kind of client," said Jeremy, "he represents money, lots of it. Thus I spend all the time he wants."

"What kind of money, I mean, what do you do for a living?"

"Actually, Carla, I'm in investment banking."

"Oh," she said for the second time that evening. "Tom here makes laser instruments for the medical industry. His company has won international awards. We travel a lot. We were in Japan last month, eating with chopsticks you know. We also have places in Connecticut, Sun Valley and Nassau. So you can see that we're busy. I have three daughters. They're all married."

"How nice," said Jeremy, nodding to Tom and then turning to David. "Dad, did you happen to see my mobile? Last time I had it was when I stopped by your office."

"Don't think so," said David, "but I'll look tomorrow."

"You had it last night," said Fiona.

Carla swung around to look at her. "You two know evidently know each other. How sweet. Where did you meet?"

"Picked her up at a pub." Jeremy looked at Fiona. "Around midnight last night, wasn't it?"

Fiona grinned. "Eleven-thirty I think."

Carla said "Oh," again and then had a thought. "Well, yes, that is a coincidence; I mean here you are, and your families are friends, and you must not have known that. Nice."

Jeremy grinned at her and then winked at Fiona. "Nice indeed."

And so it went, on through dinner, except for a few interesting discussions Tom initiated concerning his business. Carla kept mercifully silent, concentrating on her dinner with voracious pleasure. Tina had seated Jeremy and Fiona together, so there was an undertone of their intermittent and whispered remarks, culminating in Jeremy bursting out laughing and then looking around at the instantly silent group and apologizing for the interruption.

"You two are behaving like toddlers," admonished Tina, which rebuke had little effect on either of them.

Chapter Eighty-three

Paris

Friday morning at breakfast the three of us rehashed the previous evening, mildly reproaching ourselves for mimicking Carla. Alex then said, "I've got a better idea than Scotland. You two were going to Paris to see Enid. Due to her delay in getting here, time is running short for Fiona, and we've got the theatre tonight, so why not fly out tomorrow and spend a few days in France. Fiona can go back from there. I don't have to be here until Wednesday afternoon."

"But Jeremy said . . ." interrupted Fiona.

"Tell him to come along," said Alex.

I glared at him. He glared back.

"Well, I could. Do you think he'd find that . . ."

"Either he would or he wouldn't," said Alex. "Either way you'll know what he's thinking."

"I have to be in Spain for work Wednesday morning, so it'd work. Gran, you can call Enid and find out," said Fiona. She pulled her phone out of her bathrobe pocket and rushed out of the room to call Jeremy.

"I'll fix it," said Alex as he rose from the table and went to find his briefcase. "Meanwhile I have a meeting with the Wilding people and their attorneys to discuss what they've found out. David and I don't want to have to sever the relationship with the Chinese, but depending on what happens today, we may have to. I have a feeling they were as much in the dark as we were, but who knows?"

"Alex, if the Wilding patents were hijacked as well, is there anything legal they can do to get the rights back or can the Russians go forward with production?" I asked.

"Don't know; it'll be a chore to untangle. I'll call you later if there's any news; otherwise I'll see you this evening. We'll eat after the theatre, so get a hearty tea."

A little more that twenty-four hours later, following a thoroughly enjoyable evening seeing *Flashdance*, we were on our way to Paris. Alex had nothing to report except that the experts Wilding had hired to look into the potential hacking of their computers had concluded that not only had a good deal of research material been stolen but also their financial information. The hackers were based in Russia, where several rings had recently been uncovered, people who stole drug information and sold it to other countries as original research. As to the effort to keep Alex's rights to the one patent he had, it looked good, since contracts had not been finalized, and he had the documents from Switzerland giving him the sole rights. Future legal snarls aside, he at least felt exonerated.

Enid was thrilled at the prospect of our arrival and said there was plenty of room at their flat for the three of us with Fiona sleeping on a rollaway cot in the living room, so Alex cancelled the hotel reservations. Fiona did ask Jeremy if he wanted to come, but he said he had shooting plans that weekend with friends in Scotland, plans made long ago, and begged off. She was disappointed but making the best of a jaunt to France. He had promised to try to get off work and fly over on the Monday, so perhaps she'd see him again before returning to Spain.

We travelled by train to Paris, a trip of over two hours, and Enid and Evan were both waiting for us when we arrived at their flat, a huge marble-floored area that overlooked a small garden with a few benches. Area in the flat was apportioned by the type of furniture. Sofa and chairs, dining table, drawing table, lateral files, and a desk were scattered, and in the central area there was a kitchen. To the rear of the room was a parquet-floored hall with two bedrooms and two baths opening off it. The whole was light with shutters at the windows and a few Moroccan rugs near the sofa.

"Oh, Mum, it's been ages," said Enid as she flung herself into my arms. Both she and Evan were dressed in jeans and heavy sweaters, and drawings littered the floor around the drawing board.

"What are you up to?" I asked, pointing to the large sheets of paper.

"Oh, Evan was showing me the sketches for his new series, sea turtles. Come look."

We moved across the room, and indeed the drawings bore a resemblance to sea turtles, although abstracted into great mounds and whorls.

"No more mothers and children?" I asked.

Evan shook his head. "You'll see why. Worked my way through the various manifestations and called it quits. On to the real thing." I looked questioningly at Enid. She took my hand and led me to the sofa.

"And now my dear mother, we have news for you." I looked at Evan. He was beaming. He pointed at Enid's left hand where I noticed a large emerald. My hands flew to my face. Alex was sitting on my other side, and Fiona was on the floor looking up at Enid.

"Oh, Enid," I cried. "Not really."

"Yes really," said Enid, "and today. I mean we were off to have a quiet ceremony anyway, and then you called, so we decided to surprise you and wait until afternoon."

Tears were spilling down my cheeks. "Oh, dear, I'm being a sentimental old fool. Why after all these years? I mean, I thought it wasn't going to happen, ever."

Alex took my hand while I blubbered away.

"Okay," said Evan. "Hold on to your hat." I looked up at him standing with the light from the window making his face a blur. "Enid is pregnant. We are pregnant."

Fiona stood up. "Yipee, this is the best." She looked over at Enid. "How old are you, Aunt Enid?"

Enid laughed. "Very old indeed, my dear. Forty-four."

"You'll be okay, won't you?" asked Fiona.

"She's strong as a rhinoceros," said Evan.

Enid looked at me. "Flattering comparison. Evan has this way about him; irresistible."

Unfazed, Evan continued, "The doctor says she should have no problems. So, after lunch today, we go off to the registry office where a few of our friends will meet us, and Elise, you and Fiona can be bridesmaids, well Matron of Honor and bridesmaid, and Alex can be my groomsman along with my best friend, Jean, if that's okay."

"I'd be honored," said Alex, "but haven't you got pals you'd rather have?"

Evan looked at him. "Well, old man, rumor has it that you have stolen my soon-to-be mother-in-law's heart, so we thought as a virtual part of this family, we'd make the wedding your initiation. Too late now, it's settled."

"Are we dressing up?" asked Fiona. "I have smart new clothes Alex bought for me."

"Oh, do wear them," said Enid smiling at her. "All the pictures Penny has sent me over the years have you in torn jeans and a man's hat. It'll be a lovely change."

Fiona scowled. "Well, I can look civilized from time to time."

"You certainly have recently," Alex teased. Fiona fixed a scowl on him.

"What's this?" asked Enid.

"Oh, nothing," answered Fiona.

"Jeremy is nothing?" pursued Alex.

Enid raised an eyebrow. "Jeremy?"

"Well, he's sort of a new friend," said Fiona shyly.

"I see," said Enid. "Okay now, group — Alex and Gran, you're in the bedroom to the left down the hall. Fiona, I guess you'll have to park your things in here. Both bedrooms have a bath, and there's a powder room by the front door over there you can use, Fiona. If you want a shower, you can use

Evan's and mine. Now, I'll get us lunch."

Before four that afternoon, we assembled by the elevator, having put ourselves together as best we could for the wedding. We walked to the local town hall and met Enid and Evan's friends, eight of them, who were already there. Evan introduced us. There were a couple of lawyers from Enid's firm, and the rest were artists of one sort or another. Evan's friend, Jean, told me they had planned a surprise reception at a restaurant nearby.

The ceremony was simple with predetermined language, so there was nothing personal. Afterwards, Enid and Evan had to sign simple documents that would be filed with the county registrar. As witnesses we signed paperwork as well. Then Jean announced that Enid and Evan were to follow him, and we walked four blocks to a restaurant where the proprietor met us at the door and led us to a private room at the back. There the group had arranged for a violinist and a beautiful wedding cake with sea turtles delicately marching around on the frosting.

"Mon Dieu!" shouted Evan. "This is amazing. You people; how did you pull this off without our knowing? I mean we changed the time until Elise could get here, so how?"

"Ah," said Jean, "we are magicians, no?"

Dom Perignon champagne was poured, and one by one we made toasts to the bride and groom. A beautiful dinner followed with a filet of beef, green beans, and roasted potatoes. Then Evan and Enid cut the cake, a sponge with marzipan filling and fondant icing.

When it was over, we decided that it would be in our best interests to walk home after such a big meal, so we ambled along, talking and stopping to gaze into shop windows, relishing the twinkling lights of Paris at night.

Later I crawled in beside Alex who was already under a down comforter, lying on his back with head cradled in his hands. "I'm completely exhausted," I said.

"Really? Can't imagine why."

"It is exciting, isn't it?" I asked.

"Not half as exciting as I find you right now," said Alex, turning towards me and reaching his hand up under my nightgown. It was a while before we fell asleep and late the next morning when we awoke.

Chapter Eighty-four

Love

Sunday's brilliant sunshine allowed four of us to walk out for brunch and then stroll for an hour in the Bois de Boulogne before going to the Louvre. Evan had gone off to his studio. Everyone was in high spirits, not least Fiona who had heard from Jeremy that he would arrive Monday late morning and be able to leave near the time she had a flight to Madrid late Tuesday afternoon.

Alex was walking ahead of us in the park, and Fiona ran forward to join him. He took her hand, and together they broke into skipping along the wide path.

"Mom, he's so cute," said Enid. "How come you waited all this time to see him again?'

"It's a long story. You know the first part, how he was your grandmother's doctor and all. He had young kids and a wife back then, and I, well I was married to your father, and of course that wasn't going to change either."

"Wait a minute. Are you telling me that you two, back then, I mean were you attracted to him?"

I realized my phrasing had been transparent, so I switched gears. "Enid, it wouldn't be hard. He's cute as you say. And he was so close to my mother that it was easy for a friendship to grow. But no, there was little thought of leaving your father, especially after he had his first stroke, although he seemed to recover pretty quickly. And I did love Dad. You must believe that. As you know, once he was improved, he had another, slightly more damaging but still, he could function pretty well. The last one left him so helpless and sad, it broke my heart."

"Well you were wonderful."

I looked over at her and smiled. "It's a funny thing. When you take care of a person, a dependent creature in other words, you develop an attachment that is sustaining; at least it was for me."

"I think I can see that. If something happened to Evan, I know I'd always do what I could to make him comfortable." She paused and then said, "So, okay, still you two could have gotten together sooner."

"Oh, I don't know, Enid. Time passes. There were other considerations. I had my life in Baltimore, good friends, books, trips with first Arthur and

Potter, and then after Arthur died, I traveled alone with Potter and helped with the editing of his books while I did my own writing. My payment was lovely free journeys to exotic places."

"Did you and Potter ever . . .?"

I laughed. "No, love, Potter is gay."

"Oh, wow, I never knew that."

"In retrospect it was pretty obvious, but then Arthur had already told me about it around the time your grandmother died. I know everyone in Baltimore suspected, but back then the subject wasn't really discussed."

"I'm glad things like that are more in the open now," said Enid.

"Me too. Otherwise you wouldn't have an ancient mother already moved in with her younger boyfriend." Enid threw her arm over my shoulders and gave me a hug.

"Randy old fools, both of you," she laughed.

I patted her stomach. "The pot calling the kettle what?"

"Careful of my pot. It's full of baby," said Enid.

We spotted Alex and Fiona up ahead talking to a couple with a pair of Salukis. "What beautiful creatures!" exclaimed Enid. Fiona was kneeling down and patting the dogs and looking up at the owners.

"Gran," she yelled when she spotted us. "Look at these babies. Aren't they gorgeous?"

When we were abreast of the group, it was clear that the dogs were the centerpiece and that Alex didn't know the couple, but they were chatting happily to him in French. Surprisingly he was holding his own in the conversation. Finally he pulled Fiona to her feet, and without complicating things with introductions, he moved us all towards a path that led out of the park.

"Let's get a cab and go to the Louvre," he said.

Enid looked at her watch. "Good idea. Evan will be home around four, but there's no hurry."

Chapter Eighty-five

Monday

On Monday, Jeremy arrived in time for a late lunch at Enid and Evan's flat. If a human body could be said to glow, then Fiona was incandescent. After making plans — what, where, and for how long — they flew out the door, leaving us gasping in their wake.

"Time for a nap," said Enid. "I'm exhausted. One forgets the energy required around young love."

"Old love is more restful?" asked Alex going to the window. He looked down. "Come look, I think this thing has evolved more than we realized."

We rushed to the window and looked down. Fiona and Jeremy had emerged from the building and were wrapped around each other, a bundle of heavy coats and puffs of hot breath in the cold air.

"Oh my," I said.

"Resign yourself," said Alex, putting his arm around me. "I'm sure you can remember what it's like."

I glanced up at him, and we both grinned.

We retired to our rooms and sank gratefully into bed for a long nap.

It was nearly dark by the time we emerged and gathered for cocktails prior to dinner. Enid declared herself on the edge of starvation, so we hurried along to a nearby restaurant and spent a long time savoring food and wine and catching up on our lives.

"So, what are your actual plans?" asked Enid.

"Regarding what?" answered Alex.

"Well, I guess regarding the rest of your lives. I mean are you going to stay shacked up, or are you going to marry?"

Alex stood and cleared his throat. "Well, no time like the present," he started. "You may have noticed a rather large ring on your mother's hand. It was originally intended as a sentimental gesture, the anniversary of when we first met. However, as it turns out, I'm going to make an honest woman of her, that is if she'll have me."

I looked around at Enid and Evan, who were smiling, hardly surprised. "This is embarrassing; immediately after your wedding day, and with Fiona and Jeremy wrapped up in each other. I mean it's getting indecently maudlin."

"Oh, Mum, stop it. It's wonderful, and I will positively toss you out the door into the street if you don't accept on the spot."

"Where will you live?" asked Evan.

"I've bought a house in London," said Alex. "Splendid place — two houses made into one in Kensington. I still have a job at least, as your mother-in-law is expensive. We'll also spend time in Cornwall where I have a modest little cottage."

"Mom? Are you really going to move over there? I mean give up Baltimore entirely? Penny? Matthew?"

"Penny and Matthew know how to travel, and I haven't forgotten how either," I said. "I heard from Helene the other day, and she and Louise are already planning a visit in the spring. I expect Potter won't take that long to get here. He's in Asia right now and will probably come round this way before going home. He has research to do in Turkey."

"All coming to see if I'm up to their standards I suspect," said Alex. "Want to wager on their conclusion?"

Enid patted his hand. "I think you might squeak by," she said.

When we finally went to bed, it was nearly midnight and no sign of Fiona. I read for a while and, unable to stay awake, curled up and slept fitfully until I heard whispers in the living room. I put on my bathrobe and went out. They were standing at the refrigerator with the door open. Nearly half its contents were already on the kitchen table.

"What time is it?" I asked.

They glanced up, startled. Jeremy looked at his watch. "Three," he grinned.

"Three. Ah. Yes." and feeling awkward, I added, "Well, goodnight."

"Goodnight," they said in unison, and I headed back to a snoring Alex.

Tuesday morning we arose late and found Jeremy asleep on the sofa and Fiona on the cot near the street window. Both had their clothes on. We roused them and, finding little left in the refrigerator, went out to breakfast.

The thing I remember best about the day was how happy we all were and the toast Alex made with orange juice to smooth sailing for everyone and the baby to come.

Chapter Eighty-six

Life Moves On

When we returned to London, Alex started the process of paperwork, and the next month we got married quietly with David and Tina Lowther as witnesses. After a celebratory dinner — the four of us — we resumed our lives, and for several years after that, Alex and I floated in self-indulgent euphoria. I flew back to the States several times to see Matthew and Penny and to take care of the Baltimore house. After a few weeks on the market it sold, near the price I wanted, and thus I wound up my life there.

I had a few of my belongings shipped over, others either sold or distributed to Penny and Matthew, and we moved into the new house after having it painted and decorated. Friends came and went, meeting Alex and enjoying London. In March, Matthew and his wife, Juliana; Penny and Christopher and Enid and Evan came for Drew's wedding in Ireland with their children. Jeremy arrived with his parents along with our other English friends. There were over two hundred guests — thirty-one of us stayed at the castle, others sorted themselves out in hotels nearby. A lengthy picture-taking session took place by the lake, interrupted when one of the children fell off the pier into the water and was rescued and whisked away by her parents. It was elegant — funded in part by a generous infusion of Anne's and Alex's money, as the bride's family was clearly not wealthy.

With my family and Alex's other two sons, we stayed on and spent ten days in a rambling old house Alex leased in Glaslough, near where the wedding was.

By April, Alex and David wound up the debacle with Wilding, severed relations with the Chinese company and managed to hold onto and sell Alex's patent to an American firm. They lost the first installment of their investment in the Chinese firm, one of five planned over five years.

One evening near the end of April, Alex suggested we go down to Cornwall for a week.

"May's the time to be there, flowers in bloom along the roadsides, splendid," he said. "And, I do want you to meet my friend Lady Bromley. I've never told you about her, have I?"

"Not really. You've mentioned her once or twice, and David did too when I first got over here. He said then that Tina was madly curious as to what your relationship with her is."

Alex chuckled. "Ah, Tina. She has to be up on everything."

"I thought you liked her," I said.

"I do, I do. I adore her. But you have to admit she's distinctly maternal with me. 'Alex, did you remember to . . . ; Alex, you simply must . . .'" he mimicked.

"Oh, that. Yes, I noticed it, but that's because she cares about you."

"And so she does. Anyway, Lady Bromley, Sarah, I met at a dinner when I first got over here. She's a big Wilding shareholder, and this was a business thing, stuffy and boring. It was in a club, and there was a balcony. She was my dinner partner, and a writer at the table was rambling on about his recent book retracing the financial meltdown. She poked me in the ribs and said, 'Do you want to escape as badly as I do?'

"I smiled at her and nodded. So, as soon as people got up from the table, she grabbed my hand and led me out to the balcony, pulled a pipe out of her purse and started smoking it."

"How marvelous," I laughed.

"She is unique. So, we had dinner a few times and enjoyed each other hugely. She invited me down to Cornwall to her place for a weekend. I was lonely and knew few people at the time. She had another couple there, from Australia, an authority on butterflies who had published his third book."

"What kind of place does she have?"

"Mammoth pile. The husband left everything to her, fifteen hundred acres around it too. Dripping with art and priceless furniture and carpets. Has a chapel as well. One of those places Henry VIII gave his pals in the mid-fifteen hundreds. The stables are several times the size of our new house."

"And she lives there alone?" I asked.

"Well, alone except for help of one sort or another. She's rather reclusive actually, but she does stage the odd weekend house party and has a few offspring and grandchildren slipping in and out."

"How old is she?"

"Well into her eighties by now, but you'd never know it, agile as a kangaroo. Still rides every day."

"She sounds daunting. Will she be open to your bringing me along?"

He grinned at me. "Oh, you will get looked over, no doubt. I've been her sort of, hmmmm, I don't know what, the other man on weekend gatherings and dinners here in London. She won't want to give that up."

"Well, she'll have to, won't she?"

"You're the one to make that clear."

"Me? I don't think so," I replied.

"I'm teasing. You're right; she'll have to find another convenient male."

"Have you told her anything about me?" I asked.

"Yes, yes, of course. I even went so far as to tell her we'd be there soon."

Lady Bromley wrote Alex a note the beginning of May, urging him to come down and bring me.

> *The weather here is typically transient, one day blue skies and weak sunshine, the next grey with mizzle, but the spring flowers are beginning to decorate the hedgerows, with celandines, primroses, and daffodils brightening the dull remains of last year's undergrowth.*

So, the second week of May we set off for Cornwall, and Alex was right, it was beautiful. His cottage was small, one bedroom, low-beamed ceilings, and cozily furnished with a well outside the back door. The kitchen was tiny with a refrigerator to scale, so we shopped in the village every day. He drove me around, stopping to lunch at pubs on wonderful meat-and-vegetable-filled tarts called *pasties*, typical of Cornwall. We took long walks along narrow lanes and over fields, and we had quiet evenings talking and reading. On the fourth evening we went to Lady Bromley's for dinner, driving up a long lane and turning in at imposing iron gates. A butler met us at the door and took us into a large library. She sat by a window, two Great Pyrenees dogs at her feet.

"Oh, here you are," she said, pushing out of her chair and coming across the room, both arms held out for a hug with Alex. The dogs looked up but did not move.

She stepped back and looked me over. "Well, I can see I'm no competition for this lovely thing," she said to Alex. Then she extended her hand and shook mine. "I do hope we'll be friends," she said.

"I'm sure we shall," I said.

"Well, one never knows, does one?" she said with a smile.

"No, I suppose not."

She flapped her hand and moved back to her chair. "Sit, sit. Alex do go over to the chest and pour us drinks." Turning to me, she asked, "And how do you find our wild countryside down here?"

"I think it's dazzling."

She snorted. "Yes, it is, but I'm not sure life's up to American standards for convenience. It takes nerve to drive on the narrow lanes, and as for getting anything done, well you learn patience. People take their time."

I smiled. What could I have said anyway?

"So," she went on, looking at Alex. "The big news here is that that decaying heap of an estate I showed you has finally been settled after forty years of tangled entailment. We're all thrilled. It finally went to an American descendant who's planning to sink a fortune into shoring it up. Probably rent it out for fairs and weddings, but no matter, it'll be nice to see life over there."

"Ah, yes, you've fretted over it for years. One complaint we won't have to listen to now."

She grinned. "Am I that tiresome?" She took the glass of whisky that Alex handed her. "Yes, I suppose I am." She turned to me. "Getting old, you know. It's no picnic, let me assure you. And if you say it beats the alternative, you're off my list forever," she added, looking at me.

"It hadn't occurred to me to say much of anything," I said.

"Oh, well, that's good, isn't it?"

"I expect it beats the alternative."

"Ha!" She grinned at Alex. "She's got spirit. I'll say that."

"So she does," he said.

"Now, I need to tell you I've finished my play. Hellish struggle it was, but I think this one's good. I showed it to Julian, and he thinks it has great promise. He's got a pal in London he's shipping it off to, fellow who's a producer. We'll see."

"What's it about?"

"The play?" she asked.

"Yes, the play," I answered.

She wriggled back in the chair and took a sip of the whisky. "Well, it's revolves around an old man whom everyone thinks is going gaga, but it's an act. He's trying to figure out how to settle a significant fortune, and by playing dumb he gets to watch his relatives in full venomous flower as they decimate each other, make unlikely alliances, and say dreadful things about him."

"A comedy?"

"Hardly. This is a jab in humanity's ribs. Not meant to be funny, but I must admit there are humorous lines sprinkled throughout."

"Perhaps a metaphor for political corruption?"

She sat upright and stared at me and then looked at Alex. "Your friend and I might get along, Alex. Do fetch us another drink and then tell George we'll eat in twenty minutes. Oh, and bring my shawl from the hall will you?"

On the way home Alex commented, "Well your presence certainly reduced me to a lackey in a few minutes. Alex, get me this; tell George that," he laughed.

"I like her," I said, "Crusty old thing that she is."

"Not really, she's the product of years of distillation."

Chapter Eighty-seven

Cornwall Weekend

By 2013, Alex and I were making regular weekend jaunts to Cornwall and more often than not staying well into the following week. We added a big room to the back of the cottage. It had a fireplace and a view to the now lush perennial beds I had dug with Sarah Bromley's help in planning and cuttings from her garden. Above was our bedroom and bath, leaving the original bedroom downstairs as an office for me with a sofa bed for guests, mainly used by Jeremy and Fiona whose cohabitation had become permanent.

On the Friday of June fourteenth, a few days after the Queen's Birthday, we were expecting them by dinnertime. With Alex's urging, Fiona had gone on to the University of Edinburgh, so she was with us a great deal. She and Jeremy got engaged in January, and the wedding was planned for August in Cornwall. I assumed Fiona intended to finish her education in Edinburgh and reminded myself to ask her how she'd manage that.

I sat on the sofa with papers spread out around me trying to make sense of the logistics of putting up family and friends in surrounding inns and bed and breakfast places. Lady Bromley had made four of her bedrooms available as well, so Penny and Christopher and Fiona's brothers would be staying there along with Enid and Evan and two-year old Catherine. Matthew and his family, along with Alex's sons would fill the neighboring hostelries.

"Have you got it figured out?" said Alex, coming into the room. He had aged in the last few years with a full head of grey hair. I thought him still the fetching fellow who had greeted me that first night in Hopwood, although I clearly did not think so then. I was aware of lines crisscrossing my face. For goodness sake, we were old.

"Not quite," I answered. "I still have Louise and Latimer and the Filmores to place."

"Oh, Helene and Anthony are coming after all? That's great news. What about Fiona and Jeremy's friends?"

"Some of them are staying in Liskeard with Jeremy's uncle and aunt, others are at a hotel or staying with a friend of Fiona's near there, not sure where, but she and Jeremy have taken care of those details. Sarah has been a marvel. What a lovely place to have the bridal dinner and wedding."

"She's been remarkable, I agree," said Alex, passing by the back of the sofa and kissing the top of my head. "Makes me want to marry you all over again in a grander manner, maybe get Lady Elizabeth Anson, the famous party planner, to stage it!"

"You sentimental old fool. We've done pretty well to stay together three years as it is."

"Well it's entirely due to my good nature and patience given your fierce temper and complete overhaul of my lovely little cottage."

"You know you love it as it is now."

"Perhaps I find it charming in a decorative *Country Life* way, but I did love its rustic untidiness before."

"Rustic? It was a mess. Remember the rot under the kitchen sink and the tub that wouldn't drain? And then there were the holes in the bedroom floor covered with scatter rugs? Do you want me to go on?"

He was standing gazing out at the garden with his back to me. "Oh, yes, please. You love this conversation."

"Oh, do shut up." I laughed. "Get me a drink. If they don't get here soon, I may get drunk."

He went over to the bar and started fussing with glasses and ice. "That'd make a pretty welcome for the bridal couple."

We heard tires crunching on the gravel outside and doors slamming. "Here they are anyway," said Alex, handing me my glass and heading for the front door. It burst open pinning him behind it, and Fiona and Jeremy flew into the room.

"Gran, Gran, come see," shouted Fiona. "Jeremy's bought the most obscene car — a Ferrari. He's in love with it." Alex inched out from behind the door, and she wrapped her arms around his neck and said, "You too. Come out."

The three of them spilled out the door, and I got up and followed. And there it was, pale blue. "It's a California," said Jeremy. "Got it secondhand; left hand drive — a drawback."

Alex was already circling it like a dog examining a fresh bone. He ran his hand along the hood. "Pretty thing. How's it run?"

"Like silk," said Jeremy. "Come on, I'll give you a ride."

"Now?" I said. "It's nearly time for dinner."

"Now," said Alex. "Elise, do you want to go?"

"No, maybe later."

"You want to drive?" Jeremy asked Alex.

"Sure," Alex answered. "I'd love to." Jeremy flipped the keys across to him. Fiona and I looked at each other and shook our heads.

"Gran and I will wait here," she said. "Take the cases out, Jeremy, and put them in the house."

Jeremy looked at me and shrugged. "Already ordering me around, and I haven't submitted to vows yet. Doesn't bode well for the future does it?"

"You'd better call the whole thing off. Fiona is a terror."

"We won't be long," said Alex, looking back at me.

"Good," I said. Fiona and I went into the house and could hear the engine start up with a roar and then fade as they went back along the lane.

"Two kids with a new toy," I said.

"Jeremy's mad," she said. "Clearly bonkers. What if we have kids? Can you see car seats and strollers in a Ferrari?"

I patted her shoulder. "I think you're looking too far ahead. Time enough for sense. Have fun." I paused, "Follow me into the kitchen. I have to check on the roast."

Sniffing the aroma, she said, "Ooooh, lamb? You are a love. My favorite. Do you have mint sauce?"

I nodded and opened the oven, glancing at the thermometer. Not ready yet. I turned to her. "By the way how did the job interview for this summer go?"

"Oh, that. It's not a serious group. Collecting money for the environment but spending it the wrong way. The director, or director-ess I should say, was an absolute harpy. Couldn't stand her. No, that's not going to work. But I'll find a job, don't worry."

"Have you found a flat?"

"Yes to that. Adorable. Not far from his parents and plenty of room. We'll have to start furnishing it, and you'll need to help me with colors. I'm hopeless, and Jeremy's worse."

"You are going to finish your studies?"

"Oh, yes, I'll go back up for the final bit in the fall; come home on weekends."

We went into the living room, and Fiona got a bottle of wine out of the refrigerator and followed me. We looked over my plans. Penny was bringing over the dress she had worn, as Fiona was insistent on wearing it; they were the same size. Alex and I were buying her a veil. I caught a glimpse of the large diamond Jeremy had bought her, round cut and bordered with more diamonds. I pointed to it. "Be careful of that."

"I know. No gardening in it, right?" And she grinned.

I looked at my watch. The men had been gone nearly an hour. "Where could they have disappeared to?" I asked.

"Oh, probably stopped by the side of the road tinkering with the engine or having a pint at a pub," said Fiona taking a sip of wine. "Come on, Gran, let's go outside so you can have a smoke."

Chapter Eighty-eight

Derriford

The Police arrived while Fiona and I were wandering around the garden. I heard the doorbell faintly but knew it was unlikely that Alex or Jeremy would ring it. Fiona and I looked at each other and rushed into the house.

The rest is a blur. I remembered to turn off the oven, and we got to the Derriford Hospital in Plymouth, where they'd taken them, by following the police car. We found Jeremy on a gurney in the hallway waiting. Alex was nowhere to be seen.

"Mr. Lowther has a broken arm and facial bruises but no other injuries that we can see," the doctor told Fiona. "We'll get him into the operating room as soon as possible. Meanwhile we've given him painkillers, so he's drowsy." Fiona rushed over to him, and I saw Jeremy reach up for her with his good arm.

Then the doctor took me aside. "They're checking Dr. Creighton. He's been started on steroids to reduce swelling. Could be a spinal contusion. They're checking to make sure there isn't a lung contusion as well."

"Oh no. No, no, no. What happened? The police only said there had been an accident."

"From what I can gather, your husband was driving on one of the back lanes, fast I think, and a lorry came around a corner. The Ferrari is a left-hand drive, so he was on the side that hit the stone wall when he swerved to avoid the lorry. The lorry hit the middle of the car on the passenger side. That's it. The lorry driver wasn't hurt, just shaken up with a few bruises, so he was treated at the Liskeard Community Hospital and released."

"So what's going on with Alex? Please. He'll be okay, won't he?"

"Well, *okay* is a relative term, Mrs. Creighton."

"Yes, go on."

"If the injury had been higher on his back, we'd be facing paraplegia, but since it is below L2, there's a chance of recovery, although it might take up to a year or even more. We think this is a spinal contusion, in the lumbar region. All we can do for now is use steroids and wait and see, get him stabilized. We're taking an MRI to see if there is a disc displacement or any loose bone fragments, in which case we'll have to operate. However it goes, he'll be in a wheelchair and need to have skilled nursing care at first and then rehab."

"How long?"

"As I said, we don't know. He could recover anywhere from weeks to months. He might not. We simply have to wait." He patted me on the shoulder. "Meanwhile we'll get Mr. Lowther patched up, in a cast and to a bed. He's going to hurt, but he'll be fine. You can see him when he comes 'round, and then you can go home. Dr. Creighton will be pretty well sedated."

"No, I'm not going home and leaving Alex here," I said.

"At any rate, as soon as we're through with him tonight, you can see him. We can possibly set up a cot in his room, if we can find a private one. Otherwise, I suggest The Lodge on Blunts Lane. It's here for relatives of patients. We'll have to keep him for a while." He glanced at me. "You may want to go get a bite to eat while you're waiting."

I sat down in a nearby chair. Food was the last thing I wanted. I saw several nurses wheel Jeremy towards what I supposed was an operating room. Fiona came over and sat down beside me. "Jeremy said the car isn't beyond repair. There he is on a gurney, banged up, and he's more worried about his car. He's pretty drugged up, so I guess that accounts for his screwed up priorities. They do think he'll be okay, thank God. How about Alex? What did the doctor say?"

I told her, and we held hands and waited, stunned, beyond tears. There wasn't much else to say. Eventually, I got up and went outside to clear my head. Fiona came out after a while, and we took a walk away from the hospital. The night was mild, stars clearly visible in the sky even with the lights from Plymouth competing. A perfect June night. We should have been finishing our dinner by now. I couldn't grasp the enormity of what had happened.

When we got back to the hospital, we made do with tattered magazines, and after waiting what seemed a long time, another doctor came towards us.

"Mrs. Creighton?"

"Yes," I answered.

"The good news is that there is no disc displacement or loose bone fragments. We're taking Dr. Creighton to a room now."

I looked at Fiona. "You stay here and wait for Jeremy. Come find me later, and we'll figure out what to do for the night." I followed the doctor through the hallways to Alex's room. After I was seated next to a bed, the doctor left. Presently I heard Alex being wheeled along the hall, and there he was, eyes closed, pale and pathetic. I walked over and took his hand. His eyes fluttered slightly but remained closed.

"If you'd step aside, Mrs. Creighton," said one of the two nurses, "we can get him into bed."

And so began the long night, long weeks, and long months.

Chapter Eighty-nine

Christmas

Six months later we were still in Cornwall, and the weather had turned cold, wet, and miserable, day after dreary day. Alex was in a terrible mood, anchored to his wheelchair, parked by the back window and staring at the skeletal shapes in the garden, brittle reminders of the lush summer we'd left behind.

That morning I had attempted to put Christmas decorations around the living room, holly, pinecones, a pretty angel I had found at the Oxfam shop in Liskeard.

"What on earth are you doing?" Alex asked.

"Trying to make things look a bit festive," I said. "Fiona and Jeremy will be here tomorrow for Christmas dinner."

"Ridiculous," he said. "I don't know why you don't pack up and leave. I'm no use to you or anyone else. I wish I'd died. You don't have to do this. Hire a nurse and be done with it. First Karl and then me. Nice life for you."

"Stop feeling sorry for yourself," I snapped. "It accomplishes nothing."

I was losing patience with him. He might at least hold up his end of the bargain, show a ray of hope and make an attempt to engage himself. I'd bought books, paints, DVDs. He rejected them all. All he wanted was classical music or television all day long and meals on time. He was nasty to the people who came to give him physical therapy, nasty to me, showed no interest in anything. I had taken to sitting in my study and writing most of the day. We couldn't leave Cornwall. The positive note was that I had nearly finished another book, and I thought it was good — deeper observation.

The wedding had gone off as planned. Alex had still been in rehab, learning to live with paralysis of his lower body, so I was free to attend and try to put a good face on the festivities for family and friends. Of course they were solicitous and treated me like a fragile piece of glass, which exacerbated the situation. I was indeed fragile, and the slightest show of pity brought me to tears.

"Alex, do you want to go back to London? Would that cheer you up? I think we could manage it soon," I offered.

"It doesn't matter where we are, does it?" he replied, turning his head to look at me.

"Well, the difference would be more friends around to distract you.

Honestly, you're like a bear down here. You won't help at all."

"So leave. Put me in a nursing home. God damn it, Elise, you have no idea how I hate watching you trot back and forth here with a wretched forced cheerfulness, fetching things for me, helping me bathe, bringing me meals. It's awful. I'll never get better, and having you say I will is like salt in a wound."

I couldn't take any more. "Well, *God damn it* back to you, you wretched spoiled, whining child. You can get better. The doctors say it's entirely likely. Yes, it could be a while, but you won't make any effort, and you drag me down. I don't mind caring for you. For pity sakes, I love you, Alex. Does that count for nothing? What would you be doing if this had happened to me?"

He turned his head and stared out the window again. The silence had its own cadence, pounding and relentless. Beyond it I could hear water dripping off the roof. I wandered over and poked at the fire and threw on another log. Sparks flew, as the blaze rose up. The phone rang. It was Edward, Alex's son, so I carried the phone over to him and went into the kitchen. It was nearly dinnertime. I could hear him delivering monosyllabic replies to his son's remarks. This had to stop. Truthfully, I didn't think I could go on unless he changed his attitude.

I heard the news on the television. Alex must have finished his conversation and used the remote. Depressing news had flowed that month. Ukraine had been in revolt against President Viktor Yanukovitch about his refusal to sign free trade agreements with the EU. Nelson Mandela had died of a lung infection. India had banned gay sex, and in England tidal floods along the North Sea had pitched houses into the water, and thousands had been evacuated. The meager positive news, if you could call it that, was that two members of the singing group *Pussy Riot* were being released from a Russian jail. The news anchor droned on while I carved chicken and spooned carrots and potatoes onto our plates.

After dinner, I began the lengthy job of getting Alex ready for bed, and when that was accomplished, I returned to the kitchen to do the dishes. Mrs. Mabin, my cleaning help, would be coming the morning after Christmas, Boxing Day, and I could get out for a few hours. Three days a week she arrived and kept an eye out for Alex, giving me a welcome respite from the routine that bound us too closely to the whole miserable calamity. I planned to get my hair done, refresh our food supply, and shop for hooks for the bedroom closet and nice soap.

Christmas Day's weather showed no change for the better. I heard the roar of the Ferrari's engine around eleven when I was in the kitchen basting the rib roast. When they came in. I heard them talking to Alex and went into the sitting room.

"Hi, Gran," and Fiona came over to give me a hug. Jeremy was grinning.

"We have a lovely present for you and Alex," he said, shrugging off his sheepskin jacket and throwing it over the back of a chair. They were carrying nothing, so I was puzzled.

Alex was scowling at Fiona but showing interest. A good sign at least. "So what is it?" he asked.

"Are you ready? Jeremy, go get it." Jeremy went back out the front door and quickly returned leading a black Scottish Terrier. The door slammed. I looked at him in horror.

"You can't be serious," I said.

"Oh, yes, we're serious. She's a rescue. Name's Abigail."

"For us?" asked Alex. "What the hell are we going to do with a dog?"

"Oh, Alex," cried Fiona. "You have to admit she's adorable. She's here to make you happy. Please cooperate."

Jeremy detached the leash, and Abigail ran around sniffing the furniture and finally Alex's leg.

"She's going to pee," said Alex, looking helplessly at his immobile leg.

"No," said Fiona. "She's fully housebroken. We've had her a week. She's an angel. A year old."

Alex looked at me. "Elise, you tell them this is patently ridiculous. I mean she'll be one more thing for you to look after, and she will clearly annoy me."

"So what," I said under my breath to Fiona. "Everything annoys him." I was warming to the idea of having cheerful company.

I sat down on the sofa and called the dog over to me. She came bounding up and into my lap, leaning up to lick my face. I ran my fingers through her hair, soft wiry clumps of blackness. "Hello, Abigail." She wagged her tail. I stroked her for a while. Finally, I got up and said, "Well, I guess I'd better get luncheon. Jeremy you can pour sherry or whatever you want before we eat."

I heard Fiona go outdoors again, and presently she came into the kitchen carrying a shopping bag, which she put on the counter. "Dog food and bowls," she said by way of explanation. "Keep the kibbles out all the time, and give her a couple of spoons of the canned food morning and evening. She also loves chicken, if you want to cook it; chop it up and keep it in the freezer. There are three tennis balls in here too. She likes to fetch them."

"Good Lord," I said. "This is overwhelming. I don't know."

"Gran, stop it. You know you love animals. Abigail will also give Alex something to think about; maybe he'll stop being an old grouch. Come into the sitting room. I'll show you."

I followed her. She had one of the tennis balls in her hand and called the dog who came tearing over to her. She crossed the room and handed the ball to Alex. "Throw it," she directed. I suspect Fiona was the only person in the world that Alex would have listened to right then.

He tossed the ball across the room, and Abigail scurried after it, retrieved it, and dropped it at his feet. When he didn't lean over to get it, she picked it up and stood with her paws on his knees and deposited the ball in his lap. He gazed up at Fiona. "Clever, isn't she?"

"So throw it again," said Fiona.

He did, and this time Abigail didn't hesitate before jumping up and putting the ball in Alex's lap. He actually smiled, truly the finest sight I'd seen in months. Tears sprang to my eyes, and I had to look away.

Before lunch, I took Abigail out to the garden. There was a stone wall around the whole perimeter, so I didn't use the leash. She bounded around, sniffing, and at one point dug in the rose bed. "Stop that," I shouted. She looked up, startled, and then wandered across the lawn, stopping to squat and pee. I called her, and she came back inside with me.

Jeremy wheeled Alex to the table, and we had lunch.

"I've finally found a job for the summer and possibly for when I'm done in Edinburgh," said Fiona.

"Oh, good," I said. "Where?"

"It's actually a private thing, an Anglican priest who has moved into his family's place. It has a huge garden that's been neglected. He wants to do a complete overhaul of the beds and has an idea about replicating the character of Giverny — ordered but hectic. It'll take a long time. There's a pond at the bottom of the property, so obviously we have to go for water lilies."

"It can't be in London with that much land," said Alex.

"No, but it's an easy commute. No distance at all."

"Sounds perfect for you," I said. "What's the priest like?"

"Young, good looking, wildly knowledgeable."

I raised an eyebrow and glanced at Jeremy. "Yes," said Jeremy in reply. "Who could resist Fiona, especially in cruddy old boots, blue jeans, gardening gloves, and mud on the end of her nose?"

I noticed Alex's hand repeatedly easing pieces of beef from his plate and handing them to Abigail under the table. "Alex, slow down with that," I said. "You'll make her sick."

He looked up, surprised that I had caught him. "Won't hurt her," he said.

"It might," said Fiona. "As long as she throws up on you and not the rest of us." Alex shot her a disgusted look, wrinkling his nose, and resumed eating.

After lunch, we went back into the sitting room, and I gave Jeremy and Fiona their presents: a green cashmere sweater for Jeremy and a navy wool jacket lined in red from Selfridges for Fiona. Jeremy immediately tried on the sweater. "I love it," he said coming over and doing a model's dip and turn.

"Thank Alex too," I said.

"I didn't have anything to do with it," Alex retorted. "Spends my money like crazy."

"I beg to differ," I said. "It was my money. What does it matter anyway? We both decided what we wanted to get them."

Abigail had been lying at Fiona's feet, and she got up with the ball in her mouth and delivered it to Alex's lap. He threw it. She raced out into the hall where it bounced and raced back to Alex, dropping it on the floor, heaving for a moment and then throwing up on Alex's shoe.

"Good Lord!" shouted Alex, raising his leg and staring at it in horror. We gaped at him.

"Alex, oh my God! You lifted your foot," I whispered in awe.

Epilogue

Today Alex and I *Google* what we forget. Our teeth and eyes need greater attention. Our aches are allowable as a subject of conversation. We are consummate bores on the subject of grandchildren, and the chill gets to us.

Mostly we stay in London. We sold the place in Cornwall — negative memories — and Lady Bromley died shortly after Alex started to regain mobility. My latest manuscript is with the publishers, and I am at loose ends, not ready to begin another book, restless. Alex is still having occasional physiotherapy. He gets himself there and back now and walks with a cane. Miracles do happen. Our life is nearly normal now, and Alex is absorbed in a new venture with David, this time on a more altruistic scale, organizing clubs for poor boys who could not otherwise participate in the national passion for rugby. Donations have flowed their way, and the program is expanding. In other words, Alex is happy. We are happy. We haven't ventured to Brighton on walkers, but we are older and probably not a grain wiser.

Friends from the States visit from time to time, and even my sister Suzanne has made the trip and stayed with us. She and Alex, while not exactly loving in-laws, have a sort or restless peace that has its comic moments.

Best of all, Alex and I are still in love and able to prove it.

About The Author

An unrepentant New Englander, Cynthia Osborne Hoskin has had a long career in writing that has been an eclectic pastiche of journalism embracing profile writing; culinary and lifestyle columns; art-focused articles; and general business; as well as corporate public relations; co-writing client memoirs; and PR for corporations and not-for-profits.

Despite a modestly kept footlocker of short stories, poems (well, several were published with obscure awards), and personal memoirs, this is her first full-length novel. It's gestation and birth would rival that of any dinosaur, but now it's here and contemporary, she is speeding up with more flights of history and fantasy that have been percolating in the wings.

Hoskin's first poem was written at age seven on a blackboard just unloaded from a moving van in Cohasset, Massachusetts and was about heaven and angels, a subject she has never had the temerity to attempt again.

Hoskin lives in Northern Kentucky with the charismatic star of the book, Abigail the Scottie, and her beloved, humorous, patient and very, very smart husband, Richard, author of the magnificent *The Miner & the Viscount*, a rousing tale of his native Cornwall, England.

NOTE: If you've enjoyed this book, you'd do a great kindness by going to *amazon.com* and writing a review. It's easy. Just locate the book by using the search box at the top of the Amazon page and write away! The more reviews authors receive, the better is their exposure. Also, feel free to visit Hoskin's blog at *osbornehoskin.com* in which she'll feature adventures from Elise's and her era as experienced at the time. And of course, thank you for reading *Fall's Bright Flame*!

Made in the USA
Middletown, DE
16 September 2017